FORETOLD

The Tale of a Highland Village

Elizabeth Sutherland

For David
with love & best wishes

Elizabeth Sutherland

1

The Inverally Predictions

Tha an latha a'teanadh...the day is coming when the big sheep will chase the people from Glen Mhor.

The day is coming when the very hearthstones will weep for the children that are no more.

The day is coming when water and fire will flow together through the streets of Inverally.

The day is coming when the bonny lands of Inverally will fall into the hands of the son of a fisherman. Woe unto that man for his world will be stained with blood.

I see into the far future: the day is coming when the ancient inhabitants of Glen Mhor shall return and take possession of the lands of their ancestors.

Fiosaiche of Glen Mhor.

Athough the plot of Foretold is loosely based on the Brahan Seer prophecies that predicted future events in the Highlands and in particular the estate of Rosehaugh in the Black Isle, Inverally Hall, the village, the characters, events and outcome are entirely fictional.

I have dedicated my story in loving memory of my Aunt Meg (Mary Jane Coventry of Shanwell, 1860-1935 known as Meg) who was the inspiration for my main character. ES

ISBN: 978-1-910205-87-7

Printed and published by For The Right Reasons
fortherightreasons@rocketmail.com
60 Grant Street Inverness IV3 8BS
2016

Acknowledgements: My thanks and love to Kate Cutler, Julie Gamble and to Richard Burkitt and Kevin Swanson at FTRR for all their hard work and for Stewart Forbes of FTRR for his imaginative cover design.

Also by Elizabeth Sutherland
The Black Isle (nf) 1972, Lent Term (f) 1973, The Seer of Kintail (f) 1974, *Hannah Hereafter* (f) 1976, *The Eye of God* (f) 1977, *The Prophecies of the Brahan Seer* (ed) (nf) 1977, *The Weeping Tree* (f) 1980, *Ravens and Black Rain* (nf) 1985, *The Gold Key and the Green Life* (ed) (nf) 1986, *In Search of the Picts* (nf) 1994, *The Pictish Trail* (nf) 1996, *The Five Euphemias* (nf) 1997, *Lydia, Wife of Hugh Millar of Cromarty* (b) 2002, *The Bird of Truth* (d) 2006, *Amendment of Life* (f) 2010. *Boniface, Bishops and Bonfires* (nf), *Children of God* (m) 2010, *One of the Good Guys* (f) 2011, *How Nessie Became A Vegetarian* (c) 2011, *Of Sinks and Pulpits* (m) 2011, *Columba and the Monstrous Wurrm* (c) 2012. *Spoilt Children* (f) 2013, *The Great Triduum* (ff) 2015.

4

Inverally Village

Inhabitants of The Hall

Colonel Jock Murray-Myers, 53, **Laird of Inverally**
Grizel Murray-Myers, 48, his wife known as the *Aingeal*
Isabella Janet, 19, their eldest **daughter**
Meg (Margaret or Megaidh),14, their second **daughter**
Andrew John, 12, their **son** and heir to Inverally

Indoor Staff
Cuthbertson, **Butler**
Miss Enid Fraser, **Governess.**
Mrs Jean Shanks, **Housekeeper.**
Jenkins (Jimmy), batman turned **Valet**
Nanny Gilchrist, (retired) **Nurse.**
Mima Black, **Table Maid**
Effie Macreedie, **Housemaid**
Ina Munro, **Kitchen Maid**
Bessie Sharp, **Nursery Maid**

Outdoor Staff and Tenants
Ian Wedderburn, **Factor**
Bob Paterson, **Head Gardener**
Mrs Marie Paterson, his **wife**
Jenny Paterson, his **daughter**
Hugh Finlay, **Game Keeper**
Ewan Mackenzie, **Stalker**
Sam Stuart, **Groom**
Councillor Ronny Mackay, **Farmer** at the Mains
Ivor Wilkie, **Factor**

Relatives
Very Revd George Myers, the laird's younger twin, **Dean of Westchester Cathedral**
Mrs Georgina Myers, his **wife**
Victor Myers, 23, their older **twin son**
Revd Cedric Myers, 23, younger **twin son**
Mrs Susan Myers, his **wife**

Friends and Acquaintances .
Lord Moncrieff, Perthshire **landowner**
Lady Moncrieff, his **wife**
Miss Maria Kennedy, her **sister**
Captain the Hon. James Moncrieff 26, **RA Indian Army**, their **son**
The Hon. Harriet Moncrieff, 24 (Lady Harriet Barraclough) his **sister**
Sir Hector Macdonald, **MP** for Point and Inverally
Lord Donald Morton, **Laird of Point**
Dowager, Lady Morton, his **mother**

Children
Andrew Moncrieff, born 1900
Ruth Stuart, born 1895
Eli Stuart, born 1897
Daniel (Danny) born 1900
Adela Morton, born 1905

Inhabitants of Kirkto+ n

Revd Hugh Vass, 32, **Episcopalian Priest** of St Moluag and **Schoolmaster**.
Mrs Emily Vass, 27, his **wife**.
Wee Hamish, 1, their **son**
Mrs Helen Macfarlane, 27, (widowed) **friend**
Miss Rosie, **Assistant Teacher** in St Moluag's School
Mr Arthur Gordon, **Lay Reader**, (assistant teacher after Miss Rosie)
Miss Caroline Budge, St Moluag's **Organist**
Mr Shaw, **Headmaster** of Inverally Parish School
Revd Sorley MacQueen, **Free Kirk Minister**
Revd Caleb Carruthers, **Church of Scotland Minister**
Revd Solomon Carrruthers, **son** and **depute Minister**
Miss Martha Carruthers, **daughter**
Miss Dorcas Carruthers, **daughter**
Dr Charles Anderson, **Doctor**
Miss Rhona Anderson, his daughter, **PianoTeacher**
Morag Macmurdo, **Schoolhouse Maid**.
Minnie Macmurdo, her sister, **Schoolhouse Maid**
Misses Sarah and Agatha Smythe, **Neighbours**

Inhabitants of Milton

Joshua Gallie, 42, **Owner and Manager** of the Timber Mill
(Victoria Cunningham Gallie, his deceased **wife**)
Aaron Cunningham Gallie, 12, their **son**
Miss Agnes Gallie, 45, Joshua's spinster **sister** and **Housekeeper**
Sara Munro, 30, **Servant**
Hilda Spencer Gallie, Joshua's **second wife**
Cynthia Spencer, her **daughter**
Kenneth Ross, **Chandler**

7

Fanny Ross, his **daughter**.
Mrs Mack, their **Housekeeper**
Jessie Rose, **Maid**
Jared Macreedie, 21, **Chandler's Apprentice**
Miss Constance Ross, (Bearsden) Fanny's **aunt**
Miss Eliza Matheson, **Dressmaker**
Constable Rossie, **Policeman**

Children
Young Kenny Macreedie, born 1895
Connie Macreedie, born 1898

Inhabitants of Fisherton 1890

The Macreedie Family known locally as **King**
Sine, 72, 'The Old Mother'
Ezra, 41, her son, **Fisherman** on the B*right Star*
Marsali Gansey (Munro), 37, his **wife**
Jared, 21, their son, Chandler's **Apprentice**
Jonas, 19, their son, **Labourer** in fish curing factory
Euphemia, 17, (Effie, their daughter) **Housemaid** at the Hall
Donnaidh,12, their son, **Schoolboy**
Mrs Anna Munro, Marsali's **Neighbour** and mother of Ina
Jeemock, **Labourer**
Ephraim Cooper, **Inmate**, Poor House, Point
Evie Cooper, his **daughter**

Children
Seth Macreedie, born, 1895
Cathie Macreedie, born, 1898

Inverness Connections

Malcolm Macmurtrie, **Law Agent**
Lachlan Golland, **Inspector**, Inverness Police Force
Angus Grigor, **Sergeant**, Inverness Police Force
Anton D'Olio, **Music Teacher**
Josiah Higgins, self-styled '**Businessman**'

American Connections

Aaron Morton, Lord Morton's distant **cousin**
Fraser Gemmell, **Rancher,** High Cloud, Wyoming
Angeline Gemmell, his **wife**

Indian Connections

The Hon. Mrs Clarissa Moncrieff
Major Arthur Thomas, Royal Artillery, India

Before

In any family there is a natural pecking order, a dynamic that shapes decisions, attitudes and perceptions. In this respect, the Murray-Myers family of five did not differ from the norm.

Colonel Jock, retired from his battalion in the Royal Artillery on his inheritance of Inverally Hall in Ross-shire, managed his estate, or rather was managed by an ageing factor called Wedderburn who had run the place, not particularly profitably, but, there again, not disastrously, for the past twenty years. Thus the Colonel was able to spend much of his time visiting retired fellow officers in mourning for their youth that was India or entertaining them at his home. During the shooting season those same friends, with or without wives, visited Inverally for the estate boasted 1500 acres of grouse moor and woodland covey. He was genial with his fellow officers, polite to his wife, and kindly, if a little distant, to his children. He read the first lesson at Matins regularly at St Moluag's, the local Scottish Episcopal Church, (better known, if inaccurately, as the 'English' Kirk) which he attended with his family on Sundays, and read prayers dutifully, if un-inspiringly, for the assembled household on Sunday evenings when he was at home. He was a man of habit, disliked untidiness or unpunctuality, and was motivated by an ingrained sense of his family's worth. He spent a great deal of his time cleaning his guns, walking the estate thereby exercising the dogs, and reading the day-old *Times* starting at the obituaries. Apart from the occasional flutter on the stock market, (mostly unsuccessful), Colonel Jock was generally considered to be 'a sound chap' In truth he was comfortable with two people only, his valet, Jenkins, a cheeky, foul-mouthed Cockney known as Jimmy, who had been his batman in India, and Nanny Gilchrist, his childhood nurse, a humourless Free Presbyterian now retired to a cottage on the estate, whom he visited most days.

Grizel Murray-Myers had been indoctrinated with religion by her father, a charismatic Episcopalian priest, socially well-connected, who had laboured in the slums of Edinburgh, until his heart failed a few months after the decease of his wife when Grizel was ten years old. Adopted by her father's wealthy maiden aunt, the daughter of an earl, who was renowned for her charitable works, Grizel met and married Jock Murray-Myers on furlough from India without knowing much about him. He had come home to find a wife. She was good-looking in a statuesque way, un-flirtatious and not in the first giddy flush of youth. She was also heir to her relative. The Major, as he was then, was thirty-six and herself two months over thirty. By the standards of the day, it was, therefore, a suitable match. Grizel was better-looking in middle age than she had been as a girl. She had grown into her strong nose, her wide mouth and her large blue eyes. She did all that was asked of her and more because she was by nature dutiful and conscience-driven. She was strict with her children, fair to her servants and efficient in her housekeeping. If she believed that Jock drank too much whisky, she kept that thought to herself. She seldom smiled. She was known among her large acquaintance as 'a good sort', dependable, if not exactly popular. None of them saw her when she visited the cottages on the estate with food from the Hall kitchen, sat with dying fisher wives in their pitiful hovels, dispensed beef tea and hot house grapes to their sick children. To them, Mistress Myers was beautiful, not just Lady Bountiful, more of an angel from heaven.

Jock and Grizel had three children. Isabella, the eldest, was the family beauty, compliant and conventional, all that her parents could hope for. At eighteen she had been launched

11

into society by a cousin of her father's who lived in London. Isabella knew what was expected of her; a good marriage, sons and a position in society. She had many admirers, fancied herself in love with at least three of them and spent much of her time reading romantic novels, arranging flowers, receiving callers and travelling in the brougham with her mother to leave cards or attend tea parties at neighbouring estates. Very occasionally, she would accompany her mother on charitable visits to Fisherton where she was gazed at with awe and admiration. She was exceedingly pretty and had a beautiful smile. 'Your face is your fortune,' one of the old wives in the village once told her with a deep sigh as though this were not something to wish for. Isabella took it as a compliment, for she loved the way she looked, her life, her position in society, her gentlemen admirers and her prospects. If she was vain, she was also charming. If asked, she would say that she was happy, especially in the company of men, no matter what age. She thrived on admiration.

Meg, her younger sister, was clever. In spite of her angular, nose-dominated appearance which she had inherited from her mother and her maternal grandfather, she had a remarkably pretty mouth, vulnerable and shapely and no one could discount her brain. At fourteen she was two inches shorter than her twelve-year old brother and still in the schoolroom. Meg was analytical, curious and critical. She found it hard to tolerate those whom she considered to be fools. Fortunately her governess, Miss Fraser, if not exactly clever, was at least better informed than she. Unfortunately, Miss Fraser's interest and talent lay in literature and in particular the Romantic poets For this reason, Meg was able to respect her though she never learned to share her governess's passion for Lord Byron. She preferred the practical sciences. Ever since she attended a lantern-slide lecture given by a missionary on furlough she had decided she would like to become a medical lady missionary, not in India, which she saw as decadent and peopled with polo-playing sahibs like her father's friends. She preferred the Transkei in Africa, where the Episcopal Church had a strong presence. Other young women were training in Edinburgh for medicine. Why not Meg? Thus she argued with her mother who understood her longing to serve, recognising that she had inherited this ambition, together with her appearance, from her clerical grandfather. Gently she pointed out to Meg that she had been born into a position in society and thus could never aspire to become anything so unfeminine as a missionary or worse, a doctor. However, she saw no harm in her furthering her education. To this end, and to keep her argumentative daughter quiet, she allowed Meg to be coached in Latin by Mr Vass, schoolmaster and rector of St Moluag's Episcopal Church. Twice a week she walked, rode or preferably bicycled, the mile down the Brae into Inverally village to have lessons at the rectory. Above all, she loved her bicycle.

Andrew at twelve was the only son, the heir, and therefore held a unique position in the family. Inverally was his undisputed birthright which Isabella and Meg, far from resenting, were first to recognise and respect. Andrew was an enigma to his sisters. They hardly knew him. From the age of seven he had attended a prep school in the Borders and at twelve was about to go on to Wellington where his father had been before him, destined to become a soldier. They knew, however, that they loved him. Everyone loved Andrew. He was good-tempered and non-judgemental, the same to his sisters, his parents, the servants, the estate workers and the village lads with whom he spent a great deal of his time. His parents were not particularly concerned, believing that he would soon make lasting friends of his own sort at Wellington. He laughed a lot. He made people feel important because he listened to them, or appeared to listen. He was presumed to be as happy at school as he appeared to be at home because he was popular without trying and a threat to no one. Although he was not particularly intellectual, he was certainly not a fool, coming in the middle of the class in exams, middling good at cricket, middling good at athletics. He was a reasonably good shot on the grouse moor, which pleased his father. Did he have a world within his head like Meg? Did he have passions like Isabella? Nobody knew. He presented himself as happy, genial, friendly and kind. His mother and father and his sisters were as one in their pride and affection for him. One person, perhaps, knew Andrew a little better than his family and friends. He had once met Mr Vass, the rector, on the road and stopped to ask him a strange question. 'If God asks you to do something, can you say 'no'?'

'Tricky question,' Mr Vass had replied. 'Theoretically you can say no. You have a God-given mind and a God-given will. The choice is yours. Just think, though. Where would we be today if Mary had said no to Gabriel?'

'Righto,' he had said. 'Thanks. I just wondered.'

Mr Vass had opened his mouth to probe but the boy had already walked off. Mr Vass wondered if he had been talking about a vocation to the priesthood like his grandfather, which would present him and his family with problems. Andrew had not mentioned it again.

This, then, was the family that lived at Inverally Hall, a large red sandstone mansion that had started life as a farmhouse for a Murray tacksman. Over the years it had been enlarged and improved several times on money made in the Glen Mhor cotton planatations in Guyana until finally the old Earl of Glen Mhor had added a handsome Georgian front intending that one of his sons should live there for part

14

of the year at least to keep an eye on the crofters he had evicted from his glens. It consisted of a conglomeration of small rooms, passages and unexpected stairways tucked behind an impressive beautifully proportioned suite of public rooms. Behind the house and arranged around a cobbled courtyard were stables for some dozen horses, various other outhouses and the factor's office. The extensive grounds consisted of a walled garden, three hothouses, a shrubbery, beech wood and a croquet lawn. The whole estate, which included two longish carriage drives and a scatter of cottages for the outdoor staff, was surrounded by a six foot high stone wall which had been built for the old Earl, Jock's great-granduncle, by those of his evicted crofters too scared, too old or too stubborn to go to sea.

Inverally Hall stood above and a little to the west of the village of Inverally on the south-facing coast of the Firth of Point in the north-east Highands of Scotland. The village itself consisted of three separate communities physically linked to each other, yet socially separated from each other by the Brae, a steep road dreaded by travellers and horses alike.

Kirkton, higher in rank and elevation, than Milton and Fisherton, housed the professionals – the doctor, ministers and teachers – also the small or impoverished gentry, mostly retired serving officers or their widows. Its substantial stone houses were surrouded by pretty gardens and had stunning views across the firth. Here Thomas Wilson's elderly spinster daughter (recently deceased) had lived in some grandeur able to keep an eye on the school and handsome chapel her father had founded for the children of his largely English mill workers. The current schoolmaster, the Revd Hugh Vass, previously a curate in Edinburgh (though a Highlander by birth), was persuaded by an evangelising Highland bishop to come north to his diocese not only to teach in the school but also to grow the church and provide regular services. Mr Vass convinced his frail young wife Emily to give up Edinburgh city life to settle in the north of Scotland to which she had agreed, not because she wanted to come, but because she loved her husband. He never knew just how homesick she was, because she never allowed herself to complain.

Milton, lower in rank and elevation than Kirkton but above Fisherton, boasted the High Street and was the trading hub of the community. The High Street housed the grocer, the ships' chandler, the baker, butcher and bank. The shopkeepers lived in tight accommodation above their businesses. Milton straddled the Ally, a river powerful enough to supply a pond and two mills, one of which was the small wool mill founded by a benevolent Englishman of Scottish extraction called Wilson. Here too lived the tradesmen and artisans in cottages and small houses of varying prosperity. The mill workers were housed in a row of tidy, terraced cottages built by Wilson for his work force on one side of the road. Across the handsome bridge, which had been designed by Thomas Telford, some half-mile up-river was the timber mill and yard owned by the grandson of the founder, a widower called Joshua Gallie, an upstanding, taciturn fellow, who, since the death of his wife in childbirth, had courted several widows but as yet had committed himself to none. He had one son, Aaron, aged twelve, a quiet, resourceful lad, who, though still at the parish school, was intended to follow his father in the timber business.

Fisherton was nearest to the shore, its small squalid cottages huddled gable-end to the sea and clustered around the harbour and curing yard. Fisherton had been hastily built by the said Earl of Glen Mhor for his cattle-owning crofters whom he had evicted during the clearance of Glen Mhor to make way for the more profitable Cheviot sheep. Fisherton folk were deeply respectful of old customs and the old ways. They still spoke Gaelic among themselves, were nourished on folk tales of the Celts, visited healing wells and believed as gospel in the predictions of *Fiosaiche*, (Fee-sa-her) their much-loved and long-dead local seer.

Three families dominated Fisherton: the Macreedies, the Munros and the Macmurdos. These names were seldom used except on birth or marriage certificates. Each family had a distinguishing bye-name. Thus the oldest late resident (he had lived to be 92) who was known legally as Solomon Macreedie of 2, Silas Lane, one-time skipper of the *Bright Star* was known in the village and to his mates as King Solomon; his children and grandchildren thereafter belonged to the King family. Donnaidh Macreedie at twelve thought of himself as Don King and Marsali, his mother, was not Marsali Macreedie or even King. She was Marsali Gansey from that branch of the Macmurdo family, who, two generations back, had invented a new pattern for the fishermen's thick woollen garment, now no longer a secret but still respected as such by the other families. Though they all could speak English, their preferred language was Gaelic and their culture indelibly Celtic.

Above and beyond the town stood Inverally Hall with its stables, gardens and a scattering of dwellings that that included the Mains farm which supplied the 'big house', as it was called, with the necessities of life. The farming folk did not mingle socially with Kirkton, Milton or Fisherton. Fisherton folk kept themselves to themselves. Only the laird's factor and the fisherwives moved freely amongst the four communities, the one to collect the rent from the others who sold fish to pay for it.

Chapter One

1890

Kirkton

Meg noticed things. Sometimes she wished she didn't. Like today, her bicycle ride of half a mile into the village, was marred by three mildly irritating flaws. The lower half of the east avenue had not been weeded recently. Several branches needed trimming from two of the beech trees which dipped untidily over the carriage way, and the wooden gates were wide open to the world. Wedderburn needed to pull his socks up. Just because the family mostly used the south avenue was no reason to neglect this one. She wished she could be indifferent. It was undoubtedly a curse not only to notice imperfections but also feel compelled to comment on them. 'You are far too critical, Meg,' her mother occasionally rebuked her, but she was not able to let go of small irritations, trivial though they were in the scheme of things. 'No, they are not trivial,' she argued with herself. It was well known, because her governess was never tired of telling her, that slackness in small matters led to carelessness in greater concerns.

Dismounting from her bicycle on that breezy April afternoon to close the gates she noticed that several of the wooden spars had rotted and that the whole gate needed a new coat of paint. With an impatient sigh she closed the latch firmly and added the state of the gate to one of the lists she kept filed in her head, and, as she remounted, pulled out another, a list of Latin irregular verbs learned for the forthcoming weekly lesson at the schoolhouse.

She liked Latin. It was a neat language, tidy, economical, and, apart from the irregular verbs, logical. She much

18

looked forward to the weekly lesson from the Reverend Mr Vass, the Episcopalian schoolmaster of one of the two local schools. He also happened to be her rector at the small local Episcopal church of St Moluag, the 'English church' as the inhabitants of Kirkton and Milton called it, the incomers with pride for many of them had English roots and all things English must *ipso facto* be superior, the Scots with scorn for they were suspicious of all things English. Fisherton dubbed them 'Piskies' which satisfied Mr Vass, who was never tired of pointing out that the Scottish Episcopal Church, although now in full communion with the Church of England, had its own hierarchy and superior origins that had nothing to do with Henry VIII.

He had, however, a particular fondness for the psalms which he would have Meg translate from the Book of Common Prayer, sometimes into, sometimes out of Latin. Occasionally, he could be diverted into discussing the proper names for wild flowers and their herbal uses which were her current interest. She would pick a handful by the hedgerows and take them to him. Always he knew what they were called. '*Bursa pastoris*, Shepherd's Purse. Good for open wounds,' he explained, and make her write down the declension of both nouns. 'You would do well, however, to study the Gaelic herbology,' he had advised. 'Their remedies are, on the whole, more appropriate to the neighbourhood.' She had been immediately interested.

'I never thought of Gaelic as having much sense to it.'

'That is what you are supposed to think,' he answered sadly. 'It has been the policy of the government for many years to denigrate the Gaelic language in the hopes of eliminating it altogether.'

'Why?' she demanded.

He pushed back his chair and crossed his legs. 'Politics and religion, Miss Meg, politics and religion. Jacobite politics and the Roman religion. Someday perhaps I will explain. Sufficient for you to know that Gaelic is God's own language - in my opinion.'

She was not sure if he was joking. Gaelic was the language of the kitchen maids and Fisherton.

'I'd like to know about their medicine.'

'We'll see,' he said with a smile. He had remarkably good teeth, she noticed not for the first time, though he rarely smiled. Her first impressions of people were formed by the state of their teeth. Good teeth were rare, bad teeth all too common, alas, and, in Fisherton, no teeth at all was the norm. Papa had difficult teeth. He attended a dentist in Edinburgh from whom he would emerge white and shaking and in need of brandy. Although he had served courageously in India as a soldier, had a rack of medals to prove it, that bravery did not extend to the dentist. Mama too suffered occasionally from her teeth, and, although she seldom complained, she often emitted a heady aroma of oil of cloves. Andrew's teeth were strong and a little crooked like hers whereas Isabella had perfect teeth, like Mr Vass, white, un-crowded and even.

'The Gaels had a cure for most diseases,' he was saying as she switched her attention off his teeth and back to his words.

'Even toothache?'

'*Ola cas easgainn, bainne cich circe...*,' he began, then translated the old cure-all rhyme into English:

'Oil from an eel's foot,
Milk from a hen's teat,
The tallow of midges
In the horn of a pig,
And rubbed on with the feather from a cat's wing.'

He was teasing her now. 'I am telling you, the Gaels had all the answers.'

She laughed as he intended she should and suggested that for home study she should translate the rhyme into Latin.

'Could you teach me Gaelic?' she asked impulsively.

'Certainly I am able,' he replied pedantically and immediately she saw her error.

'Would you, I mean? That is, would you be willing to teach me Gaelic?'

'Ah, well now, put like that I would be willing, but you will need your parents' permission,' he replied.

'They wouldn't mind,' she assured him.

'Are you sure of that?'

She was not at all sure. She remembered the last occasion, the only occasion, the language had been mentioned. She had overheard two of the maids, talking together in the boot-room as she passed and had stopped to listen.

'Mama,' she said later while they were sipping China tea in the garden, 'did you know that Effie and Ina can speak Gaelic?'

'Of course, ' she said.

'Does anyone else?' she had asked.

'At least half the village,' her father answered as he refolded the two-day old *Times*.

'Surely you knew that?' Isabella remarked, more surprised than scornful.

She had known, of course, but she had never thought about it. 'Why don't we know any Gaelic?' she asked curiously.

'*Cha Gaidhlig agam*,' her brother declared and added, 'Speak for yourself.'

'It's nothing to boast about, Andrew,' their mother said mildly.

Meg was only partly surprised. Her brother at twelve had the freedom to go and do as he please, mix with whom he chose. She considered him to be outrageously indulged.

'Gaelic is an uncouth language and not to be encouraged,' her father declared dismissively, ignoring Andrew.

'Why?' she asked a little truculently.

'Because, my dear,' her mother interrupted. 'It is divisive. It separates and divides a community whereas a common language unites them. It is our duty to encourage the fisher people to speak better English. Mrs Shanks would not be pleased to know that any of the servants were speaking Gaelic in the house.' Mrs Jean Shanks was the housekeeper who together with Cuthbertson the butler ruled the staff below stairs with a flat iron. They were both, in the eyes of the villagers, incomers, as was Jenkins, Papa's vile batman, now become his valet.

'In the old days - .' Meg had been about to say that Mr Vass had told her that everyone had spoken Gaelic. English was considered to be uncouth, but she was interrupted by her mother who told her not to be so argumentative.

She closed her mouth into a thin line, put her cup and saucer back on the tea tray and asked her parents shortly if she might be excused.

He mother sighed. 'Meg is becoming quite difficult,' she said to no one in particular, but Meg overheard her as she stalked away.

'If you are going for a walk, would you mind taking the dogs?' The Colonel raised his head from the *Times* just long enough to call after her.

Realising that this was not the time to suggest she learn Gaelic, she had summoned the two eager animals and taken the path that led up to the hill above the house. She was annoyed without quite knowing why. Within twenty minutes of hard walking she had reached the grouse moor that overlooked the estate, and, below that, the pall of smoke that hovered above the village. She found the old grey boulder that sheltered her from north winds and flung herself down on the heathery turf. The whole bay lay below her, a view she had taken for granted all her life but now, for the first time in her fourteen years, she studied it through critical eyes.

From here she could see the divisions clearly. The stony beach with the fishing nets hung out on lines to wash the salt from them, the small square sandstone tidal harbour where the zulus ingathered on Sundays, the large unsightly curing shed next to the tavern whose stench of ale almost out-stank the stink of stale fish. Fisherton was a quadrant of narrow lanes with the thatched cottages built gable-end to the sea. The cobbled streets sloped towards a central gutter down which the waste water oozed unpleasantly to find its way eventually into the sea. Middens, peat stacks and the occasional patch of kale crammed the narrow spaces behind the cottages where pigs rooted close to the two wells from which Fisherton took its water. If the wind was from the south the miasma reached the Hall.

Each street had been named for a Biblical hero chosen by the evangelical factor of the old Earl, who, some seventy years previously, had evicted the crofting forebears of the current inhabitants from the glens of their ancestors in favour of Border farmers and their Cheviot sheep, forced them to sell their cattle and become reluctant fishermen. Thus Abram Row ran parallel to Moses Street, Daniel Terrace to Silas Lane, Jemima Road to Deborah Path. Fine names indeed for the rows of cottages which had been barely adequate when they were built and were now damp, cramped and evil smelling hovels.

Meg's attention shifted from Fisherton to Milton where the trades-folk ran their businesses. She could count nine shops, including a chandler and a bank, haberdasher, two grocers, two butchers, a stationer and a post office spaced either side of the main Inverally High Street built wide enough to take two carriages side by side. At the far end of the busy street stood the station, a fairly recent and highly popular addition to the community, and, beside it, the Royal Station Hotel, a handsome red sandstone building with two bars, public and private, well patronised by strangers and locals alike. She could hear the faint whinny of a horse from the hotel stables. To Meg, it sounded like a pathetic protest against the 5.15 train that was building up steam on the platform ready for departure.

Her eyes shifted again to Kirkton. She knew that Kirkton folk despised Milton just as Milton folk thought themselves a cut above the fisherfolk The two communities socialised on Sundays and at the occasional village function such as a lantern lecture on Galvanism or the flora and fauna of Africa, but both ignored Fisherton folk, apart, of course, from the fisher-wives who sold them herring and haddock from creels at their back doors when the boats came in.

A child's cry drew her gaze on to the schools and the churches. Over the years a shift in the school attendees had gradually taken place. Most of the Milton and Kirkton children changed to the parish school because the bare-footed, ill-clad fisher bairns preferred the Episcopalian establishment. The reason for this was that Mr Vass distributed oranges or sugar mice on church festivals such as Epiphany and Easter, and these were rare treats for the impoverished Fisherton children. Occasionally some of the fisher children attended St Moluag's church, squashed together in two of the un-rented pews at the back, persuaded by Mrs Vass on the promise of a mint ball, but their parents never attended. Meg always knew when there were fisher bairns in church for their distinctive odour overpowered the sweet peas and roses on the altar. There had been complaints from time to time, but not often. Mr Vass had a way of making the complainers wish they had held their tongues.

She had always been told that the fisher folk were devout Christians. She had wondered about that, for, although the boats were usually in harbour and the streets quiet on a Sunday, none climbed the Brae to attend any kirk. All three ministers, Free Kirk, Presbyterian and Episcopalian visited Fisherton to take funerals and, in the case of the Free Kirk minister, hold an occasional service in the Mission Hall, a corrugated-iron roofed shack, yet converts to the three main churches were seldom made. She also knew that none of the three ministers emerged from their manses on the mornings that the boats set forth, the men perched on the backs of their wives if the tide was wrong to preserve their precious leather sea boots. Ministers were considered to be bad luck. This Meg found to be slightly shocking.

Gazing down at the village in the slanting sun of the late afternoon, Meg thought of the fisher folk she knew. Many of the estate workers and most of the lesser house servants were from Fisherton, distinguishable from the others by their distinctive Gaelic accents. It occurred to her that the estate was like another manufactory providing employment for those who could not go to sea or find work in the mills or the farms. But what did she know of them, their lives, their dreams? Did, she wondered, they think at all? She had always taken them for granted, a little like the family dogs, but not so friendly. Treat them well and they served you well. She had been taught to be polite but to keep her distance. 'Give them an inch and they'll take a mile,' was her father's maxim. He saw them not unlike his Indian servants, a sub-species, who, in exchange for a small weekly wage, a pound of tea and a joint of beef at Christmas, existed to provide a service.

She thought about Mr Vass. He too had a Gaelic accent, though his voice was gentler, less throaty than Effie and Ina's. That rhyme he had quoted was full of humour and wisdom, a mind-opener to her. Gazing down at the village in the fading evening sunlight, she was aware of a shift in her thought processes. She had always known in her intellect that the fisher folk were human beings like herself, but she had not recognised them as equals in any sense of that word. She began to understand why Mr Vass disliked Mrs Alexander's popular new hymn with the verse that stated: *The rich man in his castle,/ The poor man at his gate,/ God made them high or lowly,/ And ordered their estate.* It was not God who ordered their estate but men like her father. But that was not fair either. Her father employed them, leased them their cottages at a fair rent, made it possible for them to earn a living. That they lived in poverty at home and in danger at sea was not God's will, but nor was it entirely her father's fault or indeed their own. This was how things were, but did it always have to be that way? She had risen to her feet, called to the dogs and walked thoughtfully home, her mind made up.

'I should like to learn Gaelic,' she told Mr Vass firmly at their next meeting. He assumed, incorrectly, that she had her parents' permission and told her that he would be delighted to teach her.

The trouble with education, Meg thought, as she free-wheeled down the Brae was that for her it could not lead anywhere. Andrew was cramming for exams to get him into Wellington. He would go on to join the Royal Artillery, serve a spell in India and return to take over the estate. Isabella would marry. Why should she not have a career, go to the university and study medicine? It was not absolutely impossible in these modern times, but she did not think her

26

parents would stand for it. The hints she had dropped had fallen on particularly stony ears. 'Any Tom, Dick or Harry can become a doctor, Meg. You have been born to different responsibilities,' her mother had said. She knew without asking what they were, marriage, children, a large household, a role in society. It occurred to her that, in her way, she was just as restricted regarding her future as any of the fisher folk. They were cemented into a way of life through lack of education and money and class. She was equally trapped in her life by convention, her sex and social standing. She could no more change her circumstances than if she had been born in Silas Lane. Maybe Mrs Alexander was right. God had ordered their estate.

At least she was now allowed to bicycle on her own to her classes with Mr Vass and take walks by herself. It was only because she had recently celebrated her fourteenth birthday that she had been considered old - and hopefully sensible - enough to go out without her governess or one of the maids tagging along beside her. But, she thought, I am free in my mind to go where I choose, think what I like, achieve the impossible. We are all free in that other world within our heads. This was a revelation. Physical freedom to go, do and say what you liked was probably impossible for everyone, even her father, who was as bound to his estate as the fishermen to their boats. Mental freedom was available to all. A flood of relief like the rush of the wind in her face filled her with hope.

She arrived at two o'clock sharp that Tuesday to be greeted by the rectory maid who ushered her into the study. Although Mrs Vass chaperoned her lessons, with her baby in a cradle at her feet, she might just as well not have been present. She crouched in a low beaded chair by the window sewing little garments intended for African babies but which, Meg later discovered, usually found their way into Fisherton.

She would glance up briefly at Meg and smile, but Meg doubted that she actually saw her.

Emily Vass was delicate, no doubt about that. Gossip among the parishioners murmured that she was 'a poor soul' and that the rector should have married someone like Miss Caroline Budge, a hearty, capable farmer's daughter who played the harmonium behind blue curtains for Sunday matins. Mrs Vass's baby never seemed to cry, but lay back contentedly under his embroidered coverlet, a trouble to no-one. Meg who, unlike Isabella, was not much interested in babies, never gave Mrs Vass or the baby much thought. Not then.

Sometimes there were distractions. The schoolhouse was attached to the two form rooms, where, in Mr Vass's absence, the assistant teacher, Miss Rosie, struggled to keep the two classes - one consisting of fourteen boys between six and twelve and the other of a dozen similarly aged girls - under some sort of discipline. It required the patience of Job to quell the restless unruly classes with two teachers in control. When Mr Vass was otherwise occupied, Miss Rosie's only assistant was the strap.

Meg had barely pronounced her newly-learned Gaelic greeting before shouts and screams issued from the courtyard outside Mr Vass's study window. Usually he paid no attention, until, under the surprisingly dire threats of Miss Rosie, the noise died down. On this occasion, however, a stone hit the study window. Mr Vass exclaimed with exasperation, and, seizing his cane which lay ever-ready on his desk, strode out of the room. Meg went to the now cracked window to watch. A full-scale battle raged between Mr Vass's boys and the parish school pupils across the road. Stones were hurled, sticks brandished and, at the school gates, the bare-footed Vass 'loons' as they were called faced a crowd of jeering, stout-booted parish scholars from the school across the lane. The quines had crowded to their schoolroom window to egg their brothers on.

A few choice words from Mr Vass, with his cane under his arm, quelled his boys while the headmaster of the school across the road dealt similarly with his own pupils. The two men confronted each other with icy politeness. 'I would thank you, Mr Shaw, to keep your pupils to their own grounds,' said Mr Vass. 'If you would but install some discipline among your hooligans, Mr Vass, we would have none of this,' retorted the parish head teacher.

Both men nodded stiffly at each other, and, after some sharp words from Mr Vass, which she did not catch, his boys filed back into their classroom and the quines were released to their own yard at the back of the school.

'Discrimination,' Mr Vass was muttering as he came back into the study. 'I cannot abide discrimination.'

'Be calm, my dear,' Mrs Vass said gently, looking up from her sewing.

'How can I be calm in the face of this continual harassment?'

'I don't understand,' Meg said.

'Well then,' he replied roughly. 'You shall learn. What is the good of all this study, if you have no understanding of the humanity on your own doorstep?'

She was shocked. No one, apart, occasionally, from her father, had ever spoken to her in such a tone. For a moment she thought she might cry.

'Hugh!' Mrs Vass put down her needle. 'Miss Meg did not deserve that.'

He was immediately contrite. 'I beg your pardon, Miss Megaidh. I had no right, no reason, to speak to you so sharply. I tend to take out my frustration on whoever is within earshot as Mistress Vass can, I fear, confirm.'

He sat down again, silent, and Meg could see his dejection. All thought of tears vanished. 'Teach me, then,' she said impulsively. 'What is it I must learn?'

He looked up at her and sighed. For a moment their eyes met and held. She knew he was seeing an indulged and ignorant child. Why should he waste a moment more of his time on her? She was the first to look away, down at her hands. She had always been rather proud of her hands. She had crooked teeth, a nose that her mother called 'aristocratic', mouse-brown straight hair that hung down her back like a sleek waterfall and smoothed away from her brow by a petersham ribbon, eyes that were neither blue nor green or yet hazel, an indiscriminate mix, but her hands were pretty, were they not? Pretty, but useless. She hid them in the folds of her blue linen skirt. For the first time she saw herself as he must see her, worthless, idle, not particularly clever, privileged, a waste of his time.

He was still looking at her. She twisted her head away. 'Meg,' he said for the first time not using her title. She did not look up. 'How old are you?'

'Fourteen,' she whispered. It had always seemed a good age to be. Now it sounded ridiculous.

'Do you believe that God created all men in his image to be equal in his sight?'

She nodded.

'Ah, but do you? Do you really believe all people to be equal in the sight of God?

Jeemock, for example, who sits all day on the harbour wall and blasphemes at whoever passes by. Do you see him the equal say of, say, Mr MacQueen, or your father?'

What was she supposed to say? Mr MacQueen was the venerable Free Kirk minister who looked and preached like an Old Testament prophet. Surely he was not to be spoken of in the same breath as Jeemock, whom she would cross the street to avoid. Could he be the equal of her father, who was a gentleman and a soldier? In the eyes of God?

After a moment, she nodded again, '*The rich man in his castle, the poor man at his gate?*' she quoted.

'*Ceartas,*' he said lapsing into Gaelic as he leaned towards her, 'Certainly.That is just how it is. In spite of the hymn, do you really think that is how God intended it to be?'

She wanted to say 'no' but, truthfully, she was not at all certain what she believed. 'I'm not sure,' she said in a low voice, but then, quite suddenly, she was sure.

'Well, now, you are beginning to understand. Tell me this. Do you think that God has favourites?' She shook her head. 'Do you think that God is punishing Jeemock for his sins, but has rewarded Mr MacQueen because he is a good man?'

Again she was not sure. God was a jealous God, was he not? He was well able to punish those who were disobedient to him. And what about the sins of the fathers being visited upon their children? He was waiting for an answer so again she whispered, 'I'm not sure.'

He leaned closer. 'So you have led a spotless life, Miss Megaidh, you, your father, your ancestor, the old Earl, who provided work and cottages for his homeless crofters?'

She saw the futility of her argument. 'Indeed no,' she answered shamefully

'Does it not, therefore, follow that if God created all men in his image to be equal in his sight that his created creatures should see each other as reflections of his creation?'

She nodded.

'Think very carefully, Miss Meg. Jeemock, filthy, drunken, foul-mouthed Jeemock, a reflection of his creator?'

She was beginning to understand. The Jeemock she saw was not the Jeemock God had created, nor the Jeemock God saw. He was the Jeemock that poverty and ignorance, and yes, though it hurt to think it, her father, herself, had made. Again she nodded.

'Therefore should he not be treated with respect? With kindness? With love?'

She had a sudden image of Jeemock, filthy, leering, drunk.'I suppose,' she said a little doubtfully.

He leaned forward on his elbows over the top of his desk, his hands clasped, his expression intense. 'Don't think it easy, Meg. Never think it easy. It's far easier to act like the pupils across the road who treat my loons as dogs, worse than dogs, for they love their dogs. They have no love for their God-created brothers because they do not consider them to be sons and daughters of the same creator God; brothers and sisters. Do you understand?'

'I think so,' she murmured. If what he was saying was true - and she had never thought to doubt the gospel he taught - then she was as guilty as the boys at the parish school, for never in her life had she thought Effy and Ina, or any of the servants as being equal in any way. There were stratas in society, classes, barriers. Did Mr Vass think them all wrong, then?

'Your mother is an angel,' Mrs Vass interrupted at this point.

My mother, an angel, how? Meg wondered. She never thought of her mother as anything but her mother.

'Indeed, 'Mr Vass was saying, 'Mrs Murray-Myers is rightly known as the *aingeal* of Fisherton. You have made my point for me, my dear. An angel, however, is not a sister.' He turned back to her. 'Your mother is generous and kind to all those who are sick or impoverished in the village, but does she - and there are others in the community who follow her example - do they see those they succour as sisters and brothers of the same father, God.'

'I'm sure Miss Meg's mother does, dearest?' his wife rebuked him mildly.

It was not news to Meg that her mother visited Fisherton with baskets of eggs and posies of flowers. It was something that Mama did, with one of the servants to carry the baskets and another to drive the pony trap. Once she had taken Isabella, but never again. For some reason Isabella had fainted. 'It was the …smell', she had whispered afterwards to her sister as if she had spoken a rude word. Meg thought she would like to go but Mama would not permit it. She had thought her too young. She also knew that Mama did not see Fisherton folk as equal to her family in the eyes of anyone, let alone God. Mama was from the top drawer of society. Her family was a great deal older and nobler than that of her majesty, the old half-German Queen. It occurred to her that Mama did not see anyone in Inverally as her equal. And in one sense she was right. She was, after all, the great grand-niece of an earl.

'Mama always says that because we are privileged, we must be responsible. She would say that less is expected of people like Jeemock because they own less.' Even as she said it she knew it sounded wrong. If Jeemock was to be considered equal to the laird in the eyes of the Lord as much must be expected of him as of her or her mother.

Mr Vass was instantly contrite. 'I certainly do not mean any disrespect to your mother, Miss Megaidh. She is, as Mrs Vass has said, an angel of mercy and God knows that angels such as she are in short supply. It is discrimination that I detest, discrimination in the church, in the village and in the country.'

'Mr Vass wishes to change society beginning with pew rents,' Mrs Vass added with a hint of laughter in her voice. 'He is running uphill, is he not, Miss Meg?'

'I think I understand,' she said seriously. 'It's not what you do so much as why you do it.'

'Motive certainly,' he agreed, 'but it is more than that. It is a matter of recognising the creator God in each one of his children. It is a matter of humility.'

'How can people change?' she asked.

'Ah,' he said. 'That is the hardest question of all.' he was silent for a moment, his head sunk upon his chest. Suddenly he looked up. 'You start with yourself, Miss Megaidh. We must all start with ourselves.' Taking out his pocket watch, he studied it for a moment, then changed the subject. 'Your Latin exercise, if you please. We will start with the verb 'to be' in all its tenses.'

Obediently she took out her Latin notebook and switched her attention to *sum, es, est...*

The Hall

Twenty minute later she was out of doors again, bicycling past the little church, and, as she pedalled past the stone houses and pretty gardens as far up the Brae as she could manage, she remembered that conversation. Indeed she would never forget it. She knew she had learned more in those few minutes with the rector than all that her governess or parents or text-books had taught her. She had always known that there had been people in history, still were people, politicians, Whigs mostly, who tried to turn society upside down, radicals, her father would call them. It had never occurred to her that she could ever be one of them. Did she even care enough to be one of them? Did she want to change the way society behaved? Beginning with herself?

Dismounting to climb the Brae and still thoughtful, she passed a fisher-wife on the road with her creel slung over her shoulders, her striped petticoat hitched up to her waist, her brown legs and splayed calloused feet, bare, coated in dust. Meg had seen her, or one of her neighbours, countless times on the road, acknowledged their passing with a curt nod, but had never before properly looked at them. Now she did. The woman looked tired, her mouth sunken into her jaw for she had no teeth at all, her brown face a network of lines, her bare arms strong and sinewy, and her back bowed.

She stood aside and for a moment their eyes met. Shyly Meg found herself saying '*Feasgar mhath*'. The woman looked at her with astonishment and suddenly came out with a spate of Gaelic which left Meg speechless and bewildered. Then she heaved off her creel and there at the bottom lay a couple of silver herrings. Finding a dock-leaf in the hedgerow she wrapped the fish in it and held it out. Meg backed her bicycle and protested in English that she had no money. The woman shook her head vigorously. 'For you, Miss. It is a gift.'

She did not want the fish. She cared little for herring but she knew she must not refuse. '*Moran taing*,' she said, for 'thank you' was almost the only Gaelic term she could remember.

The woman smiled toothlessly, nodded and hoisted up her now empty creel and with a wave of her hand walked away.

As Meg placed the fish carefully in the wicker basket in front of her handle-bars along with her Latin primer, she was filled with exaltation. She stood for a moment looking back at the retreating fishwife. Could it really be this easy?

In that moment of contact, she made up her mind. She would be one to build bridges. She would be one to break down the conventions that kept society divided, Inverally class-ridden.

How would she do it? By learning the language of Fisherton, by befriending the fisher folk? That was what her mother did, the angel lady, who descended from a great

35

height and dispensed largesse. As she pushed her bicycle up the east avenue she remembered the jeering lads at the school, the stones and the language which she could not understand yet knew to be shocking, the girls who shouted encouragement to their brothers from the open class-room window. Her life was so different, structured and privileged, nurtured and controlled, that she did not really know where to begin and she was overwhelmed with a sudden sense of hopelessness. All those other people who had tried to change society had failed, had they not? Mr Vass surely was one of them. If he could fail, what hope had she? Unless…Unless she became a person of importance. A minister was out of the question, a nurse perhaps like Miss Nightingale…a doctor? The idea that she had already half rejected came storming back into her mind. Society would listen to a lady doctor, would it not? This time she would not give up so easily. Mr Vass would help.

Pushing her bicycle over the large sweep of gravel in front of the house, she noticed two vehicles, a brougham and a gig drawn up in front of the house. One of the grooms stood by his horse calming its restlessness. The other sat back his hat pulled over his eyes obviously asleep. There were callers in the drawing room. She knew who they were. Leaving her bicycle in the harness room, she slipped into the house through the library French window hoping to escape to her room unnoticed, but nothing went unnoticed in the big house. Jenkins, her father's manservant, was crossing the hall. He eyed her boldly, that look of contempt and awareness that she particularly hated. Without catching his eye she handed him the herring. 'For my father,' she said curtly. As he took them from her, he moved to stand between her and the staircase, too close. 'They are h'all in the blue drawing room h'in case you was wondering,' he said as she inched past. His breath stank of onions.

'Thank you, Jenkins,' she said aware of his insolent stare. 'I'll be down directly.'

'Please yourself,' he muttered rudely. At least that was what she thought he said. She ignored him. On the first floor landing she met her governess. 'Oh, there you are, Meg. You are very late. Mr Vass should not keep you so long. You look over-heated, and - how is it possible? You have a distinct odour of fish. As soon as you have changed and tidied yourself you are wanted in the drawing room.' Miss Fraser looked pinched and flustered. Meg saw by the look of her eyes that she had a migraine, but knew better than to comment. Miss Fraser did not like it to be known that she suffered from migraines.

'Please don't wait for me,' she said sympathetically. 'Why don't you lie down?'

'Thank you but I am perfectly well.' Miss Fraser wanted, needed, to keep her job. She had an invalid mother in Perth to support.

Stripping off her linen skirt and high-necked blouse, Meg poured cold water from the tall china ewer into the basin and washed her face and hands. The pink sprigged muslin afternoon dress lay across her bed. Though it felt cool and fresh, she hated it. Pink was not her colour, but, as yet, she had little choice over her clothes. She brushed back her long hair and changed the navy ribbon to one of pink satin. In the looking glass she thought she appeared faintly ridiculous, like a silly doll. She was too old to be dressed in sugar candy like a child.

Her door opened and Miss Fraser came in. 'What an unconscionable time you are taking, Meg,' she said a little crossly. 'Please come directly.'

Annoyed by the intrusion, Meg said nothing. Why should she not have a lock on her door like her sister? She would speak to Mama. Somewhat truculently she followed her governess down the stairs. Jenkins was still hovering. She thought she heard him snigger as Miss Fraser opened the drawing room door and stood back to follow Meg into the room. She caught the expression on her governess's face and was suddenly angry for her. She hated Jenkins.

There were four women present, grouped in comfortable chairs around the tea table laden with silverware, gold-rimmed Wedgewood china, and heaped with an abundance of scones and cake. April daffodils and narcissi brightened every available polished surface and the room smelt as it always did of flowers and wax polish.

'Ah, here is Meg,' her mother said ignoring the presence of Miss Fraser who, as was her custom, took a low chair behind the grand piano. Meg saw her put her hand to her head. The migraine was still bad, then. Poor Miss Fraser. She might, or might not be offered tea, depending upon which of the maids was serving. Today it was Mima, a well-trained, middle-aged table-maid from Inverness. Miss Fraser would be served, eventually, when everyone else had finished and the tea gone cold. Meg knew this but had never thought much about it. Today she noticed. When Mima brought her a cup of fragrant China tea and placed it with a plate and napkin on the small table at her elbow, she said in a low voice, 'Please take this to Miss Fraser.'

Mima was visibly outraged by the implied criticism. Meg, aware of her pressed lips and averted eyes, held her ground. Lifting the cup and saucer, she handed it back to the servant. 'Please,' she repeated, but it was not an appeasement, it was a command. Mima, with a bad grace, did what she was told but managed to spill tea in the saucer as she did so. Miss Fraser, far from being grateful, kept her head averted. Meg sensed that she felt humiliated. Nor did Mima bring Meg more tea or offer her any food.

Mama's visitors included Lady Moncrieff, her sister Mrs Maria Kennedy and her daughter, Harriet. After she had had some conversation with Harriet who was in her middle twenties and wore a cluster of diamonds on her engagement finger, Meg, now hungry, crossed over to the tea table, poured herself a cup and helped herself to a scone. No one noticed, or so she thought, except a glaring Mima, because, at that moment, Isabella came in through the French window escorted by the Honourable Captain James Moncrieff, one of the three men her sister professed to love. Isabella looked ravishing in white muslin, her yellow hair scooped up in a loose knot at the nape of her neck and escaping in tendrils to curl around her ears and on her brow. Her cheeks were flushed and Meg knew immediately what had happened. Within seconds her father and Lord Moncrieff entered the drawing-room looking pleased with themselves. The Colonel then announced somewhat pompously that his daughter and Captain Moncrieff were engaged to be married.

The Moncrieffs were not as aristocratic as their name and title suggested. Lord Moncrieff was the grandson of (whisper it softly) a pedlar, a travelling chapman who had, through the invention of a cure-all called Jackson's Elixir, made himself a fortune and thereby earned a peerage. His grandson had married into the Moncrieff family, taken his wife's name, inherited the Moncrieff estate in Perthshire, enjoyed rather too extravagantly his father's fortune and educated his sons at Eton. James, his younger son, had two older siblings - Angus, his father's heir who was currently abroad, and Harriet, engaged to an English industrialist. James was an officer (like his prospective father-in-law) in the Royal Artillery and exceedingly handsome. It was a good match for Isabella. If Mama thought the family a little beneath her own, she kept her opinion to herself. After all, one can't have everything. Isabella, as the future Honourable Mrs James Moncrieff, would be established for life.

As the congratulations, the handshakes, kisses and embraces, flew around the room, Andrew, home for the Easter holidays came in, scruffy as always, smiling as usual. As Meg watched him shaking hands with the Moncrieff family, she wondered, as she so often wondered, what made Andrew so special. He had a presence, as if an extra lamp had been lit in an already sunny room. Everyone suddenly seemed to be laughing, at ease, happy. She watched James' sister, aunt and mother, all of them elegant, sophisticated women, at ease in society, become animated, witty even in his presence.

Munching a scone he came over to her, smiling. 'Beat you at croquet when they've gone?'

'You will not,' she retorted.

'You know I will,' he said over his shoulder as his father summoned him to speak to Lord Moncrieff.

She crossed the room to offer her sister her congratulations. 'Are you sure he's the right one?' she whispered curiously. Isabella tended to talk freely about her lovers to Meg and she knew that James was only one of three, less amusing than one, less well-to-do than the other, albeit decidedly the most handsome.

'Of course,' she said flushing prettily. 'It was always James. He looks so splendid in his uniform.' It always came as a slight shock to Meg to realise, as she had only recently recognised, that her older sister was perhaps a little silly.

The wedding was to be in three months time in early September towards the end of James' furlough after which she would accompany him back to India to join his battalion.

'It will be your turn next,' Harriet, her future sister-in-law, said to her kindly, when, after tea, Mama suggested that as the sun was warm enough they might like to see the garden. The herbaceous borders in the walled enclosure blazed with blue grape hyacinths, scarlet tulips and paper-white narcissi and the air hummed with newly awakened bees as she considered this remark. She had always liked Harriet, probably because she bothered to be friendly. Most of Isabella's contemporaries ignored her.

'I shall never marry,' she said decisively and when she saw Harriet's smile of disbelief she added with a touch of defiance. 'I think I might like to become a lady doctor.'

'Really?' said Harriet with surprise. 'Will you parents allow that?'

'I suppose not, no,' Meg shook her head.

'Are you serious, or is this just a whim?'

'I'm not sure,' she answered. 'I know I want to do something useful with my life.'

'Well then, I do know of some one who might be able to help you. You should write to Miss Jex-Blake. Do you know who I mean?'

'Do you actually know Miss Jex-Blake?' Meg was impressed. Sophia Louisa Jex-Blake was famous, or rather infamous, for campaigning to allow women to qualify in medicine. She had actually founded a medical school in Edinburgh a few years back although, so far, no women had been allowed to graduate. Miss Fraser had told her she was considered to be a controversial figure.

'The thing is, Meg,' said Harriet,' if you want something badly enough you have to fight for it, especially if you are a woman.'

Meg looked at her curiously. 'Did you?'

'Not hard enough,' she said, twisting her engagement ring. 'Seemingly I was destined for marriage, but, just because I failed to go to university does not mean that you need fail. I could send you Miss Jex-Blake's address.'

The Moncrieffs left soon after Meg's conversation with Harriet, and Isabella went with them to spend a few days in their Highland home, a shooting lodge in Wester Ross. When they had gone, Meg turned to find Andrew at her elbow. 'Come on,' he said, 'time for croquet.'

The game did not go well. She could not concentrate. In her head she was already composing her letter to Miss Jex-Blake and forming the words she might use to persuade Mama. Andrew noticed. 'Isabella will be all right, you know,' he said misinterpreting her silence. 'James is nice.'

'What would you say, Andy, if I told you I want to be a doctor?'

He lined his ball up to hers preparing to smash it into the rhododendrons. ' I didn't think girls could be doctors,' he said hitting the balls hard.

'They can't, not yet, but I want, at least, to learn,' she said as she followed her ball across the lawn and aimed to hit it back at his.

'A lady doctor!' he said. 'I can just see you with your little Gladstone bag and your silver spoon. Open wide, if you please, madam. Say ninety-nine, sir.'

They both laughed as her ball amazingly clicked against his. 'Now it's my turn!' she said in triumph as this time she clocked his ball into the rhododendrons.

After the guests had gone, Mama, on her way to change for dinner, joined Meg in the schoolroom and sat down in Miss Fraser's chair. Miss Fraser had already gone to bed and Meg was trying to compose a letter to Miss Jex-Blake.

'Meg, my dear,' Mama began. Meg sighed inwardly. Her mother only called her 'my dear' in that tone when she wanted to reproach her. 'What happened in the drawing-room at tea today?'

She knew exactly what her mother meant. 'Mama,' she said, 'the servants are always so rude to Miss Fraser.'

'And you were rude to Mima. You hurt her feelings.'

'She hurt Miss Fraser's.'

'No, my dear. Both Mima and Miss Fraser know their place. It is not for you to teach them.'

'Mr Vass says we are all equal in the sight of God.'

'Mr Vass is well-known to be a radical but even he would know better than to hurt the feelings of one of God's children, and, in so doing, embarrass another.'

Meg was suddenly on fire. 'I hate these foolish divisions in society, Mama, between lords and grooms, table maids and governesses, men and women. I have quite made my mind up. I want to become a lady doctor.'

'My dear Meg, you are barely fourteen. You are not old enough to know what you want. God may well have other plans for you. If, in three years time, you are still of the same mind, we can discuss the matter again.' She stood up to leave the room.

'I won't change my mind,' Meg said stubbornly.

Mrs Murray-Myers smiled. She had an extraordinarily sweet smile, Meg thought, just like Andrew. 'When I was your age,' she was saying, ' I wanted to become a nun. I wanted to join the Sisterhood of St Margaret in East Grinstead but God had other plans for me.' She opened the schoolroom door. 'As I said, we will discuss this when you are old enough to know what God has in mind for you. Meanwhile you should remember that in society there are boundaries. If you try to cross them there are often unfortunate consequences. I wonder if perhaps you should stop your Latin lessons with Mr Vass. I'm not sure his influence is altogether good for you.'

She was appalled. 'Oh please, mama, I love Latin. All Mr Vass said was that all people are equal in the sight of God.'

Mrs Murray Myers thought for a moment, then she said calmly,' I can't argue with that. As long as you realise that we also have to live in society.'

'Then I can continue with my Latin?' she asked anxiously. She said nothing about Gaelic.

Mrs Murray-Myers put her two hands on her daughter's shoulders and kissed her on the brow. 'My darling, I am not condemning you or Mr Vass for your opinions. Far from it! I'm proud of you. If, I repeat, in three years time, you still want to become a doctor, I promise to speak to your father.'

Meg gazed at her mother in awe. For the first time she saw her as a human being, a person in her own right, not just a figure of authority to be taken for granted, respected and obeyed.

'Did you really want to become a nun?' she asked awestruck.

'Yes, I did.' Mrs Murray-Myers smiled again. 'I wanted to change the world through the power of prayer but God had other ideas for me. You were one of them.'

She had one more question. 'Mama,' she called after her as her mother opened the door, 'please take me with you next time you visit Fisherton. After all I am fourteen.'

This was not the first time that Meg had asked. Mrs Murray-Myers had always refused, her excuses being twofold. She was too young and the dangers of infection from the miasma that surrounded the cottages too great. This time however, her mother paused outside the door and turned her head. 'I should be delighted,' she said and smiled again.

Meg went back to the schoolroom and over to the window which looked out over the flight of stone steps that led from the front door down to the sweep of gravel with the wide lawn beyond, fringed at the far end by a stand of beeches. Half hiding behind one of the stone pillars at the foot of the steps, she could see Donnaidh Macreedie, first and best of

Andrew's Fisherton friends. Bare-footed and bare-legged, he skulked. There was no other word for it and she knew why. If Cuthbertson caught sight of him anywhere near the Hall, he would chase him off with a scolding. As she watched, Andrew emerged from the front door and ran down the steps. Donnaidh came out of hiding to greet him. Andrew flung his right arm around his friend's neck and must have made a funny remark, an Andyism, as Isabella once called it, for Donnaidh, as dark as Andrew was fair, doubled over in laughter. Still she watched as they raced across the lawn until they reached the fringe of trees. There Andrew bent down, took off his boots and stockings, tied them together and slung them over his shoulder. Then they both ran off and quickly disappeared between the trees

Meg shivered suddenly. She noticed, or it may have been hindsight, that the beeches on the far edge of the lawn were thrashing, for the wind had risen.

Milton
'Where is that confounded boy?' Joshua Gallie slammed his fist down on the table top sending the cutlery jingling.

'Here, sir.' Aaron entered the dining room as his father spoke and slid into his chair between his father and his Aunt Agnes.

'You're late', he grumbled as he reached for a bannock and his sister ladled out the hot beef stew and piled his plate with potatoes and carrots.

'Sorry,' his son mumbled as he reached out for his own plate.

'What were you doing? You know I like to be sat down at six sharp? And look at the state of you.'

There were times when Joshua Gallie could not bear the sight of his son. When he asked himself yet again why the boy had survived and Victoria had not, he felt no shame, only anger. He looked so like her, the same deep-set grey eyes, the same fine brown hair, the pale unblemished skin, but he was not her, not even an acceptable substitute. Why was this? How was it he could not love his son for the very attributes he had adored in his wife? He did not understand himself and the less he understood himself, the more angry he became with the boy. But, he told himself, it was only in his looks that he aped Victoria. In character he was as unlike her as sand is to sawdust. Victoria had been lively, teasing, talkative, quick to laugh him out of his moods, persuasive, but Aaron was timid, dour and silent, a boor of a boy. He had once said as much to Agnes, but she would not see it. 'Aaron's a good lad. You put the fear of the devil into him, Josh. You have made him what he is,' she told him boldly. 'I'm sorry if the truth pains you but it needed said.'

He ranted at her for a while, but he knew she was right. He knew Aaron was a good lad, respectful, liked by the men. Even so, he himself could not bear the sight of him.

'You should marry again,' Agnes advised, 'have more bairns. Then maybe you'll learn to appreciate the son you've got.'

And yes, he knew she was right. He had courted several fine lasses, but loved none of them. Victoria had spoiled him for other women. There was no one in Inverally he even fancied. The station master's younger niece was too plump, the doctor's daughter simpered, Miss Budge who played the organ in the English church too opinionated, and Janetta, a game keeper's widow, was too nippy by half. There was only one woman he could bring himself to admire and she was unattainable, the laird's lady. His Victoria had been a lady too. A wealthy Glasgow tobacco merchant's daughter, well out of reach to a small-time timber merchant from the Highlands, she had fallen in love with him on a visit to her cousin, a retired Creenock ship-builder and his wife who lived in Point, and there was no gainsaying Victoria. About once a month on a business trip to Inverness by the new railway, he visited a certain house across the river where all his needs in that direction were adequately taken care of. The only reason for marrying again would have been for more children but there was no woman among his acquaintance, apart from the unattainable Mrs Murray-Myers, at whom he would glance twice.

Tonight he had a genuine bone to pick with his son. 'I hear there was trouble again at the school. Were you involved?'

'No sir.' Aaron kept his eyes lowered on his plate of beef stew.

'What was it this time?' Joshua continued. 'Those bloody brats at Vass's, I'll be bound. That Macreedie lad the ringleader, eh?'

Aaron said nothing.

'Well?' his father grumbled. 'Was he or wasn't he?'

'What sir?'

'Are you deaf? Was the Macreedie lad involved?'

'Might have been,' the boy mumbled.

'How often have you been warned to stay away from that family?'

Agnes, who rather liked the dark, curly-headed mischievous Don Macreedie protested. 'He's good enough for the laird's lad.'

'The laird's lad is well out of it, He'll be back to his grand school come May.'

As he uttered the words, he knew the solution. It has been at the back of his thoughts for weeks now. 'I've half a mind to send you off to school myself. See how you like that'

Not a muscle on the boy's face twitched. Nor did he reply.

'Well?' his father goaded.

'Whatever you want,' he mumbled, not looking up from his plate. The gravy was already congealing.

'Whatever I want! When was it ever what I wanted? It doesn't much matter what I want or what you want for that matter. You're going. There's that school in Glasgow where your uncles went – the Academy. Let's hope they can knock some sense into you. It's easy seen you've learned nothing in the parish school.'

Not a twitch of his features nor a blink of his eye betrayed what Aaron thought. Inside his head, he was dizzy with anticipation. He knew if he showed his excitement, a suspicion of how he really felt, the prize would be snatched away.

'Well then, you dozy blockheid. You'll be off just as soon as they'll take you.'

Agnes, put up a heartfelt protest. 'You surely don't intend to send your only bairn away to strangers?'

'My mind's made up,' Josh told her while shovelling meat into his mouth. 'The sooner the better.' Then he turned to his son. 'Away to your books. I cannot abide the sight of you.'

'He hasn't finished his dinner yet,' Agnes protested but not too hard. Neither father nor son paid her any attention. Aaron rose and without looking at his father or his aunt left the room.

'Well,' Joshua growled, 'let's hear it then. Get it off your chest. I'm a cruel, no good father. How could I think to send away my only son to a pack of strangers,' he mimicked in a whining falsetto.

Agnes screwed up her eyes, a habit she had developed in childhood when she was thinking. Truth to tell, she thought it the right decision. He was a strange boy, right enough, secretive, prickly, unloving. 'Maybe it's for the best,' was all she said.

'Of course it's for the best. He's a lazy, good for nothing lay-about,' he blustered. Deep down he was appalled at himself. What would Victoria have thought? He pushed aside his plate.

'Will you take some Dundee cake with your tea?' his sister asked.

'Hang your tea,' he muttered. 'I've books to do.'

She was left alone at the table and not for the first time. For a meal to end amicably was an unusual event these days. Joshua would stump off to the office to go over the orders and the accounts, while Aaron... God knew where Aaron went, but it was certainly not to his room. She always checked but he was seldom there. She never mentioned it to Josh. He never asked.

Neither of them noticed Aaron slip into the kitchen but Sarah did. Sarah Munro, seaman's widow from Fisherton and maid-of-all-work to the Gallies, knew exactly where he was going.

'I'm for off then' he called out to her from the back door.

'Be good,' she called out after him, 'and if you canna be good, be careful.

Fisherton
Marsali automatically counted the heads gathered together for the evening meal. Only Ezra was missing. Without Ezra the room seemed half full. She knew exactly where he was. The men gathered most evenings at the tavern when the boaties were in. 'Don, away you to the tavern and tell your father that his meat is on the table,' she told her youngest son. She needed money for the rent, for oatmeal, for wool, for Donnaidh's school fee, a penny a week and there were three weeks owing, not that Reverend Vass ever insisted, may heaven bless him.

There was no thought of waiting for the man of the house. Two of his three sons had been at work all day, Jared as an apprentice to the chandler on the High Street and Jonas as a labourer in the curing shed at the pier head. Donnaidh, the youngest at twelve, was still at Vass's school up the Kirkton Brae. They ate their pork and onions with mealie pudding and potatoes in silence and with relish. His daughter Effie lived in at her work in the big house kitchen.

'Was that the wee runt, then?' Jared asked indicating his pork dinner.

'It was,' said Marsali. The family sow was supposed to be kept with the others in a small park beyond the bridge but few could afford the rent in the lean days before the white fish season properly started so it rooted mainly in the small back yard beside the water closet until funds allowed it into the park again. The runt of last year's litter had also stayed in the back yard and would now keep the family fed for the next week or so.

When they had eaten, the two elder lads scraped the scant remnants of bone from their plates into the swill bucket and with a brief word to their mother left the cottage. Jared was courting, Jonas off to the pier for craic with the other village lads. Don came in as they left and fell upon his plate of rare meat.

'Is he coming then?' Marsali asked in exasperation.

'*A dh'aithghearr,*' said Donnaidh, 'soon,' with his mouth full. He scraped the last of his gravy off the edge of his plate with a hunk of bannock. 'I'm away out,' he told his mother from the door.

'*Cait a bhaeil thu 'dol?*' she asked, as if she didn't know where he was going.. He and his two mates were not above a bit of poaching on the sly.

'See you and behave yourselves,' she told him in Gaelic. What she meant was, 'see you and don't get caught.' The laird's factor had already threatened to involve the law.

Marsali ladled a plate of food from the pot, cut the meat up into small pieces and carried it through to the wee room in bye where Ezra's mother lay on her mattress propped up on three straw pillows covered in rough striped cotton. Her breathing was bad tonight. Marsali removed the Gaelic Testament from the stool by the cot, sat down and prepared to feed the old woman. It took a while because without teeth and with the palsy that affected so many of the fisherfolk, she could not hurry the business. The old soul seemed worse this evening, for the shaking exhausted her frail body and her cough was bad. Her mind, though, was still alert. She loved to hear the village craic.

'I was seeing that girl, the *Aingeal*'s quine, on the road today,' Marsali told her in the Gaelic for it was the only language the old woman spoke these days.

'The one with the yellow hair in it, or the other?'

'The one they call Miss Megaidh. She was speaking to me in the language!'

The old woman paused in her munching. Under the thin white thatch of her hair, her eyes, quiet dark pools in the wrinkled network of her skin, were curious.

'What is that you are telling me?'

Marsali held out another spoonful, 'I was thinking of asking if there was work for Donnaidh at the Big House.'

'I thought he was going for an education?'

'So he was but there is no living in it. I am thinking the young laird would speak for him and the *Aingeal* - and maybe the minister.'

'It is better that he should stay at the school.'

'That is what I am thinking. But then there is Ezra who is wanting him on the boat.'

51

'Leave Ezra to me,' the old woman said turning her head away. She could stomach no more food. Marsali leaned forward and wiped her chin with a cloth.

At the same moment the door opened and Ezra stood there in his stocking soles.

'What does my mother want of me now,' he said good-humouredly. The drink always made him mellow. He was also good-humoured because the word in the tavern was that the haddock were on their way.

'Read me a verse of two from the Testament,' she told her son in the Gaelic.

'Aye, when I have had my meat.'

'Now' she insisted and he did not argue. The only person in the village that Ezra obeyed was his mother.

'Donnaidh,' she said before he had started. 'He is not for the sea.'

'You are in the right of it. He will never make a fisherman but he is of an age to work,' Ezra said as he shuffled through the Testament till he found the words he knew best. Ezra was not that good at the reading but the words of Matthew were so familiar to him that he did not have to read them.

'No, son.' The old woman was agitated. 'Not the sea, do you hear me?'

'I hear you, mother,' he said to humour her.

'I have had a dream,' she said, still agitated, the words shaking with her body. 'He is not for the sea.'

His mother's dreams were to be respected. 'I hear you,' he repeated and launched into the Sermon on the Mount. '*Is beannaichte iadsan a athat bochd 'n an spiorad…*'

The old woman joined him in the words, '*oir is leo rioghachd neimh…*'

Marsali took the plates outside to wash them in the pail by the back door. Her neighbour Anna called out to her across the picket fence. 'Have you heard the latest? Miss Isabella is to be wed!'

'Is that so?' Marsali replied, dragging her mind off Donnaidh and his education.

'I thought your Effie would have told you,' she said with a hint of triumph. She was not usually first with news from the big house. Her youngest son laboured in the timbermill. He had an eye for Effy who skivvied in the Hall kitchen but Effy was sweet on Sam Stuart who worked in the stables.

Marsali had seen Effy that afternoon when she had taken her fish up to the Hall kitchen. She knew there had been visitors upstairs but nothing had so far been said, though much suspected. This was good news. A wedding at the big house meant a week's free rent and other perks.

She and Anna discussed the bride and prospective groom for a while, but Marsali's mind was not engaged in the gossip. Donnaidh was on her mind. Mr Vass had told her that his schoolwork was well above that of his contemporaries. 'He has a gift for learning,' he had said meeting her outside the school not long after she had given the last of her fish to Miss Megaidh. 'He could go to the university at Aberdeen.'

'Could he be a teacher?' she had asked.

'He could become anything he set his mind to,' Mr Vass had told her. 'He has the ability.'

Marsali loved all her children; Jared for his charm, he could sweet talk his way into anything he wanted. That was how he had got the coveted job at the chandler. Jason for his weaknesses, he had neither charm nor good looks. He would always find life hard. She loved him because he needed her love, and then there was Effie, her only daughter. Effie was Effie, her ally, her other self and the image of her father in looks. Donnaidh was her baby. There was no doubt that he was a favoured child. Good to look at with his rich dark brown hair that curled all over his head, and blue eyes on him that were always laughing, always alert to her moods and wishes. But he was not her only baby...

Donnaidh was putting on his working jacket. Already too short in the sleeves, it had belonged to Jared and Jonas before him and bore the stains and darns of all three. Soon Don would outgrow them all, she thought, and then where would his clothes come from?

'What's that on your jacket?' She asked, noticing the black smear across the cuff. He pretended not to hear. It looked like pitch. If so, it could only have come from the local carpenter, undertaker and boat-builder. He kept it in a big barrel in his yard and anyone could take a jug-full for a few pence. But what would he be wanting with tar?

'What are you up to, the three of you?' she asked, and, knowing he would never tell her, did not wait for an answer. 'I'll need you up by six on the Quaking Sands. The tide 'll be right for the lugworms.'

'Aye,' he said cheerfully. 'I'll be off then.'

Where are you going, she wanted to ask, but knew better. The answer would be 'out' which told her nothing at all. What are you up to, she would have liked to insist, but knew the answer would be 'nothing'. She could only trust that he would be safe with his two companions, Aaron from the timberyard and Master Andrew, the young laird from the Hall. Her three bairns, she called them, for so they once had been, Aaron, a girner from his cradle, Andrew, the bonniest loon she had ever suckled, her own included, and Don, the leader of the pack.

She hoped it would not be rabbiting again. Aaron kept the ferret in one of the sheds at the back of the timbermill, but it was Donnaidh who had wheedled the snare out of the gamekeeper in exchange for an hour's labour in his prized garden. The factor had warned them twice already. A third

54

time he swore he would hand them over to the law but by that time Master Andrew would be out of it, safely hidden away in that great school of his. She sighed as she drew out her knitting needles tucked into the pouch at her waist for her fingers were never idle. They knew what to do while her thoughts wandered off in several directions. The old *mathair*, her health failing fast... Ezra with the rheumatics already gnawing at his back... Jared walking out with that grand lassie from Milton. There would be trouble over that. A chandler's daughter was considered too good for a fisherman's son.

She remembered again Miss Megaidh who had spoken to her on the road. She was a great one for the book learning, so it was said. Marsali imagined her future, bonny dresses, parties and marriage spread out before her, servants like Effie to answer every request. She would sail through her life without a care in the world, sunshine all the way. What did she need with book learning?

Not for the first time, she considered the unfairness of life. It was not that she grudged Master Andrew and Aaron the privileges they had inherited of an assured future at the big house or in the sawmill, not at all. It was just that she wished the same security for her own sons, particularly her youngest. Had he not always had to take third place, even at her breast? If he had been ambitious like Jared or argumentative like Jonas, she would not have cared. But Don was special, brighter than his brothers, bigger than his two companions not only in height and girth but in character, inventiveness and in leadership. Whatever the three of them were up to, Don would be in control. What might Don not do with an education, a position in society, wealth. He could be Prime Minister.

The old *mathair* was calling. Poking her knitting back into its pouch, she hurried to attend to the old woman's needs.

Her mind, however, was made up. She would remind the schoolmaster of his promise to speak to Mistress Murray-Myers and she herself would have a word with Miss Megaidh.

The Hall

What exactly happened that night they never knew for sure. Certainly there had been a storm, a sudden quick temper of wind which had flung a drift of twigs and new leaves over the lawn and died before daybreak. Meg was in the schoolroom next morning with Miss Fraser studying *The Tempest* when Mima knocked on the door to summon her downstairs to the library.

Both her parents and Wedderburn were standing mute, still as statues, grey as ash, facing the long windows that looked out on to the lawn.

Her father turned. 'Meg, my dear, when did you last see Andrew?' His voice was strange and cold.

'Yesterday,' she answered. 'We played croquet. Why? Where is he?'

Her father turned away, nor would her mother look at her. She stared out of the window, dry-eyed, stricken.

'Why?' Meg insisted. Her inner organs seemed to collapse in on themselves. 'What has happened?'

It was Wedderburn who spoke. His moustache hid his mouth but his huge greying brows could not hide the devastation in his eyes. 'A boat has been found upside down and drifting in the bay. Two local lads are missing. Andrew may have been with them. Did he tell you where he was going?'

'Is it Donnaidh Macreedie and Aaron Gallie?' she asked in a shaky voice.

The factor nodded.

Then Andrew would have been with them. They were inseparable, had been from the cradle, always up to something. She knew because Andrew had told her they had been building a boat. It had been Donnaidh's idea, Donnaidh's design and Donnaidh would get the tar. Aaron could get timber and nails from the yard and Andrew was always the willing go-between.

She remembered very clearly when she had last seen her brother. They had played croquet but he had not turned up for the six oclock schoolroom supper with Miss Fraser. Nothing significant in that. He often begged something from Cook if he was going out in the evening. She told her father in a flat voice that she had seen him from the schoolroom window. He had been crossing the lawn and Don Macreedie had been with him.

There is no pain like the agony of a lost child. She, her mother and her father stood apart unable to find comfort even in each other. Her father was the first to move.

'Where are you going?' her mother cried out unnecessarily.

He did not reply as he crossed the room in three strides and flung open the door.

'I'll go with him,' Wedderburn told her and followed him out of the door. Meg ran into her mother's arms. She was crying now. Her mother, dry-eyed, held her for a moment. 'That poor, poor woman,' she was saying, 'I should go to her. Ring the bell, Meg.'

Cuthbertson answered, his voice and eyes lowered, as her mother ordered the carriage to be sent round.

'I'm coming with you,' Meg said.

'Dry your eyes then,' her mother ordered but not unkindly. 'Pull yourself together,' she added but Meg knew that these were instructions to herself, for she was on the edge of hysteria.

'It will be all right, Mama,' she said playing the adult role. 'We'll find him.'

Her mother said nothing. In silence they mounted the closed carriage. For a while they sat opposite each other in an agony of silence until Meg noticed her mother's hands twisted together, the knuckles white bone under taut skin. She could not bear the agony of those twisted hands so she crossed the coach to sit beside her and forced her own fingers between her mother's clenched fists. Mrs Murray-Myers seized on her hand and held it tightly between cold fingers.

The whole village, it seemed, were waiting at the pier, Fisherton, Kirkton and Milton folk united in anxiety for the three lads.

Donnaidh from Fisherton, Aaron from Milton and Andrew from the Hall had been friends from the cradle, more than friends for they were also foster brothers. Not that Meg knew this at the time. Much later she learned that Marsali, who had been nursing Donnaidh, had been summoned to the big house. Meg's mother had been ill after Andrew's birth and because Andrew was unable to digest cow's milk, the doctor had recommended Marsali. Some three months later, Aaron's mother from the timber yard had died in childbirth and her infant put to a wet nurse who had been taken ill with a fever so Marsali had suckled that little lad too. The three young boys were inseparable until Andrew at seven had gone away to boarding school, but he still spent his holidays in their company. Aaron at twelve, who attended the parish school, was to be apprenticed to his father, the timber merchant, while Donnaidh, who was noticeably quick and bright, remained at Vass's, his future uncertain. As they grew older, all of them had learnt new ways of mischief, Aaron had discovered ale, Andrew had acquired a savage little jill ferret which Aaron housed for him and Donnaidh, who 'had the brain in him', devised the boat.

It was a revelation, the crowd and the silence. The carriage clattered noisily over the cobbles to stop as close to the pier as the coachman could safely manoeuvre. Mama had stood for a moment with one foot on the carriage step, scanning the faces until she had seen Marsali and a whey-faced Effie, flanked by two women standing a little apart from the silent mass. Ezra, his sons and those men not already at sea, united in anxiety, were already out in their boats scouring the waters of the bay for any sign of the missing lads.

The silent crowd stepped back to let the laird's wife through. Meg followed. To her surprise she saw that Marsali was the fisherwife she had spoken to on the road the previous day. Was it only yesterday? That encounter seemed so long ago, a lifetime away. To her shocked surprise, Mama put her hands on the woman's arms and drew her close. They stood there for an immeasurable moment, beyond tears, beyond comfort.

'They are in God's hands,' Mama murmured.

'*Ochone, ochone, ochone,*' Marsali keened. They clung to each other united in agony. Presently some of the men returned. They had news. It was Mr Vass who came over to tell them. The bodies of Andrew and Aaron, wrapped in each other arms, had been recovered, stranded by the tide and torn by the rocks off Point headland. Their boat was later found submerged and drifting half a foot below the surface of the water a good mile from the shore. It had been pronounced, by the men who found it, a good wee boat, well-constructed and safe enough in calm waters, but the sudden night squall had been too great and the boys'seamanship inadequate. Although there was as yet no sign of Donnaidh, none doubted he had suffered the same fate.

The whole household went into mourning. The dress-maker was summoned hastily to make Meg the obligatory black dress which she had not as yet needed to acquire. The funerals were delayed as long as possible in anticipation of Donnaidh's body turning up, but sadly, though the fishermen scoured the waters and shores for miles, no trace of him was found. 'Likely he was swept out to sea,' they told each other sadly but without surprise. Death by drowning was all too familiar an event in Fisherton. Meanwhile a devastated Isabella had returned immediately from her betrothed's home. A week passed and as there was still no sign of Donnaidh the funerals could be delayed no longer.

Although Aaron and Andrew had died together, they were to be separated in death. Andrew's coffin, palled in purple, led by the local piper, with the whole county in sabled attendance, was taken to the family vault in the churchyard outside the kirk of St Moluag. Aaron, in an even more splendid ceremony drawn by four black plumed horses was buried beside his mother by Mr Carruthers in the Church of Scotland kirkyard The only links between the two funerals were the identical wreaths of white lilies fresh from the Hall hot-house. Colonel Murray-Myers attended both ceremonies in full Highland regalia.

Day after day, thereafter, the county called to offer flowers and condolences. Black-edged mourning cards and letters poured in from all parts of the country. The question no one quite liked to ask was answered voluntarily by Mrs Murray-Myers herself. Most certainly Isabella's wedding would go ahead as planned for the 17th September. To wait a further five years for her fiance's next furlough was out of the question.

Meg, caught up in a whirl of activity, dutifully sat for fittings, made lists of the gifts as they began to arrive, lists for her sister's trousseaux and lists for the great camphor

60

scented boxes that would contain household linen, china and the other necessities for setting up a household in India. It was all done quietly without laughter. Without Andrew, there was no joy in it.

But life went on. Decisions were made and discarded. Instead of the six bridesmaids Isabella had originally planned, she was to be attended by Meg alone, and although Isabella was to wear pale coffee-coloured lace, Meg would be in mauve as befitted a mourning sister. Her mother would change from black to purple temporarily for the occasion.

Meg's Latin classes were halted. It was now high summer, and lessons with Miss Fraser also ceased. She too was roped in to help with the preparations until summoned to Perth to attend to her mother who could no longer live alone. She was hardly missed. Poor Miss Fraser wept to leave the household. She knew she would not be coming back. Meg who had grown tolerably fond of her hardly noticed her absence.

The wedding service itself was to be quiet, conducted in St Moluag's by the bishop with Mr Vass in attendance, immediate family only, after which Isabella and James would travel south to spend a few days in Edinburgh and from thence to Liverpool to embark for India. The garden party planned for a hundred or so guests was cancelled in favour of a quiet luncheon for family and intimate friends. A list of every gift and its giver was recorded in the Northern Chronicle from mother-of-pearl handled butter knives (no less than three), to a splendid inscribed silver salver from the estate tenants. Two days before the ceremony, the gifts were crated and entrained to Liverpool to join the ship that was to take the newly weds to India.

After the wedding luncheon Meg watched the carriage retreat down the south avenue lined with cheering tenants. Now what will we do, Meg thought... now there is only me.

Nothing was said, however, and nothing decided. Isabella, whose new husband seemed a sensible fellow, was now presumed to be the colonel's heir. The estate, however, was entailed in the male line and the laird had nephews, the Dean of Westchester Cathedral's two sons. At Andrew's funeral, the dean had not been slow to promote their interests, tactfully of course. 'If you need some help with the estate, I believe Victor could be persuaded,' he had said placing a brotherly arm around Jock's shoulders. 'You need a man at a time like this. Victor is young, I know, but he can learn the ropes.' Jock, inarticulate with grief and outrage, had said nothing

Then Grizel had told him of Meg's ambition to be a doctor. 'Never!' he had declared. 'Never in a thousand years.'

'There is one way to keep her at home,' she told him. 'She's a clever girl. Break the entail. Make her your heir.'

He said nothing but he knew he should make a new will. As a soldier, he was well acquainted with the impermanence of life; as a father, he now understood its frailty. He was well over fifty years old. Isabella's husband was a good chap, but he was also a career soldier. Was it fair to encumber him with Inverally? He remembered his own resentment at having to leave the army to take over the estate. There was always the possibility, a strong possibility, that Isabella might have a son. That was the answer; wait and see. He did not care for his twin brother, the Very Reverend George Myers. He had two children, twin sons. Cedric the younger, a deacon soon to be ordained priest, somewhat pompous, was now a curate in a prosperous country parish with excellent prospects. Victor, the elder, was still at home with no ambition to go into the church or join the army; a useless silent sort of fellow or so he seemed to his uncle. Jock had been piqued because none of the family had come north for

Isabella's wedding, considering it unseemly so soon after Andrew's death. Certainly the dean had brought his family north for Andrew's funeral, but his demeanour had been both greedy and critical. Apart from hinting that Jock make Victor his heir, he had considered that Andrew had been allowed too much latitude. Had he been under a stricter regime at home, the accident might never have happened. It had always been understood in the family that the evangelical dean had disapproved of Grizel's father's connections to the Oxford Movement with its Catholic leanings. Jock, who did not want either of his nephews to inherit Inverally, said nothing.

Make Meg his heir? The thought had never occurred to him. Grizel was right in her remark that Meg was the clever one in the family, no doubt about that, but she was argumentative and self-willed, and now all this nonsense about wanting to train as a doctor. A doctor for God's sake! He knew he should make up his mind. Isabella's as yet non-existent son, Victor or Meg? Breaking the entail would be a costly troublesome business. Meg will marry, he told himself, but if it were to be known she was an heiress, all the gold diggers in Britain would be after her for the estate. So, partly for that reason, partly in the hopes that Isabella might soon give him a grandson, but mostly because his grief had made him deeply depressed, he did nothing.

Meanwhile Grizel's grief found an outlet. Always a religious woman, - how could she escape? - her dead father had somehow become confused in her mind with God - she persuaded her husband that in Andrew's memory the church should be improved by a stained glass window. Christ walking upon the water. Grizel's private wealth exceeded that of the colonel so expense was no problem. Mr Vass was summoned. The plan for a window was chosen, approved by the bishop, and a stained glass artist (vastly expensive) recommended by the diocesan architect. She pored over colours and designs. Her visits to the poor and sickly in Fisherton increased and sometimes Meg accompanied her, but more often she preferred to go alone, and, when alone, it was to Marsali's cottage she went. There she stayed and there she sat while the fisherwife's needles clicked. They spoke hesitantly at first, then freely, of their lost sons. Sometimes she drank tea. Once, on a hot day, she sipped a cup of water.

Kirkton

After the wedding Meg begged to be allowed to continue her Latin lessons. Neither of her parents had the heart to argue with her so, twice a week, she continued to bicycle down to the schoolhouse, or, if the weather was vile, and, if her mother had no need of it, she took the pony trap. On those occasions, she wrapped herself up in a mackintosh cape and tied a scarf over her hat. She lived for her lessons.

Mr Vass was not always free to teach her. Miss Rosie, the assistant teacher, was poorly that winter, and, as there was no improvement in her health come the spring, he was confined to the classrooms; nor was Mrs Vass always able to chaperone her. It had become generally known in the village that there was consumption in her family. Indeed her mother and sister had already succumbed and Emily Vass's high colour and bright eyes told their own story. She was, as often as not, resting while the little boy, Hamish, who was now walking, was left in the care of the maid, Morag Macmurdo, a quine from Fisherton. It was Morag who told Meg that Mrs Murray-Myers spent many hours with Marsali. 'My mother says they are come together in their grief,' she whispered. Meg's heart ached for them both.

Meg herself had found some consolation in the rector's little boy. If Mr Vass was occupied in the classroom and Mrs Vass resting, she sought out Morag in the nursery above the study and together they played the whole hour with little Hamish. His sunny temper and smiling welcome as he staggered over to the door to greet her, reminded her of Andrew, but not in a painful way. He filled her heart with joy as he leapt up into her arms and cried her name, 'Megaidh!'

'Miss Megaidh,' Morag prompted him, but Meg was too busy lifting him aloft, tickling and cuddling him to notice.

Morag had a lover, and once during a March storm when the boats were in harbour she asked Meg if she could watch the little boy so that she could steal an hour with him. Meg was delighted. Thus it was that when Mr Vass returned from the classroom, he found them together. He said nothing when she explained as tactfully as she could that Morag had been called away. Instead he caught the little boy up in his arms, laughed and said something to him in Gaelic. In that moment of revelation, Meg was reminded that it was not just the little boy that she came, twice weekly, to see, not only the Latin and Gaelic knowledge she had come to acquire. Just for an instant she saw Hugh Vass not as a priest, her teacher, the father of Hamish, nor as the husband of a delicate wife. He had become changed from being a god without feet of clay into a mortal man. It was a delicious moment, that put brightness back into her eyes, lifted her spirits and gave her a renewed reason for living.

He looked at her over the little boy's head. If he saw anything different in her expression, he did not acknowledge it. 'I am sorry, Miss Megaidh. There will be no Latin today. As you can see my hands are full.'

'*Tha mi dulich*,' she murmured disappointed, '*A mairaich*? Tomorrow?' she asked hopefully.

65

'*Gle mhath! A marraich.* Good afternoon, Miss Meg. You will excuse me. As you can see, I must attend to my son.'

She rose to go. He followed her while the little boy wriggled like a fish in his arms.

'Is there any news of Donnaidh Macreedie?' she would ask him occasionally in those sad autumn months.

'No news. I doubt there will ever be news.'

'Do you think then that he was drowned too?' she asked. It was what most of the village thought, apart from Marsali, his mother, whose belief in her son's survival was unshakeable.

'I fear so.'

She nodded and turned to go. After a time no one asked any more.

Milton

Agnes was concerned for her brother. She seldom saw him during the day for she was busy with household concerns, he at the mill. Dinner now was a largely silent affair. Though, as the days passed, she attempted conversation asking him about his day, his workers by name, his health, he seldom answered with more than a grunt. When he had eaten, he would go to his office and get out the whisky bottle. Hours later she would hear him pass her bedroom door, stumbling, cursing, muttering, to fall into a stupor on his own bed.. Agnes hated whisky for she had seen how it had killed their father when Josh had been not much more than Aaron's age. He knew how drink could ruin a man and his family with him, yet here he was repeating the very pattern that had destroyed his own father. And now he had no son to step into his shoes. Bowed down with her own grief for she had loved the gentle boy who was so like his pretty mother, she was

66

not only concerned for Josh but angry with him too. Thus the dinner hour was painful in the extreme for she wanted to shout at him, tell him to pull himself together, accuse him of having been too harsh with the boy when he was alive. What right had he to indulge himself, to play the grieving father when she could not believe his grief to be real. He had always been so hard on the boy. A pretty sight for Sara when she brought in the vegetables, Josh black with rage, herself with tightened lips, her own anger ready to explode.

Three days after the funeral, she could contain her resentment no longer. He had brought the whisky bottle to the table. 'I'm thinking of leaving,' she said suddenly and abruptly.

He said nothing. Instead he took a mouthful of the steak pie on his plate. 'It's your own fault. I won't sit by and watch you drink yourself into the grave the same as my father.' Still no reply. 'Did you not hear what I said?' she added sharply, 'or do you not care?'

'I heard,' he said coldly. 'You'll no doubt do as you please, though where you're likely to go is another matter. And how you'll manage on what our father left you is yet another matter entirely'

'I'll manage,' she retorted quickly. But they both knew he was right. Agnes had a hundred pounds a year left to her by her father. Otherwise she was entirely dependent on her brother.

'Don't expect me to bail you out.'

Agnes felt miserable. She had been her brother's housekeeper for twelve years now, since Victoria's death. Before that she had cared for her own widowed mother who had retired to a small house in Kirkton where she had moved on her son's marriage. Apart from those short two years of Josh's marriage, she had lived her whole life in The Timber House. The thought of leaving it was terrifying. She had no

67

friends outside the town and she was now forty-six years old. The only man who had ever loved her had been entirely unsuitable as a husband for he had been a Macmurdo from Fisherton, a relative of Don Macreedie, a fisherman who had drowned not long after she had refused him. She had always had a fondness for Donnaidh because he was so like his uncle Ethan in looks and in his speech. And now Donnaidh and Aaron, like Ethan, were all gone. It flashed through her mind that if she had married Ethan, she might have persuaded him out of the fishing and he would be alive today.

'I could get work,' she began defiantly.

Joshua laughed bitterly. 'Don't expect a reference from me.' He pushed back his chair, picked up the bottle and left the table, his meat half eaten.

Fisherton

The old mother was always thirsty. She was the first to die of typhoid, long before Doctor Anderson had had a chance to test the water in the well at the end of the street. By that time, the flies, the filth and the contaminated water had done their worst. Mrs Murray-Myers had taken her the mildest of broths, the tastiest of dishes, had even sat with her and read some verses of the New Testament, but it was too late. The old woman died later that night with her family gathered around her bedside.

Three days later, Grizel herself was taken ill. She knew that she would die and she was glad to go, or so she told Effy in her delirium. Who would have thought that God could be so merciful? She was not particularly sorry to leave her daughters because she truly believed that she would still be able to care for them from the next world where she would be with her respected parents and her beloved son once again. It seemed to her to be a fair exchange. Isabella had her own life to live and Meg had her father. Her only real regret was the stained glass window. She would never now see it installed.

During her sickness, she would not allow Meg near her, so Effy, Marsali's daughter now promoted from the kitchen to housemaid, who had been in contact with the old mother, became her constant companion, her nurse and her comforter when the diarrhoea prostrated her and the headaches blinded her and the fever sent her into a gabbling delirium.

Typhoid was endemic in Fisherton. Sometimes it was the water in the well that was polluted by the privies of Milton and Kirkton which were built on higher ground, but often the fever attacked when the water was pure. Doctor Anderson told Wedderburn that it was a disease caused by poor sanitation, and, until conditions changed, Fisherton would never be free of it. Wedderburn, who had heard it all before, did not tell the laird. He had tried to make changes before, but the colonel had told him that there was no point. That was the way things were among people who knew no better. It had been the same in India with the cholera. Wedderburn, who was ageing and thinking of retirement, did not argue.

Meg wrote to her sister on the day her mother died as she did every week, knowing it would be months before she received a reply. There was nothing Isabella could do, especially not now with a baby on the way.

Dean Myers with his wife arrived the following afternoon. The colonel aroused himself from his grief sufficiently to inform him that Grizel had left instructions that Mr Vass was to conduct the service in exactly the same way as he had done for her son. The dean was offended, and his wife more so, when the colonel asked his fifteen year-old daughter to take his wife's place at the head of his dining table. ('She's not even out yet and her hair is not up,' she had complained to the dean in the privacy of their bedroom). They left as soon after the wake as was seemly, but not before the dean had said what he had come north to say. 'Since Andrew has entered into glory, you need to think seriously about an heir, Jock. As I told you last year, Victor is willing to come north and learn the management of the estate. Wedderburn won't live for ever and this is a man's task.'

'I'll think about it,' Jock replied gruffly. He did not like to be reminded that his own son was dead.

'Victor is not academic. He would be ideally suited to country life.'

The colonel nodded abruptly. He could not trust himself to reply. He was consumed with anger every time he thought of his twin brother's greed. George, he reckoned, had always been jealous of his inheritance which had been due solely to seven minutes of seniority. Now he wanted it for his son. In spite of his irritation, Jock knew that the offer was sensible. Wedderburn had already hinted that he would like to retire; Isabella's husband had recently been promoted to major in the army where he was seen as general material, or so he had been told, and even if her forthcoming child were to be a boy, it would be twenty years before he would be fit to run an estate. 'Think about it,' George had advised as he prepared to join his wife in the carriage that would take them to the local railway station. Again Jock did not reply. He did not want to think about it.

Without a word, he strode past Meg who was standing on the top step of Inverally Hall waving goodbye to her uncle and aunt as they drove off. He called to Jenkins to fix him a whisky soda and disappeared into his study. He was still angry.

He was always angry these days. Since Andrew's death, his brows had been drawn together in a perpetual scowl, and, since Grizel's death, the lines had deepened. He believed that fate had dealt him a blow too many. What had he done to deserve such a punishment? He once murmured something of the sort to the parson and got little sympathy. Deep down inside his soul he believed both deaths might have been something to do with himself. He supposed he had loved Andrew but, in his heart, he had also considered him a bit of an idiot. Once in the warmth and darkness of the marital bed, he had whispered as much to Grizel. 'Is Andrew all right, d'you think?'

She had not immediately reassured him. Instead she had said, 'Why do you ask?'

'Spends all his time with those young village louts,' he had muttered.

'He'll grow out of it,' she had said sensibly.

But Andrew had not grown out it. He hadn't lived long enough and now Grizel, the woman he had never loved with passion but had always respected, was gone leaving him alone with Meg. He had never approved of Grizel's close involvement with the fisherfolk. He should have put his foot down. They had both known that typhoid was endemic in that slum. He looked at his daughter down the length of the long dining table, beyond the two tall candles and did not know her. Grizel had been a handsome, if not a pretty woman. Isabella was considered beautiful with that mass of corn yellow hair, but Meg with her thin face, crooked teeth and intelligent eyes, was like a stranger to him. He wondered if she still had ambitions to study medicine. If so, he had better squash that one stone dead. Meg must marry someone of whom he approved, a man he could trust with the estate.

He opened his mouth to say as much but she was already speaking. 'Father,' she said quietly, 'something must be done about Fisherton.'

71

'What are you talking about?' he asked roughly. Unreasonably, his seething inner anger rose to the surface.

'Mr Vass told me of a village on the Moray Firth not unlike Fisherton where the laird has provided boxes at the end of the streets for the removal of rubbish which are emptied once a week and disposed of in a disused quarry.'

He stared at her in amazement. 'What are you talking about?'

She held her ground. 'Miasma and filth and flies,' she said with spirit, and added in a low voice, 'I am talking about mama's death.'

'My dear child! Do you think a few boxes at the end of the street would change the habits of generations? These people live like savages because that's what they are. They would create a pigsty out of a palace. They know no better.'

She leaned forwards. In the candlelight, her eyes gleamed, almost beautiful. 'Papa, have you ever visited any of the cottages? I have. Mama did. They are poor yes, but most of them are clean and swept and cared for. It is the streets and the middens and the privies that are filthy for there is nowhere to put the waste.'

'You don't know what you are talking about.' He sounded dismissive.

'Perhaps not,' she replied, only a little daunted, 'But Doctor Anderson knows. Mr Wedderburn knows. Go and see for yourself. Mr Vass says -'

'Mr Vass says, does he. That well-known radical! How dare that jumped-up fellow of a parson stir up trouble in my village? Never cared for him. Boxes in the street! What next.'

'I thought it might be a suitable memorial to mama,' she said quietly

Suddenly the anger left him. He was immensely tired. 'I think you can trust me to find your mama a better memorial than that, my dear,' he said coldly, and to show he hadn't forgiven her, he added. 'It's time you grew up. That ridiculous idea of studying medicine must cease. No more Latin, if you please. You are, for the time being at least, mistress of a considerable estate. Your responsibilities lie here.'

Until that moment, he had not known that he was going to tell her. Indeed he had not been sure up to the moment of speaking that he intended her to be his heir. But the words now said could not be unsaid nor did he wish to unsay them. She was a good girl most of the time, strong-willed but nothing wrong with that, so long as she did what she was told when it mattered.

She said nothing. The news was not a surprise. She had taken it for granted since the death of her mother and brother that she would sit at the head of his table at least until Isabella and James returned from India.

'I mean it,' he blustered. 'No more Latin.'

Her father had said nothing about Gaelic. Of course he did not know about the Gaelic lessons and she was not in the mood to inform him. I must have something to lighten my life, she told herself.

Apart from Sunday church and his formal visit after her mother's funeral, she had seen nothing of Mr Vass lately and she missed her lessons.. Now that she was considered to be temporarily mistress of Inverally, the familiar gossip of Effy and Ina and the rest of the army of servants who lived parallel lives in and around the big house no longer reached her. Although she felt no different, she was aware that she was considered to be different. It left her lonely but with plenty to do. Mrs Shanks now came to her with the menus and accounts. Gradually, under the housekeeper's tactful guidance, she began to take over her mother's household duties. The accounts, correspondence, keys, personal

73

problems, illnesses and complaints of the house staff became her responsibility. In addition to these duties, her mother had kept up a correspondence with several missionary workers in Africa and India, had supported the Aberlour orphanage and numerous other Christian organisations, to which she was now expected to contribute. She could afford it as she now owned a third of her mother's personal estate.

First and foremost of her duties was to complete her mother's heartfelt tribute to Andrew, the stained glass window. She persuaded her father to enlarge it to include a memorial to her mother. When he questioned the expense, she told him that she would pay it from her own bequest. It was all surprisingly expensive, but, in her opinion, worth every pound. St Moluag's little church glowed with colours that were reflected in the stone every time the sun shone. In due course the window was unveiled and dedicated by the bishop in the presence of an admiring and congratulatory congregation who assured her that it was indeed a fitting tribute to a wonderful lady and her fine son.

Chapter Two

1895

The Hall

Meg sat at her bureau in the breakfast room on a fine May morning. Now that she was more or less her own mistress, her life was more regulated than ever it had been in the schoolroom. The week lay before her as planned as a ship's log. Any deviation from the norm put the whole household into a fluster. She glanced down at her maroon leather-backed Charles Letts diary but in fact she had no need to consult it. She knew exactly what she had to do and when to do it.

Today was Monday. The new week brought no prospect of change to the routine. Rise at 7, take the dogs out for half an hour, notice if the grass needed cutting, the gravel had been raked and weeded, the maids up and at their housework. She had no real need to check the former for it was Wedderburn's job, or the latter for Mrs Shanks continued to oversee the household as efficiently as she had always done. Now Meg made it her business to keep an eye on the ageing housekeeper's health. Though Jean Shanks would not admit to seventy, she had been sixty-nine for at least three years, having always, and wrongly, assumed that no one would notice.

At 8 am Meg breakfasted in the morning room, the menu unvaryingly the same, porridge, toast and scrambled eggs. At 9 am she visited her father's ground floor apartment. Colonel Murray-Myers had had a stroke two years past which had paralysed his left side. In some ways his mind was as sharp as ever but emotionally he had changed. Her aloof undemonstrative father had turned into a child, she the

75

parent. She could not have coped without Jenkins whom over the years she had learned to respect, if not like. She dared to believe the feeling was mutual.

'How is my father?' she asked him, as she asked every morning when he opened the door to her knock.

'Bullish. We've 'ad news,' he said winking.

Meg had got used to Jenkins' winks, having realised long ago that they were neither conspiratorial nor a sign of over-familiarity. Whenever Jenkins had news, his left eyelid seemed to work of its own accord. The tic had never been more noticeable than on the day he had to tell her, a couple of years back, of her father's apoplexy.

'Good morning, Papa,' she said crossing the great Indian carpet to where he sat, dressed and at his breakfast in the spacious room whose French windows opened out on to the flower garden. It had been converted for his use from the old library .

'There you are, Meg,' he said crossly. 'Show her, Jenkins.'

Jenkins handed her the opened letter. It was from his twin brother, Dean Myers. Meg glanced through its contents.

'...I've heard on the grape vine that Wedderburn has finally decided to retire, and high time too. Now, therefore, might be the time to consider employing Victor as your factor. It seems to me entirely sensible that the young people get to know each other now so that when the time comes – and I pray God it may be later rather than sooner – Meg will have the support of her family, and the estate will once again find itself in capable hands ...'

'He never gives up,' Colonel Jock said the colour rising in his face. 'What does he mean "once again in capable hands"?'

'Canny, canny, sir,' Jenkins said smoothly, the tic once again shuttering his eye 'We don't want to make h'ourselves h'ill again, do we?'

'Stop nannying me, Jenkins. Shut up, can't you.'

'My Uncle George is right about one thing, Papa. Mr Wedderburn is well over seventy. He must be allowed to go.'

'I suppose he must,' the colonel said truculently. 'But that boy, what's his name - Victor - is a bloody idiot. What does he know about running an estate? Just wants to get his hands on Inverally.'

'Perhaps we should advertise the post,' Meg suggested calmly.

'Advertise?' the colonel echoed, appalled. 'Let any Tom, Dick or Harry apply? Over my dead body! I suppose the boy had better come. Wedderburn can show him the ropes before he goes. Write to your uncle. If Victor wants the position, he had better come and try it out. Three months should be long enough.'

Meg sighed. She remembered her cousin Victor without much affection, a thin gangling young man who seldom uttered. The situation however was tricky. Isabella still had no children, her two pregnancies having miscarried. Unengaged herself at nearly twenty and with no suitors in mind, Meg was practical enough to realise that the estate which she now knew to be entailed in the male line would eventually have to go to someone. If neither she nor Isabella were to produce an heir, Victor or Cedric would automatically inherit Inverally. That being so, would it not be better if Victor learned the ropes from Wedderburn than inherit knowing nothing? They should be thankful it was not his younger brother Cedric, now a vicar near Bath and the most odiously sanctimonious of young men. For all she knew, Victor might have improved with age. He would be about twenty-five, she reckoned.

The truth of the matter was that she itched to manage the estate herself and believed it was within her capability, provided of course that she had someone to collect the rents and prosecute the poachers. It could be a blessing to have a young vigorous factor, hopefully with radical views, who would at least listen to her ideas. Every small change she had managed to inaugurate had been achieved only after endless discussion and delay from old Wedderburn. She had finally managed to introduce waste boxes at the end of each small street after three long years of objections both from her father and the factor by paying the bulk of it from her own fortune. Now it was her ambition to bring running water into each home but knew it would never be done while Wedderburn remained at the helm. As the factor had aged, so his views had narrowed. Conservation of the status quo and retrenchment were his trademarks. Innovation, especially when it cost money, was always to be avoided. Hopefully her cousin Victor would have more enlightened views. Surely he must do.

At ten o clock she called in at the estate office, a stone building at the end of the stable block, cold even in the summer. Today, with an early May mist on the ground, Effie, Marsali's daughter and now the groom's wife, who earned a few extra pennies by keeping the office clean - not a hard task as the old factor was meticulously tidy - was lighting a fire.

'Morning Miss Megaidh,' she said cheerfully getting up from her knees and smoothing down her apron over her noticeably pregnant bulge.

'How's your mother?' Meg asked after she had inquired for Effie herself. The baby was due in three months time.

'There's been news,' Effie said. 'I was not meant to say anything yet, but there was a message. Donnaidh's been seen again.'

Meg closed her eyes briefly. Although it was now five years since the three boys had gone, Marsali's belief in her son's survival was fuelled from time to time by sightings. Although her hopes were continually disappointed, her trust was unshakeable. Fishermen had returned with word that Donnaidh had been seen in Wick or in Ullapool or as far afield as Ireland and Cornwall. Once it had been Jamaica.

'Where was it this time?' Meg asked. Though, unlike Andrew and Aaron, no body had ever been found, like the rest of the village, she had long ago given up all hope of seeing her brother's friend alive.

'Chicago. A crofter from Skye who is a cousin of Ina swore that he had seen him across a road.'

'Did he not try to speak to him?'

'Seemingly he disappeared into the crowd.'

'So once again your mother's hopes are raised,' Meg remarked quietly.

'Well, but it could be true, Miss Megaidh,' Effie said hopefully. 'Mam says -'

At that moment Ian Wedderburn opened the door, saw Meg, and, frowning, pulled his watch from his fob pocket. He did not like to think he was late.

'I'm a little early,' Meg said smoothly and sat down in the chair opposite the old man's desk.

Effie put a couple of logs on the now blazing fire, picked up her bucket of ashes, bobbed to no one in particular and left the office.

They spoke of estate matters for a few minutes. Mrs Shanks had reported that the servants' hall chimney was smoking again and Meg herself had noticed on walking the dogs that the fence to the east meadow was faulty by the water-gate.

Ian Wedderburn duly made notes, asked for the colonel as he always did and then mentioned his own retirement.

'I was coming to that,' Meg said smoothly. 'My father wishes to offer a three months trial of the post to my cousin, Mr Victor Myers, provided you would stay on to train him?'

Wedderburn frowned. Meg knew he had hoped to be gone in three months time. 'If I must,' he agreed stiffly, 'but I have to say that, in my opinion, the colonel would be better advised to employ the Mackenzie lad from the Point estate. He knows the work and he knows the people.'

Meg had met Ewan Mackenzie, a son of the neighbouring factor, a courteous young man who from his boyhood had from time to time stalked for the Colonel and his sporting guests before his stroke. 'It may well come to that. My cousin Victor has no knowledge of the Highlands,' she said. 'He may be unsuited to the work. However he is my first cousin and my father wishes to give him the opportunity.'

No more was said on the matter, and after a few more minutes spent on estate matters, Meg rose to go and the old man rose with her.

'Have you had time to look into the matter of piped water for the cottages?' she asked.

'It could only be managed,' he told her, 'if the rents were to rise in proportion to the expense but I would not advise it. The herring season has not been good this year. The tenants will not like it.'

'But of course they will!' Meg insisted. 'Have you not seen the daily struggle of the women at the wells, their bowed backs, the children weighed down under their pails?'

'It is not the women or the children who have to find the extra rent,' Wedderburn rebuked her, but mildly. He could see the sense in 'Miss Megaidh's improvements,' as they were generally called, but he had also costed the project.

Meg was silent. It had been the same with the dustbins. Now the fisherwives wondered how they had managed without them but their menfolk were a stubborn lot. What had been good enough for their mothers was good enough for their wives. At least Wedderburn had come to see the sense of piped water, though he baulked at the cost. She had high hopes of Victor.

That afternoon, as soon as she had roughed out a letter to her cousin on behalf of her father, she sent for the pony trap to ride down the Brae to the schoolhouse. She had neither the leisure or inclination to ride her bicycle. Morag had left to marry her fisher-lad, and her place taken by her sister Minnie while Mrs Macfarlane, an impoverished widow and school friend of Mrs Vass from Edinburgh, had joined the household. She had nursed her consumptive husband until his death and now not only looked after the schoolhouse occupants, but also played the harmonium in St Moluag's. With the rector and his six year-old son both in school and Mrs Vass an invalid, it was Helen Macfarlane who opened the door to Meg's knock.

Emily Vass was in bed, where she was now forced to remain for most of her days for her consumption was nearing its final stages. She looked so beautiful, her skin flushed, her eyes bright, ethereal, that in her presence Meg felt loud and clumsy. She handed over the basket of flowers and delicacies from the Big House to Mrs Macfarlane, who produced a vase so that Meg herself could arrange the bunch of lilies-of-the-valley that Emily Vass so loved.

'I think God has given me permission to stay alive just for these,' the dying woman whispered, reaching out for Meg to bring the flowers close so that she could bury her face in them. 'They are beautiful.'

'A little like you,' Meg murmured as she held the vase out to the sick woman. Her admiration and affection for Mrs Vass had grown over the years of sickness so patiently born.

'Meg, dearest,' she whispered, 'come and sit by me for a little, if you can spare the time. Tell me what you have been doing.'

Meg drew up a chair close to the bed and took the thin hand which felt feverish and dry. She could talk to Emily Vass as to no one else, so she told her of her father's decision to send for her cousin.

'He is thinking about the future and he is quite right to do so, I know that,' Meg said, her voice rising, 'but what does my cousin Victor know of the Highlands, the fisherfolk or the farmers?' She paused and then it came out, what had been on her mind, but on no one else's, or so it seemed. 'Why could he not have asked me what I thought? Have I not a mind of my own? Do I not know these people as well as he does? Am I not as capable of running Inverally at least as well any Englishman?'

Emily Vass tightened her grip. 'Of course you do and of course you are,' she replied, 'but Meg, you are the laird's daughter You need help in running an estate. He had Wedderburn. You will need someone too. Why should it not be your cousin?'

Meg shook her head. 'No,' she said firmly. 'I will not be running the estate, at least not for long. My father is frail. The estate is entailed in the male line. If neither Isabella nor I have a son, it will go to my cousin. I shall end up mouldering in the Dower house in Kirkton. It's not fair.'

Emily was quiet for a moment. Then she said.' No, it's not fair. It has never been fair but that is the way of the world. You are a woman. That is your only fault. Shall I ask Mr Vass to speak with the colonel?'

Meg smiled in spite of her anger. Hugh Vass, that 'well known radical', could only further harden her father's heart. 'I think not,' she said, 'only tell me I am not wrong to resent my cousin's appointment.'

'You are not wrong.' Mrs Vass smiled. 'There is, of course, a solution.'

Meg looked up eagerly. 'There is?'

'You could always marry him.' She paused.

Meg stared at her. 'You are teasing me, I think.'

'Perhaps a little,' the older woman answered still smiling. ''But this may be in your uncle's mind, possibly also in your father's.'

'The idea is outrageous,' Meg insisted. She felt herself blush.

'No, my dear, it is not outrageous. A marriage of convenience is always worth a second thought.'

'I could never love him,' she said quickly, but she could not look at the sick woman. They both knew who it was that Meg thought she loved.

'Meg, my dear,' Mrs Vass began, her voice barely perceptible. 'Do you know why Helen is here?'

It seemed a strange question. 'To look after you,' she replied.

'That certainly - ' but Meg would never know what had been in the sick woman's mind to say, for she began to cough, a painful sickly cough. She pressed her handkerchief to her mouth and Meg saw it was bright with blood. She rang the bell that hung within reach of the sick woman, and, within seconds, Helen Macfarlane was at the dying woman's side.

Meg hovered for a few seconds. 'What can I do?' she asked wretchedly. Helen Macfarlane looked up at her briefly. 'Find Mr Vass,' she said quietly.

So Meg left, went straight to the boys' classroom and opened the door. Nineteen pairs of eyes switched round to stare at her. She stood there, speechless. Hugh Vass, seeing her, put down the book he held in his hand.

What can I do for you, Miss Meg?'

'Mrs Vass,' was all she said, for she did not want to alarm the pupils. He strode towards her between the desks, ushered her out and shut the door firmly behind them before questioning her carefully. Meg tried to explain but the tears were thick in her throat. Without another word, he opened the schoolroom door again and briefly instructed the boys to take out their reading books. Then he called to his son. Before they hurried off together, he remembered she was still standing there. Briefly he pressed her hand. 'Thank you, Miss Megaidh.'

The impression of his fingers on her wrist stayed with her and her heart beat faster as she continued her journey down the Brae to Fisherton.

Fisherton

Marsali's foot rocked the cradle on the hearth that kept Jared's bairn contented, while her fingers flew over the dark blue gansey on her knitting needles. Ezra's clock ticked loudly over the fire. A fine instrument, it had been presented to him by the skipper of the *Bright Star* after a particularly good herring season, three years past now, but that was not the reason. He had saved the life of the skipper's son, a lad of seven years who had tripped over his own feet and fallen off the harbour wall. Ezra, who had been aboard the boatie doing repairs at the time, had jumped into the murky water and rescued the lad, a brave thing to do considering neither of them could swim, and not in character. Ezra had grown sour and silent since the disappearance of Donnaidh, his pleasure in life broken.

Marsali could not even in her deepest mind think of her youngest son as drowned, but she had learned to keep her hopes to herself. To so much as suggest to Ezra that the loon might still be alive would be to bring the lash of her husband's tongue down on her, but never, thank the good Lord, his fist. There were plenty in Fisherton who had no choice between the tongue and the fist.

But she could think her own thoughts, and her head was full of Anna's whispers. 'Did you not hear yet what they're saying in the street? Your Donnaidh's been seen again.'

'Where? What are they saying? Is he well?'

'Ina got it from the cattle-man at the Mains? He heard it at the Dingwall mart. Chicago I think was the name.'

Marsali sighed. There had been so many rumours over the five years since the accident and it was sometimes Chicago. A relative of a Fisherton family once went to Chicago and Marsali thinks it's the only place name they know in all the Americas. She tried to imagine Donnaidh at eighteen. Would she still recognise him? If not her, would anyone else? Loons changed so much in five years. She tried to imagine him now and blinked away the tears that blurred the intricacy of the navy-blue wool on her needles, and started up at the knock on the door.

She knew exactly who it was. Miss Megaidh was the only one to knock. Neighbours walked in.

'*Feasgar mhath*, Mistress Macreedie. I hope I haven't called at an inconvenient time?'

Miss Megaidh was always so polite, and kind, so like - yet unlike - her mother, the *Aingeal*, who would descend on her cottage as from a starry height. Miss Megaidh approached her on near level ground.

Marsali switched her mind from the Gaelic she thought in, and answered in English

'*Failte! 's e de beatha* - a thousand welcomes, Miss Megaidh. Will you sit?' She did not offer any sort of refreshment for it was always in her mind that the *Aingeal* had died from water drunk in her house, or so it was said.

After Meg had admired Wee Kenny, the sleeping baby, and inquired for the health of the family she said, 'I've come to pick your brains, Mistress Macreedie. I need advice.'

From me? she thought. That'll be the day. Marsali looked at the anxious young face, under the broad brimmed hat, the marino wool dress, the high collar with the pretty brooch at her neck and the coat that she has loosened. Why me?

'Mr Wedderburn wishes to retire. He has a certain Ewan Mackenzie from the Point estate in mind as a successor, but my father wishes to give the job to Victor Myers, my cousin from England.'

'Oh aye?' Marsali encouraged her. It sounded sensible. She could not think why the quine should object.

'He knows nothing of the countryside let alone the Highlands.'

'Can he not learn? Can Master Wedderburn not teach him? And yourself? There is not much you don't know about our ways, Miss Megaidh.'

You think it's a good idea then?' she asked.

Marsali could see her anxiety. She was after all not yet twenty years old. 'I think it will relieve you of responsibility. Has he got a wife, this cousin of yours from the English? If he brings her here you can then be free to follow your own path. Was it not the university that you were wanting?'

Miss Megaidh had once, not long after her mother's death, poured out her heart to Marsali; how she wanted to become a doctor and cure the many sicknesses that plagued Fisherton.

Miss Megaidh sighed. 'That was before my father took ill. There can be little hope for me or my foolish dreams now. I'm afraid my cousin Victor has no wife.'

'Well then, but can he not support you in your care of the laird?' Marsali suggested encouragingly. It seemed to her like the perfect solution for the young quine. She was curious to see the loon for herself.

'So you think I should give way to my father in this instance?'

Marsali's hands flew over the needles. 'That is not for me to say,' she said. carefully, 'but Miss Megaidh, think on this. You might grow to like the young gentleman.'

'I suppose,' she said with a sigh. 'Mr Wedderburn is none too pleased,'

'Mr Wedderburn will do what he's told, I should think.' Like the rest of us, she thought to herself.

'I suppose so,' Meg said reluctantly and changed the subject. 'How is Mistress Munro? I promised Ina I would call in and see her.'

Marsali switched her thoughts to her neighbour. Anna's palsy was worse. She shook like an aspen leaf and the more she trembled the frailer she became in mind and body. 'She will be glad to see you, Miss Megaidh,' she answered honestly.

'Is there any new sickness in the street?' Meg asked.

They spoke for a few more minutes of Marsali's neighbours. Diarrhoea was still endemic but there had been no further outbreak of cholera or typhoid. 'Not since the laird gave us the bins,' she said.

'And there will be running water next,' Meg told her fiercely. 'I promised it and I will keep that promise.'

Marsali thought of the changes that had come since Donnaidh's disappearance; the rubbish boxes at the end of each street, and, more recently, the ruling over pigs. Mr Wedderburn had threatened eviction of any family that let their pigs roam freely in the narrow streets. They were to be kept penned either in the patch of ground behind each of the cottages by the earth closets, or on the strip of common land between Inverally and Point. Poultry still roamed freely but

87

at the owner's risk, so most were kept cooped and out of harm's way. Although some of the fisherfolk ignored the rules, the village was already a far cleaner place. That was due to Miss Megaidh, she thought with pride. Poor wee Miss Megaidh. She had never before thought to pity one in her class and of her social standing, but today she did. There was something lonely and vulnerable about the quine. Maybe this cousin of hers would turn her head in a more satisfactory direction.

They talked a little about Effie and the forthcoming baby. 'He is to be called Donnaidh if he is spared,' Marsali told her. 'Ruth, after Sam's mother if it is a quine.'

Miss Megaidh rose. She never stayed more than fifteen minutes and Marsali knew she would make several calls in Fisherton before taking the pony trap for the long push up the Brae. The baby began to girn. Although it was eighteen years since her breasts had provided sustenance for Donnaidh, Andrew and Aaron, they still ached at the sound of a baby's cry. Fanny would be in shortly to feed her.

Fanny was the only child of the widower, Kenny Ross, ship's chandler, in the High Street where Jared had served his apprenticeship. Theirs had not been an easy courtship, clandestine and disapproved of, for it crossed both the acceptable class and age conventions. Fanny was from Milton and now at 28, was five years older than Jared's twenty-three years. Although the quine was of an age to make up her own mind, Mr Ross had come after Jared with a shotgun. The couple were forced into separation and had it not been for Jared's stubbornness and the lassie's cunning, the affair would have long since ended. She had been sent to an aunt in Glasgow, a gullible old romantic who had easily been persuaded to support her niece's love affair. During that time in Bearsden, Fanny had dutifully attended her indulgent aunt's church and sworn her to secrecy by

88

pretending a pregnancy. (She had been no more pregnant than a billy goat). The banns were duly read three Sundays running. Jared had borrowed enough money from his friends to get him to Glasgow and they had been married quietly the next day with old Aunt Constance in tearful attendance.

They had come back to Inverally with the marriage a *fait accompli*. The ensuing row included a threatened disinheritance and some heated words, until Fanny, steel under marshmallow, was able to convince her outraged father of Jared's worthiness to be his son-on-law. After Jared's suitable period of penance in the proverbial wilderness as a delivery boy, his daughter's genuine pregnancy melted the chandler's heart. Jared was promoted to the counter and the couple were invited by Mr Ross to make their home with him above the chandler's shop. It was a happy arrangement because Fanny intended that it should be. The old man grew to tolerate his son-in-law's presence at the dinner table, even to value his services at the counter. It freed him to indulge his passion for fishing the Ally. By the time the baby was born, the young couple were more or less running the business.

Once a week, Fanny travelled by the new railway to Inverness to place orders and interview suppliers while a nursemaid was left in charge of the bairn. On this particular day, the nursemaid, little more than a child herself, had taken her one free afternoon in the week to attend a funeral. At Jared's suggestion, Fanny had called upon Marsali to care for her grandson. She and Fanny, if not exactly friends, respected each other for Fanny, being naturally forceful, lively and controlling, worked hard at getting her own way. She had twisted her old aunt round her little finger, just as she had re-entwined herself into her father's heart and more importantly kept the admiration of her handsome husband. As a couple they had further ensnared the chandler by

89

naming their baby for him, Kenneth Ross Junior. Fanny still had some work to do where her mother-in-law was concerned.

She arrived at the moment of Miss Megaidh's departure. She bobbed a small curtsy as she had been taught at Fernleigh, the young ladies establishment she had attended in Inverness, and they exchanged the usual pleasantries which included Miss Meg's admiration for the baby and Fanny's gracious appreciation.

Marsali sometimes wondered what Fanny saw in Jared, apart from his obvious good looks. Although she loved him as she loved all her bairns, she was not unaware of his weaknesses. She reckoned Jared was competent enough behind the counter, but he was too easy going, enjoyed a dram a little too much and was too easily manipulated. Maybe that was the attraction for Fanny. She controlled her husband just as she controlled her father and just as, one day she would own and control the business. She took off her hat, sat down, unbuttoned her bodice and with a twist of his brown head, Little Ken latched on to her right breast like a leech.

'That's a relief,' said Fanny as the pressure on her breasts relaxed. She looked up curiously over the baby's nuzzling head. 'Is it true then that you nursed three at the same time. Jared was telling me.'

Marsali's needles clicked. Fanny's directness always surprised and pleased her. She was slowly growing to admire and cautiously like her daughter-in-law. 'Aye,' she said without expanding as she remembered the three heads, the one near bald, the other a thick fair thatch and the third, her Donnaidh, brown as the good earth and wavy as the ocean. She twisted her mind away from the image.

'And were they all as greedy as this little monster?' Fanny said dotingly as she switched Little Kenny to her other breast.

'Aye,' she replied as her mind flooded with the memory.

'I'll wager it was Donnaidh came off best. Jared told me he would probably push the other two aside to get what he wanted.'

It was a long time since anyone had spoken to her so freely about Donnaidh. She found to her surprise that she liked it. 'He never got the chance, poor wee loon, but he always got his share. I made sure of that.'

'Jared was telling me he was sighted in America,' she looked up expectantly .'Do you think there's any truth in the rumour?'

Nobody had asked her that either. Her heart told her yes but her head said no. 'There have been so many stories over the years.' she said aloud.

'Think if there were none,' said Fanny. 'Would that be worse?'

Marsali shied from the thought. 'I always have hope,' she said quietly.

They were silent for a while. Then Fanny said, 'I'll need to go. I can't think what's keeping Jared. He said he'd be here with the trap to help with the baby.'

'You don't need Jared, a fine lass like you!' Marsali said putting aside her knitting. She crossed the room and opened a kist that held her clothing and after a bit of rummaging pulled out a massive grey shawl. She had last used it for Donnaidh. 'Give me the bairn,' she said. Wee Kenny, who was as intrigued as his mother, was silent as Marsali bound him to Fanny's front as tightly as any Indian papoose. She hoped her daughter-in-law would not be offended or ashamed to carry her bairn like the fisher wives did. She was not. She laughed. 'I hope the Misses Sarah and Agatha

Smythe are at their window when I pass. I don't often get the chance to please them,' she said laughing. 'Good day to you, Mother Macreedie.'

Marsali watched Fanny as waving she picked her way over the cobbles with wee Ken strapped to her chest. Any doubts she had concerning her daughter-in-law's suitability as a wife and mother vanished at the sight of that wave. She and Missus Jared would get along just fine.

Milton

Fanny's confidence faltered as she met face to face with another woman with a baby tightly shawled to her breast and a creel on her back, at the end of the street. Although she smiled and murmured, 'Good day,' the woman stared at her, speechless. Fanny felt ashamed as if she had been play-acting the part of a fisherwife in order to laugh at them. She felt the blush start on her neck and burn her cheeks crimson.

She intended to climb the Brae out of Fisherton and walk the length of the High Street in full view of her neighbours but inwardly she quailed. She knew she had already outraged the hard-working respectable shopkeepers and mill-workers of Milton when she had married Jared. Some of them had clawed their way up from the dregs of Fisherton and here she was parading the road with Kenny shawled to her body like any common fisherwife. She was ashamed of her mixed feelings, lifted her head high, whispered to her bairn who was obviously loving the sway and swing of her walk.

The Brae, however, seemed endless and the bairn was heavy. Fanny stopped, and halted a second and third time to catch her breath. Once again she wondered at her own impulsiveness. Her courtship of Jared had been much the same, an act of bravado, which having started she had been determined to finish. Had her father and her circle of friends not been so set against it, she might well have let the affair drift. It was her need to win any argument, get her own way that drove her sometimes to make mistakes. Yet she could not help herself. At the least sign of conflict or criticism, she had to win. Fortunately Jared was an indulgent husband. She might have had worse, but it was not a marriage of equals and never would be. Jared reminded her of the china dog on the mantelpiece, pretty to look at, decorative on the surface but hollow, cheap, lightweight. Did he even like her? She suspected he might not be faithful. At least she had her baby. She would always be grateful to him for that. And, best of all, she had the business.

The clip-clop of pony hooves behind her drew her attention. She turned to see Miss Meg on the Brae behind her in the pony cart. It would be Miss Meg, she thought, her bravado quelled in an instant. She turned her head away hoping she would not be recognised. The pony stopped.

'Mrs Macreedie!' Meg called out giving Fanny her full title. 'Can I give you a lift up the Brae?'

Fanny had a choice. To stick to her guns and walk it out, or to drive into Milton beside Miss Meg. No choice really. 'I would be grateful,' she said, forcing herself to sound confident, and then realised that she could not climb on to the cart with the child shawled to her. Meg noticed. She climbed down from her high seat, and together they unwound wee Ken from his cocoon.

'Goodness me, he's heavy,' said Meg as she held the gurgling child. 'Adorably heavy,' she added with a laugh. 'I love babies.'

He was adorable, Fanny thought as she climbed up to the seat and took her child from Meg's outstretched arms. 'Thank you, Miss Meg,' she said gratefully.

'I sometimes wonder how they manage, the fisherwives, with creels of fish as well as babies to carry.'

'They', Miss Meg had said, not 'you'. For that small pronoun Fanny was so grateful that her confidence flooded back. 'It's a nice safe feeling,' she said.

'I believe you,' said Meg. 'How is Jared these days?'

Fanny remembered that Miss Meg knew her husband's family almost as well she did, that her brother and Jared's brother had shared the same fate. 'He still misses his wee brother,' she said.

'Yes,' said Miss Meg quietly, 'as I do mine.' They were silent for a long moment. The High Street branched off from the Brae and there were the Misses Smythe from Kirkton with their shopping baskets over their arms nodding and waving at them. 'Miss Sarah and Miss Agatha seem in lively form,' said Meg as she and Fanny both lifted their hands in acknowledgement of the sisters' vigorous greeting. It was a small moment of triumph for Fanny.

Miss Gallie from Kirkton too was out in the street. Fanny was a little scared of Miss Gallie but she was also sorry for her. Her brother had thrown her out, or so it was rumoured, when he married the widow of an Inverness wine and tobacco merchant. The two women could not agree, so it was said, and that she could well understand. Miss Agnes was a critical spinster of particularly slender means. She eked out her income by teaching piano and making preserves. Her pupils were small and timid. If she managed to keep them for a year she was lucky for her frequent use of a ruler across small knuckles made her mightily feared. Small pupils much preferred to learn from Miss Rhona Anderson, the doctor's daughter, who taught from a sunny room behind the surgery in Kirkton for a larger fee certainly but with happier results. The preserves could be found behind several counters in Milton, the chandler's included. It was not easy to refuse Miss Gallie. Besides, her bramble jelly was exceptionally good. Neither Fanny nor Miss Meg commented on Miss Gallie, though both smiled and nodded at her as they passed. Neither of them liked her much but where Meg was incurious, Fanny was cautious. Miss Gallie was after all a customer.

At the sound of the pony, Jared, swathed in a white apron, came out of the shop, bowed a little obsequiously to Miss Meg, which was how his father-in-law, Mr. Ross, has taught him to treat important customers. He handed her down first, saw her up the three steps into the shop. There was some light banter between them before he turned to Fanny and took the baby from her. He was full of apologies and questions. 'I couldn't leave the counter. Your father is at the fishing and the lad still out on deliveries. Did you find my mother well? Was she pleased to have wee Ken? Did he behave himself?'

Fanny laughed. 'Yes, yes and yes. Your mother taught me how the fisher women carry their babies. I walked up the hill with him shawled to me. Imagine that!'

Jared frowned. 'You never did! You walked the Brae like any common fishwife?'

'I certainly did – till Miss Meg took pity on me.'

'She saw you like that?'

'She surely did.'

Jared's frown deepened. 'How could you do such a thing? You are not a fishwife, Fanny. You are above such behaviour. I can't believe that you would lower yourself to behave in such a way. You shame me.'

'How?' she asked, prepared to be annoyed but also curious. 'Does your mother shame you, then?'

'No she does not. My mother knows her place and she keeps to it. You are not my mother and to ape my mother is to bring shame on her - on us all. Suppose the Miss Smythes had seen you?'

'I don't care two halfpennies for the Misses Smythe's opinion or anyone else, for that matter.' Fanny declared warmly. 'You were not there with the trap so what else was I to do?'

'You could have waited for me, I suppose. Mr Ross would have come back eventually.'

'Why should I? Your mother is a busy woman, and, so, for that matter, am I.' She left him then to take the baby to his nursery in their flat above the shop. 'Have you forgotten? Your customer is still waiting,' she told him coldly and shut the door in her husband's face.

Jared was becoming more like the Misses Smythe with every day that passed. Fanny laid wee Kenny down in his cot. His nappy was wet. She glanced at the watch pinned to her jacket. Where was the nursemaid? She was due back from her afternoon off at five and it was already ten past the hour. Once again she had serious doubts about Jessie as a nursemaid, but Jared had been so against hiring one of the Fisherton quines, as he called them, and she could understand why. Jessie's father, on the other hand, was employed by Master Gallie in the timberyard and Jared's connection to that family particularly tender.

The baby lay half-naked and kicking on Fanny's lap when Jessie returned, breathless and pushing the wisps of her hair into her cap. 'Sorry, I'm sorry Ma'am!' she repeated until Fanny cut her short. 'Don't let it happen again,' she said as sternly as she felt was required. Fanny could be very stern when she needed to be. Now was not one of those times. She enjoyed having her baby to herself for short periods but was equally thankful to hand him over when it suited her. 'Just see to his bath. He's more than ready for it.'

It was not that she did not adore her baby but that she also loved her father's business and she had the shop accounts to see to. Now that Jared was an established fact, her father had begun to leave more and more of the chandler's business in their hands and accountancy was something that Jared could not do. He was capable of taking orders, giving change and charming customers but book-keeping was well beyond his powers.

'You could learn,' she once said to him as, night after night, she totted up the figures, checked supplies and issued accounts. She had been taught by her father from the day she left Fernleigh Dames' School. 'It's a good business, Fanny, and it will be yours one day. You've a great head for figures on you. When you marry it will still be yours. I've seen to that.' He made doubly sure when she came back a bride with Jared. 'He'll not get his fishy fingers on my business if that's what he's after.' He refused to believe that Jared could want his daughter for any other reason. It was not that Fanny was plain exactly. She had bonny eyes and a lively expression, but she was no beauty either with a snub nose and an over-wide mouth. A lad as youthful and handsome as Jared could have had his pick of the Fisherton lasses. There had to be another motive for his courting of Fanny. That was what her father believed and he was not slow to make his opinion known. Fanny had appeared to submit to him, but she had gone off to her Glasgow aunt and come back married just the same. It was not that she did not believe her father but that that she wanted the handsome Jared too. She would soon teach him the business, or so she had thought.

But after a few sessions with Jared, she had come to the conclusion that he would never learn accounting. He had neither the brains nor the inclination and after a short while she gave up trying to make him focus. What he did, he did moderately - no, give him his due - very well, and for that she was thankful. She disliked counter work herself, found it fatiguing and unrewarding, but Jared was in his element. As for her father, though he was not that old at sixty-five, his mind was failing. He forgot important messages, he repeated himself, he spent all his time out on the burn after the salmon in season, or perch from Loch Point. Sometimes he forgot where he was going and once he had been brought back by Constable Rossie, the local police officer. Granted he was full of whisky at the time. Fanny had come to the conclusion that there was only one person fit to run the chandlers and that was herself. All the taboos against women in business had risen up to confront her and one by one she had demolished them. She could do it and she would. Though she sighed and complained from time to time at her responsibilities, secretly she was pleased. She enjoyed ordering supplies, dealing with the skippers, finding new outlets for stock. She knew she was getting better at it all the time. She could spot a poor payer or a downright fraud at a glance and she could be ruthless with debtors. So, if there were times when she thought she would rather play the housewife and full-time mother, there was more times when she was content to leave her baby to Jessie and the housekeeping to Mrs Mack. The elderly widow who had been her father's servant and her own devoted slave since her infancy was pleased to continue managing the household thus leaving Fanny free to devote her time to the business.

It had been daunting at first but she had learned through experience that men rated her as she rated herself. If she held her head high, produced accurate figures and stood no flirtations nonsense, she could close a deal. The timid little lady act failed every time.

Mrs Mack had not been pleased about the marriage however. She had already made out a list of suitable husbands for Fanny, and Jared had not been one of them. Nor had she liked it that Fanny had taken the baby down to Fisherton to bide with a fishwife, though she was his grandmother. 'I could have kept him,' she complained to

Fanny. 'You don't want him picking up something nasty from that dirty place.'

Fanny pretended not to hear. She lifted the lid from one of the pots on the range. 'Oh good,' she said. 'Mince and tatties. Jared's favourite.'

Mrs Mack was not mollified. 'Did you not hear me? I said …'

'I heard what you said, Mrs Mack, but I wasn't listening. I fully intend that wee Kenny is at much at home in his nanna's house as he is in his grandfather's kitchen That's the way it's going to be.' Besides, she thought, much of my business depends upon the fishermen. It did the business no harm to have a firm foot in all of the Inverally communities

'You'll live to regret it, mark my words.'

Fanny did not answer her. Her mind was already running ahead to the following morning's meeting with Mister Gallie at the timber-yard. The meeting was scheduled for 11 clock at his office. If she were to place a big order for new shelving, she would offer a reciprocal favour. Those four-inch nails, for example, needed shifting and she had a nice line in beeswax candles. She left the kitchen and went into her father's tiny office - her office now - and opened the register.

At half past six Mrs Mack called her for dinner. The old housekeeper still presided at the foot of the table as she had always done and Fanny would no more have thought of shifting her than of moving her father from head of the table. Jared had washed and changed from his shop clothes. How handsome he is, thought Fanny with a flush of affection. How fortunate I am. She turned to her father. 'I saw Mair's manager this morning, father.'

'Ah,' said her father as Mrs Mack served him first with a generous plateful. 'Mince and tatties! Mrs Mack knows her way to a man's heart!'

'I was saying father, that I saw Mair's – '

' What was that?' Mr Ross asked, 'Mair's manager did you say? A surly fellow if I remember aright.'

'We came to an understanding.'

He did not ask her how. He showed no interest. She came to the realisation yet again that her father no longer was concerned. A shame really because she had no one with whom she could discuss the business side of the chandlers, no one to pat her on the shoulder and tell her what a good job she was doing, or perhaps not. Grow up, Frances, she told herself.

Meanwhile Jared was asking him about his day on the Ally. He answered at length while shovelling food into his mouth. She glanced at Jared and they held eyes for a moment across the table then got on with their food.

There was rhubarb and custard to follow and finally a cup of strong tea. After it was over, her father disappeared probably to the Royal Station Hotel (so called because Lord Point, chairman of the County Council, had invited minor royalty to open the new branch railway line a decade back,) to meet his cronies.

Jared spent a reluctant twenty minutes going over the day's sales leaving her to cash up as usual. 'Where are you going?' she asked for he was clearly restless.

'To see my mother,' he told her. 'I'll not be late.'

She was resentful for about ten seconds then she put on her reading spectacles and turned her attention to the accounts, as she did every evening.

The Hall

The house dogs met her at the door. Three of them. Goldie, her mother's ageing spaniel, and Tommy and Tucker, her father's over-weight, under-exercised labradors.

'Have they been out?' she asked Cuthbertson who had nobly undertaken the task of taking the dogs for an run in the afternoons after the colonel's stroke. Cuthbertson was getting on himself these days, and inclined to portliness, so she was never quite sure whether the run extended itself beyond an amble to the gardener's cottage at the foot of the south avenue where he had a friend in Bob Paterson's wife, famed for her scones and gooseberry jelly. She made a note to take them out herself on the hill after dinner.

First however she had that letter to write.

She sat down at her bureau in the breakfast room across the hall from her father's quarters that she used as an office and drew a sheet of notepaper engraved with the address Inverally Hall, Invernally N.B.

Dear Cousin Victor, (though he was by no means 'dear' and she had no desire to write to him at all.)

Mr Wedderburn, my father's factor, wishes to retire before the end of the year. My father wonders if you would be interested in taking on his duties under Wedderburn's guidance for a trial period of thee months with a view to becoming factor of the Inverally estate. There is, naturally, a house and salary attached to the position which will be a matter of negotiation in due course. Meanwhile my father hopes you will stay at the Hall as his guest. We look forward to hearing from you.

My father sends his good wishes to your family.

Yours sincerely, Meg Murray-Myers.

She read it over then took it to her father. He was silent for a while, his head sunk on his chin.

'It's not what I had hoped for,' he said eventually.

'I know,' she said briskly. 'But it's not too late. Isabella may still have a son.'

He did not immediately reply. By all accounts two miscarriages had left Isabella a shadow of herself. Both had been boys.

'I should take the dogs out before dinner. Tommy's putting on weight.' she moved to the door.

'Which room will you give him?' her father asked abruptly.

She did not need to ask who. Victor lay heavily on both their minds.

'The Blue Room, I thought.' The Blue Room was situated in the west wing of the Hall away from her own quarters in the South wing and even further from her father downstairs in the library.

The colonel nodded. 'That damned entail,' he muttered.

She knew that he had done his best to break it but the expense was beyond reasonable. 'Good night, father,' she said from the door. 'Goodnight, Jenkins.' He was winking as he opened and closed it for her.

She returned to the breakfast room, sealed the letter and put it out on the tray in the hall for postage the following morning. There - it was done. Then she called the dogs

Inverally Station

The two-coach branch train drew up with a screech and a final puff at Inverally platform. The station master who lived in a standard stone house in Milton overlooking the platform and a little apart from the row of cottages that housed the other railway employees, was shouting somewhat unnecessarily, 'Inver-ally. Inver-ally Station,' for this was the end of the line.

A porter flung open the door of his first class compartment, doffed his cap with its rail company insignia, and offered to take Victor's bag. 'The trap from the Hall is waiting, sir.'

102

How did he know that, Victor wondered as he handed over his Gladstone bag. This was his first indication that everyone in Inverally knew the Hall's business sometimes before it happened. If he had hoped for anonymity in the Highlands he had come to the wrong place.

It was the wrong place for so many reasons. For years now his father, the dean, had wielded Inverally over his head like an axe. If you don't want the ministry...if you can't pass your exams...if you won't try law...work in the City...there is always Inverally. It was not that he wouldn't take Holy Orders, if he could only have read the prayers without stuttering. He found it impossible to sound consonants so how could he read a collect or preach a sermon? The ministry was all words. The Wwword of Gggod... He stuttered even in his thoughts. Supposing he could have prayed as fluently as his father, or as fervently as Cedric, he could never have passed the necessary exams for he found writing as hard as speaking. His handwriting was still as unformed and ill-spelled as it had been when he was a child. Even if he could have learned to write, he could not place the letters in the right order, apart from his name. He had memorised the picture it made and though it was an effort to control and shape the correct letters, he could just about manage that, but alas he could hardly read. So what could he do to earn a living in this difficult world? His father had the answer: Inverally.

The groom doffed his cap and hefted his trunk into the back of the trap. Victor chose to sit up on the bench seat beside him. When the young man had stowed his trunk and bag, he leapt up to take the reins, Victor's heart turned over. No, he said inwardly to himself, nnnot again. Ppplease not again. Victor had these feelings for sturdy men of powerful physique and he could not understand himself. One of the reasons why he had agreed to accept his father's suggestion

103

he come north was to escape the attentions of a lay clerk in the catheral choir, a handsome man over six foot tall. Yet there was something not quite honest about that statement. It was not Hilary's attention he had wanted to lose; rather it was his own overwhelming feelings for the tenor that his father was determined that he should lose. Not that he had ever succumbed to those feelings, at least not openly. What he did at night in the dark of his own room, though another matter of shame and disgust, was at least private.

Silence in the presence of a servant would not normally have caused him a second thought. On this occasion however it intruded and expanded like an air balloon. To prick it, he asked for the fellow's name. He responded respectfully, 'I'm Stuart, sir, Sam Stuart, the colonel's groom.'

Victor couldn't say it. 'Ssss...' was as far as he got. The fellow looked at him briefly and curiously. 'Sam, sir,' he repeated carefully. Victor did not even try to pronounce it. He nodded briefly. His eyes switched to his hands on the reins. Strong, brown, large, working hands. On the back of his left hand he noticed a half-healed scar. He could not take his eyes off it. 'Hhhow dddid you ggget that?' he asked nodding towards it

Sam's surprise showed in his tone of voice. 'That, sir? Stable cat. Went for me when I tried to shift her litter of kits.' He laughed. 'Right wee de'il, she is.'

Victor had a sudden urge to pick up that hand and carry it to his lips. He forced himself to look away. They had joined the steep Brae that wound upwards from Fisherton through Milton past Kirkton to the Hall. Suddenly, or so it seemed to Victor, who had not been expecting it, Sam leapt down from the trap but still kept hold of the reins. 'The old lady's getting on a bit and the Brae's awful steep,' he explained briefly.

Victor nodded. His grandmother had done the same, insisted the children climb down from coach or carriage and walk up hills to spare the horses. He stretched out his hand.

'No need for you to walk, sir.'

'Of cccoursh I'll wwwalk. Jush gggive me a hand dddown.'

Sam stopped the horse and held out his hand. In that moment of contact, Victor knew that for him nothing had changed. He held that warm rough hand seconds too long.

'You mmmarried, Sss...?' he asked as they walked side by side up the Brae.

'Aye' he said. 'And I've a wean on the way.' He sounded defensive. Victor could sense him recoil.

'Cccongratulations, Sss...'

'Thank you, sir,' he replied impassively.

They passed the junction road to Kirkton. 'That's the Anglicccan church, shhhurely?' Victor said, pointing at the red sandstone cruciform building standing in its own graveyard beyond a stand of yew trees. He remembered the last occasion he had been there five years ago at the funeral of his Aunt Grizel. His father had been somewhat contemptuous of the small church and the rector's inappropriately personal eulogy. He also remembered with a flicker of resentment his cousin Andrew, whom he had met once as a small child on a family visit. Andrew was, if through no fault of his own, the reason for his being here in this remote God forsaken spot in the north of Scotland. Andrew... All he knew of his first cousin, Andrew, was that he had drowned under tragic circumstances leaving Inverally without a direct heir and that if Isabella or Meg produced no son before Uncle Jock died, the estate would be his. Probably. He was also well aware that no one relished the idea, least of all himself.

He remembered that uncomfortable interview with the dean. 'You could, of course, make sure of it,' his father had said.

'Of whwwat, sssssir?' he had asked naively because he had no idea what his father had meant. Cedric had spelled it out for him later.

'Marry the girl, of course,' he told him. 'Don't look so scandalized. It's been done before and it will be done again. You need a career, brother. What's wrong with marriage? It's done me so harm.'

Cedric knew what he was talking about. He had married the daughter of a bishop His future in the Anglican hierarchy was rosy. He already had one daughter but had not given up hope of a son; a son who might one day inherit from his uncle, provided he owned Inverally in the first place. But that was looking too far ahead. Victor might well have sons of his own. If he did his duty. If he chose to do his duty.

The horses turned into the south avenue. Mistress Paterson was there outside the lodge to open the gates. She bobbed a curtsy to Victor who acknowledged her with a wave and looked about him with interest. The fields on either side of the long line of mature trees - he did not know their name - seemed trim, the two horses that browsed in the meadow behind wooden palings, contented, the stony drive weedless, the great clumps of rhododendrons, as they approached the big house, in glorious crimson blossom. He knew next to nothing about managing an estate but said to himself to cheer himelf up, 'how difficult can it be?' Compared with sermon writing, collect praying and Bible reading, it seemed an alternative he might be able to manage. He could see himself ambling through these fields, stick in his right hand, poking at the fences with a friendly labouring fellow at his heels with whom to converse. A fffellow like Ssss... He began to feel more cheerful.

'That's you, sir,' Sam said to him somewhat unnecessarily as he halted the trap on the gravel outside the front door. He leapt down but did not offer his hand to Victor who descended more slowly to find his cousin Meg and the butler - he had forgotten his name - there to greet him. Three dogs bounced up eager to share the welcome. He stepped back to avoid their exuberant paws.

'Cousin Victor!' she exclaimed, holding out her hand. 'Welcome to Inverally.'

He took her hand which was small and smooth and warm, as unlike Sam's hand as it was possible to be, and saw that she was rather plain. Apart from her intelligent eyes and pretty mouth, her nose was too long and her hair, scraped back into a neat bun, mouse brown. What a relief. He had expected - what? A gorgeous flaxen-haired beauty such as he remembered Isabella to be, who had scared the daylights out of him. He could not remember Meg as he had last seen her as a teenager. Meg as a plainish, ordinary young woman, some five or six years his junior was almost comforting.

'Tea is ready and Papa anxious to meet you. How was your journey? Are you well?'

He did not really have to say anything apart from a murmured 'How ddd'y dddo, Cccc ...Mmm....' He handed his hat to Cuthbertson, remembered to thank Sam who was shouldering his trunk off the trap and followed his cousin across the wide hall strewn with colourful Indian mats and the walls crammed with prints and sporting trophies of the colonel's Indian years. The dogs bounded ahead of them.

'This used to be the library but Papa moved downstairs after his illness,' she explained as she opened a door that led into a large light room. The first person he saw was Jenkins.

'Can we have tea now, Jenkins,' Meg asked but it was not a question. 'This is my cousin, Victor Myers. You've met before, I think.'

107

Jenkins winked furiously as he acknowledged the introduction. Victor instantly thought, he cccan see rrrright through mmme. Though he was soon to learn that the winking was merely a nervous tic, that feeling of his own inadequacy as seen through Jenkins eyes was never quite to leave him. He believed from that instant that Jenkins could see him the way he saw himself.

He turned from the servant to his master. His uncle, a shadow of the man he remembered, seated in a bath chair, a tartan rug over his knees, was drawn up to a small table covered with a white cloth and a gold rimmed tea-set. Wedgewood, he recognised. He had an urge to pick up a saucer and examine it more closely. If Victor could be said to have an interest, it was in fine porcelain but now was not the moment.

'Well, Victor,' said his uncle a little testily. 'Here you are, then. You left your father well, I trust?'

There was nothing wrong with his voice though his right side was paralysed from the neck downwards.

'Th...thank you, sss ...uncle, I dddid.' His stutter was more pronounced when he was nervous. He wanted to say that his father sent his best wishes, but could not get started. Meg was swift to notice his difficulty and took over the conversation.

'I do hope you'll be comfortable. Mrs Shanks, our housekeeper - perhaps you remember her? - has put you in the Blue Room. You 'll have your own staircase and door so you can come and go as you wish. We thought it would be nicer and more private for you. I've arranged for you to meet Mr Wedderburn tomorrow morning in the estate office. You'll like him even if he is a bit conservative in his views ...'

'And thank God for that,' the colonel barked. 'My daughter tends to be too radical by half.'

The silver tea things meanwhile had been brought in by a maid escorted by Cuthbertson bearing a stand of tiny paste sandwiches, scones and Dundee cake. Meg began to pour the tea. 'I'm afraid we only have Indian. My father prefers it to China tea, but if that's what you prefer I'll ask Mrs Shanks to order it. Milk, Cousin?'

He only had to nod.

'Thank you, Mima.' Meg dismissed the maid and Jenkins also slipped out of the room ostensibly to give the family some privacy, in reality to have a smoke with Mrs Shanks in the housekeeper's private sitting room.

The colonel was able to speak more freely. 'What you've got to realise, Victor, is that I'm not made of money. We are constantly having to retrench. Wedderburn does his best but he's getting on these days.Wants to retire. What I need here is a man with ideas, how to make the estate pay its way, keep an eagle eye out for slackers and poachers. '

'Let Cousin Victor settle in first, father,' Meg said calmly.

'Of course. Goes without saying. Three months should be long enough to find out if you like us enough to take on the job.'

'I'll dddo my bbbesht, ssssir.'

'I know you will, my boy. I know you will,' the colonel said impatiently. 'Wouldn't have suggested it, if I hadn't thought you could do it.' Changing the subject abruptly he asked about his twin brother.

An agonising fifteen minutes passed as the colonel questioned and Victor struggled to answer. Meg, quick to understand her cousin's speech impediment, intervened as often as she could to her father's visible annoyance. 'Let the boy speak for himself,' he exclaimed testily.

Victor sipped the tea and wished it had been brandy. Brandy helped with the stutter. Fortunately he had his own supply.

Meg was silent for a while then changed the subject. 'I expect you'd like to see your room and get settled in before dinner? You must be tired after such a long journey.'

She had risen. Victor rose with her. She led him up the main staircase along a number of corridors to his spacious room in the west wing with its four-poster and rich blue patterned carpet. His trunk had already been unpacked and his dinner jacket laid out ready. The brandy bottle was not in evidence, thank God.

'I hope you'll be comfortable here, cousin. I know it's a big change for you after city life, but I trust you'll be happy with us.' Though her words were warm her tone was cool. She dddoesn't want mmme here anymore than her fffather does, Victor thought gloomily; any mmmore than I wwwant to bbbe here.

'Ring for anything you need. Dinner is at eight. I usually take the dogs up on to the hill at this time so we'll meet again later.'

'Th..thth… you,' he said, inwardly cursing his wretched disability.

When he closed the door behind her, he began to tremble; another of his hated weaknesses. Any stressful situation could set him off. The fit lasted only for seconds but left him tired and even more depressed. He found the brandy on a tray with a carafe of water and a glass on his bedside table half-hidden by one of the great damask bed curtains. He poured himself a small measure, lay down on the vast bed and tried to compose his thoughts. Now that he was here, the job a reality, his relatives substantial, could he cope? Did he want to cope. Probably not. Did he want to try. Yes. He thought he did. He found that he liked the reality of Cousin Meg a great deal more than the image he had conjured up. He would try to please his uncle. If after three months he was found to be, as he knew he was, inadequate, he could tell his father he had at least tried.

At dinner there was wine, followed by port. Speaking became a whole lot easier. Meg left them, uncle and nephew, to make the best of the situation. Jenkins, who had been at hand to cut up his master's venison too had retreated. The colonel's useless right arm was strapped to his chest while the sleeve of his dinner jacket hung empty.

'Not my idea, you know, to offer you the job,' the colonel said abruptly.

Victor swallowed a mouthful of port. It had been his father's idea enthusiastically encouraged by Cedric. He had always known that. He sensed his uncle's hostility. 'I'll dddo my bbbest, sss...'

The colonel looked at him. Suddenly he pushed his port away with his functioning left hand so rapidly that it tipped over spilling its contents on the polished dining room table. Victor rose. ' Leave it, leave it,' the older man commanded him impatiently. 'Can't stand the stuff. Let's have a proper drink. Sideboard.'

Victor opened the sideboard cupboard doors and took out the brandy.

'Not that,' his uncle waved his good arm. 'I said the proper stuff. Whisky of course.'

Whisky was not a drink that Victor knew. His father had never kept or offered it. Called it a kitchen drink. Reluctantly Victor returned the brandy. There were at least half a dozen whisky bottles in the cupboard. He chose one. Uncle Jock nodded. 'Best malt. You haven't lived till you taste this.'

He was right. The liquid like smooth fire burned away the worst of his stutter. His uncle offered him a cigar. The strings of both their tongues loosened. 'How d'you get on with what's his name, your brother?'

Victor did not see the question as odd. 'Ccedric?' It had been a long time since he had been able to utter his brother's name.

'Cedric,' the colonel repeated. 'Can't stand my twin. Your father. Never could.'

Victor lifted his glass and looked into the amber depths. He could say it. He could actually say it clearly without hesitation. 'Nor can I.'

'Ah well…' the colonel took another mouthful. 'Meg's a good girl,' he said, 'a good daughter. Needs watching, though. Gets bees in her bonnet.'

Victor said nothing.

'Gets ridiculous ideas in her head. Wants to put running water into the cottages. Absolute nonsense. There are two good wells in Fisherton. What more do they want?'

He had heard the same from his father about the almshouses behind the close.

'I'll lllook into it,' Victor said

'You'll put a stop to it, I should hope. Speak to Wedderburn.'

'Of cccourse, ssir.'

'Well, well…Glad we've had this chat. Ring the bell for Jenkins, there's a good chap.'

Victor staggered a little as he wound his way up to the west wing. It had been a long day.

The Hall
Meg knew that Victor would be a disappointment to Ian Wedderburn. He had been a shock to her. She had no memory of him at all as, she realised, he had none of her from his previous short visit to attend her mother's funeral. She remembered Cedric for his pomposity and blonde undeniably good looks. She remembered his mother for her

112

disapproving glances and his father for his unctuous domineering demeanour, but Victor had escaped her memory altogether. The reality was a shock. He was small, not above 5 foot 3 inches, she reckoned, which was a little above her own height, but where she was adequately covered in glowing flesh, he was thin, all of him from his wispy moustache to his nail-bitten fingers. He was also unhealthily pale and his complexion permanently scarred from the spottiness of youth. Added to that he could not speak without stuttering on consonants and agonising pauses.

She had taken him round to the estate office after breakfast where Wedderburn had been waiting and introduced them. She would have stayed during that first interview, curious to see how it went, but after the formalities, Wedderburn had politely dismissed her. 'You will be wanting to see to your own duties, Miss Meg. You can safely leave Mr Myers to me.'

She was reluctant to go but Victor, whose manners were faultless, opened the door for her and held it open. His mouth gaped and she knew that he would have liked to say something but no words came. Instead he swallowed and gave her a quick haunted glance. She knew from that momentary glimpse exactly how he felt, inadequate, unprepared and useless. It was then that she decided not to hate him. She did not think he would last a month.

The rest of the day passed much as usual. She returned to the Hall, wrote a long letter to Isabella describing Victor in perhaps not the kindest of terms. She visited the kitchen, drank mid-morning coffee with Mrs Shanks, listened to her concerns, then went out into the gardens where she admired Paterson's lay-out and choice of annuals for the half-moon summer beds.

Victor did not turn up for luncheon which she took in her father's room. He was loud in his criticism not of Victor but of his brother George for suggesting his son for the position of factor. 'I've nothing against the poor boy,' the old man raged. 'He's no more desirous of the work than I am to employ him. He can't help being an idiot. God knows what Wedderburn will make of him. It's his father I blame, putting him - and me - into such a wretched position.'

He fulminated quietly throughout the meal. Meg said very little. She could only agree.

Tuesday afternoons she was at home to callers. It was not Meg's favouorite occupation. She would rather visit the schoolhouse or walk the dogs but found it marginally better than Thursdays when she paid calls on those of her neighbours who expected her to visit. She was sitting in the drawing room looking at her old Gaelic exercise book when Cuthbertson announced that she had a caller and brought in her card. 'The Lady Harriet Barraclough.'

It took Meg a moment to recognise the name as that of Isabella's sister-in-law, now married to her wealthy English industrialist who owned a shooting lodge on Loch Ness, but she had not forgotten her.

'Lady Barraclough! How do you do,' Meg exclaimed with pleasure. She had always liked Harriet.

'Miss Murrray-Myers - little Meg - I am well, and you?'

The formalities over, Harriet's health noted, the health of their respective parents duly commented on with the proper concern. (Lady Moncrieff was severely rheumatic) they talked at length about Isabella. 'Sadly I don't think there will be any more babies,' she said. 'Those miscarriages have taken their toll on poor Isabella's health.'

They were both silent for a while. What was there to say? Harriet changed the subject.

'And what of you, little Meg? I suppose medicine is now quite out of the question?'

Meg nodded. She had not thought of doctoring since her father's stroke. 'There is a lot to do here,' she said somewhat lamely. 'The estate…. the tenants…

'Indeed,' said Harriet, 'Your duty. But what do you do for yourself?'

Meg was bewildered. 'For myself?' she repeated. 'Well I try to keep up my Gaelic…'

Harriet laughed. 'You mistake me, Meg. I'm trying to ask you if you have fallen in love?'

Meg blushed. Mr Vass in his Sunday robes flashed into her mind and was as instantly dismissed. She shook her head.

'How old are you, Meg? Nineteen? Twenty? Have you thought at all about the future? What do you want in life?'

Before she could answer, before she could think, the door opened and Victor stood there on the threshold, hesitant and embarrassed. He would have left as abruptly as he had entered had Meg not called him in.

'Cousin Victor, come and join us.' She turned to Harriet. 'Lady Barraclough may I present my Cousin Victor Myers. Victor, Lady Harriet Barraclough is Isabella's sister-in-law.'

'How ddd'ye ddd…?' Victor managed to say as they shook hands.

Meg explained briefly that Victor was staying at Inverally for a while but not that he was in line for the factor's job.

'And what do you do, Mr Myers? Your father is in the church is he not?'

Meg had the feeling Harriet knew exactly who Victor was and why he was here.

Meanwhile Victor nodded. 'I'm the nnnew …' he swallowed 'Essssss…' but got no further. 'Factor,' he said abruptly.

'Ah yes,' said Harriet. 'I heard that Wedderburn was retiring. Do you think you'll like the work, Mr Myers?'

115

Victor opened his mouth to reply, but 'yes' was an impossible word. Instead he nodded.

Half an hour later she rose. 'I must go. It's been a pleasure to meet you, Mr Myers. I do hope you'll be happy in the Highlands.'

Meg rang for Cuthbertson. At the front door she turned to embrace Meg. 'You should marry him, Meg, and have a son,' she whispered. 'That would sort out the entail.'

Meg was astounded. She felt her mouth open but she said nothing. Unthinkable.

Victor was still in the drawing room when she returned, 'How did you find Wedderburn,' she asked 'Did you visit Fisherton?'

'Cccousss...Meg, 'he said ' I dddo ssso agggwee with you.' He had become visibly excited, animated even. 'Wwwater,' he said 'Every cccottage shshshsh...have ppp... wwwater.'

She was so surprised, so delighted she leaned forward and involuntarily kissed him on the cheek.

Milton

Wedderburn found Joshua Gallie preparing to leave his office for the day. They discussed the price of the estate's order for 500 5ft stobs for fencing the Brae meadow which were due for delivery during the week. It was an uphill struggle to get Josh to budge an inch when it came to payment, unlike Kenny Ross who would reduce the bill by a substantial amount in exchange for a couple of day's fishing on the private upper reaches of the Ally. A bottle or two of Highland nectar would sometimes do the trick. Not today however. At least not so far.

'Word's about you're training an English fellow up for the estate,' Josh said, reaching for his coat.

'Aye' said Wedderburn shortly. Joshua was not deceived. 'Come up to the house. Mrs Gallie'll be pleased to welcome you.'

The Timber House as it was called, stood on the outskirts of Milton, on the far side of the Brae separated from the timber mill by a stand of Scots pine, too fine for the yard to cut. They were Joshua's personal treasure. He loved those trees. 'Remnant of the old Caledonian Forest,' he would boast. 'You'll not see many left in these parts.'

Mrs Gallie met them in the hall. She beamed her welcome. 'You'll stay for your tea, Mr Wedderburn?' she asked.

Hilda Gallie was not a woman you would want to say no to. Ian Wedderburn envied Gallie his choice of a second wife. She was round in every direction, of bosom, thigh and smile. A comfortable creature who could make a man feel cherished in spite of her high shriek of a laugh which could be heard trilling above the liveliest of conversations. Maybe,Wedderburn thought, for she was laughing now at some remark of Josh's, because of it. Any woman who laughed so whole-heartedly at her husband's jokes was certainly to be cherished. He hoped that Josh appreciated his good fortune. It seemed that he did for he was growing as round as she was, round of belly and round of chins. Together with a generous table and the vinter's comfortable fortune she had also brought him a daughter, Cynthia. She was a forward young miss of seventeen who attended a dames' school in Inverness, boarding there during the week and returning to Milton by the railway for weekends. Josh doted upon her.

Wedderburn hesitated. 'Of course he'll stay for his tea, woman,' Josh said good-humouredly. He guessed that the factor had not had a good day and the reason for it. Schadenfreude improved his own mood. He might even be prepared to take off a couple of pounds, round the account down for the stobs.

Tea was lavish. Steak and kidney pie, boiled potatoes and mashed turnip followed by apple pie and cream washed down with strong Indian tea. Under Mistress Gallie's womanly concern for their appetite and their comfort, the two men ate their fill with enjoyment and relaxed.

'So what's he like, this young fellow from England?' Josh asked between mouthfuls.

'Mr Myers? Seems a nice enough lad,' Wedderburn replied carefully. He too had been appalled by Victor's frail appearance and speech impediment, but he was not going to tell the timber merchant, especially not the timber merchant's wife. He had learned the hard way to keep his personal opinions to himself.

'Is he wed?' Hilda asked innocently. Both men knew that there was nothing innocent about the question. She was ambitious for her daughter.

'No ma'am, he's not married.'

'You must bring him round, Mr Wedderburn. The poor young man will be lonely so far away from his family. We'll make it a Sunday dinner when Cynthia is at home. The young people should meet each other,' she suggested, beaming at him.

Ian Wedderburn smiled inwardly. Cynthia, as he remembered that articulate, ringleted young lady, would not spare his successor a second glance.

'Thank 'ee, Mistress Gallie. I'll pass the message on.'

'So what about yourself, Mr Wedderburn? What are your own plans?' she asked solicitously. 'Will you be staying on in Inverally after your retirement?'

It was a question he had been asking himself on and off for the past five years. It would be a wrench to leave the place which he knew so well from the inside of a Fisherton cottage to the laird's backyard. On the other hand he knew he would not be able to stand seeing the estate go to the dogs which it surely would do if Victor Myers was in control.

'I'm for off,' he said. 'Got a place in Perth.' That at least was true. He had a widowed sister in Perth who had been pressing him to live with her. He had hummed and hawed over a decision long enough. Had he been able to appoint his own successor he would have accepted the colonel's offer of a house on the estate. The Dower house, in fact, whose elderly tenants were leaving for Yorkshire to join their son.

'Agnes will be sorry to see you go,' Gallie said slyly.

There had been, according to Inverally's principal gossip-mongers, an understanding between Joshua's sister and Ian Wedderburn, but the friendship had really been between Agnes and Ian's deceased wife. Wedderburn saw to it that Agnes received a present of game from time to time from the estate, but nothing more. He rather regretted abandoning the acquaintance, especially when he saw how well Joshua had settled into a second marriage, but somehow the opportunity had passed him by and it was too late now.

'How is Miss Agnes?' he asked out of politeness rather than interest.

'Well enough,' said Joshua heartily. 'Runs a charity for orphan fisher bairns. On the Poor Law committee.'

Hilda said nothing. It was well known in Inverally that there was no love lost between the timber merchant's new wife and her sister-in-law.

'When do you plan to leave us, Mr Wedderburn?' she asked instead.

He didn't know. He didn't want to think about it. 'Not for a wee while yet,' he answered evasively.

'Got to teach that young English fellow the tricks of the trade, eh?' Joshua asked.

'Something like that,' he replied blandly.

119

Joshua said nothing. His lost son Aaron flashed through his mind for a sickening instant. He had no one to leave the business to. It would be sold to strangers. He had long ago made up his mind to that. Of course if Cynthia were to marry wisely, he might think again. If she were to marry the young factor for instance... Now there was a thought.

Wedderburn took his leave as soon after the meal as was polite. 'What about Sunday week?' Hilda suggested.

'Sunday week?' he asked as she helped him on with his coat.

'Dinner at 2 o clock and bring young Mr Myers?'

'I'll ask him.'

In the somewhat chilly comfort of his own home, he poured himself a whisky and took the game book on to his knee, but his mind was not on last season's records. On the whole, the day had been a disaster. He had taken Victor to meet various of the fisher families including Ephraim Cooper and his large improvident family who were in debt to the estate for six weeks rent and would have to go to the Poor House in Point if necessary. Jeemock the local drunk was poaching again. He would need to be watched. When he pointed out that the rents would have to rise when the herring season got underway, Victor had said nothing but he had held his handkerchief to his nose in the Cooper hovel. Wedderburn had fumed inwardly. Ephraim was a scrounger and a shirker no doubt about it, but he deserved a little respect. Myers had been unforgivably rude.

Wedderburn had also taken him to Kenny Ross's chandlery and various other merchants in Milton. They had trudged the moor field to check the fencing, met the gamekeeper, inspected the game chicks, heard about the poachers, examined the accounts and other records meticulously kept in the estate office. Victor had seemingly taken it all in, but there was no knowing. He had barely glanced at the estate accounts and he had asked no questions, hardly answered when spoken to; held his nose in Ephraim's hovel.

With a sigh Wedderburn realised that Victor would not do. He did not have to wait three months to know that. He would have to tell the laird. If he wanted the estate to survive, it needed a safe pair of hands. Otherwise it would become mired in debt; with any luck it would see the colonel out but then, what? Without a factor who knew what he was doing, he gave the estate two years.

Kirkton
On Sunday morning Meg took Victor to church.

There were three churches in Inverally built within half a mile of each other in Kirkton, and a Mission Hall with a corrugated iron roof in Fisherton. The Presbyterian Church of Scotland and the Free Church of Scotland were large stone barns dominated by imposing wooden pulpits and serried rows of pine wood pews while the Episcopal Chapel was cruciform, flower-filled with - daring this - a pair of brass candlesticks on the altar.

The elderly Presbyterian Church of Scotland minister, the Reverend Dr Caleb Carruthers lived in a fine stone manse with his two ageing, unmarried daughters, Martha and Dorcas and his son, Solomon, who was also his successor and a peacemaker. He had learned from an early age to steer a skilful path between the rivalries and ministrations of the eagle-eyed sisters. In his seventies, Caleb had once been a tower of a man, strong of voice and purpose, respected and admired by his large congregation. His daughters were tall and steely of purpose, twin Amazons who had stepped into the role of his meek and ailing wife. It was not his fault that old age had shrivelled his limbs, weakened his voice and enfeebled his mind. He clung literally to his pulpit like a cripple to his stick while his successor, his son and depute minister, trudged the streets, attended interminable meetings and bided his time.

The Reverend Ewan MacQueen of the Free Kirk was nowhere near as impressive. He was a mild-mannered little man who had married a dragon. Woe betide any backsliding family. The dragon would be on their doorstep breathing fire on Monday morning. They too had a large congregation but fewer children.

Fifteen minutes before 11 am on a Sunday morning, Inverally echoed to the sound of bells; St Moluag's mellifluous tinkle and the parish church's sonorous boom. No sound at all came from the squat turret of the Free Kirk. Mrs Macqueen, whose unlikely Christian name, Belinda, was largely unknown and never used even by her husband, believed bells to be a popish intrusion on the Sabbath.

For some half hour the Brae and the streets of Kirkton were crowded with carriages, pony traps and ambulant families clad in their Sunday best. Almost everyone in Milton and Kirkton went to church. In Fisherton with the boats safely in harbour, the majority stayed in bed, not having the clothes or the pennies to go up the Brae to Kirkton for Sunday worship. Many, however, attended the Mission Hall in the evening to hear the latest itinerant missionary from the Bible College who was hot on hell and damnation.

Some of the fisher children however attended the afternoon Sunday schools held in all three churches. The Episcopalian Sunday School was particularly well attended for Mrs Vass, (latterly Mrs Macfarlane) usually found some small treat to distribute with the collects and chants. Oranges were the most popular. The Piskie chapel was famed for the numerical strength of its Sunday School, mostly bairns from Fisherton.

Meg led Victor into the family pew, front right of the aisle under the pulpit. There was no mistaking where to go for the cushioned front pews were rented annually, an important addition to the church accounts. (The meagre sixpences and shillings or pennies would never have paid either stipend or coal bill.) Some of the congregation including Mr Vass and Meg (who did not count) were vociferously against pew rents seeing them as divisive and discriminating The other half which included the colonel and vestrymen realised that the church relied on the income. Some were afraid that strangers, possibly Fisherton strangers, might sully their property so to speak, but in view of the rector's well known opinion, no one quite liked to say so. When gradually over the years the pews lost their tenants, they remained quietly unlet.

Unlike the Church of Scotland and the Free Kirk whose congregations were middle-class worthies, farmers and shop keepers mainly drawn from Kirkton and Milton, the congregation of St Moluag crossed class barriers. English incomers earned it its soubriquet, 'the English Church'. Upper middle class county families whose attendance at English public schools instilled in them a familiarity with Matins and a knowledge of the English Hymnal, attended *en masse* at Christmas, Easter and Harvest, seldom throughout the rest of the year. Clan members whose affiliations had once been (and indeed some still were) Jacobite also attended the Scottish Episcopal Church which had, a century before, been persecuted for its presumed Jacobite leanings; but what is a century in time after all, and Highlanders have long memories. Retired serving officers many from the Indian Army read the lessons. Occasionally tradesmen attended, two families in fact, and the even rarer Fisherton family in the form of the Macreedies whose loyalty to the late Mrs Murray-Myers, brought Marsali out most weeks. As

123

the token fisher family, Marsali was condescended to, made a fuss of, and, truth be told, quite enjoyed the patronizing attention (of which she was perfectly aware). Of the two shop keepers, Kenny Ross the chandler whose late wife had been English, was a sidesman thus Fanny had been brought up in St Moluag's as had Jared Macreedie. The Sunday congregation numbered an average of thirty souls not counting the five choir members and Mrs Macfarlane, who had taken over the harmonium when Miss Budge's hands had become too arthritic to play.

All eyes that May morning were on Victor Myers. Fanny, seated between her husband and the factor, who had been on duty that morning handing out prayer books and hymnals, watched him with interest as he followed Meg up the aisle. 'We'll ask him to tea,' she thought as Mr Vass robed in surplice and black scarf entered from the vestry door. But here was a difficulty. If he was staying at the Hall as no doubt he was, she would have to ask Miss Meg, would she not? Indeed she would like to ask Miss Meg, but at the big house they ate dinner at 8 pm, not high tea at 6 pm. She would not at all mind eating dinner at 8 pm but she knew her father and Jared too, for that matter, would dig their toes in. She might be able to persuade Jared to change the habit of a lifetime for one meal but never her father. Besides Meg might not come. She would be charming of course, but she would be firm in her refusal. She supposed she could ask Mr Myers with Mr Wedderburn. Her father got on well with Mr Wedderburn. The business needed to keep in with the big house. Yes, that was what she would do, ask young Mr Myers with old Wedderburn and see that they had a good tea.

'*Dearly beloved brethren, the Scripture moveth us in sundry places…*'Mr Vass intoned from the prayer book Matins. Why 'brethren' she thought, her eyes lifting from

124

her prayer book. There were far more 'sistren' - if that's what you called them - in church. It always annoyed her. The moment passed as she turned over the pages to find the psalms for the day. 'Sistren' didn't count for much in this world, she thought sparkily. We'll see about that. It was all change at the chandlers if not in St Moluag's.

The pointing of the psalms was different from Inverness cathedral which she had attended from school, and after a while she gave up trying to sing and turned her attention to Victor. What a thin, pale, young man he was; nothing to get excited about. She wondered if he would be robust enough in the factor's office. He looked as if a feather could blow him away. He might be easier to deal with than old Wedderburn. She had noticed that the Hall account was again overdue. Her father had told her somewhat dismissively that the matter was in hand. She knew her father. The business would be in real trouble if left to him much longer. She had already, unknown to him, sent out letters to a number of customers hinting at legal intervention and as a result most of the outstanding accounts had been settled. Not the Hall, though. Mr Myers would be a push-over she thought. She wondered what Meg made of him.

Meg had made a discovery that Victor could not keep hidden either from her or the old factor. She had not believed it to be possible until this morning. Mr Gordon, the lay reader and assistant teacher at the parish school had met them at the door. He spoke to her as he had not yet been formally introduced to Victor.

'Commander Macintyre has been taken ill. Would Mr Myers like to step into the breach and read the first lesson?'

Unsurprisingly, Victor had shaken his head vigorously. He had pointed to his throat. 'You mmmusht excccuth me, pppleath,' he had mumbled.

Meg said nothing. There had been no indication of a sore throat in the carriage.

Settled in the pew, she had murmured. 'I didn't know you were unwell.'

'I'm nnnot,' he whispered. 'Bbbut I cccan't - .'

'I understand,' she had said quietly.

He had said nothing but she knew he was stating a simple fact.. His refusal to read was not only on account of his stutter. He was - quite simply - unable to read. There had been indications over the past week but she had refused to believe them. If he can't read, he can't write. My God, she thought. What next? Can he count? She watched him carefully as the hymns were announced. He found them eventually, but it had been a slow fumble through the green hymnal. He could sing too without stuttering, but then the hymns were all familiar. He probably knew them by heart. Did Wedderburn realise his inability to read or count? He must have guessed by now, she thought. He would have to tell her father of course. He would be found unsuitable for the job and sent back to the deanery, but was that what she really wanted?

It took the whole of Matins, sermon and all, to work out the answer. It came to her in one word: Inverally, the land, the house, the church, the dogs, the sea, the moors. the people, every stick and stone and flesh and bone. She wanted it all, to tend, to keep, to inhabit, above all to love. She also knew what she would have to do to obtain it. It was an awesome revelation.

Before she knew it, they had reached the last hymn, *Praise my soul the King of Heaven.* Impulsively she touched Victor's arm. 'You have a really nice singing voice,' she whispered encouragingly.

He said nothing, but she could see that he was pleased.

Chapter Three

1898

The Hall

It had taken three years from that moment of revelation in church to her wedding day.

Meg stood in her wedding dress at the window of her childhood bedroom for the last time. She no longer asked herself was marriage to Victor the right decision. It was the only one. She had managed to convince herself that she liked Victor. She had liked him from the moment he had asked why the fisher cottages had no running water. Apart from his stutter and other disabilities there was a vulnerability about him, a complete lack of male arrogance that had appealed to her from that Sunday morning he had told her he could not read. In the carriage home from church he had explained, without looking at her, that apart from his inability to pronounce consonants, he could read only a little, stumblingly, and though he could guess at some words, the letters seemed to dance and twitch on the page and he could never hold them long enough in his sight to make sense of them. He was better with numbers and could even manage simple sums but a column of figures was impossible. As for writing, he had learned to sign his name and half an hour of concentration might produce a couple of ill-spelled sentences. He had a brain deficiency, one of his tutors had told him, but his father insisted that he lacked application.

'Mmmy fffather sssees mmme as a shshshirker,' he told her. 'Nnneither he nor my bbbrother take my …wwweaknesses… ssserioushly. I thought ppperhapth the jjjob of fffactor might be ssss…do. I had not wealitsed how mmmuch pppaperwork wwwas involved. Ssstupid of mmme.

127

'Bbbut there you are, Cccousin. I'm sss... a ff fool. ' He had turned to look at her then. 'If I cccould ssstay until the end of the ththth.. mmmonth I cccould tttell them at hhhome that I hhhad tttried. I sssuppose I ought ttto lllearn how the estate wwworkth. '

She had been silent for a while, long enough for him to look out over the south avenue and sigh. In fact she had been thinking feverishly. What to do now.

'The tttruth is Cccousss... Mmmeg, I lllike it here. I know it's only bbbeen a fffew dddayth bbbut I ccccould be hhhappy here and I think I cccould even be useful. Bbbearing in mmmind that one ddday....' but he could not say it.

She finished the sentence in her head. Bearing in mind that if neither she nor Isabella had a son before her father died he would probably inherit Inverally.

'Whwhwh.. ever hhhappens there wwwill always be a hhhome for you hhhere, Ccc...Mmmeg,' he said turning to face her

She ignored the remark. 'You could still be factor, Cousin.'

'Have you sss...bbbeen in Wwwedderburn's office?' he asked

She nodded. Filled from floor to ceiling with game records, account books, tenants' agreements, plans of the estate, maps of Inverally, she knew it well.

'Wwwedderbbb... wwwill tttell my uncle that I am unsssuited to the wwwork and my fffather will fffume and my bbbrother will jjjeer.'

How dare they! She was full of indignation on his behalf. The carriage was approaching the front door. Cuthbertson was waiting for them on the top step.

'Not if we work together,' she said without moving.

He looked at her in astonishment. 'Hhhow?'

128

Their eyes locked. He has nice eyes, she thought, gentle when they were not scared. 'Exactly what I say. I could do the books and keep the accounts.'

His mouth opened in astonishment. 'Wwwedderburn wwwon't like thththat,' he said doubtfully.

Meg's eyes flashed. 'You mean you won't like it.'

'I dddon't know,' he said doubtfully. 'It hhhardly ssseems rrr-right for a lll…'

'Well then,' she said, smoothing off her gloves, 'go back to your family. Neither Wedderburn nor my father will detain you.'

Sam had opened the carriage door. She gave him her gloved hand. The dogs burst past Cuthbertson and surrounded her joyfully, but she ignored them and strode into the house.

After a fairly silent lunch in the presence of the servants, he had sought her out later that afternoon as she returned from walking the dogs on the moor. After apologising for his ungentlemanly behaviour in the carriage, he asked her if she had 'ssspoken to her fffather yet.'

She had told him 'No, for he would have thought exactly the same as you.' She paused. 'You're probably right,' she added briskly. 'I know every inch of the estate. I know every one of the tenants. I can keep accounts. I can write letters. I can speak - in Gaelic to the Fisherton folk'. (She had been about to leave it at 'speak' but hastily added 'Gaelic' for she knew she had sounded cruel and it was not his fault that he was the way he was.) 'But I'm a woman,' she continued on a spurt of passion. 'Worse still, I'm a 'lady'. I know my place.'

'The tttruth is, Cccousin,' he said humbly. 'I wwwould vvvvalue your hhhelp, if you are ssstill wwwilling to gggive it to me?'

It had worked after a fashion.

They became friends, almost good friends over the books for he was never patronising in his attitude towards the tenants, had an ability to see the best in people and was far less critical than she was, but they were not and never would be lovers. The word 'love' had never been mentioned between them. 'Like' would have to do. 'Like' would be enough. Wouldn't it?

On Wedderburn's advice, her father had wanted to send Victor back to the English deanery long before the three month's trial period was over. Wedderburn had warned him that the estate would be ruined if left to Victor. Meg had somehow managed to persuade him otherwise. 'He's excellent with the tenants, Papa.' That she could say in all honesty. Victor seemed far more at home in the village than the Hall. So Wedderburn left, not just the job but also the district and Victor had, on the face of it, taken over.

At six o'clock on most evenings Meg had visited the office where he would usually be waiting. None of the tenants or estate workers were there at that hour so they were undisturbed. She examined the invoices, kept the records up to date and, if he was there, they discussed the business of the day. She opened the mail, replied to the letters, wrote out the cheques - a lot of them - for him to sign in her father's name. Apart from that, she saw surprisingly little of him. She did not ask him where he went but others were quick to tell her that he spent a good deal of time at the timberyard or in the Royal Station Hotel, getting to know the tenants, she supposed. And so the months went by. She was busier than she had ever been and felt the better for it.

It was Helen Macfarlane who told her what was common gossip in Inverally. The young factor had set his cap at Miss Cynthia Spencer, Mr Gallie's pretty and available step-daughter.

'Does she care for him?' Meg had asked naively.

Mrs Macfarlane was silent for a moment, her head bent over her crochet work. Then she looked up and said, 'I don't think love comes into it. A marriage to the heir - Mr Myers is your father's heir is he not? - would please her mother greatly.'

Now it was Meg's turn to be silent. She knew Cynthia slightly, an attractive clever girl, whose glorious hair and pert prettiness sapped her own confidence. Victor would marry her and move into the factor's house which at present stood empty. Her father would not live forever. Then what? The Dower house for her? Or freedom. Through her mother she had a little money of her own. She could travel, she supposed, visit Isabella in India, find herself a husband. The idea did not appeal.

Less than a week later the colonel had another seizure, not enough to kill him but a warning nonetheless. Meg knew immediately what she would have to do.

In the end it was easier than she could have imagined. A few days after the colonel's stroke she and Victor had met in the office as usual. Meg had noticed that Victor seemed distracted, anxious even and his stutter was more pronounced than ever. She thought something must have gone wrong in the estate. There was a perpetual wrangle over the hill boundary line between Lord Point, the neighbouring landowner and Inverally which had flared up again. She had the most recent letter in her hand.

'Is something troubling you, Cousin?' she asked outright. 'I notice that the Point people are making a fuss over access to our moor. Macmurtrie will deal with it.' Macmurtrie was the estate law agent whose office was in Inverness.

He had no idea what she was talking about, not having read the letter. 'What's wrong, Victor?' she persisted.

So he told her in his convoluted roundabout way. He had been spending much of his time at the timberyard. He was interested in wood and some of the stable block needed renewing. Mr Gallie, however, had misinterpreted the visits and had asked him outright what were his intentions concerning Miss Cynthia. He had indicated that he would welcome him as a son-in-law.

'What about you, Cousin?' Meg had asked him anxiously. 'Do you love her?'

He looked astonished. 'Lllove her? Shshshe's a pppretty gggirl but nnno I dddon't lllove her and I dddon't wwwant to mmarry her. I'm not the mmmarrying sssort.'

'Then marry me,' she said without looking at him. She felt herself redden from her toes to her cheeks.

After what seemed to her like an endless silence, he said quietly. 'Dddid you nnnot hear me, Mmmeg? I'm not the sssort of mmman that lllladies mmmarry.'

She had no idea what he meant. She thought it was because of his stammer, his lack of looks, his inability to read. That gave her confidence. 'I heard you,' she said looking up at him, 'and I don't care. Will you marry me, Victor?'

He still said nothing.

'I know you don't love me,' she continued in desperation. 'I don't love you either, but we like each other, don't we? And we both love Inverally, don't we? Don't we?' she insisted forcing him to look at her.

His eyes shocked her. She saw wretchedness, fear and anxiety written there as clearly as letters in a book. 'Victor?' she pleaded.

The look intensified. 'I'll lllet you dddown,' he prevaricated. 'I cccan't help mmmyself. I lllet everyone dddown.'

She had a sudden image of Hugh Vass whom she believed she still loved, still dreamed of, older, unattainable. What was she doing proposing marriage to this unprepossessing young man? But Mr Vass belonged in the world of dreams. Victor was real.

'I'm willing to take that risk, if you are,' she said holding out her hand to him.

After a moment he took it. He raised it to his lips. 'I'd bbbetter ssspeak to mmmy uncle, then.'

That had been over a year ago and now finally her wedding day had come.

She had learned a lot more about her husband-to-be during that year. She knew his weaknesses; his love of brandy, his pleasure in the company of handsome rugged men, his extravagance. Helen Macfarlane had warned her, 'Don't expect too much.' She told herself that she did not care. If she could not have Mr Vass she would make the best of Victor. Run the estate herself, if need be.

Mrs Shanks adjusted the small pearl tiara over the silk net veil.

'You look very fine, Miss Meg,' she said admiringly. 'Mr Victor will be fair proud of you today.' Mrs Shanks was one of Victor's admirers. She was sorry for him of course, for his stutter, for his lack of robustness, but he was unfailingly polite to her, even after he had taken a dram. He awakened her motherly instincts.

'I am doing the right thing, aren't I?' Meg asked as she faced herself in the mirror.

'I'm sure you'll be very happy, Miss Meg ' Mrs Shanks answered. She had no idea and had never been married herself. Hers was a courtesy title. Meg had not however been speaking to the ageing housekeeper. It was her own decision she queried. Especially now, for her father let it slip only that morning when she had visited him after breakfast that Mr Vass had asked him to put a stop to the marriage.

'Why, Papa?' she had asked. 'Why would he do that?' Could it be because he loved her? Ridiculous thought. She had tried hard to dismiss it.

'He keeps bad company,' was all her father would tell her. 'Drinks too much.'

'What did you tell him, Papa?'

'Told him to mind his own business. I already know that Victor's a useless factor and an apology for a man. He wouldn't be my choice for a son-in-law. I wish it didn't have to be this way but there it is. Your future is secure, thank God. You have my blessing for what it's worth.'

It was as much as he had ever said to her at any time. She thanked him. 'Victor's not that bad, Papa. I know what I'm doing.'

He grunted. 'At least you'll have a roof over your head when I'm gone.'

As she gazed at her own image in the looking glass, the question crept back, why had Mr Vass tried to stop the wedding? It stayed with her as she descended to the basement to show herself to the servants, when she visited the colonel who was now confined to his room. He wept. Her father actually wept! Since his last seizure, the tears were never far away.

The bridesmaids, Victor's two nieces, were waiting for her in the drawing room, dressed in pink silk and carrying white roses. Her own bouquet of pink roses was handed to her by her soon-to-be mother-in-law while her father-in-law in his clerical frock coat came forward to greet her. He was to give her away.

And all the time the secret thought that Mr Vass had tried to stop the wedding, coloured her cheeks and animated her eyes. It did not take much imagination to pretend that it was him who was waiting for her at the chancel steps, because, of course, he was.

Kirkton

Helen Macfarlane wheezed through her repertoire of voluntaries. She found the harmonium hard work and wished that the vestry would hurry up and raise the money for a new pipe organ. There had been promises for the past year or so, but several bazaars and bequests had not yet raised enough cash.

Hugh was robing in the vestry with Hamish and a Fisherton loon, as his two servers. Hamish was nine this year, a sturdy lad, the image of his father in looks and temperament. There was nothing of Emily in him that she could see.

Emily had been dead for nearly two years and Helen was expecting Hugh to make an offer soon. She supposed she should have moved out of the schoolhouse when Emily had died, but with Hamish and his father both so devastated, she knew it would have been cruel to abandon them. There had been some gossip in the congregation which flared up from time to time, but as housekeeper and the child's carer, she had ridden it out. She had taken over Emily's role in the parish in every respect except the one she still hoped for. She had loved Hugh for a very long time now. Emily had known this and had brought her to Inverally as a youngish impoverished widow to look after her husband and child when she first learned her own prognosis. She suspected Hugh knew it too, but he had never so much as held her hand.

She also knew of Meg's crush. She gave herself away at every turn. She and Emily had even spoken of it.

'She'll grow out of it,' they had told each other indulgently, but Meg had seemingly not grown out of it and now here she was about to be married to a man she did not love and who, she suspected, did not, could not love her. A marriage of convenience. How sensible, she had thought. How wise of

Meg. That was before she had heard the rumours; that he was after young Mrs Macreedie at the chandler's, never away from the place, and then he was chasing that pretty Miss Spencer at the timber yard; that he spent too much time in the Inverness taverns or the Royal Hotel saloon. It came as quite a shock to hear that he was actually marrying Meg.

She had told Hugh over tea in the rectory, just the bare facts because she knew the rector could not abide gossip. 'Have you heard? Miss Meg is to marry Mr Myers.'

'What?' he had exclaimed angrily.

'Do you not think it an excellent solution?' she had asked curiously.

'No, I do not,' he answered shortly.

She was surprised at his tone. Perhaps, she thought, he has feelings for Meg himself. That had never before occurred to her.

'I know he's not perhaps the ideal husband for Miss Meg, but this may settle him down.'

'It must not happen,' he had said rising so abruptly that he knocked over his half- drunk tea-cup. He did not even apologise when she picked up a napkin to mop the spill.

'But Hugh, don't you see. The estate is entailed. If she has a son…'

'She will never have a son or any child by that man.'

'Why ever not?' she had asked, shocked by his vehemence.

He had not answered her. Instead he strode from the room leaving her to guess at his meaning. Perhaps he had one of those frightful diseases she had barely heard of. She knew Hugh had gone straight to the Hall to see the colonel, but he had not told her what he had said. Whatever it was had obviously had had no effect, for here they all were in church and the bride about to arrive.

At that moment Mr Myers and his twin brother, as his best man, stood up as Hugh and his servers processed in from the vestry.

At a prearranged nod from the usher at the west door, she started to play the Wedding March.

Pleased with her own new pale green silk gown, specially designed by Miss Eliza Matheson, Inverally's foremost dressmaker, Fanny was eager to see what Miss Meg had chosen for her wedding dress. She hoped at least that she would equal that of Miss Cynthia Spencer who looked ravishing in pale yellow satin. Fanny was wary of Cynthia but not enough to make an enemy of her. Fanny was far too shrewd to antagonise any of her customers (she thought of all the Inverally inhabitants as customers), and, after the estate and the Fisherton skippers, the timberyard was one of the most profitable. So she smiled and nodded at her as she followed her mother, the second Mrs Gallie and her husband, up the aisle into their allotted pew.

The whole of Kirkton was here, she thought, and a good deal of Milton as well, while the street outside was lined with Fisherton and other tenants - as well it might be. A Hall wedding brought with it a week's free rent

The susurrus of whispered conversation died down as the congregation turned to a woman to see what the bride was wearing. There stood Meg, her slight figure encased up to the neck in cream lace. An awed whisper flew round the church that it had been her mother's wedding gown. Certainly it was very fine. Meg looked different. Not pretty exactly, at least not pretty as Cynthia was pretty with abundant curling hair the colour of corn, but today she looked what Fanny had never suspected of her, vulnerable. Fanny liked Meg. Since the day she had given her a lift up the Brae she had felt that there was a bond between them.

And yes, the Hall was in debt to the chandler, but she trusted Meg.

Her eyes followed the bride's progress up the aisle on her soon-to-be father-in-law's arm until they stood beside Mr Myers.

She sighed. The truth was she did not care for Mr Myers. There he stood in full Highland regalia wearing the Murray tartan but neither badger sporran nor neck ruffle, *skian dhu* or velvet doublet could disguise the fact that he was a poor specimen of manhood. With his thin frame, round shoulders and wispy moustache how could Meg want him for a husband? The answer seemed clear enough. It was the estate she wanted. Everyone knew that this was a marriage of convenience. He could not help how he looked, poor wee mannie, or how he spoke. Those were not the reasons for her dislike. It was his habits she detested. His drinking habits.

Sometimes in the rare few quiet moments in her life, maybe at dawn, she would have a small tweak of regret that she had married for love. It was not that she did not still care for Jared, or love the way he looked, especially today for he too was in full Highland regalia, the Ross tartan, an anniversary gift from herself to him which was worth every considerable penny of the cost. But their's was not a marriage of equals. She knew that. This was nothing to do with class, though perhaps that was the basic cause of it. Jared was uneducated, had no ambition and was completely uncultured. But, as she reassured herself time and time again, what he lacked in education he more than made up for in other ways and she had two children to prove it. She could see only one compensation for Meg where Mr Myers was concerned and that was the Hall. Would it be enough?

Her reason for disliking Victor had in fact nothing to do with his lack of looks or his unfortunate stutter. It was the influence he had on Jared, or, she wondered, could it be the other way round? Maybe it was Jared leading the wee factor astray. For a while they had met nearly every evening in the Royal. Jared would come home the worse for wear, stinking of whisky. When she remonstrated, he would say, 'How could I say no to the wee factor? He's a good customer.'

'Could you not just go for a walk, or fishing like papa?'

Jared had treated her remark as a joke. 'Aye, that'll be right, A wee walk maybe with the wee factor!' Then he added seriously. 'That stutter of his almost disappears after a dram or two.'

Maybe Mr Myers needed a dram but Jared certainly did not. She told him so in no uncertain terms and for a while he was content to spend more of his evenings at home but not all of them.

Not for the first time she felt sorry for Meg up at the altar making her vows to love, cherish and obey. Och well, she thought optimistically. Maybe marriage will settle him down.

Cynthia, watching Meg make her vows, came to a decision. When I marry, she thought. I shall not wear my mother's gown. I want white taffeta, with leg of mutton sleeves and a long train with six bridesmaids also in taffeta with blue sashes carrying violets, so then I shall have to be married in May. But who to choose for her groom? She sighed. At present she was being courted by three gentlemen, one of whom resided in Kirkton, the minister's son, young Mr Carruthers, not so young perhaps, nearly forty in fact, but a minister himself, ready to step into the shoes of his father and in need of a wife. She quite fancied herself as a minister's wife.

The other two gentlemen were the brothers of school friends in Inverness and both at the university in Aberdeen. Cynthia sighed. How she missed Inverness and her life there.

She even missed school. All the giggling and chatter and company. She sighed again audibly this time. Her mother glanced at her sharply.

Poor Miss Meg. She would not care to be married to Mr Myers. No indeed. Cynthia had no time for men who spurned her, and there was no doubt about it. Mr Myers had been rude. She had worn her most ravishing gown, flashed him her most brilliant of smiles. Mr Myers was the laird's heir, so it was said, and yes, if asked, she would really enjoy being the laird's wife. But Mr Victor Myers had spurned her. He had taken her hand when introduced and what a limp, damp handshake it had been. She looked into his eyes in that irresistible way (one of the Inverness young gentleman had told her that her eyes were irresistible) but he had not even glanced at her. Not once during that Sunday dinner had he looked at her or spoken directly to her and after the meal he could not wait to make his excuses to leave. He was often to be seen in the timberyard, but he never called at the house. Not that she cared. There was always Mr Carruthers. He would propose any day now, she felt sure of it, but how would she answer him?

Did Miss Meg love Mr Myers? How could she? He was so feeble, somehow. Not that Miss Meg was all that beautiful herself. Too big a nose and too short in height. There they stood side by side while Mr Vass prayed over them, stuck with each other for life. In that moment she realised that she did not love Mr Carruthers at all. She decided that would refuse him and wait for Mr Right to come along. After all she was only twenty. She had years to fall in love.

She sighed again so loudly that her mother turned her head to look at her, and, raising her eyebrows, whispered, 'do you require some *sal volatile*, dearest?' She shook her ringlets impatiently.

Mr Vass announced the next hymn. '*Oh God of Bethel, by whose hand…*' God's hand seemed to have had very little to do with it, she thought, as she sifted through the pages of her hymn-book. After a verse, her eyes shifted restlessly round the congregation and lighted on Fanny Macreedie. Her gown was delightful. She must find out who had been her dressmaker. Fanny's husband moved and for a moment obscured her vision. How handsome he looked in his kilt, without doubt the most handsome man in the church. She considered Jared Macreedie to be near perfect until he opened his mouth. He spoke with the strong Gaelic accent of the Fisherton folk and sometimes sounded so broad that he was impossible to understand. Fanny had married for love. The whole town knew that for a fact. They had more or less eloped. She could well understand why Fanny had fallen in love with him. She could also understand why Jared had leapt at the chance to improve his position. Fanny was nothing special to look at. Jared had chosen to better himself. Store-room lad to proprietor at one stroke of the pen! Two bairns already. But did he love her? Her eyes lingered on Jared. She imagined, not for the first time, his mouth on hers and thought it still could happen. Outrageous, she scolded herself, you are outrageous, Miss Cyn Spencer!

The last verse over, she craned her neck and ears to watch and hear the exchange of vows.

Fisherton

Marsali took out the letter from the front of her bodice for the umpteenth time. She did not need to look at it for she knew the contents by heart. It was from a neighbour's son to his mother who had emigrated to the Americas some five years back. It was not addressed to her but it contained that snippet of news on which her heart relied.

'...Last week we halted the cattle outside a wee town called Dust which is well-named! They call it a city but it is just a wide dirt street with a few wooden stores and a tavern. As it is the only civilised spot for miles, it was busy. Several fights broke out but the sheriff came and that night the jailhouse was full. Some of the loons I knew, a lad from Point and the King boy, at least I thought it was the King boy, one of those three loons that was believed drowned. I had a dram with the Point loon, Davie Sutherland's lad, Cal, but he was from a different ranch. He's doing fine with the cattle. I could have been wrong about the King lad. I never got to speak to him....'

It was another scrap to put by in her kist. There were five of them now. Surely not all of the sightings could be mistaken? At the same time she took out her best dress, black bombazine that came out for funerals, weddings and the kirk. The Mission Hall was having a do in honour of Miss Megaidh's wedding, a proper sit-down meal with meat, ale and cakes from the Big House. The meat and tatties, bannocks and cheese had come from the Inverally Ladies Charitable Fund, served by the committee and organised by the chairlady, Miss Agnes Gallie. Highlight of the evening was to be a visit from the newly weds and the presentation of a gift from the Fisherton tenants. This was an inscribed silver salver which had cost each family the rent for the week. When Miss Megaidh had heard where the free week's rent had gone, she had insisted on two weeks free. She was getting more like the *aingeal*, her mother, with every year that passed. What would she have made of her daughter's marriage?

It was not that she disliked the wee factor. As she said to Anna, 'How could you dislike a poor wee lost city loon like yon?' Her Jonas would have a better idea of the work.

142

Mr Wedderburn may have been tough over the rent but at least he saw to it that the roofs were watertight. He had been known to evict persistent rent offenders and had to her knowledge sent one widower, Ephraim Cooper, to the Poor House in Point. It only happened once. Mr Wedderburn thereafter had sent his man to every house on a Friday night when the boaties were safe in harbour, before the tavern opened and the money spent. Mr Wedderburn had been known to confiscate a pig for rooting among the cobbles and he'd take poachers as young as eight years old to the law. No excuses. The wily Fisherton wives could twist this wee factor round their fingers what with their tears and tales. He was soft, he was, and the gamekeeper was getting past it, so Jonas reported as he slung another rabbit on the kitchen table. The estate was going to the middens, so Ezra said. She wondered what the laird thought of it all, if he could think at all, poor gentleman… and Miss Megaidh.

By the time she had changed, Ezra had come back. He spent much of the day on the pier head gossiping with the other old or idle men. It was not that Ezra was that old, not yet sixty, but the business with Donnaidh had finished him with the fishing. He hated the sea as a living enemy, spat his phlegm in it every morning and last thing at night. If it were not for Jonas who had taken his place on the *Bright Star* and Jared, of course, doing so well and her own fingers forever busy at the knitting, they might be in the Poor House themselves. That, she thought with relief, would never happen, not with Missus Fanny in the family. My, but she was a hardy lassie, Missus Fanny. How had Jared, the big soft loon, ever managed to capture such a bride?

'Get yourself shaved,' she told Ezra who had settled into his chair by the range. 'The dinner's at six. *Nach cuala tu e.'*

'I'm not going,' he said taking his pipe out of one pocket and reaching for his baccy in another.

Please yourself, she wanted to say to him. Why should he go if he didn't want to? She didn't want to go either but there would be ale and venison and the company of his cronies. So she argued and he gave in as indeed he had always intended to do, and at ten to six they set out for the Mission Hall with the rest of Fisherton.

Long trestle tables had been set up with white cloths and long benches. The fisher folk knew to bring their own cutlery, horn spoons for the most part and gutting knives. Marsali and Ezra took their seats beside the Munros. After Mr Carruthers (junior) has welcomed them and intoned a long grace, the committee ladies of the charity, still wearing their wedding hats and swathed in long white aprons, emerged from the hall kitchen with a great cauldron of broth and baskets of bread.

The cock a'leekie soup which had come from Mrs Gallie's kitchen was delicious. Fanny as a newly elected committee member had provided a vast dish of minced lamb. The beef stew came from another Kirkton kitchen while a great platter of mashed tatties and neeps came from the Mains farm. The Big House had provided the ale which flowed freely and the Misses Dorcas and Martha Carruthers presided over the tea urn. It was a fine spread topped with a slice of wedding cake rich in dried fruit and coated with hard white icing.

As the feast neared its end, the doors opened and the wedding party arrived. It was formally welcomed by the county councillor representing Inverally who happened also to be Mr Mackay from the Mains farm, and the Member of Parliament for Point, the elderly Sir Hector Macdonald. Speeches over, the bridal couple were toasted and the presentation made by a Mackay granddaughter whose name Marsali could not remember.

To a person, the audience wondered how the wee factor would manage to reply but it was Miss Megaidh who rose to her feet, and why shouldn't she, Marsali thought, ready to do battle with any critic - and there would be plenty - who would not like to see the bride in such a position. You could see that some of the platform party were surprised.

Gracefully she thanked them all. Her voice was clear and the words appropriate. Then she added to the surprise of all, 'and we have a gift for you, one that you have been promised before, but this time we intend it to happen. As from Monday the streets of Fisherton will be busy. You will all be vastly inconvenienced for the next six months, your lives disrupted and the noise excessive.' Miss Megaidh was smiling as she spoke. 'But I think, I trust, I know that you will be delighted to have piped water in your own kitchens. No more trudging to the wells, no more drainage into the streets. Fisherton will greet the new century as a modern village. This will be our wedding gift to you.'

The news was greeted in absolute silence. Then someone on the platform started to clap. A few joined in but by no means all. Marsali was one of them. Ezra was not.

Miss Megaidh was still on her feet. 'I know that this is a lot to understand. That is why we have brought along Mr Jarvis, the engineer, who will be in charge of the project. He will answer any questions you might like to ask.'

To begin with no one would speak. Then the questions came slowly, tentatively. 'Where is the water to come from?' 'Where would the waste water go?' It was Ezra who asked the question that concerned them most.. 'Will the rents rise?'

'That is a matter for the estate,' Mr Jarvis replied smoothly, 'But I think I can safely promise you that the ladies present will find water at the turn of a tap to be well worth a few more pennies on the rent.'

The answer was greeted in silence. Councillor Mackay, made a graceful closing speech extolling the virtues of piped water newly installed at the Mains. At a nod from Mr Carruthers, the local fiddler struck up a lively reel. The trestles were folded, the benches pushed back against the wall and gradually a few of the more lively lads found partners for a reel. The women congregated on one side of the hall and the men on the other. The gist of the men's conversation consisted of grumbling. 'The women have always managed fine. What's wrong with the wells? Who needs taps anyhow?'

Marsali and Anna took seats by each other. 'What are you thinking of these taps?' Anna asked. 'My Ina up at the Hall says she wouldna be without them.'

'Miss Megaidh thinks it for the best,' Marsali said loyally, but like Ezra she was concerned for the rent.

Inverally
After the presentation in the Mission Hall, Victor and Meg had taken the closed carriage to Inverness to start their wedding trip in easy stages to spend a week in Fort William. It was to have been Rome but with the colonel so frail, Meg had decided they had better not go so far in case the worst happened. Naturally she was disappointed but it had been her decision. It was also her decision not to take Ina Munro who had been promoted from the scullery to the house as a personal maid. Ina had been disappointed but Meg was firm.

Victor elected to make all the arrangements and had chosen Sam Stuart, the Hall groom, to be in charge of the horses. A small excitement possessed him every time he thought of Sam Stuart as their coachman. With the help of the aged office clerk who came from Point by train three mornings a week, he engaged rooms for all three of them in the various inns and hotels *en route*. That way he could ensure that he and Meg had separate rooms without any awkwardness and that Sam would at least be under the same roof. He liked Sam. They could have a brandy together.

Victor sometimes wondered how much Meg understood his predilections. If she did, she was remarkably phlegmatic. If she did not, she would soon learn. Would she mind? He thought not. Meg, he realised, nursed a hopeless passion for the rector, a strange taste for the rector was, in his opinion, singularly unattractive. Victor preferred big men, with bronzed limbs and sky-blue eyes. Like Hilary. Like Sam. Not like Anton, though, who was dark and beautiful.

He also knew that the rector did not approve of this marriage, had done his best to advise his uncle against it. What had been said, he had no idea for his uncle had never spoken about the visit. Jenkins had done it for him. He was also wary of Jenkins, 'Jimmy' as the colonel called him. Jenkins had followed him out of the colonel's room not long after the enagement and winked. 'We 'ave our h'eye on you, Mr Victor... sir. We know your sort.'

Victor would have scurried away but Jenkins had his hand on clamped on his arm.

'Lllet gggo of me,' he had blustered indignantly.

'Oh, h'I'm on your side...sir.' He had given his arm a playful pat before letting him go and winked again.

Victor was continually confused by Jenkins. He seemed friendly enough but his words always contained a hint of menace. What could he know?

Once or twice a week Victor had escaped the goldfish pond of Inverally where everyone knew his every move, his every action. Cedric had once warned him not to foul his own nest. Cedric had been disgusted and horrified to find him a pet of one of the masters at the minor boarding school they had both attended. Victor did not want to remember that appalling time. In public, Cedric had lied for him, protected him, given him alibis, but in private he had lashed him with his tongue, shown his disgust and punished him with his fists. Then there had been that episode with the under-gardener in the deanery shrubbery. That had eventually resulted in his banishment to Inverally. But he had learned his lesson. In Inverness he could be anonymous. Oddly enough, it was Jenkins who had first told him about the Bonnie Prince club. 'A private place, see? Young gentlemen like yourself meet there for a dram and maybe an 'and or two of cards.' He was winking madly as he said it, but Victor, on Meg's advice, had learned to ignore the winks, choosing to perceive them to be friendly rather than sinister. He memorised the address which had been quite hard to find down an obscure wynd off the High Street and it was there that he had met the beautiful, dark-eyed passionate Anton who had rooms near the harbour. There they were safe, hidden from prying eyes, as safe as it was ever possible for perverted creatures like himself to be. And yes, that was how he saw himself, as a perverted creature, close to the toad in nature, or a beetle to be trodden under foot. He would have to be careful with Sam. He knew he would have to be content just to look, perhaps share a glass of ale at the end of a long day's travel, but not to touch. Meanwhile he would try his best to take care of Meg. He had grown to admire Meg, almost to like her. That could continue so long as this marriage didn't involve ...intimacy.

They dined that night at the Caledonian Hotel in Inverness. Meg, he thought, was rather silent. Usually she maintained a flow of trivial conversation about estate affairs for in those matters they thought alike. Victor tried to amuse her with his stuttered comments on some of the wedding hats.

'Wwwas it a bbblue bbbird or a ppparrot?' he wondered, that had crowned Mrs Gallie elaborate coiffure? 'Mmmy dddear, I thought it would pppeck me when we shshook hands!'

Meg laughed as he intended she should, and the rest of the meal passed pleasantly enough as they together remembered the highlights of the day.

'You mmmuth be tttired,' he said as they rose from the table. 'It's bbbeen a lllong ddday.' Outside her room he took her key, opened the door to let her in. Then he took her hand and raised it to his lips, an awkward gesture, but he could see that it pleased her. 'Ggggood night, Mmm… Mmmyers,' he said.

She looked surprised. 'Are you not coming…?' she began.

'I'm dddown the ccccorridor,' he interrupted firmly. 'Gggood nnnight, my dddear.'

But he did not go to his room.

There were two bars in the Caledonian Hotel with separate entrances. He found the public one which was crowded with customers. He saw Sam half way across the room but he was not alone. He watched him for a moment with a glass of ale in his hand talking and laughing with a couple of other working men. Across the crowded room he caught his eye. Without any sign of recognition, Sam turned away his head, raised his tankard and proposed a toast to which the others boisterously agreed. Victor left quietly. It was not too late to visit Anton.

Chapter Four

August 1900

The Hall

Isabella came home to have the child. Macmurtrie, the colonel's law agent and executor had made it clear to the family that if Isabella was carrying a son at the time of her father's decease, that child would be his heir. Failing this, Inverally would go to Meg's eldest son, should she have one. If neither of his daughters were to produce sons by the time of his death, the estate would go to Victor as his closest male blood relative.

Little more than a vegetable with a day and night nurse on the premises, Jock clung on to life determined to see not just his eldest daughter once again but above all the grandson he so desperately hoped for. He had been quietly dying for a week.

Isabella, sitting by his bedside, hoped beyond hope that this time all would be well. She blamed India for her two miscarried children, both of them sons. Surely in the cool clean climate of Inverally her baby would survive. She dreaded the ordeal ahead.

It was her first trip home since her wedding ten years past. Home furlough occurred every five years but she had been too ill to travel in '95. She and James had gone to the hill country around Simla and gradually her health and some of her happiness had been restored. James had been very patient with her, if not entirely faithful. She did not blame him. Indian women were so beautiful. There was at least one child that she knew of. Somehow, like servants or pet dogs, Indians did not count. She could not reproach him. If she despised the wife she had become, how must he regard her?

150

Her skin had coarsened, her hair lost its lustre, her voice had shrilled and her eyes were forever bright with unshed tears. She was aware of her failings, her uneven temper, her misery, yet she could not seem to change, could not turn again into the butterfly she had once been.

The door opened quietly and Meg came in. 'How is he?' she asked the nurse who sat knitting by the window.

'Much the same, Madam. Resting peaceful.'

Meg put her hand on Isabella's shoulder. 'I'm going down to Fisherton in the trap. Marsali would love to see you. Come with me?'

'Fisherton?' Isabella was horrified. 'You can't honestly expect me to risk my child's life in that dirty place,' she whispered, horrified. 'I'm surprised that you would even ask.'

'But that's the point, Bella. Fisherton's changed. There have been no cases of fever since the streets were cleared of rubbish and a proper water system introduced. I really want you to see it.'

Isabella covered Meg's hand with her own. 'And I will. I will, but not yet. Perhaps when the child is born.' Perhaps not, she thought with a shudder, as she remembered her mother's death. Infants are so fragile. She thought of all the dead babies in India, not just her own. 'But thank you, Meg. Don't let me keep you indoors. I can see it's a beautiful day.' She remembered how sick she had got of the sun in India, how she had longed for a grey day.

'Well then, shall we call on the Mortons in Point?' Enemies in the estate office but friends in the drawing room, Sir Donald's estate marched with Inverally. 'Or what about visiting the rectory? You haven't met Mrs Macfarlane yet.'

'You go.' Isabella patted her hand. 'I'd rather stay with papa.'

151

Meg sighed. She leaned down and kissed her sister on the cheek. 'I worry about you, Bella.'

And I, thought Bella, as her sister left the room, worry about you. If she had changed, so then had Meg. At twenty five, Meg still had the tiny-waisted, petite figure she had had as a child, but now her leanness had a slightly haggard appearance, her features were almost gaunt. She looked older than her years. Not for the first time she wondered about her sister's marriage.

In the privacy of their own room, James called Victor 'the village idiot'. She had remonstrated with him. 'That's hardly fair. He can't help his stutter. He seems to manage the estate well enough.'

'No,' James had said. 'Your sister manages the estate.'

'Meg?' she had said, surprised.' Are you sure?'

'The village idiot can hardly read, let alone keep the accounts.'

'How do you know?'

'Jenkins told me. Knows everything that goes on in the village not to mention this house….Well, all that will have to stop if…when…'

They were both silent, unwilling to jinx the future by tempting providence.

Sitting by her father's bedside, she allowed herself carefully to contemplate the future. James' leave was nearly over. If the worst happened she would go back to India with him but if she had a child, what then? She could not imagine herself with a child, a living baby in her arms. The thought was too painful, too sweet. Her musings stopped at that point.

She rose abruptly and went over to the window where the nurse was sitting. James was crossing the lawn his gun broken under his arm. He stopped to have a word with a gardener who was trimming the edges of the lawn. He had been shooting rabbits. Finlay, the head keeper, had complained that the estate was overrun and it gave James something to do. Dear James, she thought with a rush of love for him. She knew he was getting bored. They were both in limbo, she thought, waiting for the child to be born, her father to die. Meg and Victor were, no doubt, anxious too.

Standing there while the nurse shifted her father's position in the bed she felt a movement within her womb that was different from the child's familiar kick.

Kirkton
Meg stood outside the schoolhouse. Still that feeling of anticipation, that metaphoric standing on tiptoe that she had always felt as she waited for this particular door to open. It needed a coat of paint, she noticed, and the gutters should be cleared of dead leaves and winter debris. Since her involvement in the management of the estate she had become even more aware of deterioration wherever it was to be found. She sighed involuntarily. On the surface, the estate seemed to be going well enough, rents came in fairly regularly, yet money was perpetually short, the bills delayed and sometimes not paid at all. The piped water had been expensive. The rents had risen accordingly, and the fisher folk had been predictably bitter for the herring season had been poor. She knew that Wedderburn would have had no scruples at all about adding an extra shilling or two to the weekly sum, but she had maintained to Victor that since the tenants had not asked for taps they should not be expected to pay for them. Nevertheless out of necessity they had paid up but the burden of the estate debt had not noticeably lessened. She was worried, felt out of her depths so had decided to confide in the rector. If Isabella had a son there would be changes, she knew.

153

The rector himself came to the door. It being a Saturday he had no classes.

'Miss Megaidh!' he said '*Ciamar a tha sibh?*'

'*Gle mhath*,' she answered stepping over the threshold.

'Mistress Macfarlane is out, I fear. You will have to make do with me.'

'It was you I came to see,' she told him seriously. 'If you can spare me some of your time?' She peeled off her gloves. 'How is Hamish?'

'As noisy, as untidy, as clumsy as ever.'

'But you love him.' She smiled.

'I love him.'

They were silent for a moment as they seated themselves. She knew he would be wondering why she had no child on the way since she was now two years married. So many people wondered. Their eyes flew briefly to the flatness of her belly. That was something she could never tell him nor indeed anyone else.

'We are old friends, Miss Megaidh, are we not? How can I help you?'

So she told him about the constant effort to pay the bills, the never-ending cycle of repairs, re-fencing, the tenants, their problem, the poachers, the pensions, the salaries, the continual lack of money. She did it all without once mentioning Victor's name. He was not so careful.

'Where is Mr Myers in all this?' he asked bluntly. 'I thought he was the estate factor.'

'He is,' she said quickly and after a moment repeated less forcefully, 'he is.'

Suddenly she was telling him everything. Like vomit that won't be kept back, it all poured out. To begin with, she and Victor had worked together amicably, but - she could see it now - she had become too critical, too controlling, too curious. He had not liked to account for every movement in

154

his day, for every penny spent, for every absence. From hindsight she could not blame him, though at the time she had been contemptuous and angry. He had demanded a salary so the estate paid him what Wedderburn had earned but that was not enough. It was never enough.

To begin with, their frail friendship that had been forged over his enthusiastic support for her Fisherton improvements had gradually leaked from their relationship. Victor's heart had never been in the estate, she knew that now. He liked the idea of himself as factor and heir presumptive but hated the reality of Fisherton with its smell of poverty, the fields and the farms with their stench of dung. He pined for his old city life and as a result spent too much time in the taverns of Inverness. At least that's where she supposed that he went. Sometimes he spent whole days and nights away with no explanation.

Rows of momentous proportions had flared up over the slightest event from the failure of a fence to keep a valuable animal from plunging to its death over a ravine to his absence at dinner. The bruising arguments had recently disintegrated into silence, silence in the estate office - he was never there - at the dinner table in the presence of servants and in the bedroom he had never shared. His last threat had been 'Thththings will be dddifferent when I'm the lllaird.'

Then Isabella had come home pregnant.

'She may well have a son.' Meg told the rector. There she had said it.

'And he will inherit Inverally?' Hugh asked.

She nodded. He was silent for a moment. Then he leaned towards her and said earnestly. 'Might this not be your opportunity, Miss Megaidh?'

'How so,' she asked.

'Did you not once want to become a doctor? That might not now be possible but Fisherton needs a place for healing -

not necessarily the ills of the body - a place where the sick at heart might be eased, paupers fed, the anxious comforted. The Poor House is only a hated last resort. There is so much that needs to be done. Mistress Macfarlane and I have often talked of this. The calling is there for the one who hears it.'

Her mind was racing ahead of him. 'The Duff cottage will soon be empty. Since her man was drowned, Mrs Duff is leaving to live with her sister in Aberdeen,' she began then thought again. There were at least two families she knew of in need of housing. By solving one problem she was creating another.

She sighed and rose to stand by the window that looked into the schoolyard. 'And what of Mr Myers?' she asked in such a low voice that his sharp ears only just heard. 'What of Victor?'

'Surely Mr Myers will keep his job. Even if Mrs Mackenzie has a son, Inverally will still need a factor will it not?'

'One who can hardly read, barely write and who cannot add more than a single column of figures?'

He was beginning to understand. 'So, these past years you have ....?'

She nodded. 'If the estate is left in Victor's hands, it will fail. If Isabella has a daughter, Inverally will come directly to Victor when my father dies. It will fail all the sooner.'

'But surely if you are there, as you have been these past years...?'

'Victor no longer listens to me.' She could not look at him. She longed to tell him more, how he countermanded her orders, spent the money set aside for the accounts, ignored repairs, but now there were tears in her eyes and her throat was choked with them.

There was a tap on the door which opened immediately. Mrs Macfarlane stood there still in her outdoor clothing

'Excuse me, Hugh,' she flashed him a look and turned to Meg. 'Sam Stuart is here from the Hall. Mrs Moncrieff is in labour, Miss Meg. He has the trap waiting at the door.'

Milton

'I don't know,' Miss Cynthia was saying, her head cocked fetchingly to one side. 'I think perhaps the blue taffeta, but the white silk is adorable. Is it not adorable, Mrs Macreedie?'

'It is indeed,' Fanny replied, feeling a yawn start at the back of her throat. Was that where yawns usually came from? She had never given it a thought, but then she was seldom so bored as she was at this moment.

Miss Cynthia was choosing material for the Chamber of Commerce Ball in Inverness. Granted that it was an important day for any eligible young lady but this was Fanny's third visit to the Gallie house, her third batch of materials for Cynthia to peruse. Since the chandler's business had expanded to include fabrics and haberdashery, she had never been so busy. Normally she would have passed on this job to her lady assistant, but the Gallies were important customers. Miss Cynthia could so easily have taken her custom to Inverness. Still could. Metaphorically she gave herself a small shake. 'The silk will fall in folds like a smooth river while the blue taffeta will look like a frothing cataract,' she said dramatically. She could hear the mockery in her tone but could not stop herself. 'Which would you rather be? A frothy cascade or a shining meander?'

'I don't know,' Cynthia wailed. 'I can't make up my mind.'

157

'Would it help to ask advice from Mrs Gallie?' Fanny knew this was a risk. Mrs Gallie wanted Inverness outfitters to supply all their gowns.

'No. Yes. I don't know. Have you anything else?'

She had, and now was the time to produce it. The red brocade was heavy, figured and very expensive. Cynthia wanted it immediately. Mrs Gallie was summoned and she too approved. The price was not even considered. The order placed.

Fanny's cab was still waiting for her in the yard. The groom, wearing oilskins over his great coat for it was now raining, opened the door of the coach and took up the reins. Fanny no longer walked anywhere, not because she had become too grand or because it was too wet, but because she had no time. The business had grown immeasurably over the past two years. Jared had three counter staff, a seedsman and a lad while she employed an older lady who travelled from Point by train each morning to attend to the haberdashery. It had been Fanny's idea to expand the business into an Emporium This had required an extension into the garden at the back of the building. Ross's Emporium was now a large store which sold every necessity to community life. Jared had supported her enterprise, and, she soon realised, relished having a small staff under his personal control. She had long ago realised that it was his particular slightly pompous counter manner that brought in the customers and more importantly kept them coming in. He knew the life story behind every regular client, the names of their children or their boats or their horses. She realised that the questions he asked, the interest he took in each of them was an important part of being a shopkeeper. To begin with, Mr Ross, her father, had resented the changes, and spent more time than ever on the Ally or in the Royal Station Hotel lounge. There he was continually surprised but pleased to hear such good reports of his business. He was gradually coming round to a cautious approval.

She looked at her watch. She had about an hour to spend before returning home to supervise the children's dinnertime, a task she had no need to take on, but chose to do.

She should call in on the Estate Office to speak to Mr Myers. An account needed settling and already another large order had come down from Hugh Finlay, the game keeper, for wire netting. It was difficult to pin Mr Myers down for he was seldom in his office. She sighed. This was the hardest part of her business, securing payment from some of her customers. The skippers of Fisherton she trusted to pay up at the end of the fishing season and they seldom let her down. The farmers were more or less reliable especially after a good harvest, while the Inverally Estate could be described as bad customers. There were just so many debts the business could carry. Perhaps she should speak to Miss Meg. The trouble was she admired Miss Meg and disliked the idea of discussing business with her. There was, however, someone else she could confide in and whose judgement she trusted.

Rapping on the back of the coach she told the groom who was a Fisherton loon, kin to the Munros, to turn down the Brae. That would please him. He could spend half an hour with his kin while she warmed herself at her mother-in-law's hearth.

Fisherton

The narrow cobbled streets of Fisherton ran with rain and there was not a soul to be seen, not a zulu in the harbour. The men were away at sea, the bairns at school or indoors where she found Marsali, her length of navy knitting tucked into her apron, her fingers busy as they flew over the tiny needles seemingly of their own accord. The wonderful close intricate patterns of the ganseys had always intrigued Fanny and she had now taken on the sale of the fine oiled wool in the Emporium at a more competitive price than the Inverness traders. At her insistence, Marsali had made one for Jared. 'He'll not like it, though,' she had told Fanny shaking her head. 'How could he not?' she had argued, but Marsali had been right. Jared had refused to wear it, 'I'm not on a boatie,' he had told her, offended. 'It would not be right.' So she had given it to her father who was happy to make use of its warmth under his fishing oilskins.

The inside of the cottage was gloomy for the rain clouds had darkened the day. Marsali rose as she entered. Ezra did not. He cowered behind the *Courier*, and only at Marsali's insistence lowered it to nod to his daughter-in-law. As she sat and removed her hat, he quietly left the room.

Marsali did not offer any sort of refreshment to Fanny nor was she expecting it. Jared had told her how Meg's mother, the *Aingeal*, as he called her, had died from water drunk in the cottage. Though the water came from a tap these days and was clean, Marsali would never again take such a risk.

They talked of the children, Kenny who was four past and little Connie who was now well into her second year. Marsali saw her grandchildren regularly for Jared took them down to Fisherton on Saturday afternoons while Fanny finished her books. Fanny would tell Jared to bring her back for her tea but she seldom came. Marsali was not at her ease with Mrs Mack who patronised her and watched her like a policeman. Mrs Mack was from Point and, though she had got used to Jared, she regarded fisher folk as an alien breed.

Marsali poked the red coals behind the iron bars of the old black range on which a pot of mutton broth simmered quietly. The cottage may have been gloomy but it was cosy and comfortable. The big clock on the wall ticked away the minutes.

'And how is wee Kenny's mam?' she asked kindly, for she could see for herself that her elegant daughter-in-law was troubled. Marsali had never quite got round to calling her by her Christian name.

Fanny rose to her feet and moved over to the range to warm her hands. Marsali waited.

'The business would be good but we are owed more in outstanding debts than we have in stock.'

Marsali's mind flew to Jonas who had left the curing yard to take over Ezra's place on the zulu. 'The boaties are still out. Is it the *Bright Star*?'

'No, no,' said Fanny a little impatiently. 'The skippers are not to blame. There is an arrangement.'

Marsali nodded. 'It'll be the estate, I'm thinking.'

Fanny sat down again. 'There's hundreds owing. The orders keep coming in but the accounts are never settled. What do you make of the wee factor, Mistress Macreedie? He's never in his office, never to be found.'

'He's to be found all right, if you know where to look. Do you not think of sending Jared after him?'

Fanny knew exactly what she meant. She did not quite like to say that the Royal Station hotel or the tavern were the last place on earth she would send Jared. 'I was wondering if I should speak to Mistress Myers.'

'Poor wee Miss Megaidh. She has her troubles.'

There was a tap on the door which opened immediately. The doors in Fisherton were never locked. No one waited for an invitation. Anna from next door came in, unable to control her excitement.

'Excuse me for intruding but the word is out. Ina's friend - you ken the garden loon at the big house - ran down special.

Miss Isabella has had her bairn! Both doing fine. I knew you'd want to know.'

Fanny and Marsali spoke together. 'What is it?'

'Oh aye,' said Anna triumphantly. 'I forgot the best bit. It's a wee loon!'

They discussed the news excitedly. 'That'll mean big changes up at the Hall.'

'The laird 'll be pleased,' said Fanny. 'A wee boy to inherit the estate.'

'And a week's free rent from the laird – or maybe two weeks seeing it's a loon,' said Anna.

Poor Miss Megaidh, said Marsali to herself.

Milton

Victor held his head in his hands. The first class compartment of the Inverally branch line was empty as the last train of the day steamed through the darkened woodlands and fields of Point. Relief and acute anxiety battled themselves out in the befuddled depths of his brain. Relief that Anton had gone, anxiety over the means. He knew the mess he had got himself into and was not quite sure of how to solve it. There had been a ffflight over mmmoney as usual. His brain was too befuddled to remember what exactly had hhhappened. It had been ssseff dddefence, hadn't it? Anton had lllashed out ffffirst, hadn't he? To protect himself he had hhhit him over the hhhead with a ssstool and knocked him out, perhaps kkk – him, but he could not even think the word. With Joe's help he had got away, but Joe knew what he had dddone. He would have to pppay. He wanted to pppay. Anything rrrather than the lllaw. The rrrents should cover it; just. Mmmeg's income would see that the wwwages were pppaid. The bbbills would have to wwwait.

162

All would be well if Isabella had a dddaughter, disappeared with her intrusive husband back to India, and the old man dddied. He would be lllaird. He knew exactly what he would do. Employ a new factor and forbid Meg to go anywhere near the office. Pppack her off to India with her sssister, Anton had once advised. That was the solution. Pack her off to India for good. There was a reasonable chance she might never come back…Anton. Oh bbbut he would mmmiss Anton…

The train shuffled into the station. 'Inver-ally! Inver-ally!' the station master called out on two notes. He lurched to his feet, fumbled with the window but the porter had got there first. He pulled open the door, gave no sign of recognition and asked as he always asked. 'Any bags, sir?'

Victor hardly heard him. With care he manipulated the high step down to the platform and lurched towards the ticket office. No one bothered him for his ticket which was just as well. He had no idea which pocket hid it or whether he had one at all. He wove the dozen or so steps to the hotel, ordered a cab at the desk and was told it would be in the pends in ten minutes. Jjjust ttttime for a fffinal bbbwandy.

The saloon bar was quietly busy. He knew them all for they were regulars. Old Dr Mackinley who no longer practised and Major Crook retired from the Royal Artillery had the chess board between them. They greeted him cursorily. Several men who stood at the bar, acknowledged him briefly but no one offered to buy him a drink. Among them in a crowd of younger men, he recognised Jared Macreedie.

'What'll you ddwink?' he asked him at which point all eyes were on him. Jared was polite but firm. 'I'm on my way home, Mr Myers, if it's all the same to you.'

Victor knew exactly what he was thinking. If he can afford to drink at the Station Saloon, he can afford to pay his bills. 'Mmmy usual,' he told Bob the barman curtly.

'Here to wet the baby's head, Sir?' said the barman measuring out the brandy. 'I'm hearing congratulations are in order.'

He almost said 'Wwwhat bbbb...?' but changed it to 'Wwwhats that you're ss saying?'

'Where have you been?' said a voice from the crowd. 'Did you not know the baby's been born up at the big house?'

There was a stir of conversation.

Hhhow wwwould he know? He had been away since yyyesterday mmmorning.

'It'll be drinks all round, then?' another voice piped up from behind Jared. 'Now that you've heard the good news.'

Of cccourse. That wwwas expected.. 'Dddrinks all rrround, gggentlemen,' he called out and nodded to Bob. He hadn't a ha'penny in his pocket and Bob knew it. The tab would go to the office with all the others and end up another unpaid bill.

'It's to be hoped the wee lad has better luck than the last loon to be born in the Hall,' someone said. 'Here's to him!'

'Aye, good luck to him!' they all murmured, raising their glasses.

That was how Victor learned that he was no longer the colonel's heir. He was not surprised. He and Lllady Llluck were not that well acquainted. His first thought was that the bbbill was no longer his responsibility. He offered them all another round.

The Hall

Meg tapped gently on her sister's door. The monthly nurse opened it, fingers to her lips. When she saw Meg she came out closing the door softly behind her. 'They're both asleep, Ma'am. I'm reluctant to disturb my patient.'

'But she's all right? 'Meg asked anxiously. 'They're both well?'

'Baby's fine in spite of the quick birth. A healthy six pounds. A bonny baby though I say it myself.'

'And my sister?'

Nurse Dixon was less confident. 'It was a quick birth. Too quick in my opinion. Mrs Moncrieff has lost a lot of blood.'

'But she will recover?'

There was a thin cry from inside the bedroom. Nurse Dixon hurriedly returned to her patient, lifted the baby from his cot and took him to the window recess to soothe him. Meg followed her into the room. The baby's girning had wakened Isabella. She looked dreadful, grey against the white sheets, limp, listless. Her eyes were closed and her hand lay on the counterpane. Meg took it, noted with alarm its clammy coolness and enfolded it within her own two warm hands.

'Well done, Bella, ' she whispered. 'Father will be so pleased.'

Isabella suddenly opened her eyes. 'Meg?' she whispered with difficulty.

'I'm here,' she replied. Her voice sounded loud and brash. 'I'm here,' This time she too whispered.

'Don't let James take my baby to India,' she said distinctly and so loudly that Nurse Dixon turned her head. Then she coughed a little, and the pillow was suddenly flooded with blood.

'Nurse!' Meg cried.

Nurse Dixon thrust the baby into Meg's arms. 'Find the major,' she told the nursemaid, who was airing baby garments on the fireguard at the far end of the room. 'And get the doctor back.'

Doctor Anderson was with Mrs Shanks in the housekeeper's sitting room when the girl, Bessie, found him. Though he had not long left his patient, he was not surprised to be summoned back so soon. He had been consulting his notebook regarding a wet nurse among his various patients. His first thought was Effy Stuart, whose third child had been born a few weeks past. She lived near enough in the stable block. He would see her himself once he had spoken to Major Moncrieff.

Meanwhile James came bounding up the staircase, took one look at his wife and in an anguished voice demanded to know. 'Will she live?'

No one answered him. 'It was like this last time,' he told Doctor Anderson who did not reply as he counted his patient's pulse. 'I thought I'd lost her then.' He did not so much as look at the babe in Meg's arms.

'May I take the baby to show papa?' she whispered.

No one heard her for all their attention was on Isabella. Quietly Meg with the squirming infant in her arms left the room. Aware that she was holding something beyond precious, she carefully descended the stairs to her father's suite. Outside his door she paused to look properly at her little nephew. Pulling the shawl away from his face she was astounded. The little features, still so unformed, reminded her strongly of her brother. Here was Andrew born again in her arms. How marvellous was that! She was never to see the resemblance so clearly again for from that moment the small breathing bundle in her arms became himself, his own small person, not a facsimile of her brother. But the seed of love was sewn in her heart instantly, tender and unbreakable.

She found Jenkins at his master's bedside.

''e's gone, Miss Meg. You' re too late. 'e's up and gone not two minutes past.'

'Oh Jimmy, I'm sorry,' Meg whispered. 'I should have come sooner.' She waited for the tears to rise but her eyes were dry. There was no room for sorrow in her heart.

''e knew. I told 'im as soon as I 'eard myself. I told 'im 'e 'ad a grandson and 'e just closed 'is eyes and sighed.' There were tears in the servant's eyes. For the first time Meg noticed that he too was getting old.. She did not know how to comfort him.

'Come and see his grandchild, Jimmy. Isn't he beautiful?'

Jenkins stared down at the infant. 'Blimey,' he said winking away the tears. ''e's the h'image of is granddad, so 'e is.'

Inwardly she smiled. Was that it, then? Everyone projected on to a new baby the image they needed to see? Perhaps.

'Hold him, will you?' she asked, giving him no choice but to take the precious burden. Then she turned to her father's bed and after a moment bent down to kiss his forehead. The same kiss that she had given him every day of his life. He was not yet cold. The tears came then, but she was aware that they were partly tears of relief. Not that her father was dead, but that the burden of the estate would no longer be Victor's responsibility, Victor's and hers.

The Stables

The Stuarts' accommodation was immediately above the arch that linked the two halves of the stable block. The stalls that housed the horses were one side of the arch with the old landau, pony cart and closed carriage on the other side. Sam Stuart as groom and Effie his wife with their three children lived in cramped accommodation above the stables. Effie was forever nagging at Sam to ask for a bigger house, but Sam was reluctant to ask Mr Myers. 'I won't be obliged to him for anything,' he said stubbornly but refused to say why.

'Then I'll ask Miss Megaidh,' she persisted.

'You'll do no such thing,' he commanded.

'Then you do it,' she retorted. 'I can't raise three weans in two wee rooms, no water and a stair as steep as Jacob's ladder.'

'Then I'll find another job,' he said. 'I'll not be obligated to that man for all the fish in the Firth.'

'Where would you find another job?' she demanded.

'The hotel is always in need of cabbies.'

She said nothing. The cabbie's job provided no house, the hours were unpredictable and the pay dependent on tips. She sighed and moved Danny, the new bairn, to her other breast. She could not understand Sam's reluctance to be beholden to Mr Myers. He could not help his stutter and she had never known him anything but civil. Too civil perhaps. He was a queer wee mannie right enough.

That was before Eli and Daniel had been born and they were still here. Ruth, her oldest at five past was sleeping with her nan in Fisherton, but she wanted all her weans under her own roof.

Sam was still with the horses when there was a rap on the door at the foot of the steep ladder. She peered out of the window and saw to her surprise the doctor's gig in the yard. What could be wrong? Her thoughts flew to her children, especially Ruth.

Easing Daniel from her breast she placed him back in his cradle. 'Sorry, my pet,' she murmured and buttoned up her blouse. Meanwhile Sam had met the doctor and was bringing him up the stairs.

'You'll take some tea, Doctor?' she asked bobbing a little curtsy as he crossed the threshold.

'No, no thank ye. I'm awash with tea,' he said. 'I'm here to ask a favour, Mistress Stuart. Both of you,' he said including Sam who was hovering at the door. 'My! but that's a climb and a half.'

'Will you not sit down, then? 'Effie said indicating Sam's chair by the black range.

With the three adults, the cradle and the toddler Eli clinging to his mother's skirt, there was scarcely room for them all to stand. The doctor sat down and looked about him. 'Is this all the space you've got?' he asked directly.

'There's a wee room in bye,' said Sam a little defensively.

'Hm,' said the doctor. 'Well, that's not why I'm here. I've a favour to ask.'

Effie listened carefully as the doctor told them that Miss Isabella had just had her baby. 'She's a very sick woman. She'll not manage to feed the bairn. I'm looking for a wet nurse.'

Effie looked at her husband who shrugged. 'Mebbe I could do it,' she said

'Thank ee Mistress Stuart. That's a start,' he said. 'I'll just take a look at you and the bairn. Make sure you're both fighting fit, eh?' Sam nodded and left the room takng wee Eli with him.

'Well?' he asked after he had examined mother and baby and found them healthy and called Sam back. 'Will you do it?' He looked at both of them.

Sam looked at her. 'There would be a price,' she said daringly.

'Naturally,' he said.

She looked at Sam who nodded wordlessly. 'A new house?' she did not mean to be tentative but that's how it sounded.

'Aye,' said the doctor nodding approvingly. 'I'll see to it.'

Kirkton

In the end there were two funerals. Isabella died two nights after her father. The blinds were drawn, mourning clothes brushed and aired, neighbours left cards, the rector called and arrangements made. Meg had worked ceaselessly to see that everything was in order, for the household looked to her for all major decisions as indeed it had been doing for the past five years. Now there was still one more important decision to be made and quickly for James was due to return to his regiment in India as soon as possible. His compassionate leave could not extend indefinitely.

Meg had taken the closed carriage to the schoolhouse with the purpose of arranging the baby's baptism. She had forgotten that the rector would be teaching that afternoon. Mrs Macfarlane seated her visitor in the parlour and ordered elderflower cordial while they waited for Mr Vass. Though she was happy to discuss her immediate concerns with Helen Macfarlane, Meg had another decision to make which she wanted to share with the rector alone.

'So,' she was saying to Helen, 'Nanny turned up out of the blue to find Effy and the new girl Bessie ensconced in the nursery and she was not best pleased.'

Meg had been summoned to sort out the matter. 'I should have realised. The nursery has always been Nanny's domain.'

'Is she not a little old?' Helen asked.

'She most certainly is. She must be close to eighty. She was papa's nurse and then ours, but I never thought for a moment she would even want to come back to the nursery.'

'So how have you resolved it?'

'Nanny has moved herself into the night nursery and Effy is about to move into her cottage on the estate. The whole business on top of everything else has been a bit of a nightmare, actually.'

'I can imagine,' Helen said sympathetically.

I don't think you can, Meg thought. Nanny could hardly manage the stairs let alone a baby. New accommodation had had to be found for Effie and her family if she were to foster the infant for the next six months or so, and, apart from the possibility of Nanny's cottage, there were no spare houses on the estate. To remove Nanny to the night nursery

170

permanently was not the best solution. Meg had forgotten how demanding she could be. But Effy had been equally demanding, or rather, Doctor Anderson had been firm on her behalf. 'I cannot allow Mrs Stuart to take over such a responsible task unless she and her family are properly housed. Those two stable rooms may suit a stable boy but they are entirely unsuitable for a married family.'

Then there was Jenkins. He was of an age to retire and she had no need of his services but where was he to go? Meg believed the family owed him their care. Mrs Shanks had suggested that a room below stairs could be made habitable. She hoped Jenkins would be happy about that. He had always considered himself to be a cut above the basement staff.

Before Mrs Macfarlane could offer advice, Hugh Vass entered the parlour with both arms outstretched. 'Miss Megaidh! Is all well with you? How can I help?''

She accepted both his hands and the gesture of comfort brought fresh tears to her eyes. Seeing her sorrow he drew her into the shelter of his arms. She wept a little and after a moment or two her tense body relaxed. She sniffed and he drew apart to reach for his handkerchief. Murmuring words of comfort, he would have wiped her eyes for her like a child but she took it from him and blew her nose and without thinking pushed it into the pocket of her black coat.

'I'm here on behalf of James who had to go down to the War Office to make arrangements for his passage back to India,' she said shakily for tears still choked her voice. 'Could we discuss an early date for the baby's baptism?'

'I'll leave you to it,' said Helen rising to her feet. She touched Meg on the arm, then bent to kiss her cheek and left the room. At such kindness, tears again cascaded down Meg's cheeks.

Hugh meanwhile had gone to his adjoining study to fetch his diary and a prayer book and by the time he returned she had recovered a little. They settled on a date the following week, and he led her through the prayer book service of Baptism 'What is the little one to be called?' he asked.

'Andrew James Myers,' she told him, adding sadly, 'it was Isabella's choice.'

They had discussed the susbject endlessly in her last few months of pregnancy and argued good-temperedly about their mother's name. 'If it's a girl, I won't have Grizel! Don't even suggest it.'

'Let's hope it's a boy then,' Meg had joked.

How she would miss Isabella. Over the past ten years she had changed from the flirtatious rather silly teenager that Meg remembered to a tentative and fearful woman. They had become friends, *confidente*s even. 'I don't know what James will do if I lose this baby,' she told her one golden afternoon as they sat together on wicker chairs in the shade of a rhododendron bush in the flower garden.

'But you're not going to lose this baby,' Meg told her sensibly. 'Inverally is not India.'

'Oh Meg,' she had said putting aside the little garment she had been embroidering. 'How I hate India! It killed two of my babies. I'm so afraid it will kill this one too.'

'Then don't ago back,' Meg told her firmly. 'Stay here. This is your home, after all.'

She shook her head. 'Of course I must go back. James adores it there. I don't think he'll ever leave. He's expecting his half colonelcy as soon as he goes back. He wants to become a general. He needs a wife. I have no choice in the matter.'

'Surely you could stay on for a few months, till you recover your strength and the baby gets a bit stronger?'

'I would like that,' she said with a sigh. 'I'll see what James thinks.'

Hang James, Meg thought. I would not stand it with Victor. Victor... she thought. With Victor the occasion would never arise. Did she really mind?

These thoughts flashed through her head as, seated beside the rector, she told him her concerns.

'James does not think it suitable to take such a small child to India. He has asked me to raise little Andrew.'

Mr Vass nodded. 'I see. And what do you and Mr Myers think about that?'

'I haven't asked him,' she said shortly. How could she? He was never there and they had long ago ceased to communicate on matters of importance.

'Don't you think perhaps you should?' Hugh asked carefully.

She looked down at her hands folded in her lap. Automatically she covered her wedding ring No, she thought, I have long ago given up trying to talk to Victor. They had nothing to say to each other. His stutter grew worse in her presence and he would leave the room, or the office, or the garden, wherever she happened to be if she mentioned anything serious such as the unpaid bills, the overgrown ditches and his frequent nightly absences.

'I think perhaps you should try,' Hugh said firmly. 'You might well find that you are with child yourself. What then?'

'No,' she interrupted him sharply. 'That will never happen.'

If he was surprised he gave no sign of it. 'I strongly advise you to speak to him. You and he both will be in *loco parentis* to the child. His support is important.'

'And if he were to say no?' she asked in a low voice for this was the real reason why she had not spoken to her husband.

'Where else could the boy go?' Hugh asked.

'James has a sister married and with children of her own. He, no doubt, would prefer the baby to be with her rather than me and Victor - but Isabella asked for me. It was her dying request that he be raised in Inverally. What Victor thinks will make no difference to my decision.'

'Speak to your husband, Miss Meg. Soon. This is not a task to be undertaken lightly.'

After a moment Meg nodded. She knew him to be right but the idea of asking Victor for anything appalled her. After a while the conversation returned to the immediacy of the Christening.

The Estate Office

It happened that James spoke to Victor before Meg had a chance.

The law agent had explained that the child was heir and eligible to take over his inheritance on his twenty-first birthday. A trust consisting of his father, his Aunt Harriet, Macmurtrie the law agent, and Meg herself was to be set up out of the estate profits which would cover the boy's needs until such time as he came into his inheritance. Meg was left no money (she had her own capital left to her in her mother's will which so far had provided her with a more than adequate income) but she was to consider Inverally Hall as her home until the child reached his majority when the Dower house (at presented tenanted) was to become her domicile. James was either to manage the estate himself in his son's name or employ a suitable factor. No mention at all was made of Victor.

He had expected no less. Two days after Isabella's funeral, James had sought him out in the factor's office, a place he seldom stayed for longer than a hour at a time. He had been trying to make some sense out of Meg's tidy accounting. He hoped vainly that he might keep his job but knew it to be unlikely. He enjoyed the freedom and the salary it provided. What would he do now that he had no occupation and with Anton gone, no friend? He was no longer welcome at the Bonnie Prince, at least not until he had settled his debts. Would Meg stay with him? Part of him hoped not. He had grown to dread Meg, the inquisitor, the tyrant, the all-seeing scourge of his life, the Cedric of his latter years, the substitute dean. How pleasant his life had been in retrospect before Meg. Or could have been without his over-watchful, over-critical family.

At the same time he knew this to be an unfair judgement both on his parents and his wife. Their perceived contempt for him only matched his own. He knew he amounted to nothing. Even Anton, who in his own way had cared for him, at least cared for what he could provide, had gone from his life. A cloud of anxiety, self-loathing and self-pity threatened to engulf him entirely. Vainly he tried to push it aside; listen to what his brother-in-law was trying to say.

'...so you see there will have to be a few changes.' James was trying to sound pleasant but Victor realised it was an effort. 'It's not my wish to leave my son behind in Scotland, nor is it my wish to leave him at Inverally but it was Isabella's dying request and I understand why. The estate will one day be his. It's sensible that he should spend his childhood years here and learn to know and love it. I have to respect that. Meg is more than willing to take care of him at least until he is seven years old and goes away to his preparatory school prior to Wellington. I hope you understand, Victor. I sincerely hope you do.'

He tttreats me lllike the idiot I am, Victor thought, but Meg might have mentioned it. 'I under...sssee,' he muttered trying in vain to keep the bitterness out of his voice. 'I am to

175

lllose mmmy jjjob and mmmy hhhome. Of cccourse I undershtand.'

'Not your home,' James said quickly. 'Certainly not your home. This will be your and Meg's home at least until Andrew reaches his majority. Then, as Colonel Murray-Myers' will decreed, the Dower house will be yours and Meg's.'

'Hhhow very gggenerouth of you, bbbbwother-in-law.' The bitterness was like vinegar in his mouth. 'Wwwhat about mmmy jjjob?'

'Ah,' said James, turning his head away to look out over the grounds. 'I know you've done your best but I'm afraid, there will have to be a few changes. Macmurtrie is already advertising for a new factor.'

A sense of frustrated fury overwhelmed Victor. 'Wwwhat's ttto ssstop mmme from appplying?' he declared bitterly.

'Then you would be a fool.'

'Mmmore of a fff than I already am?' he declared with a humourless laugh.

James was about to retort but thought better of it. 'I'm sorry, Victor. I believe you've done your best but you must be aware that the estate is in a mess. You only have to drive up the east avenue to see the uncut hedges, the overgrown ditches, the broken fences. Then the accounts.'

'The accc are my wwwife'th dddepppartment. She pppays them,' he retorted but the fire had gone out of his protest. He knew it was unfair to blame Meg.

'Meg has done her best. You've both done your best. Now's the time to take stock. Besides you will both have a new responsibility.'

'Sssuch as?'

'My son,' he said simply. 'It was Isabella's last wish that he remain here in Inverally in Meg's care. Yours and Meg's,' he added hastily.

That was how he learned that he was to become Andrew's guardian and the thought appalled him. What little experience he had of children had not been happy. His two nieces had giggled uncontrollably whenever he opened his mouth. The deanery gardener's brats would hide in the shrubbery and pelt him with stones if he was alone. At school the boys made ape gestures and yelped at him during the break hours. Though he said nothing to James, he was deeply angry. In her usual controlling way, Meg had taken it on herself to rear the child without a word to him. It occurred to him then, because he was not the complete idiot others thought him, that Meg might have wanted a child of her own and his anger immediately dissolved into the familiarity of guilt.

He left the office ahead of James. He needed to find Jenkins.

The Moor

Three days after the funerals, the callers arrived. Sometimes they visited Meg and James in the drawing room. Sometimes they merely handed in their cards.

Lord Morton of Point was a card dropper. He was, as he later explained to the ravishing Miss Cynthia Spencer in too much of a hurry to call on her to waste a moment with his neighbours, the Murray-Myers.

'Oh but surely you must pity them for their losses,' declared Miss Cynthia, dabbing a tiny lace handkerchief to her eyes. 'I declare it breaks my heart when I think of that motherless babe.' She was laying it on like butter, hoping that Lord Donald would be touched by her tears. She wanted

Lord Donald to be more than touched. He was so nearly hers.

Being courted by Lord Morton was hard work. Never knowing when he might call, meant that she had to be ready and available at any time. It might be early in the morning before her curl papers were brushed out, or too early in the evening which might interrupt high tea in the Gallie household. His lordship did not dine until eight. So much hard work on her behalf deserved to be rewarded.

Cynthia was not in the least in love with Lord Morton, but she dearly loved what he represented, wealth, land and a title. The title alone was romance enough for her. Of her many admirers he was the only one in a position to offer the whole box of delights. So what if he were twenty years her senior? All the better, perhaps. She could imagine herself a beautiful eligible widow. So what if he had an odious mother that ruled his household? She wouldn't last forever. So what if he were six inches taller and at least a foot broader than she, that his whiskers were growing in grey and that his breath was tainted by unhealthy teeth? You couldn't have everything. The days when she had swooned over a man for his looks alone had long gone... well, almost gone.

They sat together in the parlour and talked about the weather while her mother stitched at her canvas-work. It was not that she wanted her mother present at these meetings but conformity was important at this stage in the relationship. Any impropriety on her behalf would have him running a mile with his mother hissing in his ear, 'I told you so. You can't trust the lower orders.'

Today, however, the sun was shining. When Lord Morton proposed a ride she accepted with becoming delight. It was a perfect day for a ride, she declared. If Lord Donald would excuse her, she would order her horse to be saddled and change into her habit. Left alone with her mother, his lordship chortling a little at his subterfuge, asked permission to propose to her daughter. 'I understand that you are Miss Cynthia's main guardian. Should I also speak to Mr Gallie?'

Hilda tried not to sound too eager, as she reassured him that only her permission was necessary. She was sure that Mr Gallie would be delighted to welcome him into the family. By the time Cynthia appeared, ravishing in a new dark blue velvet riding habit, the deed was done.

Cynthia was a good horsewoman, knew she looked splendid on her chestnut mare, a Christmas gift from her step-father, as they rode up the Brae and out on to the moors. Lord Donald was anxious to see for himself the state of the crumbling dykes that marched between the two estates of Point and Inverally at the approach of the shooting season. After much grumbling and many disparaging comments about the abundance of bracken that had encroached on to his land from the Inverally covers, he dismounted and so did she. It was perhaps the most romantic spot possible for a proposal. The moors were beautiful in early August, the heather in blossom, bees hummed, the occasional grouse clucked and cackled its way up into the blue sky

He proposed haltingly and she accepted prettily. He took her hand to kiss it; but because Cynthia was Cynthia and not just the pretty doll he had believed her to be, she flung her arms around his neck and kissed him on the mouth. It was mainly moustache and violently unpleasant but she did not flinch. Her impulsive action was so unexpected that he was shocked into stillness. But the feeling was so unexpected, so welcome and so arousing that he seized her roughly and planted first his mouth and then his whole body against hers. As she stepped backwards to pull herself away, she tripped over a boulder and fell.

For a moment she thought that he would fall on top of her. The look in his eyes scared her. She remembered the gossip that she had overheard in the Emporium. Two women muttering; his name whispered.

Instead he pulled himself together, reached down to help her rise. 'Sorry, old girl,' he said apologetically 'Not hurt, I hope?' He was still panting a little.

Now was the time to break it off, she thought, as they rode back in silence. Donald's person revolted her but his position in society still appealed. Which mattered most? It was no contest. She could cope with his lordship's ardour, or so she believed.

Furtively she regarded him as they rode down the Brae. This ...ardour was an aspect of Lord Morton that she had not considered. Truthfully she had given little thought to the marriage bed beyond the kissing and handholding stage. Love-making was something women had to put up with. So she had heard, so she believed without knowing exactly what love-making fully entailed. As she watched her fiancé's heavy body move with his heavy horse, something deep in her lower body stirred. By the time they reached home she gave him her hand to dismount and stumbled on purpose so that her body was thrown against his. As he held her she felt him tremble and knew that her power was more than a match for his own.

'Steady on, old girl,' he mumbled.

'When am I going to meet your mama?' she asked provocatively. She was still leaning into him.

'Name the day,' he said in her ear drawing her closer.

'Tomorrow?' she whispered allowing herself to be drawn into his embrace. If she kept her head turned she did not have to breathe his breath.

'Tomorrow it is,' he said.

Aware that her mother was watching from the front room curtains, she twisted out of his arms.

Oh yes, she thought as she watched him ride away. I can manage him.

Milton

Marsali did not often go up the Brae these days to sell fish. With Jonas married to one of Ephraim Cooper's lassies she had no need. Evie was a good girl in spite of having spent some of her childhood in the Poor House with her feckless father, or perhaps because of it. Evie had laboured from the age of ten in the curing yard and in Milton kitchens wherever she could find work. Her ambition had been to rise to parlour maid in a Kirkton household before marriage to Jonas had intervened. They now had a cottage two rows from where he was born and Jonas a wife who was not afraid of hard work. Jonas had taken his father's place on the *Bright Star* but was ambitious to rise to more than crew and Evie was ambitious for him. She was said already to have more customers than the savvier older fisher wives. Marsali sometimes helped out for Evie was near the end of her first pregnancy.

Marsali was finding the Brae harder than ever this year. Her hip jolted with every step she took in spite of the stout stick she carried to help her keep her balance with a creel on her back. The loads seemed to get heavier. She stopped at all the usual doors, old Kirkton customers where she was welcomed as a long-lost friend, given all the gossip and even offered a cup of tea and a sit-down by Minnie Macmurdo (Morag's wee sister), the quine at the schoolhouse. Never was a chair more welcome.

The main topic of conversation in every kitchen was of the double tragedy at the Hall. Minnie's version, with Mr Vass's connections to the family, was perhaps the more accurate.

181

'That poor wee motherless babe!' said Marsali as the pain in her hip gradually eased. 'I was hearing he is to go back to India and my Effie is to be taken from her ain family to nurse the wean.' Such had been the distressing gist of the gossip she had heard on the road. She had not seen Effie for a while.

'That is not the way of it at all,' said Minnie buttering a newly baked scone and placing it on a plate on the kitchen table in front of Marsali. 'The wean is to be left with Miss Megaidh. He is to be raised at the Hall by herself and Mr Myers until he is of an age to take over the estate. Your Effie is his wet nurse right enough and she is to get one of the estate cottages in exchange.'

'Which one would that be?' Marsali asked, delighted. Good news at last.

'Nanny Gilchrist is to move into the big house.'

My poor Effie, Marsali thought. Miss Gilchrist had been in charge of the nursery when she was suckling Master Andrew. All she said however was, 'is that so?'

'The bairn is to be christened next Tuesday before Major Moncrieff returns to India. Just a small party. He is to be called Andrew - after yon other poor lost loon.'

'He is to be the new lairdie, then?' said Marsali

'So it would seem.' Minnie laughed dryly. 'Not if the *Fiosaiche* is to bebelieved.'

Marsali knew exactly what she meant. The old prophecy (of which there were several versions) uttered by *Fiosaiche* of Glen Mhor before the time of the evictions, had been specific. *'The bonnie lands of Inverally will one day fall into the hands of the son of a fisherman.'*

'It's had a hundred years to happen. Why the now?'

'Why no' the now?' said Minnie.. 'We've had the *big sheep*. We've got the *running water.* We've had *the lost bairns.* Why no' the now?'

Marsali, like most of the Gaelic speakers of Fisherton knew all the prophecies by heart. '*Tha an latha...the day is coming when the big sheep will chase the people from Glen Mhor* had come to pass many years ago. *The day is coming when fire and water will flow freely through the streets of Inverally* had been quoted at every hearth when the piped water had been put into the cottages. Some now awaited the fire. Everyone knew, but seldom dared to repeat the prediction that was seen by some as a curse. '*Tha an latha...the day is coming when the very hearthstones will weep for the children that are no more.*'

'Surely no one believes all yon rubbish,' she said harshly. In her heart, and, like most of the village, she linked the loss of Andrew, Aaron and Donnaidh to that prophecy. Yet she still could not believe that Donnaidh was gone forever. Would not believe it, though it grew harder with every year that passed to cling on to her hope.

'No,' said Minnie, remembering the fisher-wife's pain. 'Certainly not. But it makes you think.'

'I must be off' said Marsali rising with difficulty, 'or the fish will beat me to it.'

Minnie laughed, counted out the coins for the herring and helped her shoulder her creel.

By the time she had completed her Kirkton round, she was so exhausted and in such pain that she knew she would need help to get home. Sometimes downhill was harder on her knees than the climb up the Brae. She had not intended to visit Milton at all that afternoon. Jared did not like to see his mother selling fish for Evie. 'If you are needing the money you just have to ask.'

'I am not needing the money,' she would lie.

'Then give up the fish. Fanny does not like to see you with a creel in the street.'

183

Marsali knew it was not Fanny who objected to her children's grandmother selling fish from door to door. Fanny would do it herself if need be. It was Jared who was ashamed. That angered Marsali. Jared sold from a shop. She sold in the street. Where was the difference? Thinking about it incensed her so much that she strode down the High Street with the remainder of her fish and up the steps right into Emporium.

Jared was behind the counter serving a couple of farmers. There was a small queue waiting. The lady assistant was busy at a different counter measuring a length of material. The apprentice lad was weighing seed.

There was a chair and thankfully she sat down and eased off her creel. There were strange looks from a couple of the queuing housewives. One of them wrinkled her nose. Jared ignored his mother. She felt worthless, and wished she hadn't come. It had been a mistake.

She was about to shoulder her creel and leave when Jared came over. 'Is there something you want, mother?'

Before she could reply one of the women waiting in the queue came over. 'Do you have any fresh haddock left?'

'Nice and fresh, ' she said. 'How many is it you are wanting?'

The deal was done.   Another of Jared's customers, an incomer to the town, came forward and took six of the few remaining herring. 'You should open a fish shop, Jared,' she said. 'Save this poor woman the burden of carrying her fish up the Brae and make yourself a wee fortune.'

Jared, embarrassed by the allusion to 'poor woman', managed to nod to the customer and quietly told his mother to go through to the house. 'What are you doing here anyhow?' he murmured as he opened the house door for her and led her through to the empty kitchen.

She would not tell him she needed a rest, a help down the Brae. 'I brought you some fish for your tea,' she told him quietly.

He was ashamed all over again as she knew he would be. He mumbled his thanks and told her to leave them on the table. 'I'll be through in a wee while,' he told her firmly closing the kitchen door. 'Don't you move.'

She had just settled into the basket chair in front of the range when the door flew open and Fanny came in. She too looked tired. 'Mistress Macreedie!' she declared and there was neither shame nor anger in her voice as she greeted her mother-in-law with genuine pleasure. She was about to reply when Fanny noticed the creel. 'Oh, you've brought us some fish! Wonderful! Haddock or herring?' She lifted the lid of the creel. 'It's the girl's afternoon off. Good! I'll cook them myself. Have you seen the bairnies?'

Marsali shook her head. Fanny's impulsive friendliness always took her breath away.

'Come on then? They'll be in the parlour.'

Mrs Mack was sitting in an easy chair, knitting. The nursemaid was folding napkins and wee Kenny was on the floor with a scatter of alphabet bricks. The baby, Connie, was fidgeting in her high chair chewing a rusk.

They all stared at Marsali as she came in then wee Kenny's little face, so like his father's, broke into a smile 'Nanna! Nanna!' he cried and ran towards her. 'See my castle.'

Mrs Mack put aside her knitting and rose reluctantly to her feet. 'Good day Mistress Macreedie,' she said coldly. There was always an uneasy relationship between Marsali and Mrs Mack and there always would be.

Marsali bobbed as she replied, 'Good day, ma'am.' She embraced the excited little boy.

'Will you take some tea, Mother?' Fanny asked. It was the first time she had called her by anything but her full title.

Marsali knew she had done it to counter Mrs Mack's coldness.

'No, but thank you for the asking.' If I drink any more tea I'll bust, she thought.

'Nanna has brought us fish for tea,' Fanny told her children. 'Isn't that nice of her?'

'Herring is it?' Mrs Mack asked icily polite. 'No need to waste your herring here. None of them will eat it.'

As if Marsali did not know that! Jared never could abide the bones in a herring but all she said was, 'finest haddock, Mistress. Fresh this morning.' She then turned and smiled down at her grand-daughter who grinned at her and spat out a mouthful of rusk. The nursemaid, who was from Fisherton and well known to Marsali, murmured *'Failte gu,'* out of earshot of Mrs Mack.

'I would like some tea please, Mrs Mack, and bring a dish of that nice new shortbread. ' Fanny told her housekeeper.

'See to it, girl,' Mrs Mack told the nursemaid. Then she rolled up her knitting and put it into a bag and prepared to leave the room..

Wee Kenny tugged Marsali forward. 'Will you play with me, Nanna?'

'Behave yourself, Kenny,' Mrs Mack scolded from the door.

Wee Kenny's face dulled with disappointment. Marsali would have liked to get down on the hearth rug and build towers with the bricks but her knees would barely allow her to sit down in the low chair that Fanny proffered.

'Come and sit with me, ma wee manny,' Marsali held out her arms to the little boy who jumped up on her knee. The pain was excruciating as he wriggled in her lap to make himself more comfortable.

Fanny was quick to notice. 'Are you in pain, Mother?' she asked kindly. 'Jared was saying that your knees were bad.'

'It's the east wind,' she told her daughter-in-law, 'gets into the bones.'

'If you can't sit still, Kenny, get down off Nanna,' his mother told him sharply.

'Is your leg sore, Nanna?' the wee boy asked. 'Me'll kiss it better.' He wriggled down to plant a noisy kiss on her skirt.

Marsali's eyes filled with tears. Fanny thought it was the pain and told her son to get down immediately, but the pain had little to do with it. Her grandson may have looked like Jared but it was Donnaidh she was remembering.

Chapter Five

1905

The Hall

The children were all ages, but it was Andrew's fifth birthday party. A violinist had been hired and the drawing room at the Hall had been partially cleared of furniture to make space for the same party games Meg herself had played as a child: *Oranges and Lemons, The Grand Old Duke of York, Here we Go Round The Mulberry Bush.* Mrs Macfarlane organised the children while Nanny Gilchrist looked on with eagle eyes to pounce on any evidence of bad behaviour, and the other grown-ups stood by and watched their own bairns with benevolent eyes. Meg was by herself at the door but it was not the children she watched, it was Victor.

Though it had been her idea to invite all the Inverally children under the age of ten to Andrew's party, it was Victor who had shown the most enthusiasm. Victor... Since the appointment of Ivor Wilkie as the new factor, Victor had changed, but that, she thought, was only coincidental. It was Andrew who had made the difference. Andrew as an infant had taken to Victor. He had smiled and cooed and held up his little arms to Victor who had been at first suspicious, then charmed and finally conquered. He had taken to the role of parenting whole-heartedly; petted the baby, spoiled the toddler and played games with the little boy. Nanny Gilchrist had not approved. A man in the nursery was, in her opinion, redundant. Andrew for no reason that Meg could understand had loved Victor from the start. He was the one he ran to when brought downstairs by the nursemaid, Bessie, to spend an hour in the drawing-room between five and six in the evening. His was the knee he clambered on, whose attention he claimed. Meg he tolerated.

But it was not altogether Andrew's presence that accounted for the change in Victor either. For the past few years he had been unwell. A minor chill turned into a chest infection which seemed to linger. Always thin and slight, he had lost weight and his clothes seemed to hang from him. Meg knew little enough about the cause of his ill-health for Victor always shrugged her questions aside, and though she has asked Doctor Anderson, he too had been cagey. 'He needs to stay off the port and rest.'

'Victor doesn't drink port,' she told him. 'What are you trying to tell me?'

'Brandy then,' said the doctor a little testily. 'He has not got a strong constitution and Highland winters can take their toll. With the whole summer before us, I hope to see a steady improvement.'

That had been several years earlier but there had been little betterment. This past winter had seen him weaker, his skin yellower, his eyes sunk deeper in his skull and he seemed perpetually anxious. Now he never took the train to Inverness and as for the Royal Station Hotel, she could not remember the last time he had been late for dinner. Of course he could be visiting the hotel or the tavern at other times of the day. She did not have time or the inclination to watch him, but she did not think so.

Jenkins had gradually taken him over. Or he, Jenkins. She was never sure. But, after the colonel's death, Jimmy had found a place for himself valeting Mr Myers. Except when Victor visited the drawing-room, the dining-room and the nursery, they were usually together. She took no part in caring for her husband just as she had taken no part in caring for her father which suited her well enough for Meg was busier now than she had ever been, even when she had covered for her husband in the estate office. Though they lived under the same roof they seldom saw each other apart from meals and not always then for Victor breakfasted in his room and on his worse days dined there too. Jenkins was also their means of communication. He would appear in the dining room and explain, 'Mr Victor h'asks that you will h'excuse 'im dinner. We are feeling poorly.'

Meanwhile Meg had been fully occupied with her own concerns. On Mr Vass's advice and with his support, she had finally opened her own premises. This one room, or shed rather, had once housed the annual coastal salmon fishers until they had moved to a more central position further down the coast. It stood just above the shore-line between Fisherton and Point, a tumble-down ruin which had been repaired by the new factor and paid for by the reluctant family law agent from her own resources. The factor had demurred at the cost to the estate.

The hut now had two rooms and a tiny kitchen. Meg had renamed it Sea Croft and turned it into a shelter for advice, rest, hot broth, the healing of minor injuries, for sanctuary, information and companionship. However it remained known locally as the Bothy, and although Meg tried hard to promote its grander name, she too eventually succumbed. The Bothy therefore it became.

On two afternoons in the week Sam Stuart drove her and Jenny Paterson, the gardener's daughter now the Hall kitchen maid, with a baking of bannocks and a tureen of broth from the hall kitchen to the Bothy where she waited in the parlour, as the main room was somewhat grandly called, for visitors. Jenny saw to the fires in winter, kept the place clean and served refreshments. Though slow to start, the Bothy over time grew so busy that when Helen Macfarlane offered to help, Meg was glad to accept. Helen took over one day in the week and Fanny Macreedie had just taken over Friday afternoons.

Women of all ages, many from further afield than Fisherton visited the Bothy. Farm women, Point women, even strangers from Inverness, and the occasional man, usually a tramp or a tinker on the scrounge but welcome nevertheless, found their way to the door.

Many of them needed money. This Meg had been willing to supply in small amounts until Macmurtrie warned her that her own pot was not bottomless. Church women from all three congregations began to collect food and worn clothing, to hold bric-a-brac sales and other charitable functions to support her, so the unemployed, the penniless and the aged had begun to receive regular food baskets. This weeded out the handful of scroungers who craved money for the tavern from the genuinely hungry of whom there were far too many. Actually Meg rather enjoyed the scroungers, some of them plausible rogues with convoluted stories to tell which made her laugh. They were offered scones and tea.

While watching the children partying, she was thinking of one particular homeless woman, an itinerant tinker, who slept out under trees, dressed in rags and stank when she arrived cold and hungry and lice-ridden.. The next item of expense the Bothy required was a bath. It could probably be fed from the outside cold water tap and warmed up from the tea urn in a curtained-off cubicle in the kitchen. There were several men on the estate capable of doing the work, if Mr Wilkie was willing to spare them.

She was going over the names in her head when she became aware of Jenkins standing beside her. He too was watching Victor playing the arch with Helen Macfarlane at *Oranges and Lemons*. Victor looked flushed and breathless, over-excited. She suddenly felt a stab of pity for him.

'How is Mr Victor?' she found herself questioning Jenkins.

191

He looked at her for a moment before his eyes slid away from her. ''e 'as 'is problems,' he said ambiguously.

'His cough do you mean?' she asked.

Jenkins looked at her again. 'Aye, that too.'

She remembered how exasperating the little man could be. 'What problems?' she demanded.

'It's 'im you should be h'asking,' he said not looking at her.

'I'm speaking to you,' she said coolly but he had moved away.

She looked at Victor again. He had withdrawn a little from the game, his place in the arch taken over by Fanny. He was leaning unobtrusively against a high-backed beaded chair. He looked dreadful, gaunt, hollow-eyed. To her surprise she found that she cared. The rows and the anger that had dominated the first few years of their marriage had calmed. These days they seldom even argued. He had supported her, one of the few, over setting up the Bothy. He had, reluctantly to begin with, more than supported her over the care of Andrew. To her surprise she realised that, after years of active dislike, she had grown first to tolerate him and finally to like him again; almost to like him. Certainly she pitied him. The word love did not occur to her. He had been a brick over the party.

The game finished, it was time for tea. The dining room table had been expanded to allow all the children to sit. There were piles of little triangular egg sandwiches, tiny sausage rolls, iced biscuits, and a cake shaped like a train with five candles instead of funnels. Andrew's current passion was trains and his daily walk with Bessie usually ended up at the railway station. Mr Vass, who had just arrived, said Grace and the children tucked in. Glancing at their pretty heads around the table, Meg knew them all from Hamish Vass, by far the biggest at a hefty fourteen, down to

Lady Morton's three year old, a pretty little girl called Adela with a head covered in artificial curls which were beginning to droop with the excitement of the occasion. Fanny's two, Ken and Connie sat with Effie's three bairns. Andrew, who had shared Effie's breast with Daniel, Effie's youngest, was now Danny's best friend. Would they have been friends, she wondered, if they had not shared the same breast? Possibly. Effie's bairns were certainly Andrew's nearest neighbours. She was saddened to see that although there were plenty of estate children round the table there were none from Fisherton. It was not for the lack of asking. The whole party had been a bit of an experiment which had not been approved by all. The dowager Lady Morton had gone so far as to quiz Meg about her guests. Milton children did not usually mingle socially with Kirkton bairns. Estate children were just about permissible, she supposed, but did Meg really think that the Emporium children should be there? Might they not get ideas above their station? Fanny Macreedie was a nice little woman but the dowager had made her opinion quite clear. She hoped there would be no children from Fisherton. You never knew what diseases they might carry.

Meg was furious. She had fulminated to Victor at dinner. 'How dare she! What is her own daughter-in-law but a Milton woman herself with God knows what antecedents?'

Victor, when he got a word in, was conciliatory. 'Wwwell, bbbut my dddear…. You did ssss-ay yourssself that the ppparty wath in the nnnature of an exppperiment?' An experiment which had worked, she told herself, as she watched the children nibble the heads off animal-shaped biscuits Nearly worked. At least Cynthia Morton had brought Adela and her nanny. Apart from the lack of Fisherton children, there were other absentees from among the neighbouring landed gentry.

After tea came the treasure hunt. Little coloured discs had been hidden throughout the drawing-room, morning-room and hall. Nanny Gilchrist and Nanny Morton presided over a table covered with toys each priced 1 to 5 discs. Victor, Meg noticed, had been adopted by two little girls, identical twin granddaughters of Finlay from the keeper's cottage with sharp eyes and nimble fingers. .

'That's not fair!' Andrew declared. 'It's my birthday.'

'Now, now, Master Andrew,' Nanny Gilchrist was quick to chide. 'Little birds in their nests agree.'

'Come on, Andrew,' Meg intervened. 'I'll help you.'

'I want Uncle Victor,' he pouted.

'Look,' said Meg, 'behind the umbrella stand.'

The twins spotted the two discs at the same time. All thirty little fingers reached out The little girls won. Andrew started to howl.

It was Victor who sorted it out. Stuttering and stammering he managed to get the children to laugh and finally share their tokens. Andrew, mollified, stopped crying and the three of them ran to the table to spend their accumulated loot.

'Going well, I think,' Meg said to Victor as they stood back. She turned to look at him. He was grey and breathless. 'Are you all right?' she asked, concerned. He started to cough. There was so much noise in the room that no one noticed.

'I think ppperhaps I'll gggo and wwwest,' he gasped.

Jenkins was at his side in a moment.

'Victor,' she said urgently. 'What's wrong?'

'I'm all wight,' he told her but his voice was weak.

''e'll be fine. Just needs 'is medicine,' Jenkins soothed. 'No need to bother the doctor.'

Because she was busy, because it was easier, because she had other matters on her mind, she did nothing.

Fisherton

Marsali missed Ezra more than she would have expected. The monosyllabic figure by the range who ate what was put before him, had been no companion but was preferable to the constant bickering at her fireside since Jonas and his family had moved into her cottage. Not that she saw much of Jonas who was at sea more often than he was at home, or Evie for that matter. Evie now ran the fish stall outside the Emporium, no thanks to Jared. It was Missus Fanny who had seen the opportunity some five years ago and converted the storage shed, or part of it into a little booth with a marble slab to keep the fish cool and a wee room behind for preparing the cod, smokies and herring as the customers required. Evie disappeared early every morning to pick up the fish and have it transported by one of the carters, or on her back depending upon the quantity required. Many of her Milton and Kirkton customers had regular orders culminating in a sell-out on Fridays. No one would buy fish on a Monday and rightly so, in Marsali's opinion. It was usually left over from Friday.

Evie was doing her best. The *Bright Star* benefited from the regular demand and Jonas had been promoted. It was Jonas who had suggested his little family - he and Evie had had two bairns in under four years - move in with his mother 'for company like'. Marsali smiled a little at the way he had asked; as if all the benefits of the arrangement would be hers. 'You will be missing my da. The weans will be company for you. No need for you to concern yourself about the rent, *a' mhathair*. It will be regularly paid. The bairns will soon be at the school. Life will be easy for you in your old age.' Indeed he had managed to convince himself that the benefits would all be hers.

It did not work out quite like that. The bairns were a handful. There was the cooking to do and the place to keep clean. Evie did nothing when she returned after six in the evening, hungry and grey with exhaustion. Nor did Marsali expect her to help with the chores, but she expected her to take control of her bairns on the Sabbath. But no. Off Evie went to the Poor House at Point to visit her father. 'I canna take the weans into the likes o' thon place. Jonas would not like it,' she explained to her mother-in-law. Marsali could not but agree. As for Jonas he spent much of the day in his bed, and the rest of it at the pier head gossiping with his mates. Nor could she blame him for that. He worked hard. They both worked hard, but she wished he had been straight with her. He and his family's need of her was far greater than her need of them. The rent barely covered it. She would not have minded however, if the two of them had been kinder to each other. Instead they bickered constantly. For some reason Evie annoyed her son. Every remark she made was criticised. He found fault with her for her lack of cooking skills, the pitch of her voice, and above all for her family which he considered to be the scum of the earth. He called her 'the fishwife' to her face and behind her back. He was ashamed of her.

He was equally unpleasant to Jared, but for different reasons. He was jealous of what he perceived to be Jared's easy life, his middle-class wife and his position in Milton. Evie's family, of tinker origin - as he was constantly reminding her - was lower than the doorstep.

Jonas had always been a difficult child, resentful equally of Donnaidh's brains and Jared's good looks. With Donnaidh gone, Marsali had thought that he might be less bitter, but if anything he was more resentful. The only person he had any apparent affection for was Effy whom he seldom saw for he was usually at sea on her rare days off. So why had he married Evie? For the simple reason that he had got her pregnant. He would have denied his fatherhood had it been possible but too many Fisherton folk had known of their affair. He would have been put off the boat had he deserted her. The skipper was a religious man. So they were stuck with each other. She did not think that Evie had any feelings left for Jonas, and how could she blame her?

Marsali pitied Evie but found her hard to love. Her slovenly ways irritated her, her shouting at the loons, her screeching laugh (which come to think of it she had not heard much lately). But Marsali's sight was a deal clearer than her son's for she saw how Evie tried to be a good wife, her fear of Jonas' tongue, her dis-ease in her mother-in-law's house, how hard she worked at the fish stall. There was much to admire in Evie. She had tried to curb Jonas' tongue. 'You'll not speak to your wife like that in my house, son,' she had told him once when they had been alone in the cottage.

'I'll speak to my wife exactly as I choose, and it's no longer your house, *a mhathair*, for I pay the rent.'

The words were harsh but the tone almost conciliatory. He was silent for the rest of the day so she supposed he had taken some heed to her words. But the moody silence was not to last. He was just as sarcastic the next day, nastier even. She was afraid it might come to blows. If Ezra had been here he would have put a stop to it. Come to think of it, Jonas resembled his father in many ways. He too had been good at the moody silences, especially after Donnaidh left but Ezra would never have spoken to her as Jonas spoke to Evie.

Donnaidh…The thought of him was like a secret pleasure to be hugged with hope in her heart. She thought of the box hidden beneath her bed which contained her treasures and the letters…

She looked at Ezra's clock. Four already. The bairns were playing peaceably with a cotton bag full of clothes-pegs on

197

the rag hearth rug lost in their own little world of dreams. Time to put on their tea. She liked to feed the bairns before their parents turned up hungry and exhausted. The mutton stew simmered gently on the top of the black range.

At that moment the door opened and Anna popped in. Marsali was glad to see her. She buried her knitting in her apron pocket and while the bairnies ran to the stranger, embraced her knees and demanded her attention, she poured a cup of tea from the pot stewing on the range. For some five minutes Anna gave her full attention to the bairns until they lost interest in her and returned to their play.

'So,' said Anna lifting the well-sugared cup to her lips, 'did you go to the Bothy, then?'

Marsali knew exactly what she was asking. 'It's difficult to get away with the wee ones.'

'Och, you can leave them with me. You should go for Miss Megaidh's sake.'

Marsali hesitated. 'I would not like Miss Megaidh to think I was scrounging.'

Anna was indignant. 'Is that what you think I was doing?'

Marsali started to protest.

'If so you are in the wrong, Marsali. It's my Ina, what she was telling me. She reckoned Mistress Myers should know and my Ina agreed.'

It was a convoluted story about one of the neighbours' pigs, hardly worth repeating. 'Did Miss Megaidh listen to you?'

'Of course she listened. That's why she's there. To listen. Something will happen. You wait and see.'

Marsali made up her mind. As long as Miss Megaidh wouldn't think her on the scrounge. There was something she needed to share with someone or she would explode.

'When is Miss Megaidh in the Bothy, then?'

'Tuesday and Thursday afternoons. Mistress Macfarlane is on Mondays and Wednesdays and your Missus Fanny on Fridays.'

'How does Missus Fanny manage?' Marsali could not stop herself from asking. Fanny had a finger in every pie, or so it seemed. She was not sure she approved. A woman's place was surely at her own fireside.

'Fine. If you get behind with the rent or payments, she's the one to speak to. Your Jared's done great for himself getting her as wife. Just like your Effie. Sam Stuart's a good lad. Miss Megaidh's right hand man,' she said with pride. (Sam was her nephew.) 'She told him."You're my right hand man, Sam," those were her very words.'

Marsali couldn't let that remark go unchallenged. 'What about Mr Victor?'

'Oh no,' said Anna complacently. 'Definitely including Mr Victor. He's a poor soul.'

Marsali was silent. She knew it to be true. The wall clock chimed five.

'Och, will you look at the time,' said Anna. 'I'll need to be away.'

She left as unceremoniously as she had come and Marsali called the bairns to the table. Tomorrow, she thought, I'll visit the Bothy tomorrow.

The Bothy

Something would have to be done about a waiting room, Helen Macfarlane thought as she caught a glimpse of the straggle of people outside the Bothy. There were benches either side of the door and down the gable ends of the shack, but in an east wind like today there was no shelter at all. Between visitors (Meg insisted they be called visitors) she went outside, and, shouting against the wind, called the queue indoors. They could wait in the parlour while she took each visitor into the small kitchen where Minnie was brewing tea. Minnie could start serving in the big room which she was happy to do. She already knew most of the folk.

It was interesting, Helen thought, how the 'misfortunates' (which is what she called them privately to herself) sorted themselves into groups according to their needs. Fanny Macreedie mostly had 'customers'; wives who could not pay their bills, disputes between neighbours, some who wanted to better themselves, practical problems that could be - if not solved - ameliorated by someone as sensible as Mrs Macreedie. Her own 'misfortunates' were usually sickly folk who could not afford to summon the doctor; women in chronic pain, children with sores or coughs, incurables who knew there was no betterment but whose pain was alleviated just by talking to her. Helen had had a smattering of nursing training before she had married Mr Macfarlane whom she had nursed throughout his last illness. Her care of Mrs Vass too had been noted and approved by all. Unqualified, she had enough common sense, enough innate skill, to know when to call on Dr Anderson whose fee, if necessary, would be covered through the charitable donations of the community.

Meg had everyone else; women with family problems, illegitimate pregnancies, law-breaking children, threatened evictions, anger, deceit, despair.

She also knew that Meg turned to Hugh for advice. She could do with advice herself, she thought, as she re-bandaged a head wound caused, she was sure, by a blow from the woman's husband's fist. She would not admit it, however hard Helen probed. There was little she could do except wash and clean the gash. She hoped it would not fester. Fortunately the well water outside the Bothy was icily

200

pure and would do no harm. She would speak to Hugh herself about the cause of the wound.

There was one matter, though, that she had not discussed with Hugh or Meg either, indeed with no one living in Inverally. That was her relationship with Hugh. Emily had been so sure that they would marry once she had gone. So, indeed, had she. But the words had never been spoken. She had thought that respect for Emily and their marriage had kept him silent for the first year after her death. Now she knew better. Now she believed they would never be spoken. Hugh respected her, needed her to run his household but he did not love her. Whatever folk might think, there was no intimacy between them and never would be. Truthfully to herself, she admitted that neither did she love him, at least not in that way. He was like a brother to her, someone to rely on, to laugh with and to care for. She was necessary to him as his housekeeper and as a nursemaid to look after his child. So she told herself, so she believed. However circumstances were about to change.

Hamish at fifteen was growing up. He did not need her as he had once done. Hugh was talking about sending him to the big boarding school in Perthshire which taught the sons of clergymen without charging a fee and trained young men for the priesthood. There he would receive the education he could not get in the village school. Without the excuse of Hamish to care for, propriety would insist that she left the schoolhouse. If so, it would be with a very heavy heart. She owned a small flat in Edinburgh recently bequeathed by an aunt, but she did not want to leave the village. She regarded Hugh and Hamish as her family, Inverally as her home.

The chance to speak to Hugh came sooner than expected.

He was waiting for her in the pony trap as he often did after her session in the Bothy. Minnie had already left, having given her arm to a young Fisherton girl who had gashed her leg on a herring box in the curing shed. The wind had dropped suddenly as it sometimes did, and it was a beautiful evening.

When he suggested taking the round-about route to Kirkton she agreed. Some quarter of a mile before Point the track divided. Automatically they both got out of the vehicle for the narrow road that zigzagged up the side of the cliffs was too steep for the ageing garron. The late spring sun beat kindly on their shoulders. Half way up, the old horse stopped to crop the verges.

'Let's sit for a minute,' she suggested. She sat down on a boulder by the track. Hugh did not sit but leaned back against a five-barred gate that led into a field dotted with ewes and their plump ageing lambs. 'What's on your mind?' he asked for she had been silent for quite a while. 'Was all well at the Bothy?'

She decided to come straight out with it. 'I'm concerned for my future,' she said bluntly. 'If Hamish goes to Glenalmond, do you want me to leave Inverally? Without your son to care for, I shall have no excuse to stay. Your name and mine would be compromised.'

She looked up at his puzzled face. 'Do you want to leave?' he asked after a moment.

'Not particularly,' she said as calmly as she could. Inwardly she was churning. 'No,' she repeated more emphatically. 'But, Hugh, you must see that without Hamish my position in your household is questionable.'

She had not meant to do it but she felt the blush scorching her cheeks. He too saw her, then turned his head to look out over the sea. A swell threw the waves noisily against the shingle below them. He was quiet for a long moment then seemed to make up his mind.

'Would it help if we were married?' he asked gently, but it was obvious to her that his heart was not in it. She knew she should refuse but she also knew she never would.

'Is that what you really want?' she asked.

He answered quickly, too quickly, but bless him for not hesitating. 'Of course. I should have asked you sooner but somehow…'

'I understand,' she interrupted him. 'After Emily…' but that was not the reason. They both knew it.

Quietly, without an embrace, they made the necessary plans. Hamish had to be kitted out with a uniform for his new school by an outfitter in Edinburgh. They decided on a quiet wedding in Bruntisfield with Hamish and a couple of her elderly Edinburgh relatives as witnesses. Hugh would make the practical arrangements. She would tell her cousins. Nothing was to be said in the parish until they returned as man and wife.

Only then did Hugh come over to her, reach out for her hand to help her rise, which he kissed. It was as much as she expected. 'Thank you, Helen.'

'Will you tell Mrs Myers?' she asked in a low voice because she could not help herself.

'Miss Megaidh?' He sounded so surprised that for a moment she wondered if he knew his own heart. 'No, no,' he said. 'I think not. Time enough for that.'

He left her to coax the old garron to climb the hill. She joined him. Silence stretched awkwardly between them. 'Hamish is quite excited at his prospects, I think,' she said to break it.

'We'll miss him,' he replied. 'We' he had said, not 'I'. That was a hopeful sign, wasn't it?

'Indeed we shall,' she told him with a sigh.

At that she changed the subject to ask him about her abused fisher wife.

Kirkton

Saturday morning. The school house was quiet. Every so often Hugh put down his pen and stared out of the window. What had he done?

Of course he had always known what Emily had expected of him with regard to Helen. Emily had thought it that easy. When he had told Hamish of the engagement, neither of them had said anything. The silence between them spread to an uncomfortable minute. Then the boy had asked a bit sullenly, 'will I have to call her Mama?'

'Of course not,' Hugh had said, relieved that his son had spoken. 'She'll still be Aunt Helen.'

'But she's not really, is she?'

'She's your godmother. Godmothers are usually called aunt.' When Hamish did not reply he added, 'Nothing will change where you're concerned.'

'Everything is changing,' he said bitterly. 'You're sending me away and keeping Auntie Helen. It's not fair.'

'Do you want her to go away too, then? Would that make things better?' he asked a little sharply.

Hamish shook his head.

'What then? Tell me.'

'I just don't want things to change.'

Nor do I, he thought, dear God nor do I. He held out his hand. After a moment Hamish took it. Aloud he said, 'I know, Shamus. I don't want you away either, but it's only for a short while and the holidays are good. You need to have a proper education. You know that.' He drew the boy close. 'I'll miss you too.'

'You'll have Auntie Helen.'

It's not the same, he thought. Later when he had gone, he held his head in his hands. God in heaven, he thought, what have I done? He knew he did not love Helen, could not love

Helen, would never love Helen, not while little Megaidh walked the earth.

He allowed himself at last to think of Meg. Thinking of her was a luxury he seldom indulged. For years now he knew she was there just below the range of conscious thought. Emily used to tease him about the little girl's crush and he would smile with her and think no more about it, but after Emily had died and Meg had become a woman there was no one to tease him out of his feelings. It was the hardest thing he had ever had to do, officiate at that sham of a wedding to Victor Myers.

But Hugh was a practical man. He realised there was no future in such feelings. He knew what Emily had planned and what Helen hoped for, knew that marriage to Helen was the sensible outcome, but he could not pretend to be ovejoyed about it. Somewhere deep down in his heart he had hoped to keep himself single for Meg. Stupid, stupid romantic fool that he was. Helen was a nice woman, a good woman, and he would do his duty by her but his heart was not free to love her, nor ever would be. He looked down at the sermon he was writing. 'Do you love me?' Jesus had asked thrice of St Peter. That one word 'love' in English was covered by three words in Greek. '*Philos*' for brotherly love, '*eros*' for sexual love and '*agape*' for spiritual love. His love for Helen was of the '*philos*' kind (as Peter's then was for Christ). It would never be '*eros*' or '*agape*' alas. He hoped *philos* would be enough.

One last indulgence. He found a book on his shelves, Tacitus' *Agricola*. There pressed between the pages was a browning, brittle Shepherds Purse. He remembered that day she had asked him to teach her Gaelic. He had loved her from that moment for her eagerness, her innocence, her mind, and because he could not help himself.

There was a tap on his study door. Helen opened it and came in. She saw the book, the faded flower. 'What's that you have there?' she asked kindly like one who is really interested.

'Nothing,' he said closing the book firmly on her question. 'What can I do for you, my dear?'

'I require some new clothes, a wedding dress, Hugh. I think I may have to tell Fanny Macreedie our news.'

'I understand. I am sure Mistress Macreedie will be discreet. Have you enough money?' He felt in his jacket for his pocket book.

'Thank you, yes.' He remembered with relief that she had a small private income which had come to the rescue before. At least they would have no money problems.

'I'll go then. It's raining so may I take the trap?'

'Of course.' She left the room as quietly as she had entered.

Enough, he told himself firmly. He picked up the *Agricola* and returned it to its shelf, sat down at his desk and dipped his pen purposefully in the ink well. Sermons would not write themselves.

Milton

Fanny spent Saturday mornings at her accounts. The children, Kenny and Connie, played quietly under the nursemaid's eye on the hearthrug with their wooden bricks. Every so often the peace was broken by Connie's delighted squeals as she knocked over the tower that Kenny had painstakingly built for her to tumble.

The task was not hard to manage for the Emporium employed an accountant these days. She liked to keep overall control, however. She had heard of too many businesses that had foundered because of careless management. She was determined that hers would not be one of them. She now thought of the business as hers for her father had signed over all authority to her, and Jared was not interested. Jared had other interests… she would not think of Jared. Deliberately she forced her mind off that particular rock face, for the time being at least.

Mrs Mack poked her head round the door. 'Mrs Macfarlane would like to speak to you, Mrs Fanny.' Mrs Mack had never been able to call her mistress by her married name. 'Macreedie' was altogether too vulgar so she ignored it.

'Show her in,' Fanny said and wondered what she wanted that could not be found in the shop.

After Mrs Macfarlane had made a fuss of the children, Kenny disappeared on one of his own ploys and the nursemaid, at a signal from Fanny, quietly removed Connie. 'Will you take some refreshment, Ma'am?' Fanny offered politely. 'A glass of Madeira, perhaps?'

Helen declined and took the fireside chair that Fanny had indicated. Mystified, Fanny inquired, 'How can I help you?'

'I am getting married,' she said, without looking directly into Fanny's eyes.

Fanny was surprised. Many years had passed since Mrs Vass's death. Folk had long ago dismissed the idea of a romance between the parson and his housekeeper. But wait… perhaps she was engaged to someone else.

'I'm delighted for you,' she said smoothly. 'May I ask who is to be the fortunate gentleman?'

Helen looked up quickly. 'Mr Vass, of course!'

'Of course,' said Fanny hastily. Widowers often married their housekeepers, did they not? All highly convenient. 'Congratulations! I am pleased for you.'

'Thank you, Mrs Macreedie… I came to see you privately because we are not announcing the engagement yet. Mr Vass and I intend to marry quietly in Edinburgh. We want no fuss. May I count on your discretion?'

'Certainly,' said Fanny. But why? she wondered. There would be gossip of course but, on the whole, Inverally would be delighted for them. Hatches, matches and dispatches were the food of village life. 'I shall be as quiet as a mouse. How can I help?'

She needed material for a gown, new underwear, nightgowns, advice. 'I'm a bit out of touch with what is fashionable these days. You are always so nicely dressed, Mrs Macreedie, and I need some sort of trousseau.'

Will you get Miss Matheson to make your wedding dress?'

Helen laughed. 'I might as well take out an advertisement in *Highland News*! No, I intend to make my own. Nothing elaborate, but nice...you know? Something I can wear again.'

Fanny was pleased. 'Let me fetch my pattern books and swatches. I see you in Madonna blue.'

'Oh, I don't think...'she began but Fanny had already left the room to come back in a few minutes armed with catalogues for corsets and other unmentionables, pattern books and samples of material.

The decisions were quickly and frugally made until it came to the dress. Together, and with some laughter they poured over the swatches. 'Not red, I think,' Helen had quipped, 'and certainly not blue. Alas, I am no Madonna.'

Having rejected purple, 'I'm not quite that old,' and green was an unlucky colour for Graham, her maiden name - 'a Graham in green should ne'er be seen.' She quipped - they found a pretty lilac fabric.

'I am going to the warehouse on Monday and I am fairly sure the material is in stock,' Fanny assured her, closing her books. 'The lad will deliver everything to the schoolhouse on Tuesday morning. Will that suit?'

Helen thanked her and Fanny escorted her to the door. 'I'm so pleased for you, Mrs Macfarlane,' she said impulsively touching the older woman's arm.

Helen thanked her calmly but not effusively and Fanny watched her go. There had been nothing of bridal excitement in her voice or in her eyes. Fanny wondered why. Mr Vass was a pleasant man, what she knew of him. Jared's family belonged to his church and his mother attended occasionally. In those early days when pleasing him was all she ever wanted to do, she had offered to give up her membership of the parish church and accompany him to St Moluag's, but he had declined. At the time, she had thought it a loving gesture towards herself, but now she knew better. Jared chose to go to the parish church along with the other worthies of Inverally for a specific reason. St Moluag's attracted the gentry and the fisher-folk. If he could never be included among the gentry, he was certainly not about to be classed with the fisher folk. He had risen out of that particular pit.

Fanny sighed. She found she preferred the liturgy of the Episcopal church to the crushingly boring *extempore* mumblings of the Reverend Caleb Carruthers. Sometimes his son would deputize for him. The Reverend Solomon did all the parish work but his father clung on to Sunday worship as he clung on to life, which was a pity because the Reverend Solomon gave a good message on the few occasions he was allowed to preach. Several of the congregation had defected to Mr MacQueen of the Free Kirk, a mild little man with eyebrows that were perpetually furrowed and an intimate knowledge (according to himself) of hell. Sometimes Fanny wondered about the three different Gods proclaimed by the three ministers. They could not all be right, or could they? Occasionally when the sermon stretched to forty rambling minutes she wondered why this particular God had not been bored out of existence. Perhaps he had been. Now there was a thought she dared not share. Fanny often had unrepeatable thoughts.

She glanced down at her accounts. All in order. Then she looked at the little watch pinned to her blouse. Nearly one o'clock. Jared would be through for his dinner in five minutes. Just time to look in on the children who ate earlier with the nursemaid in the kitchen to fit in with Kenny's school hours. They were finishing rice pudding and stewed plums. 'I hate rice pudding,' Kenny said loudly with his mouth full of it all the same. 'I hate rice pudding,' Connie mimicked him and spat out a mouthful. Connie always had to go one step further.

'Naughty girl!' said the nursemaid and slapped her wrist at which Connie burst into tears, except there weren't any tears, only sparks of rage in her bright blue eyes.

'Straight to bed and no sweets,' said Fanny at which Connie promptly shed real tears. Two sugar bonbons after lunch was the big treat of the day. The maid bore her away screaming.

'Do you really hate rice pudding?' Fanny asked her son curiously. He had finished every scrap on his plate.

'Yes,' he said cheerfully, 'but not so much as junket. Rice pudding's better than junket and semolina and frogs' spawn.' He turned down his mouth in disgust.

Fanny laughed. Kenny always did her good. He was so like Jared, the way he used to be. 'What are your plans for this afternoon?'

Kenny was ten years old now and was allowed some freedom to meet his own friends and devise his own entertainment on Saturday afternoons. He did not reply directly.

'Mother, is it true that Hamish Vass is going away to a big school near Perth?'

'I hadn't heard.' So that's why Helen's marrying Mr Vass, she thought. A marriage purely of convenience. 'Are you seeing Hamish this afternoon?'

'I'm going rabbiting with some of the lads. Don't worry, Ma, we've got permission from Mr Finlay.'

'Don't be late back, then. I don't like you out when it's dark.'

'I won't,' he said with an exaggerated sigh.

Jared was on time and her father was already waiting in the dining room when Mrs Mack sounded the gong.

The Cock a' leekie soup was followed by a roast chicken, Saturday fare for the adults who could relax over their meal as the Emporium was shut that afternoon. Jared usually visited his mother on Saturday afternoons and took the children leaving her free to attend to household affairs neglected during her busy week, sort linen and clothing, write letters, perhaps read a novel. Fanny loved novels particularly those of Charles Dickens.

'By the way,' she said to Jared as he carved the chicken. 'Kenny tells me he is going rabbiting with his friends this afternoon, so he can't visit your mother.'

'Ah,' said Jared,' that is just as well for I am not going to Fisherton this afternoon.'

'What about Connie?' she asked forcing her voice to sound natural.

'I am sure she will be just as happy to spend an afternoon with her own mother,' Jared said pleasantly.

'Where are you going?' Fanny asked. The words were out before she could stop them. Jared did not like to be questioned on his comings and goings.

'Out,' he replied shortly, 'If I have your permission?' he added wrapping the sarcastic words in a sugar-coated tone.

There was silence at the table. Mrs Mack kept her eyes on her plate but Fanny was aware of the housekeeper's fury.

Her feelings towards Jared had not softened over the years. Mr Ross, as usual, noticed nothing.

Fanny knew exactly where he was going. Or thought she did.

The Hall

Jared was not sure why he had not told Fanny where he was going, why her questioning irritated him so much; why everything she did these days seemed to annoy him. As he drove the pony trap up the Brae he tried to shake off his feelings of anger and self-disgust. He was his own man was he not? He was good at his job, was he not? He was a dutiful husband. What more did she expect of him? Fanny was always trying to change him, always suspecting him of - what? He did not know. Perhaps she thought he was seeing another quine? Serve her right if he did. There were plenty of women…one had more or less propositioned him. He grimaced as he thought of Mistress Donaldina Mackay. Always at his counter, suggesting he come round for a cup of tea or something stronger… as if! Fanny was safe there.

The south avenue gates to the Hall had been renewed and painted recently. There was a new air of efficiency about the estate since Mr Wilkie had taken over as factor. Back bills had been paid, or so he assumed, though nothing outright had been said. He knew little enough about the Emporium's finances now that the business employed an accountant, but he would have heard if the estate still owed money. Rumour, picked up in the Royal Station Hotel, insinuated that Miss Megaidh (he still thought of her as he had known her as a child) had paid all the outstanding accounts out of her own private fortune. Certainly under Mr Wilkie's management, the business side of the estate seemed to prosper now that Mr Myers had relinquished control.

It was Mr Myers he was on his way to visit. Why had he not told Fanny? Why was it that he had not even told his mother? The less they knew the better. For the umpteenth time he asked himself how he had managed to get himself into this invidious position, though he knew perfectly well that it had been and still was his own fault. There was a time when he had been flattered by Mr Myers' attention. He had even pitied the loon. He was still sorry for Mr Myers. Or so he told himself. He was acting purely out of charity, was he not? The man was sick, needed his company; enjoyed a game of backgammon. Aye, all of that, but that was not why he was driving the family trap up the long tree-lined avenue on a Saturday afternoon which he usually spent taking the bairns to visit his mother. That was not why Jenkins sidled into the Emporium every six weeks or so with instructions which culminated in a visit to the Hall. He could of course have said he was otherwise occupied. He could have refused, but there were secrets in Jared's life that he wished to remain secret especially from Fanny and his mother. There was no way he could realistically avoid the visit. He was strongly aware of the apothecary's sealed package in his coat pocket that he had picked up from the Royal Station Hotel reception desk the previous evening.

Myers, wearing a loose blue dressing gown elaborated with black frogging and seated in a cushioned chair in the window recess, had the backgammon board laid out in readiness on a small table at his knees when Jenkins showed him into his quarters on the ground floor of the Hall. He looked dreadful; great dark socketed eyes, hectically flushed cheeks, and emaciated corded neck. His frailty was only emphasised by the strength of the light from the tall French windows of the spacious room, which had been the old colonel's sick room, and was now the new laird's apartment. Not that Jared thought of Myers as laird. No one in Inverally considered him laird. He was either 'yon poor wee loon up at the big house' or 'Myers' without even the dignity of a title. To Jared he was, of course, 'sir', as befits a humble shopkeeper when dealing with a distinguished customer.

'Ah – Mmmacweedie,' he said holding out a thin hand. 'how gggood to sssee you, man. Cccome and sssiit down. Bbbwandy, is it? Bwandy, Jjmmy, bbbwandy if you ppplease'

Jared remembered now why he was willing to give up an occasional Thursday or Saturday afternoon off in order to act as a paid courier when he did not need the fee (though, come to think, when was an extra pound or two not welcome?) He realised that, although he pitied Myers, he actually quite liked the poor loon. At least he liked the reality of him if not the reason for the visit. Myers treated him as an equal. If the contents of the package which he had handed over silently to Jenkins in exchange for two envelopes, one bearing his own name, the other containing, he presumed, payment for the apothecary; brought him any relief from his sickness then who was he to quibble?

'How are you, sir?' Jared asked taking the chair indicated, warming to his host.

Myers shrugged 'Bbbetter for ssseeing you..Dddid you bbbwing my tttonic?'

'I did, sir.'

'Th-ank you, and hhhow are all my fffwiends at the Ssstation?'

Jared repeated what local gossip he had gleaned and the sick man listened avidly. It had occurred to Jared that since the poor wee mannie was no longer strong enough to visit the Station Hotel himself, he had no pleasures apart from the special 'tonic' he, Jared, regularly delivered, and probably too much brandy. But he was wrong.

The board was set up, the meagre stakes agreed, when the door was flung open and a small hurricane burst into the room demanding to see Uncle Victor followed by a large dog that yelped excitedly followed in turn by an embarrassed servant. When the moment of chaos was over the nursemaid could be heard apologising. 'I beg your pardon, sir, but Master Andrew insisted …'

'All wight Bbbessie,' Victor assured her. 'Whwhwhat is it, Andy?'

'You never said! You never told me. I need to know,' the boy demanded.

'Of cccourth you dddo. Bbbring mmme the bbbox, then.'

'What? In front of them?' He glared at Jared and Jenkins.

'They wwwon't llllook.' Jared moved away but he was curious enough to watch what happened. The boy darted behind Myers' large chair and brought out a small wooden box bound in iron hoops, a child's imitation of a pirate's treasure chest. Glaring round the room he commanded Jared, 'don't you dare look!'

'Master Andrew, behave yourself!' Bessie tried be firm but her voice lacked authority.

'I thththink,' whispered Myers, ' I think a bbblackbirds egg would be a gggood add …thing.'

Jared stole a glance over his shoulder and caught a glimpse of an eclectic collection of odds and ends that included a black feather, a round pebble, a fragment of blue and white china, a small stone encrusted with a strange beast and a polished Georgian penny coin, and he was touched. His own Kenny collected special pebbles on the beach which he called fossils and Connie pressed wild flowers.

'That's hard,' the boy told his uncle seriously as he closed the lid of the chest and turned the little key.

'Wewy hhhard. You'll need Bbb…'s hhhelp.'

'Can I tell her?'

Myers nodded. 'I gggive you thwee dddays.'

'Righto,' said the child. He returned the box to its hiding place behind the chair, hugged his uncle and within seconds the two had gone from the room.

'What a bold little fellow,' Jared said, feeling that some remark was required. 'He reminds me of his uncle Andrew.' Where that had come from he was not too sure. He had not thought of the three drowned lads for a long time.

'Ah yyyes,' said Victor 'mmmy lllost bbbwother-in-law. You lllost a bbbwother too, Mmmacweedie, dddid you nnnot?'

'Aye. Donnaidh. He was never found.'

'A bbbad ttttime,' Myers said sympathetically. 'There wwwere thwee of them, thwee bbboys?'

Jared nodded. 'At least Mistress Myers and Mr Gallie had bodies to bury. My mother still after so many years will not believe Donnaidh gone.'

'That mmmust be hhhard for hhher - fffor you all.' he paused. 'Whwhwhat dddo you think, Mmmacweedie?'

'I?' Jared pulled himself together. He was not in the mood to discuss his mother's intransigence. 'I think it's time to shake the dice.'

But now he had allowed the thought to enter his consciousness, he could not get rid of it. His mother was still so sure.

Milton

Joshua Gallie heard the carriage from the window of his office and saw it to be Cynthia. It was not her mother she had come to see. It was himself. That pleased him enormously though he knew perfectly well that she only came when she wanted something.

He watched her descend from the carriage, have a word with the groom and pick her way across the yard between the stacks of trimmed logs and rows of planed planks. What an elegant woman she was! He opened the door to welcome her. The spring air smelled strongly of sawdust. It was an odour that never tired him, full of sap and life, symbol of his prosperity. He realised, not for the first time, that he loved his business, the mill, the yard, the gift of his grandfather to his father and down to his grandson which he had cherished but to what purpose? Aaron's inheritance. In his memory, Aaron was the dutiful son who would have by now have been his manager, his heir, himself the father of many sons. And in the deepest recesses of his heart he still raged against the sea, the Macreedies and the God who had dealt so cruelly with him.

Cynthia looked bonny, dressed as usual up to the nines, grander than the grandest in the county. For a moment he weighed the loss of Aaron against the acquisition of Cynthia and wondered. Just for a moment. As soon as she touched his hand leaned forward to kiss his cheek, all doubts vanished. He adored his stepdaughter.

'How are you, Papa Josh?'

'Well enough,' he said. 'And what can I do for my Lady Morton this fine morning?'

She took his arm. 'Why should you think I want anything? Can I not call upon my dear Papa Josh just for the pleasure of it?' she pouted prettily.

'Because there is usually something behind those bonny blue eyes, Because I wasn't brought up the Clyde on a bicycle!' Because, he thought, your fine husband is not an indulgent lover and the dowager Lady Morton still has first claim upon his affections. She was looking particularly pretty this morning, the blue of her gown the exact colour of her eyes. 'So what can I do for my fine lady? Let me guess.

A new gown? A Shetland pony for Adela? Out with it, quine!'

'I am shocked, Papa Josh, quite shocked that you should think me so mercenary.'

As well you might be, my pretty lass, he thought. Don't I already give you a fair allowance. Does your mother not keep you in furs and trinkets? 'Well! I'm waiting.'

She looked down at her hands. ' Now you come to mention it, Papa Josh, there is something – '

'I knew it!' he crowed delightedly. He would give her anything; the little minx had only to ask.

'Dearest Papa, it is not for me.' She sat down in the chair opposite his desk and leaned towards him. She smelled as sweet as a summer rose, He felt himself expand with benevolence.

It was a somewhat garbled request that took him a few moments to disentangle. She wanted him to find employment for some distant relative of Lord Morton who had turned up unexpectedly from America. 'Is this Lord Morton's idea?'

'No,' she said, looking down at her fingers. Her cheeks were rosier than usual. 'Lord Morton thinks he should go back to where he came from. It occurred to me that if he were to learn the timber business from an expert like yourself, he would have a better chance to earn his living back in America.'

'And this young man, what does he want?'

She looked up and he knew exactly what the young man wanted. He would not be the first to enjoy Cynthia's company.

'So what do you think, Papa Josh? He needs help. Would you be willing to give him a trial?'

'I have nothing in the yard and even if I had there are plenty of men more suitable to the work than any relative of Lord Morton.'

'Oh, but Papa, won't you at least meet him? Please, Papa?'

'Why? Where is he? Have you got him with you?' He asked sternly half arising to look out of the window.

'Of course not, Papa! He's waiting at the Station Hotel. I could send the carriage for him, but I would rather not. You know what gossips the servants are.'

Joshua sighed. 'What sort of trouble have you got yourself into this time!' It was not a question. He did not want to know the answer. 'Go and see your mama. I'll deal with the fellow.' Get rid of him, he thought.

'Thank you, Papa!' Cynthia rose, ran to him and kissed him on the cheek.

'I'm making no promises, mind,' he warned her but they both knew that unless the young fellow turned out to be a drooling idiot, a position in the timber yard would be found.

'Oh and Papa Josh.' She paused, her hand on the doorknob, 'You won't tell Mama - or anyone else, will you?'

'Be off with you,' he told her, his voice rough with affection.

He watched her pick her way daintily across the yard and call out greetings to a couple of men she had known since her girlhood. Her mother, having seen the carriage, was outside the gate of Timber House, waiting for her.

Meanwhile Josh called for his horse, spoke to his foreman and rode down to the hotel.

A number of deals were struck and bargains shaken upon in the Saloon Bar of the Royal Station Hotel. Joshua Gallie was by no means the only businessman to be closeted with friend or rival at midday over a mutton pie and a glass of ale.

219

He greeted those he knew and took a stool at the counter to look around him.

The young man who found him was as unlike Cynthia's previous admirers as it was possible to be. No wonder Morton wanted to send him back to where he came from. He was exceedingly fine-looking from the point of view of physique. Tall, muscled, healthy, well-proportioned, tanned, exceedingly well tanned. A touch of the tar brush no doubt about it. More than the tar brush. The fellow was black. What had Cynthia got herself into this time?

'Am I addressing Mr Gallie?' the stranger asked politely. The American accent alone would have betrayed him.

'And you are?' Joshua forced himself to sound neutral.

'Aaron Morton, at your service, sir.'

Aaron? Aaron! How dare he be called Aaron? There was only one Aaron. There would always be only one Aaron. Josh closed his eyes briefly. 'Your age?'

'Round about thirty years, I reckon.'

How dare he be Aaron's age. 'From?' he asked faintly

'Wyoming, sir, but my grandaddy was born on the Morton Plantation by Kingston in Jamaica.'

'A slave?'

'A slave, sir.'

'Does Lord Morton know you're here?'

'He does not, sir.'

I am pretty sure he does not, thought Josh, with a small lift of pleasure. Joshua loathed his contemptuous, supercilious step-son-in-law with an all-consuming passion.

A few questions more and he had employed the man. They agreed terms and hours and sealed the bargain with a shot of whisky. 'Speak to my foreman about accommodation. There's a woman in Milton who takes in workers from my yard.' He settled the account, shook the man's hand and

220

added, 'By the way, you'll be known as Morton in the yard. Understood?'

That way he could cope. Equally importantly, Lord Morton would find out soon enough the whereabouts of his unwanted relative. As for Cynthia she would be pleased. He hoped her husband would not take his anger out on her. He grew hot at the thought. He would flog the brute with his bare hands if he tried anything of that nature. He also knew that his little Cynthia would give as good as she got. Look how she had already got the better of him with this black loon.

He was so pleased with himself that he had a proper dram.

Chapter Six

1910

Fisherton

Rumour whispered that Fisherton was to be sold. Marsali had known that the estate had been in trouble for a while now. The piped water was blamed. Everything had gone down hill since Miss Megaidh had given them taps and sinks and clean water, except for the rents of course. They had risen steadily. Clean water was the greatest gift that she could have bestowed upon them but it had broken the estate. So it was said. But that was not the sole reason. There had been other debts which were half known but seldom mentioned. Secrets involving Mr Myers, or so Marsali had heard from dark hints that Jared occasionally dropped.

Ivor Wilkie (still known as 'the new factor' though he had been nearly ten years in the job) had put the rents up, squeezed every tenant almost dry, retrenched where it was barely possible, sold outlying farms but it was never enough. No one knew the identity of Fisherton's prospective buyer, or if they did no one had told the tenants. Some said Lord Morton was interested, but no one knew for certain, least of all Aaron Morton. Marsali had asked him outright. He had laughed. 'Kinsman I may be, but *confidente* I am not.'

Since Jonas had reluctantly taken his family to live in one of the dilapidated cottages which Mr Wilkie had made habitable, she had taken in a lodger, not of her own seeking though the rent was useful but because she chose to house him.

Jonas had moved out with a bad grace having announced bitterly that he would not be paying two rents. She was on her own. Evie had wept a little but the two unruly children

222

Cathie and Seth (a little less unruly these days thanks to their *seanamhair*) had been excited at the prospect of a new home. It was still only half-furnished and already a midden. Missus Jared, sizing up the situation, had hired one of the young fisher lassies to mind the fish counter at the Emporium to give Evie a hand, a bright wee spark who knew her haddock from her herring and could count. It seemed to make no difference to Evie's habits. Poor Evie, Marsali thought. She needed a bit of encouragement.

Jared, who was so uppity these days, despised Evie not so much for her slovenly ways but for her family. No one was lower than Ephraim Cooper. Poor Evie. No one, not even Jared, despised her as much as she despised herself, but she still plodded up to her fish counter most days and she still endured Jonas' sarcasm. She missed her mother-in-law's comfortable kitchen, nourishing meals and her control of the children. Most of all she missed Marsali's respect. Love was not a word in Evie's vocabulary for she had never known it.

Marsali did not miss the family, (she still cared for the children for part of most days). It was not Evie's slovenliness that she had disliked so much as her son's bitter tongue. He would pick, pick, pick on his wife with one eye on his mother. Marsali was aware that his impatience with Evie was a substitute for his dislike of herself. Jonas had always been difficult, sullen as a child and jealous of his brothers. Jared he hated for his charm, his good looks and his perceived luck in life. Donnaidh he hated for replacing him, as he thought, not only in his mothers arms but in her heart. Effie he tolerated. (Effie was a girl and did not count for much in Jonas' opinion.) Sometimes, Marsali wondered, could there be some truth in his perceptions. Did she care more for Jared? She thought of her good-looking oldest son, his fine appearance, his comfortable life and smiled a little. Jared had become just a wee bit pompous. Who would have thought it? No, Jonas had no reason to be jealous of Jared. And Donnaidh? He would have been thirty-two years old. No, she corrected her thoughts. He was thirty-three past. That was the difference between her son and Master Andrew and Aaron Gallie, two or three months.

Well but there was another Master Andrew at the Big House now, a sturdy lad by all accounts. She seldom saw Master Andrew these days for he was away at a school in the south somewhere, and there was another Aaron at the yard.

It was Missus Fanny who had sent Aaron Morton down the Brae in search of lodgings but first she had prepared her mother-in-law and it was as well that she had. Marsali had never seen a black man before and she might have been disrespectful. Missus Fanny had told her that he had come into the Emporium to ask about lodgings. Seemingly the woman who took in sawyers had taken one look at him and told him she was full up. 'Well,' Fanny had said, ''that might be true.' Jared had laughed. 'Aye, likely.'

Fanny and Jared had both taken to the loon and Jared had put up an advertisement for lodgings in the Emporium window along with all the other notices for lost cats or musical evenings. Fanny had thought a little maliciously that it was the big name Jared liked, Morton.

'What about your mother?' Fanny had suggested after a while

'What about my mother?' Jared had replied.

'She must be lonely without your brother's family. Would she take him in?'

Jared had been resistant to the idea at first as Fanny had known he would be, but as he had taken to the stranger, or at least to his name, he eventually relented. 'You'll need to warn her.'

So Fanny had called on Marsali later that afternoon and told her about the new black worker at the timberyard whose name was Aaron Morton. Marsali only needed to hear the name 'Aaron'. and that had been enough.

He was a wee bit of a shock right enough, not the colour of his skin so much as the size of the man. She had seldom seen a loon taller than six feet. He was broad and where would he buy his boots? She had taken to cleaning his boots, 'more like boats,' she had jested with Anna.

Not that she saw much of him. After a big breakfast of porridge and strong tea, he was off to the yard, a couple of filled bannocks in his satchel for his dinner and a mutton stew or a bit of pork for his tea at six o'clock. Most nights he was off to the tavern or so she supposed. She was usually in her bed by the time he returned.

One night he had the cold, sneezing and coughing and sorry for himself as only a man who is never ill can be. 'Away you to your bed,' she told him. 'You're not fit to go out the door.'

He nodded but he made no move. 'I feel like death sure enough, but I've no notion for my bed,' he wheezed at her.

'Then sit in at the fire.' It was Ezra's chair she gave him with the horsehair arm rests and cushioned seat. She seldom sat there herself for the arms got in the way of her knitting. Jonas had commandeered it when he was living there. 'It's good to see it used,' she told Aaron. 'It was my man's chair. He got it from his father.'

So Aaron took the chair, leaned back in it and sneezed a few times and said politely, 'Wont you tell me about your husband, Ma'am?' Then he shut his eyes.

She did not think he was really listening but she told him all the same. 'Ezra? He was never the same after the three loons left us. It broke him like it broke them at the Hall and Mr Gallie at the Mill.'

Her eyes filled with tears. Stop it now, she told herself. You cannot weep in front of this stranger but her tears fell none the less. She was wrong about Aaron Morton. When she looked over at him after drying her eyes, she saw that he was watching her curiously.

'They told me in the tavern about the lads. Drowned together, I heard tell.'

She shook her head. The tears refused to dry up. It was difficult to speak but speak she would. She had to tell someone. The subject was taboo in her own family. The neighbours too thought she was daft, even Anna. That bleary look would come over their eyes whenever she spoke her mind.

'No,' she said as soon as she could speak. 'No, I tell you. Donnaidh was never drowned. Don't let anyone tell you different.'

He had already been told the whole story. Mrs Macreedie was a respectable widow woman with a bee in her bonnet. Just because Donnaidh's body was never found did not prove that he was not drowned.

'No indeed,' was all he said.

He had not immediately dismissed her beliefs. Would she tell him? Certainly there was no one else she could speak to. Not even Miss Megaidh. The memories for her were too painful.

Tentatively at first then more positively she asked, 'Will I show you?' When he nodded she wiped away the remains of her tears with her apron.

Aaron's eyes closed briefly. He had been about to go to his bed. His head was throbbing.

'What you need is a dram,' she said, noticing the greenish pallor beneath his dark skin. The *uisge beatha* was kept in the press on the wall and taken out only for wakes and emergencies. It had not been touched for a while, not since Ezra's death. She put a spoonful of sugar into the cup and filled it with hot water from the kettle.

'Away you and take this to your bed,' she told him for she was already regretting her offer. What if he were to scorn her precious evidence?

'Show me, Ma'am,' he said firmly.

So she crossed the room to the old kist, opened it and under her best black dress and the small treasures of her life but on top of her shroud she produced a tea caddy. Silently she handed it to him.

He eased off the lid and carefully sorted through the pitiful scraps of evidence; letters to neighbours claiming to have seen Donnaidh in Chicago and California, on a ranch, up at the gold mines. One letter he put aside to examine more closely. It was addressed to her neighbour Anna, and sent by a cousin who had emigrated to Laramie in Wyoming some years back and full of news. Her man seemingly had his own bakery. The letter contained an enclosure written in a different hand

...you'll not believe who I saw this morning. Don Macreedie! I was delivering bread to the local penitentiary and there he was, part of a work gang fixing the road. I stopped the cart to look more closely but the guard was having none of me. I suppose I could have been mistaken. Don was a boy when I last saw him but I'm pretty sure it was him. Pass this on only if you think the Macreedies would rather have a son alive and in jail or drowned and dead....

'Have you shown this to anyone, Ma'am?' Aaron asked.

Marsali shook her head. There was something in what the baker had said. Would she rather have a son in jail or a son drowned? For herself she cared little what her neighbours might think, but there was Jared and Jonas. Jared would be mortified; Jonas would be secretly delighted that his promising younger brother had disgraced himself. Both reactions were equally repellent. She had been intending to tell Miss Megaidh but Miss Megaidh had enough troubles of her own these days.

'Do you want to find him?' Aaron asked her.

'I do,' she said,' but maybe he doesn't want to be found. He's been gone these twenty years and never a word. Maybe that's the way he wants it.'

There, she said it, the doubt that had bedevilled her since Ezra had first put the thought into her head. He never believed in the sightings. He could not bear to share her hope, so she learned over the years to keep all to herself and convinced herself that it was enough to know that he was alive.

'I know the Wyoming State Prison,' he told her cautiously. Better than most, he could have added. Instead he said, 'I could find out for you.'

She was silent for a while. Suppose that baker had been wrong. Suppose Ezra and the rest of Fisherton had been right. Was she strong enough to hear the truth. It was the thought of nothing that she could not take. She shook her head.

'Leave it lie,' she said. 'He knows where I am if he needs me.'

'Just as you think right, Ma'am.'

But Aaron had no intention of letting the matter alone. He knew without a shadow of doubt that Don Macreedie was very much alive.

The Hall

The large gleaming cumbersome machine scrunched over the gravel and Mr Macmurtrie squeezed himself out of the driver's leather seat, walked round the gleaming black monster and patted its bonnet. He was not only in awe of his new purchase. He was in love with it

Mima opened the door and asked who was calling, as if she didn't know. Miss Meg's law agent was a frequent visitor to the Hall these days.

'I'll see if Madam is free.' Mima was as nippy as she had always been. Opening the door had never been her job but Cuthbertson had retired a few years back and had not been replaced, nor was likely to be. The indoor staff was reduced to herself, Ina Munro promoted from kitchen-maid to cook, Jenny Paterson from the Lodge was maid-of-all-work, Jenkins who was Mr Myers' servant and Bessie still in the nursery but acting housemaid in the term time now that Nanny had passed to her rest.

Meg dreaded her law agent's visits. He was always a bearer of bad news. This time was no exception. 'I believe the time has come, Mrs Myers, to cut our losses. There has been an offer for Fisherton.'

'Fisherton?' Meg was appalled. How had it come to this? She had tried so hard to retrench. 'You know we can never let it go,' she declared. 'It's part of my nephew's inheritance. The Trust will not allow it.'

'I have already been in touch by the telegraph with Colonel Moncrieff. He agrees with me. Better Fisherton than the Hall. Fisherton is a continual drain on our resources. As you know only too well, Mrs Myers, the rents never quite cover the outlay. Let it go and with careful husbandry the Hall and its policies will remain intact hopefully for the time being.'

'And my own inheritance? ' she asked. 'Why may I not use that to save Fisherton?' She could hear the defiance in her voice for she knew the answer only too well. Squandered. Much of her fortune that had gone towards the shiny new taps, the sparkling clear water, and then there was the Bothy. A few shillings here to save a family from the

229

Poor House, a few pounds there when the fishing season was bad. Over the years it had mounted up. Then there were Victor's debts and expenses, surprisingly high for an invalid.

Mr Macmurtrie said nothing. He did not need to. They both remembered only too well the squalid little bills he had been required to settle for Mr Myers from his wife's dwindling fortune. Mr Macmurtrie's blood had long ceased to boil at the thought of Mrs Myers' miserable excuse for a husband. What was the use? He was a sick man, a shadow of himself and still there were bills to be settled.

'The truth is, Mrs Myers, the estate owes around £10,000. Interest accrues every hour of the day. The offer for the estate of Fisherton, harbour and curing shed is £15,000. We would be mad not to accept.'

'Who is offering?' she asked. 'Is it the Mortons?' She would not sell to the Mortons of Point. Her father would turn in his grave.

'It's not the Mortons,' Mr Macmurtrie assured her, but truthfully he could not swear to it. The name of the interested party was unknown to him, and, in spite of his business connections and wide inquiries, he could find no trace of the company. It might indeed be the Mortons under a trade name but he did not think so. He had spoken to Lord Morton's factor who had laughed in his face. Fisherton was hardly a desirable acquisition.

'High Cloud Holdings is the name the company trades under. I've corresponded with their man of business, a respectable fellow with excellent references.'

'But why would they want Fisherton?' she asked.

'They wish to add the property to their portfolio. It's a good deal for the fisher folk, Mrs Myers. The cottages need more repairs, some to be made habitable.'

'The rents will go sky high. How will they manage? '

'The representative spoke of improvement to the harbour, the roads, a general upgrade. I strongly advise that you agree to the sale, Mrs Myers. An offer of this sort is not a common occurrence, I can assure you.

She rose and began to pace the morning room carpet. 'I need time to think,' she told him.

'We don't have time.'

Eventually they agreed that he could give her two days. 'I need to know by Friday at the very latest.'

Kirkton

Meg lost no time. She sent for the trap and put on her jacket and hat. She could make no decision of this magnitude on her own. Within a quarter of an hour, Sam and the pony trap were waiting at the door.

Sam was on his own now as groom with a young stable lad to help with the horses. Ordinarily she would have taken the trap herself or bicycled but her mind was too preoccupied.

'You drive, Sam,' she told him. Then it occurred to her. 'I hope you were not in the middle of your dinner?'

Sam had been, but he could see the state of his mistress. 'Where to, Ma'am?' he asked as he handed her up into the seat beside him.

'The schoolhouse.' Her hands would not stop shaking so she clasped them together on her lap. 'How are the children, Sam?' she asked because that was what she always asked.

'Well enough, thank you for asking.'

'And Effy?' She always asked for Effy who had taken Andrew to her breast and to her heart when Isabella died. Sometimes she felt a little guilty for Andrew had grown sturdy and flourished in comparison with Effy's youngest bairn, Daniel, who was a wee scrap and prone to every current ailment. Meg knew Daniel better than most of the

231

estate children for he was Andrew's chosen companion on his childish escapades.

Sam nodded. 'Aye, Effy's fine. Thank you for the asking.'

Sam was the first to break the silence that followed. 'Mr Myers? How is he doing, these days, Ma'am?'

Meg sighed. She did not want to think of Victor, not now. Once her thoughts fixed themselves in that groove they were hard to shift. She shook her head a little as if to get rid of a troublesome fly. 'As well as can be expected, Sam. No better but no worse, I think.'

And then there was silence. The early April day bloomed and blossomed as the old mare trotted down the south avenue and took the road to Kirkton.

The short schoolhouse drive was lined with daffodils and grape hyacinths, blue and gold under the three tall sycamores that overhung the playground. It was full of noisy busy children, the boys in one enclosure to the west of the school building, the girls in a shaded and secluded area behind the classrooms. Sam drove past them and stopped at the schoolhouse door. Mr Vass's assistant, a new young fellow with a flourishing beard and whiskers who was supervising the boys, hurried over and handed her down. At the same moment Helen opened the door. If she was put out at having their luncheon interrupted she showed no sign of it.

Meg thanked the young man whose name she had momentarly forgotten and allowed herself to be fussed over by Helen who drew her inside the front door. 'My dear Mrs Myers, has something happened? How can we help?'

At the same moment Hugh Vass emerged from the dining room. 'Miss Megaidh? What has happened?'

The kindness in their voices, their concern was her undoing. Meg did not often cry but to her shame the tight knot of anxiety, the sense of failure, the burden of responsibility suddenly loosened and her eyes filled with tears which tumbled and splashed, unstoppable down her cheeks.

'My dearest Meg,' said Helen, dispensing with formalities, full of concern. 'Whatever can be wrong?'. Then she turned to her husband, 'Take Mrs Myers into the parlour, Hugh. I'll brew some tea.'

Hugh put his arm around her shoulders and drew her into the parlour. A fire had been recently lit and the room was sunny and fragrant with early daffodils. The touch of Hugh's arm, the scent of the flowers, the warmth in the room was so comforting that Meg wept the harder. Her tears turned into heart-broken sobs. Hugh said nothing but led her to the sofa and still with his arm around her shoulders sat there beside her and waited until gradually the sobs subsided and the tears dried. He passed her his handkerchief as if she were a child and she wiped her eyes.

As she breathed in the faint scent of soap suds from the handkerchief she was aware that this was all she had ever wanted, Mr Vass's arm around her, his body close, herself safe. Then she remembered why she was there and marvelled that her heart's desire and her greatest dread had come together on this sofa in this moment. Even as she thought it the moment was gone. Helen came back into the room with a tray neatly set with a lace cloth, a pot of China tea and a plate of homemade shortbread biscuits. Mr Vass rose, leaving her suddenly cold and bereft on the sofa. She was about to speak but he held up his hand. 'Not a word, Miss Megaidh, until you've had some tea. *Caisg*!'

She looked up at him. His eyes were kind as always, his Gaelic pleased her as he knew it would, even though he was telling her to shut up. She noticed because she could not help herself that he had grown a little stout, his hair once so dark and abundant had thinned and grown grey. He was no longer the handsome young parson-schoolmaster she had swooned over in her adolescent dreams, but she loved him still. She loved him dearly but she knew she was not really in love with him. How strange was that. She could not remember a time when she had not been in love with him. And now she was not. That was sad. She said nothing as she sipped the scalding tea. The shortbread she could not eat.

After a moment Helen touched her husband's arm. 'I'll leave you to it,' she told him and to Meg she said, 'If you need me, I'll be next door.'

'No,' said Meg. ' Don't go, Helen. I would like you to stay. I would value your advice.' She was as surprised at herself as Helen was. Always when Meg had problems - and there had been many of them over the years - she took them to Hugh alone. This Helen understood on two levels, as a parish priest and as her chosen *confidente*.

So now she hesitated. She looked inquiringly at her husband who nodded briefly. If he too was surprised he did not show it. As a compromise she took the chair furthest from the sofa and waited.

'Now tell us what has happened, Miss Megaidh,' Hugh said 'Is all well with Andrew?'

Anxiety welled up again in Meg. She clutched the handkerchief in her lap. 'Andrew comes home for the holidays next Thursday. But how am I to tell him? How am I to say that Fisherton must be sold. Mr Macmurtrie has just told me. There has been an offer.'

The Vasses listened in silence as Meg tried to explain the history of the estate's complicated finances.

'It's all my fault,' she cried wretchedly. 'I am entirely responsible. If I hadn't insisted on piped water and that expensive drainage system all would be well. I was advised at the time that it was a mistake but I would not listen. I had to know best. I always think I know best and now see where it has led me! I have betrayed my father, let Isabella down and lost Andrew his inheritance.'

'You did what you thought was right. You cannot blame yourself for that,' said Hugh heartily. He had been one of the few to encourage her and even now he did not doubt that she had been right. 'Look at the good that was done. Cholera a thing of the past. Typhoid eliminated.'

'Surely,' said Helen, 'the estate can be run profitably without Fisherton? What about the farms, the other properties?'

She spread her hands. 'What farms? What properties? Apart from the Mains most of them have been sold to sitting tenants.'

'Your mother was a wealthy woman, was she not?' Hugh said.

'And both I and my husband have been profligate, I fear, ' she said shortly. 'I made an imprudent marriage.' She despised herself for admitting the truth for even now she did not like to speak ill of poor wretched Victor.

'What of Colonel Moncrieff, Andrew's father? Can he not help?' Hugh asked quietly. He had known, as most of Inverally knew that the estate was in trouble, but not that it had sunk so low. He was shocked and upset for her.

'James has his own concerns. Apart from Isabella's share of my mother's bequest he has litte more than his army pay. As a trustee he has already wired Macmurtrie his permission. He supports Andrew financially of course, but there is little more he can do.'

'Who is the purchaser?' Helen asked.

'The name is unknown to Mr Macmurtrie. Some company based in Liverpool that calls itself High Cloud Holdings.' Meg rocked herself in an agony of indecision. 'Oh advise me, please tell me. What am I to do?'

'What choice do you have?' Hugh asked gently.

She shook her head. 'If we sell, the debts are cleared and the estate unburdened but for how long without an income? For myself I care nothing. Victor and I can move into the Dower house. Andrew is young. He can make his own way in the world, but the fisher folk what of them? Who will care for them? I had such hopes to install indoor conveniences, even gas lighting into their houses but now that will never happen. The new landlord will no doubt bleed them dry. Oh what am I to do? What can I do?'

'How long do you have to make up your mind?' Hugh asked.

'Not long. Mr Macmurtrie is anxious not to lose the offer. A few days at most.'

'Let me at least try to identify the buyer. They may be good people.'

The Hall

At one o'clock precisely the Emporium staff dispersed, the doors were locked and Jared opened the house door. He could smell lentil soup and he was hungry but he was even more anxious to share his news with Fanny. Most of his customers had been bursting to spread the gossip. Fisherton was definitely to be sold.

Fanny nodded. 'The word is everywhere. But who is buying?' she asked him as Mrs Mack ladled out the hot fragrant soup. 'That's what we all want to know.'

'High Cloud Holdings is the name,' Jared told her. 'No one seems to know who they are. If Miss Megaidh knows she hasn't told Mr Myers.'

'The sooner the better,' Fanny said. cryptically with feeling.

Jared knew not to ask her why. She had learned from her father never to discuss the shop's debtors over the dinner table, not even with her husband. It was, however, common knowledge that the estate was heavily in debt. Rumour had it that some years past, the old laird had made a bad investment in a South American railway venture and it had crashed. So Mr Jenkins had told him somewhat furtively on one of his monthly visits to the Hall.

'It's my mother I'm concerned for,' Jared said, 'not forgetting the rest of them down there. The rents will go sky high.'

'You know my feelings on that matter,' said Fanny. 'It's high time we moved your mother to more suitable accommodation. There's a nice little house for rent up the Brae. You know the one, next door to Miss Agnes Gallie.Your mother would be much better off there and the children could see more of her.'

Jared frowned. 'I agree, but you try shifting her. You know she'll never move.'

'I don't understand it,' said Fanny. 'There's nothing to keep her in Fisherton. It would be a step up for her in the world.'

It would indeed, thought Jared whose imagination had already planted her mother in that nice, stone-built, semi-detached villa in Kirkton that shared a solid wall with Miss Gallie.

'I suppose it's Jonas and poor Evie and the bairns that keep her there,' Fanny said as Mrs Mack cleared the soup plates and brought in poached salmon with boiled potatoes and cabbage. 'Your salmon, Father,' she told the old man loudly who sat silently in a world of his own at the far end of the table. He had grown very deaf of late.

But Jared knew that it was not Jonas who kept his mother in Fisherton, nor the black loon who had become her lodger. He knew because he had always known that she still believed that Donnaidh was alive and that one day he might

237

need somewhere he would remember as home. 'I'll speak to her again, but don't count on it, ' he told his wife.

Thursday was half-day in Inverally. Every four to six weeks he still trudged up the Brae to the Hall (or if the weather was inclement he took the trap) with the apothecary's sealed package in his pocket. That he continued to return with the two sealed envelopes, one for the apothecary, remained a bit of a mystery but so far he had outlived his curiosity. No doubt there were good reasons and he did not need to know.

Mr Myers was a shadow of himself these days. Seldom left his bed, hardly acknowledged his presence and backgammon was a pleasure long past. He slept most of the time often disturbed by uncomfortable dreams. 'The tonic helps 'im sleep,' or so Mr Jenkins had explained some years ago now. Old Jenkins could do with a bit of care himself. Thin and bent and with a debilitating tremor, he somehow managed to keep Mr Myers clean and cared for. He seldom, if ever, saw Miss Megaidh.

Mr Jenkins had a glass of brandy waiting for him as usual, which he served in the old butler's pantry.

'I hear there's been an offer for Fisherton, Mr Jenkins,' Jared said.

'Right enough,' said the old man. 'They're very low about it h'upstairs, but as h'I told Mr Myers you can't 'ave your cake and eat it.'

'Not much cake in Mr Myers' life, I would think,' said Jared taking another swallow of his brandy.

'You'd be surprised,' said Jenkins.

'I would be, right enough,' said Jared. 'He's not been out of his room for - how long now, Mr Jenkins?'

'There's some things you go on paying for all your life - and it won't stop there.'

'Such as?' Jared was curious now.

'What do you think's in that envelope, Mr Macreedie?' he asked slyly.

'None of my business, I'm sure.'

'Right enough, Mr Macreedie. No one else's business.'

Jared rose to his feet. 'I'd best be on my way.' He pocketed the two envelopes as usual. His own fee for facilitating the order would pay for a pleasant hour or so at the hotel saloon bar.

Outside on the sweep of gravel he met Miss Megaidh with the two dogs at her heel. She looked small, older, thinner and he found himself remembering the bright, inquisitive girl she had been. What must it be like saddled to an invalid with all the cares of the estate on her shoulders. She was hardy. He would give her that.

'Good afternoon, Jared,' she called out.

He took off his hat as he greeted her.

'You are so kind, Jared, visiting Mr Myers the way you do. He appreciates it, you know, and so do I.'

'It's no trouble, Madam.' He wondered if she knew the reason for his visits.

'How did you find him today?'

'Not too good, Madam, to be honest. He was sleeping.''

She sighed and after a moment changed the subject. 'How is your mother, Jared? You've no doubt heard there are likely to be some changes in Fisherton?'

'Aye, Madam.' It occurred to him that his mother might listen to Miss Megaidh. 'I'd like to get her moved up to Kirkton. Mrs Myers. Could you maybe have a word?'

'Certainly. I'll do my best, Jared.'

He thanked her and watched as she crossed the gravel and entered the house. As he walked down the east avenue he was suddenly for the first time deeply curious about the other envelope simply addressed to *Mr J Higgins*, c/o *the Royal Station Hotel*. He presumed J Higgins to be the apothecary or his assistant who collected his renmuneration from the hotel. This had always mildly surprised Jared for most medications from Inverness were delivered to and collected from the Emporium. Before returning home, he would take this particular envelope straight to the hotel where, as per instructions, he would watch it locked into the hotel safe to await collection. Up till now he had been incurious as to the actual contents of the bulkier envelope. Today, however, with the future of Fisherton in doubt, he could not help wondering how much the tonic cost. Under one of the great budding trees that lined the east avenue he would not be seen.

It was easy enough to prize open the manilla flap. He would re-glue it later so that no one could tell, except, he realised, that they could. Any fool would know that they had been tampered with. A new envelope would have to be found. He did not care. His curiosity had been aroused.

The apothecary's envelope contained a sheaf of ten pound notes. Jared counted them carefully. Two hundred pounds? Every month or so? No wonder Fisherton was on the market. No wonder the estate was said to be bankrupt. But why? What was so special about the medication?

Milton

It had begun to drizzle, that fine mist-like rain that soaks everything in seconds. Lady Cynthia Morton and her daughter were in the small coach on their way to the timber yard when Adela noticed Jared on the road.

'Mama, Mama! There's that nice man from the Emporium!'

'So it is,' said Cynthia. She tapped the roof of the coach to stop the groom 'Can we give you a lift, Jared?' she called from the coach window.

Cynthia was rather pleased with herself because she was very sure that her mother-in-law would not have approved. Stopping the coach to give a lift to a tradesman was not done in Morton circles. Nor, she believed, would Jared have accepted had it not been raining so heavily. He was already uncomfortably wet.

'Thank you, my Lady,' he said climbing in and trying to keep his wet clothing to himself. 'That's a nasty unexpected shower.' He noticed the child who was only a little younger than his Kenny. 'Good afternoon, Miss Adela.'

He smiled at them both. Cynthia's heart turned over at that smile. She had always had a soft spot for Jared and she looked on Fanny as a friend. Well, almost a friend. She was not on her guest list, of course. Intimacy was out of the question. One had to be careful, or so her mother-in-law continually threatened. But Jared, out of his long white swathe of an apron, away from the counter in the Emporium, had turned from a shop-keeper into a man, a rather unexpectedly beautiful man if such a description was viable, and Cynthia was exhilarated.

'How is Mrs Macreedie?' she asked.

'Well enough, thank you. And Lord Morton?'

Lucky Fanny, she thought, to have this god of a man at her dinner table… in her bed. The thought made her blush. She felt the heat start somewhere in her belly and rise up to flood her cheeks with colour.

'What are you doing out in the rain, Jared?' Adela asked pertly.

He answered her lightly but his eyes were on her mother. He had always seen Lady Morton as a pretty woman certainly, but he had never properly looked at her. Here in the close confines of the coach where she was neither a customer nor gentry, he saw her as she was, a very attractive woman whose marriage had turned her from the daughter of

241

a tradesman, no grander than his Fanny, into one of the great folk. He was not too blind to notice that she was flirting with him, and he was certainly not too pious to admit to enjoying it.

In spite of Fanny's worries, of which he was entirely aware, Jared had been faithful in deed at least, if not always in thought. There were surprisingly few opportunities to stray. The Emporium was always busy and the female assistants respectable spinsters. The Royal Station bar where, on occasion, he was able to escape was for men only. On the other hand, Inverally was full of pretty women. They came into the shop and purchased their cotton reels and ribbons and left again with sometimes a small significant glance in his direction. Mostly he was too busy to notice.

Here in the intimacy of the coach, however, his eyes lingered. He liked what he saw and Cynthia, like all pretty women used to admiration, was entirely aware of his interest.

'Where can I take you, Mr Macreedie?' she asked rounding her large blue eyes.

'The Brae end will do fine, thank you. It seems to have stopped raining'. He had been going down to see his mother but he did not expect or want to be taken to Fisherton.

'If you're sure?'

Conversation followed on conventional lines. It was not, however, what was said but how he looked. Cynthia was astonished. How could she not have noticed, properly noticed, this Lancelot of a man? All too soon the journey was over. She tapped on the roof of the coach which stopped precisely at the cross roads at the Brae head. He thanked her and got out, waited and watched until the coach turned left towards Gallie's yard.

'Jared's nice,' said Adela waving him goodbye. 'I like him. Don't you like him, Mama?'

Cynthia did not answer her directly. 'He's Mr Macreedie to you, not Jared.'

'But you call him Jared. Everyone calls him Jared. Why can't I?'

'You can call him Jared in the shop, but out of the shop he's Mr Macreedie.'

'That's silly.'

'No. It's good manners.'

Unlike Jared, Cynthia had not remained faithful to her spouse. She had only one rule where other men were concerned. Not to be found out. She had learned to be discreet and so far she had been successful. No one, not even her hated mother-in-law, could take exception to her weekly visits home chaperoned by her own daughter. If Mama happened to invite one of her admirers to tea, offered to amuse Adela, and left them alone together for an hour in the parlour, was it her fault if sometimes a hand was held or a kiss stolen? Mama, who had grown to hate the insufferable Mortons, mother and son, took a particular delight in encouraging her daughter.

Without the admiration of men, the physical delight in a few stolen kisses, Cynthia would have long since curled up and died. She needed affection and admiration as a plant needs sunlight. Lord Morton was not an attentive husband. He showed her no affection and only the occasional rough often painful intimacy. The dowager Lady Morton was her enemy at the hearth. Adela, usually in the care of nursemaid or governess, was hardly a companion. Most of the time she felt unloved and unwanted. Today she was here to see her mother certainly, with whom she intended to leave her daughter, but also to see her stepfather and in particular her stepfather's employee, Aaron Morton.

'Stay with your grandmama, Adela. I am going to find Papa Josh.'

243

'I want to come with you,' her daughter whined.

'Don't be selfish, darling. You know how Grandmama Gallie dotes on you. You can see Papa Josh later.'

Not even Hilda knew of this particular liaison. She genuinely thought her daughter crossed the yard to see her stepfather and was glad of it. She knew Josh doted on her.

'I don't think he's back yet,' Hilda told her. 'He had business in Point.'

'I'll go and see,' Cynthia told her sweetly. 'You know how he likes me to come,' she coaxed. Hilda nodded absently. Her thoughts had already turned to entertaining her adored granddaughter. 'Ludo or Snap?' she asked. Adela taking her hand wheedled, 'could we make fudge? Pleeease?' and they were gone.

Cynthia picked her way across the muddy yard, between the stacks of sweet smelling poles, planks and beams to her stepfather's office. The scent of resin permeated the yard. She knew well enough that he was not there for he always met a business colleague for a 'pie, a pint and a pow-wow' at the Royal Station bar on Thursdays and was seldom home before four o'clock which was why she was here in the first place. Her little gold watch (one of his many gifts) told her it was only a little before three. As they had driven into the yard, she had already seen Aaron entering the office. Sometimes, she thought, the anticipation was almost as gratifying as the event; almost.

She pushed open the office door and feigned astonishment. 'Mr Morton!' she declared. 'How nice to see you again.'

He rose immediately and strolled over to her, took her hand and raised it to his lips. 'Good day, Lady.'

'What are you doing here?' she asked provocatively.

He laughed. 'I wonder,' he drawled.

Their assignations – and there had been several since the day he had visited Lord Morton claiming kinship and been virtually thrown out   for his presumption. During the summer months they had met twice in the old summerhouse, hidden from Point Castle, on evenings when Lord Morton was absent from home. During the winter only once

'I work here,' he told her. 'Had you forgotten?'

She reached up to touch his hair. She loved the feel of his tight curls, that looked like wire but felt surprisingly like wool.

'How did you know I would come?' she whispered. (She herself had suggested the arrangement at their last meeting).

'I guess I must be mighty clever,' he teased. The date had been etched on his memory.

Of course it could only be kisses. So far, at least, it had only been kisses. With one eye on the yard through the office window, her ear cocked for the sound of her stepfather's horse, she enjoyed the wickedness of it all, the danger, the thrill, and, not least, the cuckolding of her husband. She also told herself firmly that this particular affair could not go on as it was. Aaron would not always be content with a few stolen kisses. Perhaps it was time to add a new admirer to her list of conquests - a grocer. A timberman and a grocer at the same time! How angry they would be at Point Castle if they knew. She also was well aware that Aaron's kisses were not enough for her. He had somehow woven his beautiful black face into her heart.

'Dearest Aaron,' she murmured caressing his cheek. She was still deeply aroused by the contrast between his black skin and her pink fingers. 'This can't go on.'

'You don't mean that,' he said somewhat lazily as if his heart were not in the least broken. She had said it before. 'I thought you liked me?'

'I do. I do. I do care for you, Aaron,' she assured him, round-eyed and yielding. 'That's why I can't see you again.'

'That's a big shame,' he said. 'Let me tell you something, pretty lady. I am not always going to be logger in a timber yard. I have plans. Big plans, right here in Inverally. Stick with me and I can give you a real good time.'

'How sweet you are,' she murmured, 'but. you don't really want me. You just want revenge for your great grandmother.' That was how it had started and to begin with she had been happy to play along; but now?

'That too,' he admitted. 'Revenge is sweet, I'm told, but this is more that revenge, Cyn. I have never in my life met a dame like you.'

She loved that he called her Cyn. She loved everything about him.

He was the first to hear Josh Gallie's horse in the yard. Half-hidden by a shutter they watched as someone ran up to hold it while he dismounted. Aaron kissed her hand and by the time his master approached was gone, without another word, through the back entrance to the office. Aaron Morton had no wish to be compromised any more than she, not at this stage of his life. He wanted Cyn, however, and whatever she might say, he was not prepared to give her up. Humiliating his kinsman was no longer his main reason. He realised that he had fallen for her big time.

Cynthia smoothed her clothing, adjusted her hat and turned to greet her stepfather. 'At last, Papa Josh! I have been waiting ages for you.'

He grinned at her delightedly, and kissed her on the cheek. 'And what can I do for you today, Miss Goody Two Shoes?' He was as pleased as any doting parent to see her.

The Hall
Andrew jumped out of the train and looked about him on the crowded Inverness platform. Who would be meeting him

today? He hoped it would be Sam. And yes it was Sam. There he was at the barrier holding his hat, a small frown on his brow as he tried to make out which of the scrum of kilted young boys crowding the platform was Master Andrew. The holidays had started.

'Sam!' he shouted. 'Can we get a sweetie at the station stall? Please?'

'No time, Master Andrew. The Point connection leaves in ten minutes. Let's find your luggage.'

They trudged over to Platform Three where the two-coach engine steamed as it waited on the branch line to Invernally. Nearly home. This was almost the best bit of the hols, the whole four unbroken weeks of the spring break stretched out before him like a red carpet.

The third class carriage smelt of fish and, come to think of it, so did Sam,. 'You smell of fish,' he told him. 'I don't mind. I quite like the smell of fish,' he lied hastily thinking he might have offended the groom who was his third favourite grown-up in all the world. In fact he hated the smell of fish almost as much as the taste.

'Aye, no doubt,' said Sam. 'I came up on the early train with the fisher wives and their creels.' He felt in his pocket and drew out a paper bag. 'Strippet balls.'

'Thanks Sam,' he said delightedly. 'My absolute favourite.' He crammed one into his mouth, remembered in time and offered the bag to Sam, who took one too. The smell of fish was only a little less overpowering than the peppermint.

'How's everyone?' he asked. Although he was well into his fourth year at St Mary's, this had become a ritual question posed during that first hour of freedom. It took most of the forty minutes journey to ask for everyone he knew by name starting with Uncle Victor. Andrew worried about Uncle Victor. Though Danny was his best friend, Uncle

Victor was and always had been his favourite person in the world. Aunt Meg was mostly all right too as was Bessie but they were such fusspots. Why did old people always worry? What was the point? If you worried about a bad thing, and it happened, that added up to double the disaster.

'Can Danny come up to the Hall to play this afternoon?'

'Your auntie may have something planned.'

'No she won't and even if she has, Danny can come too.'

'He'll not be back from the school till four-ish.'

Sam loaded his trunk on to the trap.

'Can I drive?' Andrew pleaded. Once they were out of the traffic in Station Square Sam handed him the reins. He noticed immediately that the spring had gone out of the garron's step. She was plodding.

'What's wrong with Jess?' he asked anxiously.

'Old age,' said Sam. The boy needed to know. Old Jess was past retiring age. She should have been put out to grass long since, but there was no telling Miss Megaidh. No point. The boy knew.They all knew there was no money to replace her. 'We'll need to walk the Brae.'

'Right,' said Andrew. 'What about the others, Tom and Beauty?' Tom was his pony and Beauty was his aunt's ancient mare.

'Nobody grows any younger, Master Andrew, horses included.'

'Tom's too small for me anyhow. I need a new pony, Sam. Danny could ride Tom.'

'You'll have to speak to your auntie about that, Master Andrew.'

This was not Andrew's first inkling that life at the Hall was changing. Everything looked a bit shabby, worn out, old. Even his little Aunt Meg looked smaller, as she came out of the front door to welcome him.

'Had a good journey?' she asked briskly. They shook hands formally. 'Goodness me you've grown! Your favourite stovies for luncheon. Off you go and see Bessie. She's waiting for you.'

Bessie at least hadn't changed. He flung himself into her arms and they hugged and kissed and then he looked critically round the old schoolroom. 'Where's my treasure chest? You've moved it!'

The precious little chest which had belonged to his deceased Uncle Andrew was not in its usual place beside his play box under the nursery table.

'Leave your eyes behind you at that school, did you?' Bessie joked because of course it was there, tucked in behind the play box, safe and locked.

He had a sudden rush of anxiety. What about the key? He ran into the night nursery next door to the schoolroom and stopped in the doorway. Only one bed. His. Where had Bessie's gone?

'You're a big big boy now, Master Andrew. I've moved into Nanny's room. Now she's gone, your auntie thought it best.'

Of course. How could he have forgotten? Aunt Meg had written to tell him that Nanny had died way back in January. Not that he minded too badly. He hadn't seen much of her these past few years and truthfully he had always been a bit scared of her. She mumbled weird things and she looked at you as if she could see into right inside your head. But he would miss Bessie, that sprint into her warm bed after one of his dragon nightmares. Drowning inside the dragon.

Bessie could read his thoughts. 'I'm only next door,' she reassured him.

The key was still wound round the brass nob on the bedstead exactly where he had hidden it.

The gong boomed downstairs. 'That's your dinner ready. Mind and wash your hands first,' she called after him.

Some things hadn't changed. The stovies were trumps.

'When can I go and see Uncle Victor?' he asked.

'Please don't speak with your mouth full, Andrew,' his aunt said a little waspishly.

He sighed audibly. She was such a fusspot, worse than Matron at school. 'But when?'

'After luncheon. Ask Jenkins. Don't stay too long. Your uncle tires easily.' She paused. 'I thought we could both go down to Fisherton this afternoon. I have some calls to make. What about coming with me?'

'Need I, Aunt?' he protested. 'I've got plans.'

'Where are you going?'

'Out.' How did he know where he was going? There were a thousand and one things to do, people to see.

His aunt smiled. 'You're getting so like your Uncle Andrew. He was always going 'out' too.' Her smile shrank. 'Just be careful, won't you, Andy. Promise me you won't go anywhere near the water.'

He scrubbed the last of the rhubarb tart off his mouth with his napkin and pushed back his chair. 'Please may I be excused?'

'I mean it, Andrew.'

'Of course not,' he told her. 'I promise.' He knew what had happened to his uncle and he had no intention of going near the sea. Nor was Fisherton on his agenda. He disliked Fisherton, the predominating smell of fish, the shawled curious women, the staring bare-foot bairns. Aunt Meg was forever trying to take him down to Fisherton.

He left the dining room and crossed the wide hallway to Uncle Victor's room. Mr Jenkins answered his knock.

'Oh h'it's yourself. We've been h'expecting you.' His lined face was more monkeyish than ever.

'Hello, Jimmy. Can I see Uncle Victor, please?'

'H'I don't know. Can you?' he teased, his small bright monkey eyes twinkling.

Andrew laughed. It was an old joke and he always fell into the same trap. 'May I see Uncle Victor, please?'

'Aye, you may. 'E's been waitin' for you.'

Uncle Victor was in his bath chair, wearing his velvet dressing gown with the frogging down the front. Even Andrew could see how much his health had deteriorated. His eyes were sunk deep into his skull, the skin around them bruised almost black. His teeth, the few that were left were discoloured and his cheeks deep blotched hollows.

'Hhhail the ccconquewing hewo!' Victor croaked. His voice was barely audible. 'They lllet you out, then?'

'For four weeks,' Andrew told him.

'Dddon't ttttell me for gggood bbbehaviour?'

'Not exactly. I got beaten twice.' He had been longing to tell someone, boast just a little. Beating had a good side as well as a bad side. It was sore of course but it scored big points in the dorm.

To his surprise Uncle Victor was not amused. 'Sssods,' he whispered. 'Bbbbuggers, the lot of them.'

Andrew was elated and just a little shocked. Those words alone merited a beating at school.

'I don't mind,' he said.

Uncle Victor fell silent, literally fell. His head dropped a little sideways and he closed his eyes.

Andrew looked at Jimmy questioningly.

'Give 'im a minute.' Jimmy told him. Andrew waited.

Suddenly Victor flicked open his eyes. 'You ssstill have that tttweasure chchchest, Andy?'

Andrew nodded.

'I've gggot sssomething for it.'

He held out a frail hand to Jimmy who handed him a small brown paper parcel tied with string. Andrew unwrapped it carefully and exclaimed in delight.

He'd always wanted a decent penknife of his own. All the other boys at school had them. He'd had to lie and tell them he'd lost his, or be laughed at. Although he'd dropped broad hints to Aunt Meg and written to ask his father when he had first gone away to school, both of them had completely ignored him. When he had grumbled to Bessie, she had told him firmly that he was to young to have any sort of knife. He kind of understood the grown-ups' reasoning. His Uncle Andrew had had an accident with water; so he wasn't allowed near water. A couple of local boys at the parish school had died in knife fights so he wasn't allowed a knife. They worried about him all the time, but he could take care of himself as he was always trying to tell them.

The new knife was beautiful with a back shiny handle and lots of gadgets and a particularly sharp blade. He saw himself casually producing it at school to sharpen his pencils. It was better than most, bigger too, he thought with joy. He touched the blade carelessly with his thumb and to his delight it drew a thin line of blood. It was a proper knife. He was loud in his appreciation.

''It's nnnot a tttoy, Andy. Ppput it in your tttweasure chhchest. Kkkeep it sssafe for mmme'.

Andrew nodded wordlessly. He had no intention of hiding it away in his treasure chest. He couldn't wait to show Danny.

Uncle Victor was speaking to him. 'Sorry?' he said. His mind was miles away. Uncle Victor broke into a cough. Jimmy said. 'Your uncle was asking if you knew about Fisherton.'

Andrew frowned. 'What about Fisherton. I told Aunt I didn't want to go with her. I hate Fisherton,' he said flicking the blade open and shut.

'Tththhat's all wight then,' whispered Victor and closed his eyes.

Jimmy winked at him. You never knew exactly what Jimmy's winks were about, but he took it as a hint to go. 'Bye Uncle Victor. Thanks again.'

Victor did not open his eyes but lifted his hand in acknowledgement.

Outside the door Andrew said to Jimmy. 'What did Unce Victor mean about Fisherton?'

'Did they not tell you, then? H'it's to be sold.'

'Sold? I don't understand. I thought it was mine.'

Jimmy shrugged his thin bent shoulders. 'Seemingly they need the money.'

Suddenly Andrew minded very much indeed.

He found his aunt in the porch adjusting her hat. The trap with Tom rather than Jess in harness was at the door.

'Aunt,' he called out. 'Can I come with you?'

'Of course. Marsali will be so pleased to see you.'

There was no sign of Sam. The stable boy handed her up and gave her the reins.

Fisherton

Meg was impressed. He was still only ten but he was managing Tom splendidly. Her heart was suddenly filled with affection for her nephew. He was a dear little boy. Isabella would have been so proud of him. She would have to tell him now before she told the others. It was only right that he should know before she sent word to Macmurtrie.

But he already knew. 'Aunt,' he said in his childish treble voice. 'Is it true that Fisherton is to be sold?'

253

Meg sighed. Who could have told him? 'I'm afraid so.'

'But I thought it belonged to me.'

'It does and it doesn't,' she began. It was harder to explain than she had thought possible and she was aware that she was not making much sense. 'You know about the Trust, don't you? It was set up to look after the estate until you become twenty-one. Your father, your Aunt Hilary, Mr Macmutrie and myself are the Trustees. We are doing our best but the truth of the matter is that the estate has always been hard up. Now, partly due to a bad investment some years ago, we are seriously in debt. This offer for Fisherton is a godsend. Your father and Aunt Hilary think it best to accept. Otherwise we might have lost the Hall and we couldn't let that happen to you. If we're careful, the rest of the estate will survive. I'm sorry, Andrew. More sorry that I can say.'

He was quiet for a moment, then he said, 'don't worry, Aunt,' and she was touched by the kindness in his voice. 'I never much liked Fisherton anyhow.'

But I did. I do, Meg wailed inwardly. She knew them all, the skippers, their crews, their wives, their children, their follies and their hopes. There was now a boat named after her mother, the *Aingeal* and Marsali had told her that Jonas' skipper's new zulu half-way completed in the boat yard at Point was to be called *Miss Meg*. How was she to break the news? This looked like abandonment. She could not even tell them the name of their new landlord.

There was no room for the trap in Silas Lane so she left it in the care of a crippled lad she'd known all his life and who now haunted the harbour hoping to earn a few pence.

'Good afternoon, Jacob,' she said to him briskly. 'Will you hold Tom for us?'

'Aye, Miss Megaidh. Is he frisky today?'

'Alas, Jacob, Tom is never frisky these days,' she told him. 'I'll be in Silas Lane.'

'Very good, M'm. Is it to say goodbye then?'

'Goodbye?' she repeated stupidly.

'I never thought you'd be leaving us, M'm.'

'I'm not leaving, Jacob. Whatever gave you that idea?'

But she was. In a manner of speaking, she was. Marsali knew it. They all knew it. Jacob was only the first.

'I never thought it would come to this,' Marsali said when Meg confirmed what they had all heard. 'What would your poor dear mother have thought?' Meg was on the edge of tears. She knew if she started she would never stop.

'And what about poor Master Andrew? What does he think about it, I wonder?' she said as if he were not in the room and able to answer for himself.

'I'm all right, really,' he reassured her. And he was. He was thinking about what lay hidden in his sporran, the beautiful precious knife that he had not dared to show his aunt for fear it would be confiscated. That would have mattered a great deal more to him than the loss of Fisherton.

'Thank God for that,' Marsali told him with feeling.

Meg's tears were closer. In desperation she changed the subject. 'Jared and Mrs Fanny want you to move up to Kirkton. Would that not be a good idea?' she said forcing briskness into her voice.

'Aye mebbe,' Marsali agreed ambiguously. Meg did not press the matter.

It took two more hours to visit all the cottages. Some folk were in, but many were not, the men at sea and the women at work in the curing factory or on the shore after lug worms. Andrew had given up after the first two streets. He had noticed Seth, Danny's cousin, in one of the vennels. He wanted to show him the knife. He waited till Meg moved on.

Seth whistled in appreciation. 'It's a secret,' said Andrew pushing it back into his sporran as several older boys on their way back from school gathered round. 'One of them made a crack about his kilt which he couldn't hear properly but the others laughed, not kindly. The boy who had made the remark darted forward and tried to lift his kilt. As he swiped off his hand, Andrew remembered exactly why he hated Fisherton. He wished his aunt would hurry. It was past four o'clock and Danny would be waiting for him.

Meg returned eventually, tired and on edge, by which time the knife was safely stowed away in his sporran. Had she been less depressed, more aware, she might have seen it. She was a little disappointed in Andrew. He might have shown more interest. On the other hand, perhaps his attitude was a blessing now that Fisherton could never be his.

On their way home, Andrew prattled away about some den he and Danny were building in the wooded glen that led up to the moors. She was only half listening. Instead she was thinking that he was still so young. Why should he care about a collection of ramshackle cottages huddled together gable ends facing the sea for shelter in a storm. Why should she? But she did. She had known many sadnesses in her life but never one like this.

Milton

Aaron was supervising a new young sawyer. One of his workmates told him he was wanted immediately in the office. Now there was a coincidence. Word had come to him by telegram that the deal had been done. He had planned to speak to Mr Gallie in the dinner break himself..

'Come,' Josh called out in reply to his knock. He was expecting a shipload of pine at Point Harbour later that morning and had decided to send Morton with his foreman to inspect the load. The blackamoor (which was how he privately thought of Aaron) was proving himself to be a first rate timberman - rare enough - and as his foreman was getting on in years, Josh needed to know whether Aaron had sufficient knowledge to recognise - and the balls to reject - diseased timber whatever the size of the load. Without waiting for Aaron to speak he told him of his requirements. 'Think you can manage it?'

'I can, sir.' he told him.

'Good lad,' said Josh turning back to his ledgers.

There was no easy way to say it. 'Excuse me, Mr Gallie, may I have a word?'

Josh looked up. 'Well?'

'I'd like to tender my notice, sir. I shall be quitting your employment exactly one month from today.'

Josh was astonished and not a little angry.

'Got something better, have you?' he growled. 'Don't I pay you enough?'

'You've treated me well, Mr Gallie, but I think I told you my time here would be limited.'

He had forgotten, damn it. 'Going back to the States then?'

'Nothing like that. I'll still be here in Inverally.'

'A secret is it?' Josh snapped.

'No, sir. I shall be managing the Fisherton cottages for the new owner.'

'The devil you will! And who may that be?'

'A company called High Cloud Holdings. I'm due to take up my appointment one month from Monday next.'

'The devil you are!' Josh was astonished. Like everyone else he had heard the rumour that the Inverally estate was in deep waters financially. Like everyone else, he had also heard that Fisherton might be on the market. He had no idea that it had been sold. 'And who's behind this little venture then? Lord Morton?'

'No sir. I can assure you of that?'

'Then who?' Josh was deeply curious. It was hardly a bid for prosperity. The huddle of unsavoury cottages that comprised the Fisherton was, in his opinion, an unsightly, insanitary, deeply undesireable acquisition. The Myers' were well rid of it. Josh was his own accountant and well aware that his yard had several outstanding bills owed by the estate. What surprised him was that any one was prepared to pay good money for such a losing prospect.

'Who is the principal shareholder?' Josh was really curious. 'Wonder if he knows what he's taking on. Fisherton is hardly the land flowing with milk and honey.'

There could be no harm now surely in releasing his new employer's name. 'I was contacted way back in the state of Wyoming (no need to mention the prison) long before you employed me, Mr Gallie, by a Mr King.' No need to go into further details. For personal reasons to do with his own ancestry, he had accepted King's suggestion with interest, crossed the Atlantic on his payroll and come north to Inverally to acquaint himself with his own roots, prospect the area for Mr King, report back on the state of the village. When Aaron informed him that Fisherton was likely to go on the market, Mr King was interested to make him a further offer. High Cloud Holdings intended to put in a bid for the cottages. If the sale went through, a property manager would be required. The job was his if he wanted it. He would have been dumb to refuse.

'King, you say? Don't know the name,' said Gallie briskly. 'I shall be sorry to lose you, Morton. Don't envy you your new position. Strange folk in Fisherton, a law unto themselves. Seems to me this King fellow must have more money than sense.'

Aaron, now that he knew Fisherton intimately, could only agree, though he kept his opinion to himself. He had already

258

identified at least a dozen necessary repairs that the cottages required, the tenants were impoverished, but the pay was good and he had grown to like his landlady Mistress Macreedie. He got on well enough with most of the fishermen he met in the tavern, apart from Jonas Macreedie - but that was another story. He also knew that his presence in the area displeased his relative Lord Morton; another good reason for staying. As for his relative's wife, the desirable Lady Cynthia, she was another matter altogether.

'I shall expect you to work out your notice, Morton.'

'Of course, sir.'

Josh cleared his throat. 'I don't say this lightly and I don't say it often. If it doesn't work out with this King fellow, there will always be a job for you here.'

'Thank 'ee, Mr Gallie.' Knowing the state of Fisherton that might well be a valuable option. He was surprised that the Fisherton deal had gone through. He had been honest in his assessment of the amount of work to be done, held nothing back from High Cloud Holdings. As for Mr King, he was a much closer acquaintance than Aaron let on to Mr Gallie. He remembered the occasion they had first met. A gang of them in adjacent cages in the new Wyoming State Prison had been talking about their roots; German, Dutch, Irish – a load of Irish. 'Where you from, nigger? Darkest Africa?' someone had said not aggressively. He had said quickly before thinking, 'I got Scottish ancestors.'

That had caused some ribald laughter but afterwards a guy had come up to him, a fine fellow he was, well set up, burned brown and gold by the sun. He hadn't laughed He told him he too was a Scot and asked him whereabouts in Scotland his family came from. So he had told him what he knew: his great grand-daddy had been a Morton of somewhere called Point.

259

The fellow had opened his mouth in astonishment but before he could speak, Aaron had been dragged off and told to shut his mouth. He discovered afterwards the guy was called King. Don King. That had just been the beginning.

It was not until he had been living with Mistress Macreedie for a few months that he discovered the family bye-name. One of his mates in the timber yard had said, 'heard you got a room in Fisherton with Jonas King's mother.' He corrected himself immediately. 'Ach, of course, how would you know? It's Jonas Macreedie I mean.'

 After a few more questions, Aaron knew then for certain that Marsali's hopes had not been in vain.

Chapter Seven

Spring 1912

The Hall

Victor's brother Cedric had come north for the funeral which was surprisingly well attended. Mourners Meg had never met including some surprising local worthies in sombre black crowded the small church and overflowed into the surrounding grave yard; tavern and Royal Station Hotel habituees, tenants, shopkeepers, and gentry. She and Andrew, home for the Easter holidays, with Cedric and his wife, Susan, stood together outside St Moluag's to shake hands with the mourners and listen to their murmurs of condolence. None of them had much to say for most of them had not seen Victor for several years.

'Ah well, so my poor brother has gone at last,' Cedric said sanctimoniously on his arrival at the Hall. Cedric had grown stout and bald over the years. Otherwise he had not changed much. Meg, welcoming him, had realised almost with surprise that she had married the pick of the brothers...if you could call it a marriage. And yet...and yet... in spite of the fact they had never shared a bed, nor friends, nor many interests, their marriage had not been a complete failure. He had never been cruel or even unpleasant to her as some husbands were, or so their wives had confided tearfully to her in the Bothy, nor had she been forced into annual pregnancies like other women, aged beyond their years. Although she had never experienced the intimate side of marriage, she knew enough from all she heard in the Bothy to be thankful that she had not been forced to endure physical closeness where there was no love. Instead they had shared Andrew, had they not? Victor had redeemed himself for his spendthrift ways, his profligacy, his lack of interest in her by his relationship with Andrew.

'It is a wonder to me that Victor lasted so long,' her sister-in-law Susan contributed waspishly to which she had made no reply. It was true. He had been ill for years. A sudden wave of regret swept over Meg. Poor Victor, she thought. I could have been kinder.

She glanced at the young boy by her side, straight and tall in his Murray tartan kilt, his pale face smeared with tears and knew that he would miss him. Her thoughts flew to Jenkins. Standing a little apart dressed in a black suit that she recognised as having belonged to Victor, she wondered what on earth she would do with him. He was so bent and shrivelled and old that he could surely never work again. How he had managed to look after Victor was always a surprise to her. She thought of the cottages on the estate and remembered - as if she could ever forget - Fisherton. But she would not think of Fisherton now.

The crowd of mourners around the family mausoleum had thinned.

'Auntie Meg?' Andrew was looking at her. Almost thirteen years old, he was as tall as she was. He looked anxious and strained. 'Can we go now?'

The road outside St Moluag's was busy with departing vehicles. The closed carriage, seldom used these days, was waiting with Sam also clad in sombre black. At the same time Hugh Vass, still in his cassock emerged from the door of the mausoleum.

'Come with us?' she asked him. Helen, she knew, would already be up at the Hall for it was not the custom in Inverally for womenfolk, apart from close relatives, to attend a burial.

'Gladly,' he agreed. Still in his cassock he took a seat opposite her in the carriage. They were the last in the long line of vehicles to approach the Hall. Susan would happily be playing hostess in her absence.

Once Sam had started the horses, Hugh leaned towards her and covered her gloved hand with his own. 'How are you, Meg?'

She looked down at his broad thickly-veined hand engulfing her own and felt nothing. How her heart would have fluttered at one time, she thought sadly. Now she was comforted, but nothing more. She twisted her hand to return briefly his pressure and then removed it from his grasp.

'Well enough,' she replied, 'thank you. You have been such a support...you and Helen. The service was lovely.' Truthfully she did not know how she felt. Her heart was numb.

'What about you, Andrew?' He turned his attention to the boy.

Tears in his throat choked him so he did not immediately reply. He turned to his aunt, 'Where's Jimmy?' he asked almost accusingly.

Having given him no thought, she did not know and Andrew was right to be concerned. Hugh assured them both he would have found a lift from someone. 'I'm sure Mr Jenkins can take care of himself.'

She was not at all sure. 'What am I to do about Jenkins?' The question was directed more to herself than to Hugh. A year ago the solution would have been easy. If there were no free cottages on the immediate policies, Fisherton was always a last resort. Alas no longer.

'I want him to stay in the house!' Andrew declared hotly. Anger had replaced his grief. 'You can't turn him out, Aunt. I won't allow it.'

She was surprised, but knew, of course, he was right. 'For the time being,' she conceded. She would have to speak to him, find out what he wanted. But Andrew was right. He had

263

been an exemplary servant both to her father and to her husband. Without him how would she have managed? 'Let's see what he wants to do, shall we?' she said.

'I know what he wants,' Andrew only a little less hotly.

'Well, well,' said Hugh conciliatorily. 'Your aunt will do what's best for the poor fellow. You know that.'

Andrew was silent.

The drawing room was crowded. Mima had recruited wives of the outdoor staff including Effie to help distribute sandwiches and tea. Mima herself presided over the whisky turning a deaf ear to those she thought unworthy of a refill, with the exception of old Finlay, the gamekeeper, one of her favoured few. Over the years Meg had learned to appreciate Mima and vice versa. Mrs Shanks had retired several years past and, as part of the general retrenchment, she had not been replaced. Mima had stepped into her role as she had done with Cuthbertson. She ruled the depleted kitchen staff with a rod of steel.

'All going well?' Meg asked her quietly before starting to work her way though the room.

'Aye,' she replied. In her new role of senior servant, she had dropped the Ma'ams and Madams. If she had hoped to annoy her employer, Mima failed, for it took Meg several months to notice and when she did, she was amused. As she had written to Andrew's aunt and fellow trustee, Harriet Barraclough, she felt she should now call Mima, Mrs Black. Harriet was the closest she had to a woman friend. There was also Helen, of course, but that relationship had always been a little coloured by her fondness for Hugh.

Lord Morton bore down on her with his usual pomposity. His wife, the pretty Cynthia was on the other side of the room, flirting as usual in spite of her pregnancy. Her high tinkling laugh could be heard from time to time above the murmur of suitably subdued conversation.

'My deepest condolences, Mrs Myers,' he told her bowing slightly over her hand. 'My mother bids me pass on her regrets for your sad loss.'

'Please thank her, Lord Morton. And thank you and Lady Cynthia for your attendance today.'

'The least we could do. I was deeply sorry to hear of all your troubles. How do you do without the Fisherton estate?'

'It grieved us greatly to have to part with it. My mother would have been broken-hearted. She loved the fisher folk.'

No use pretending otherwise. The loss of Fisherton was like the amputation of a limb. Although she still kept up her visits to the Bothy, she believed she had no automatic right to visit the cottages as she had once done. Marsali had moved to Kirkton to be closer to her family, and the American, Aaron Morton, still lodged with her. She found herself resenting not the man himself so much as what he stood for. He had taken over the management of Fisherton and was in charge of the installation of the new indoor water closets. She had thought that the fisher folk would have been delighted, but far from it. The complaints voiced in the Bothy reminded her of the days old Wedderburn had installed dust bins at the end of the street. 'It's no' the same,' Anna Munro moaned. 'That black man always poking his nose in; the houses are a midden and the street no' safe for the bairns.'

'That won't last forever,' Meg had replied a little waspishly. 'This time next year you'll wonder how you ever managed without indoor water closets.'

'It aye seems to me that there is indecency in it; "going" in the hoose,' Anna murmured, her already pink cheeks reddening. 'And where is the money to come frae for the new rent? The price o' fish has no' changed.'

To her surprise she noticed that Aaron Morton was here in her drawing room tasting her whisky. She wondered at his brashness. He strode about the town as if he owned Inverally and was not just the manager of Fisherton. She was not sure whether to be annoyed or amused. There was still no sign of his employer, the mysterious Mr D.M.King. Rumours abounded as to who he might be. She had even heard the term 'minor royalty'. Watching him in conversation with Gallie and his wife from the timber yard, she made up her mind to confront him.

It took her a further fifteen minutes to work her way across the room then the rest was easy. The Gallies had moved on and Aaron was standing on his own staring out of the window at the lawns and flower beds. She was conscious that they were not up to their usual pristine spring glory. Bob Paterson had retired with acute arthritis and in his place a couple of young unemployed lads from Milton were in charge of the grounds, and it showed. The lawns had been been given their cut but the edges were ragged and the herbaceous beds between the thrusting lupins and the delphinium spears choked with chickweed. She would go out most evenings herself and dig out dandelions but there was a limit to what she could do. For a moment she joined with Aaron Morton in silent contemplation of the overgrown garden.

'Thank you for coming, Mr Morton,' she said a little more briskly than she had intended.

At the same time he spoke. 'My condolences, Ma'am.' He did not say anything about Victor, and she was glad of that. As far as she knew, he had never met Victor.

'How do you find Fisherton, Mr Morton? I hear the improvements are well underway.'

He laughed. 'Improvements, you hear? That 's not the story I hear from the fisher folk, alas.'

'We had intended the same innovations, Mr Morton. You have spared us the complaints at least and for that I am grateful.'

'You are missed a whole lot by the families, Ma'am. Please consider yourself free to visit if and when you please.'

'Thank you, Mr Morton. I'll bear that in mind. I wonder when your employer at High Cloud Holdings - Mr King is it? - intends to visit. We are all anxious to meet him.'

'Mr King is unavoidably detained. You will have to make do with me, meantime.'

He spoke with such assurance, such an air of authority and lack of nervousness that Meg wondered for the moment if she were not speaking to Mr King himself. Before she could examine the thought further, Macmurtrie bore down on her. His face was grim.

Milton.

Fanny and Jared drove down the avenue in silence. Fanny was incandescent with anger.

'Seeing we're so early, I'll take the chance to call in on my mother,' Jared told her shortly. He too was annoyed. He had been enjoying himself at the wake. The whisky had warmed him and it was he, after all, who had known Mr Myers, poor loon that he was, not Fanny. He would miss his trips to the Hall, both the welcome refreshment provided by Mr Jenkins and the little envelope that had come his way as a result. He had not yet had the chance to speak to Mr Jenkins, nor had he had a chance to approach Lady Cynthia though he had tried and failed several times to catch her eye over the crowd of mourners 'What's all the hurry?' he grumbled to Fanny. 'I was enjoying myself.'

'So I noticed,' she replied shortly.

267

'You may not like the gentry and all those great folk,' he grouched,' but they're the ones to put meat on your table.'

She did not reply. Her mouth was set in a thin line. For a moment he wondered what he had ever seen in her and then he remembered. It was not her pretty face, for Fanny had never been pretty, though she had neat little wrists and ankles. It was her determination, her wit and her cleverness that had attracted him. He had wanted a clever wife. He also wanted all she possessed and had shared with him; the children and the Emporium, perhaps the Emporium and the children in that order would be a more honest assessment. He would not quarrel with her for in a battle of words he had no chance of winning, would not want to win, for Fanny had become not only his wife but also his rock. If that rock were to crumble he knew he would founder.

'You were right, Fan. We have better things to do with our time than gossip with Lord Morton and his ilk.'

Her mouth relaxed into a small smile. 'Lord Morton?' she replied with a slight stress on the title. 'Yes, indeed, Jared. Best keep well out of his way.'

He understood then that she knew about Lady Cynthia - nothing escaped her eye - but hoped she did not know everything. They had only met twice and nothing had happened. Nothing, that is, she could take real objection to. How much did a kiss and a fumble measure in the sin list then? (Cyn list? Ha!) It equated to no more than three or four whiskies in the Station bar. How much did she know? Had she followed him? Had they been seen? But by whom? Not a soul visited that old disused summerhouse on the outskirts of Lord Morton's gardens, or so she had assured him. Somebody must have seen something, recognised the cart perhaps though he had always been careful to leave it well away from the Point House gates. It occurred to him suddenly that Lady Cynthia had maybe used the summerhouse on other occasions for other assignations. He grew hot at the thought. He made up his mind he had better give up those weekly grocery deliveries to Point…if he only had the will power. Let the lad do them.

They had reached Marsali's house.' 'Will you come in with me?' he asked.

'I have things to do,' she said coolly. ''My regards to your mother.'

Jared handed her the reins. He left her smiling with her mouth but not her eyes.

Marsali was sitting in the old basket chair in her new living room, knitting. She looked up pleased as he approached '*Ciamar a tha thu, a mhathair*?' he greeted her.

'I am well,' she told him and he saw that she was. It was as if a grey shawl had been lifted from her shoulders. He had not seen her like this for as long as he could remember. She stood straighter, her eyes were brighter and her voice confident.

'I see that you are, *a' mhathair*. You are not missing Fisherton then?'

She did not reply directly 'How is Miss Megaidh? Was there a good turn-out for the funeral then?'

'Indeed. There must have been close on two hundred at the church.'

'Were you not at the wake? You're back sharp.'

'Fanny wanted to leave early.' He could hear the sulkiness in his voice.

There was a small silence between them. 'No doubt she has work to do,' Marsali said a little tartly. If it came to an argument between them, he knew well enough that his mother would take his wife's part. She had a great admiration for Fanny.

'And Mr Morton?' she asked. 'Did he go?'

269

'Aye he was there; still is,' he replied shortly. His voice betrayed his feelings for he did not like Aaron Morton. Too pleased with himself by half. What women saw in him he refused to understand. His mother, Fanny, most of the Fisherton women by all accounts, even Lady Cynthia. Their expressions softened when his name was mentioned, lit up in his presence. If he were to probe his feelings more closely he would recognise them as jealousy. Fanny and Cynthia's approval of the blackamoor he might not like, but he could understand; Aaron was an upstanding fellow; but his mother?

'Bumptious oaf,' he muttered under his breath but she heard him

'Aye mebbe,' Marsali bent her head over her knitting to hide a small smile. 'But there'll come a day when you'll think different.'

'I doubt it.'

'I promise you,' she said confidently, putting her knitting aside. 'Now will you take a cup of tea?'

He looked around him and saw a new bottle of Point Distillery malt whisky on the shelf. 'Where did that come from?' he asked suspiciously. His mother never bought spirits.

'Mr Morton brought it in. Is it a dram you're after?'

He was so annoyed that he found himself rejecting the whisky in preference for tea. 'Does he not think to get his own accommodation? He can well afford it,' he grumbled as she set cups into saucers.

'I like having the loon about the place. He's no trouble,' she said mildly. 'How's wee Connie's cough? Did Missus Fanny try a spoonful of honey in hot milk last thing at night?'

'Connie's fine,' he said grumpily as he took the tea.

'Don't you go worrying your head about Aaron,' she told him. 'He's a better friend than you know.'

Again that secretive smile.

Kirkton

The Reverend Hugh and Helen were among the last to leave the Hall. The Gallies offered them a lift down the Brae in their coach. After the pleasantries were over, Mrs Gallie leaned across from her seat to ask them both, 'What will she do now, poor lady?'

'Who?' Hugh asked shortly. Though he knew perfectly well who Mrs Gallie meant, he refused to consider Meg as a 'poor lady'.

'Mrs Myers of course. She's a widow now.'

'I'm sure she'll manage splendidly,' said Helen peaceably 'She's got her nephew to look after. What a fine boy he is.'

'Aye well, she'll need all her wits about her if she's to hand the estate over to him,' Mr Gallie said portentously. 'Things are not good there, not good at all, I've been told.'

'I'm sorry to hear that,' said Helen and changed the subject to comment somewhat deliberately on the weather.

Hugh was silent. Privately he agonised for Meg. To him she was still the little girl whom he had for so many years loved as a daughter. 'As a daughter,' he told himself firmly and repeatedly though he knew that he had not fooled Emily, or, for that matter, himself. He was not sure how far he had fooled Helen. Marriage to Helen had proved to be an unexpected blessing. He had always liked her from the day Emily brought her as a penniless widow to live with them He knew exactly why Emily had asked her, but he had hesitated long enough over proposing marriage. It had worked, thank God. In the parish they were a good partnership. She was truly a mother to Hamish. Sometimes he asked himself in wonder why they were so content with each other because he had never been in love with her, nor, he suspected, she with him. Theirs had been truly a marriage of convenience. Perhaps that was the reason. They had had no expectations, therefore there had been no disappointments. He liked her and was happy with her but he was not in love with her. It had always been Miss Megaidh. It occurred to him as the coach rattled down the stony avenue that had he not been married, he would have been free to approach Megaidh now. The years between them no longer seemed the barrier they had once been. As quickly as he thought it, he brushed aside the idea. Helen was his wife, a wonderful loyal suitable wife. Meaaidh would always be fantasy.

'Will you come back and drink tea with us?' Hilda Gallie was asking. Hugh held his breath. The last thing he wanted to do was to drink tea, however well brewed, at the Timber House.

'Thank you, but no,' Helen replied charmingly. 'Mr Vass has much to see to. It is always the same after a funeral.' She sighed convincingly.

Hugh thought that was exactly why he had married her. His second thought was how soon could he suitably pay Miss Megaidh a pastoral visit, and settled on the following afternoon.

The Hall

'Can I go out now?'

Andrew was at her elbow by the drawing room door. He had already changed out of his kilt into more suitable outdoor clothing. The last of the guests had left.

Automatically mindful of her brother, Meg asked him where he was going.

272

'To see Danny,' he told her. It did not occur to him to resent the question. It had been part of a ritual that had started as long ago as he could remember. He waited for the rest.

'Don't go near the sea, will you?'

'No Aunt Meg,' he told her patiently.

'Be back in time to tidy yourself for dinner.'

'Yes, Auntie.'

She watched him run off as if he had been chained. Poor Andrew. What an ordeal, what a sad and boring afternoon it must have seemed to him surrounded by so many black-clad adults sqawking at him like rooks.

Her brother-in-law was still in the drawing room. He rose as Meg approached 'Susan has retired to her room She is a little tired.'

Cedric looked exhausted himself. She told him so, but he seemed anxious to talk. 'So poor Victor's gone,' he said moving towards the window, his back to her. 'I'm sorry, Meg, but I find it hard to mourn his passing. He brought nothing but shame to my father's house.'

And he didn't like you, either, Meg thought, on a spur of anger. 'Andrew loved him,' she said aloud, 'and he loved Andrew. For that I shall always be grateful.'

'Let us hope and earnestly pray then that his love has not contaminated the boy.'

Meg was so shocked that she had to hold on to the back of a chair to steady herself. 'He was your brother. Have you no pity? No regrets?'

'He was also a pervert and a criminal.'

She was silent. In the eyes of the law, Cedric was probably right, she thought. But Victor could be kind. He may have been slow and wasteful, but he had never been less than respectful to her. 'He was also my husband,' she said coldly and left the room. The conversation had left her ashamed not only of Cedric, but also of herself for her own lack of affection. She had barely seen her husband for more than a few moments each day for the last few years. She had left him entirely to Jenkins and thankful to do so. Before she could change her mind, she decided to find the old servant, thank him and assure him of a future in her care.

Jenkins was not alone. A stranger was sitting in Victor's chair by the closed window in a fug of cigar smoke. She had noticed him at the funeral, one of several mourners whose faces she had not recognised. Both he and Jenkins rose to their feet as she entered the room, Jenkins promptly, the stranger reluctantly. She looked enquiringly at Jenkins but he said nothing. It was the stranger who spoke.

'My deepest condolences, Mrs Myers.'

Meg looked at him disapprovingly. He was breathless, overweight, generally unprepossessing and he was smoking one of Victor's cigars. 'Thank you, Mr...?'

'My name is Higgins, Josiah Higgins, a...er...man of business. I am here on behalf of a close acquaintance of the late Mr Myers, your esteemed husband, I believe?'

'Well?' Meg prompted tersely. She was not aware that Victor had any business acquaintances. 'And who might that be?'

He took a couple of steps towards her, his round head with the sparse yellowish hair cocked to one side.

'Just because a fellow passes on does not necessarily mean his business passes with him. No h'indeed. It falls to his 'eirs. I presume you are your 'usband's 'eir, Mrs Myers?'. He had a strange accent, a hint of cockney overlaid with Invernesian.

She ignored the question. 'May I know what that business is?'

He sat down again. Jenkins brought forward a chair for her but he did not catch her eye. Instead he retreated to the small

274

adjoining room that had once been a butler's pantry. She ignored the chair.

Josiah Higgins leaned towards her. 'A nasty business, that you can count on.'

She sat down quickly because her knees had gone weak but she said nothing. What had poor wretched Victor got himself involved in? 'Then I'm not interested.' She forced her voice to be steady. 'Mr Myers is dead. What he did or did not do is best forgotten.'

'And so h'it can be,' he assured her. 'H'it's entirely h'up to yourself.'

She said nothing. He leaned closer towards her.

What he then said shocked her into a stunned silence.

'Did you not hear me, Mrs Myers?' the stranger asked coldly, all semblance of respect gone from his voice.

Still she could not speak. One sentence had detached itself from what he had said. 'Victor Myers was responsible for 'is death.' It echoed and re-echoed in the vault of her mind.

'Mr Myers – ' He was about to repeat himself but Meg would not listen. What Victor had done or not done was past, over, forgotten.

'I heard you,' she said sharply. She stood up abruptly and walked to the door. 'I wish to hear no more. Good day, Mr Higgins.'

He was on his feet in a instant.' Not so fast, Mrs Myers. When I say Mr Myers was responsible for the death of a friend of my client, h'I mean h'exactly that. h'It was not easy for my client to stand by and do nothing. h'It is still not h'easy for the case has never been closed… The case is still h'outstanding. You know what the police h'are like. Never give h'up.'

She was stunned into silence. 'What do you want?' she asked faintly.

'h'At last! We h'understand each h'other. As to the h'exact figure, I don't rightly know. Not to be precise. Mr Myers always paid in instalments.'

Jenkins had re-appeared. He was standing across the room with his back to the pantry door. She turned to him. 'What do you know of this, Jenkins?' she asked shakily.

The old man looked dreadful, bent, shrivelled, old – and cunning. 'Wot the gentleman says. Mr Myers paid in h'instalments. These past ten years or so.'

From my account, she thought. So that's where the money has gone. Oh Victor...

Josiah Higgins turned to Jenkins. 'Tell the lady, Mr Jenkins. Best she 'ear it from you.'

Suddenly furious, Meg stood. She held up a hand to silence him.'This stops now, or I call the police myself.'

'h'I wouldn't h'advise that, Mrs Myers,' the stranger said. 'The unnatural death of Mr Anton d'Olio h'is still a matter of urgent interest to the police. No I would certainly not h'advise that.'

'I'd like you to leave now, Mr Higgins. Immediately.' It took every ounce of self-control to keep her voice steady.

He reached for his hat which lay on an occasional table by the door. 'Certainly. h'I'll leave you to think things h'over, Mrs Myers. And w'ile you do, h'I would h'advise you to remember this. Mr Myers, your 'usband was responsible for the death of an h'innocent man. Hit 'im and pushed 'im from 'is window into the 'arbour where 'e drowned. For that 'e could have been 'anged. There are witnesses. 'e was also guilty of unnatural practices and an over-fondness for opium. Your family's good name is at stake. For h'an affordable sum of money - my client 'as never been unreasonable - you can preserve your family's good name and keep the police h'out of it. You can continue to deserve the respect of your tenants, live in your grand 'ouse and your nephew can claim an unblemished h'inheritance. Think about h'it very carefully, Mrs Myers.'

He dropped the remains of his cigar into his whisky glass, stuck his hat on his balding head and with a supercilious bow in her direction bid her 'good day'. At the door he stopped and turned. 'I h'assume you will no longer be requiring the 'tonic'? You will, 'owever, be 'earing from me in due course.'

Meg was too stunned to move, too sickened to ask questions. When he had gone, she turned to the old servant,'How could you let this happen, Jenkins? Is any of it true?'

''ow do I know? h'I was looking h'after the Colonel in them days.'

'There's a word for it,' she said half to herself. 'What that man's doing.'

'Aye,' said Jenkins, winking ferociously. 'Mr Victor called it blackmail.'

'What am I going to do?' The question was addressed to herself but Jenkins chose to answer.

'Pay 'im of course. Like Mr Victor did. Stands to reason.'

Of course she would not pay him. Her first thought was to tell Hugh Vass. He would advise her.

The Hurler

'That's jolly good,'said Andrew admiringly as Danny opened the old harness room door adjacent to the stables and pushed out the little cart they had painstakingly made together out of bits of wood and the wheels from an old perambulator Andrew had found in the stables' loft. It had been his dream to make a flying machine and he had the drawings to prove it, but Dan, the practical one, had suggested they turn it into a cart which would go by itself, downhill at least. 'A racing cart!' said Andrew fired with enthusiasm. 'We could make two and have races.'

'Aye, bye and bye,' Dan had agreed wisely keeping his thoughts to himself. Though the design and the wheels had been Andrew's, the construction was largely his and he was desperate to see it run.

Both boys eyed it proudly. Lined with an off-cut from Effy's kitchen linoleum the cart was painted green, same as the stables. It even had a steering rod attached to the front wheels. It held one rider comfortably but could accommodate two at a pinch.

'Where'll we take it?' Dan asked.

Andrew thought. There were plenty of braes to pick from. Inverally was built on a long steep hill but the roads around the village were narrow and busy. Besides he didn't want all the village children hanging on and demanding a 'shottie'.

'The Hurler,' he said, suggesting the hill where the reservoir for the Hall water was stored, (an enclosed underground vault surrounded by thistles and barbed wire to keep out the sheep). A steep brae, the Hurler was one of several foothills behind the policies that stretched upwards in humps and valleys to the grouse moor above and beyond that to the Ben. Grassy and pock-marked with sandy rabbit warrens, it was alarmingly steep as the boys had found one day when they had decided to roll themselves down and ended up giddy and sick with laughter.

Danny was doubtful. 'Do ye no' think it's a bit risky with all them sheep?' The farmer would not be pleased.

'They've got eyes, ain't they?' said Andrew, 'and legs? They can get out of our way. It's the perfect place.' He was grinning like an idiot. 'Get in. I'll pull you to the style then you can pull me.'

It went like a dream. Andrew hauled on the rope over the dirt path. Together they lifted it over the style, taking it in turns to ride till they reached the foot of the hill.

Andrew noticed that there were a lot of sheep with their lambs munching the short green turf and twice as many rabbits. Dutifully they scattered as the two boys, puffing a bit, climbed to the top. 'I'll steer,' said Andrew so Dan squeezed in behind him and off they set. The cart was fine. Steered like a dream, so they managed to avoid the worst of the rabbit warrens. To begin with. Unfortunately they had forgotten to add a brake and therefore no means of controlling the speed. Faster and faster it hurtled downwards over tufts and pebbles to stop abruptly against a hidden boulder. The two boys were catapulted out, Dan harmlessly into a bed of nettles, Andrew head first into the stony burn three feet below the bank.

'Ouch! Ouch! Ouch!' shrieked Danny whose bare arms and legs below his short trousers were soon a mass of fiery weals. Andrew was silent. Afterwards he tried to explain it to Aunt Meg and Bessie. 'There was a fellow there. No, I don't know who he was. He had a strange voice, sort of twangy. I've never seen him before. He must have been watching us. Anyhow, he lifted me. I didn't cry but it was sore. Then he carried me all the way down to see Doctor Anderson - all that way like I was a baby.'

He said this with due indignation for it would take some living down if the word got out. Luckily Doctor Anderson lived in a big house opposite Mr Vass' church on the outskirts of Kirkton so only a couple of fish wives saw him. One of them made a joke about putting him in her creel along with the fish, he remembered, but he kept that part of the story to himself. He hadn't thought it particularly funny.

His leg was not broken but the ligaments in his ankle were torn and he had dislocated his shoulder, which Dr Anderson clicked back straight off, but it was still sore.

Aunt Meg practically ignored his injuries though his puffed-up ankle was stiffly bandaged and his right arm held in a sling. Instead she told him off good and proper for being so stupid. 'You might have killed yourself,' she repeated over and over again. 'I forbid you to go near that thing.'

'It just needs a brake,' he said appeasingly.

'I absolutely forbid it.' She turned to Dan who had stuck by him. 'You can run off home now, Daniel, and get your mother to put more calomel lotion on those stings.' She gave him the bottle to take home.

'Come away, Master Andrew,' said Bessie kindly. 'What you need is a glass of hot milk and some biscuits and a wee lie down. Is it awful sore?'

'By the way,' his aunt called from the door. 'Who was he? The man who so kindly rescued you?'

'I told you, Aunt, he was a stranger. He never said who he was. Maybe Danny found out. He spoke mostly to Danny.'

'He didn't tell you his name and you never thought to ask?' She sounded anxious and cross.

'I did say thank you,' he protested. He felt two tears press against his eyeballs. I will not cry he told himself, though his ankle was really sore.

'I never cried,' he told Bessie as she helped him up the stairs.

'My brave wee soldier!' She hugged him and his tears dried up.

But others had seen the stranger and his name was soon on every lip in every household from Fisherton right up to the Hall kitchen. Mr Don King had finally arrived in Inverally, better known to a few as Donnaidh Macreedie.

Milton

It all seemed so small. He could walk from harbour to Hall in less than half a day. In fact he had walked it, starting at the station where he had alighted early, strode through Milton, passed his mother's house. He was not yet ready for that encounter. Then he had gone down the Brae to Fisherton, those tiny cottages, the narrow lanes dug up for the new sewage system that Aaron Morton had ordered. Had they always been so small? There were plenty of people about but he remembered none of them, nor they him. He walked past them without looking at them but at the same time seeing them all. They noticed him, of course they did, they noticed every stranger, but who would know him now? If he found it hard to recognise in himself the boy he had once been, how would they? Would his mother know him? Would she welcome him after all these years of guilty silence?

He had already visited Aaron in his recently acquired office, a room in Milton above the bakery, discussed the progression of his plans, seen from a safe distance the crowds who attended the funeral. He had climbed the foothills that stretched upwards into the grouse moor, stared down at the village he called home and was now returning by way of the Hurler to make himself known to his mother when he had encountered the boys.

He had seen immediately what was wrong, could have manipulated the dislocated shoulder back into place himself but had doubted the boy could stand the shock. He was white and distant with pain, his ankle swelling by the moment, beyond the balm of tears, so he had bound his arm to his chest and carried the lad as if he had been a calf and was fortunate to find Doctor Anderson, a new face to him, at his tea.

'Will you tell me your names?' he had asked the other lad as they walked down the Brae to the doctor. Danny had answered.

'Andrew?' he asked. 'Who would that be then?'

'Master Andrew Myers from the big house. And I'm Dan. Daniel Stuart. My dad's the coachman.'

'And your mam?'

'Effie, she's called.'

'Would that be Effie Macreedie by any chance?'

'Aye,' Dan replied shortly. He was unused to bearing the brunt of the conversation when Andrew was with him. Shyness tightened his tongue. He did not think to ask the stranger's name.

'Then Daniel,' he said as they reached the doctor's door. 'I reckon we'll be seeing each other again.'

So this was his own nephew, his flesh and blood and with him the Inverally heir, part of whose inheritance he had already taken. They spoke little as they climbed the Brae back to the Hall, Andrew on his back this time, his bandaged ankle stuck out stiffly in front of him. Don's mind was too full of memories to speak.

Aaron Morton had already told him all he needed to know about the inhabitants of the Hall and the members of his own family. He knew now that this lad on his back was Andy's nephew, son of the beautiful but departed Miss Isabella, raised by her sister, Miss Megaidh. You would not be thanking me now if you knew who I was and why I am here, he thought, as he left the boys on the doorstep of the Hall and bid them goodbye. He had debated with himself would he take Daniel back and confront his sister but thought better of it. There would be time enough for that. He must see his mother first.

Part of him dreaded the encounter, part of him longed to see her again, He knew that his father was dead. Aaron had told him his mother had never forgotten him, believed him to be alive in spite of all the evidence to the contrary, would welcome him home, but how could he be sure? Too many years had passed without a word. Would she forgive him? Would she accept his flimsy explanations, understand his motive?

It was a neat little dwelling right enough, in a terrace of stone houses built on the road into Kirkton with a flight of steps leading up from the wrought iron garden gate through a neatly mown slope of lawn edged with pansies.

Although he knew that twenty years had passed since he had seen her, it was still a shock to find his mother grown old. Her hair which had always been abundant and curly was now thin and white, completely and beautifully white and her skin finely wrinkled, so unlike his memory of her that he might not have recognised her had he not known it must be she.

'*A mhathair?*' he said falling back instinctively into the old language.

She stared at him disbelievingly, then knew him. '*Mo Donnaidh*! Is it really you? Can it really be you?' Instinctively she raised her arms and he found himself embraced by her for the first time in his life. Marsali had never been one for hugs and kisses. Nor indeed was he, but this time he held her as closely as she held him.

'I don't believe it!' she exclaimed over and over again.

'But mother, you knew I was coming. Aaron said he had told you.'

'I knew it in my heart but not here in my head.' She laughed and tapped her brow. 'I have known it in my heart since the day you were taken from us, but never in my head, not until now. You've grown!'

'I should hope so. I was twelve years old when we lost each other.'

283

They laughed a little. 'Wait till you see Jared. He's grown a belly!'

'And Jonas?'

'He got your father's place on the boatie.'

She had drawn him in by now and they sat either side of the kitchen range, he in his father's horsehair armchair and he drank tea the way he remembered it, strong, milky and well sugared. He told her how he had met Daniel and she told him he had seven nephews and nieces, their names and their ages.

'And now, Donnaidh, I need to know,' she said because they could not skate round the question any longer. 'Why did you never write? Did you not think your father and I would be broken not knowing if you were alive or dead?'

How to explain? He closed his eyes for a moment searching for the words that would hurt least as the last twenty years played themselves over in his mind, those that he could remember.

It started with the storm. That bit he remembered as clearly as if it had happened yesterday. A black cloud had overlain the horizon. Aaron had tentatively suggested that they waited another day, but Donnaidh would not hear of it and Andy agreed. Andy always agreed with him. They had put out from shore. They were doing well, shouting at each other, laughing, pleased with themselves. The resultant squall had quickly upset the boat and tossed them all into the gulping greedy waters. Their cries of terror as the three of them struggled were quickly quelled by mouthfuls of angry water. Andy could swim well and Aaron a little but the water was too wild. In terror they clung on to each other. By chance he had found the wreckage of their boatie for it had not sunk completely but lay upside down about a foot under the waves held up by the air trapped inside. He had held on instinctively with one hand, treading water with his feet for, out of the three of them, Donnaidh was the only one not able to swim. Had he let go he would have surely been drowned. Then nothing but shame. Their cries silenced by the angry water, they struggled to swim against the roaring waves. He had watched them drown. No. He let them drown.

The Inverness/Leith ferry had picked him up. Assuming he was a passenger who had fallen over the side, the captain had cared for him and put him off at Leith. Too shocked and ashamed to go home or write, he had signed up as a galley boy on a big ship and worked his passage to America. What a nightmare that had been.

He held his head in one hand as he remembered. 'How could I go home? How could I explain that I had let my friends drown? They were like brothers to me,' he told his mother.

'Surely it was not your blame,' said Marsali. She reached across to take his free hand in her own. He opened his fingers to clasp hers. He was moved to find her hands rough and worn, as indeed she was to find his in no better condition.

'No, *a mhathair*. It was my fault. Aaron had been the wise one. He had tried to stop us but I would not listen and Andy had trusted me. I was responsible for them. Never doubt it.'

'But you did well in yon great land?' she asked.

He told her about the crossing. The galley crew were rough but kindly enough. The chef had a fist on him as hard as any hammer. 'When I burned bread he clouted me. When I dropped plates he boxed my ears. When I spewed in rough weather he beat me. I can laugh now but I wasn't laughing then you can bet on that, yet every one of those clouts I welcomed as punishment for what I'd done.' Though he did not tell her, he had often wished that one of those clouts had killed him.

285

'Donnaidh, my son, no one thought to blame you for the accident. Why did you not return on the next boat – or send word at least?'

He had half intended to take the first passage home for he had been stricken by a home-sickness that matched his shame but then he had met Fraser Gemmell and his life changed forever. Mr Gemmell had been big and bold and charismatic and he promised good wages for hard work. Here was a man he could work for. He had not hesitated. 'He picked me and one or two other likely men off the boat to work on his ranch in the state of Wyoming. He was always careful who he chose to work for him, was Mr Gemmell. But he was not always wise in his choices.'

'You wanted to see the world. You always wanted that, Donnaidh. But you could have written home.'

Why had he not? He had intended to, but he could never find the words. Somehow the days had passed. He had never been so busy in his life. High Cloud Ranch was huge, beautiful and hard work with 12,000 head of cattle. He had to learn everything - how to hold on to a horse, how to birth a calf, how to catch a steer. He could tell her that he had had no time, that there was no such thing as mail out on the trail, but none of it would have been true. He had been the youngest by several years on the ranch. What had happened was simple in retrospect. He became the son that Fraser and his sweet frail wife, Angeline, had never had.

'You were happy, then?' Marsali asked. It was important for her to know.

'Aye, *a mhathair*, I suppose you could say I was happy enough.' But happy? He still dreamed of his drowned friends.

'You forgot us? Your father and mother, your brothers and sister. You forgot about us?'

'No, never,' he protested because he knew she wanted to hear it but truthfully as time passed, whole days had slipped by without a thought of his home. What memories he had were of shame that he had let Andy and Aaron drown. He remembered only too clearly how he had seen them drown, how he was ashamed to be still alive while his foster brothers were dead. 'How could I forget?'

'Aye,' she said, remembering the grief that had destroyed them at the Hall, that had also destroyed Ezra and would most certainly have destroyed herself had she not clung on to her belief that he was alive. 'But you were happy?' She needed him to have been happy.

'For a while,' he said. 'For a wee while, maybe.'

Now he would need to tell her the truth, but how? Fraser Gemmell's ranch had grown ever more prosperous as the years flew past, but then Angeline had died untimely of a rattle snake bite and Mr Gemmell had got angry. His patience, which had never been remarkable, grew brittle. One of his men, one of his bad choices, had a cruel way with him. He spurred his horse till it bled. Don was rowing with him in the stables. It had come to fists. Don was younger and faster but he lacked the power and weight of the older man. Fraser Gemmell had found them, seen Donnaidh's bleeding face, taken out his gun and shot Matt through the heart.

Most of the other lads had been willing to keep quiet and bury the body secretly but one of them, Matt's mate, coming into the stable untimely and finding Matt covered by a tarpaulin, rode for the sheriff. Don had taken the rap. Deliberately. Why he was never too sure. Mainly because he had wished he had been the one to deal the killer blow. Mr Gemmell was getting to be an old man. Donnaidh had grown to love him almost as a father. So when the sheriff and his men had ridden up to the ranch, he had walked forward his hands up and his confession ready. They had stuck him in Wyoming penitentiary for ten years. He had been released three months ago.

Marsali was horrified. 'You mean you went to prison for something you never did? Oh Donnaidh, my poor wee Donnaidh.'

'I intended to kill him. I had the motive but not the gun. Mr Gemmell only did what any father would have done.'

He had been rewarded, though he had not done it with any motive in mind. Mr Gemmell had died a few years later when he was in jail and left him High Cloud Ranch and a whole heap of money besides.

'And you met Mr Morton in that jail?'

'Aye, mother. Aaron told me his story and I told him mine. He was released a good while ago so I employed him to come home and find you.'

'You trusted him?'

'I did. You get to know a man well enough when you share a cell with him. I trusted him and I see that you do too.'

'I've come to respect the gentleman,' she said adding with a smile, 'you'll not mind sharing a room with him again, then? I'll not put him out and I only have the one room. to spare.'

He laughed. 'So long as it's not bread and water for my dinner.'

'And now you're home, will you stay?'

That was the question he had been dreading. 'For a whilie at least,' he reassured her.

Inverness.

Meg spent a sleepless night. What to do? Her first thought had been to tell Hugh Vass but the more she considered it the less inclined she felt to confide in him. She thought she

288

knew what he would advise because it was the same advice that she would have given to anyone in her position; be sensible, take the moral option, report the whole matter to the police. Advice which she was not yet prepared to take. Macmurtrie had murmured yesterday that he would like to visit her 'in a day or two' when she had had time to recover from her bereavement but she decided she could not wait that long. She rang for Mima and arranged for a wire to be sent to the lawyer's office informing him that she would pay him a visit that afternoon at 3pm.

Cedric and Susan had left on the early train. Cedric had asked for a keepsake and wanted the only valuable object that Victor still possessed, a small ornate porcelain snuff box. It had shocked his brother and sister-in-law to the core to find how little Victor owned. A few books of no value and unread, some worthless trinkets, some clothes of course but nothing else, not even the watch Meg herself had given him some years before. The pictures, furniture and nick-nacks that adorned his room all belonged to the Hall. They were quick to accuse Jenkins of having purloined the best of his possessions but at Meg's sharp insistence had let the matter drop. Meg too would have been appalled had she not known the truth. Instead a stab of pity touched her heart. She presumed Victor had sold his own few possessions to pay off this alleged debt before moving in on hers. Poor wretched Victor.

'The snuff box?' Cedric had reminded her but Meg had hardened her heart.

'I'm sorry, Cedric, but the snuff box was promised to Andrew.' It was a lie of course but hardly a hanging offence. Instead she handed him a small leather-bound Bible, the best of Victor's books.

He had taken it without a word. Later she found it abandoned on the bedside table in the guest-room where he had left it. She took it herself. In it she found a somewhat stilted photograph of herself with Andrew, still a baby, seated on her knee holding his arms out to the photographer. Tears filled her eyes.

Sam had already provided Andrew with home-made crutches which meant he could hobble about. She gave him the snuff box after breakfast. 'Uncle Victor would have wanted you to have it,' she told him. That much at least was true. He was, as she knew he would be, delighted. 'I'll put it into my treasure chest straight away,' he told her and hobbled out of the dining room. She saw him smear his eyes briefly as he paused to open the door.

Sam drove her to catch the 12.15 train to Inverness and she took a cab to the lawyer's office. Opposite the new cathedral, still without spires and destined to remain so, she stood staring at it rehearsing her words without seeing the oddly truncated building.

Five minutes later he bustled in full of apologies for having kept her waiting. He drew forwards a chair for her, rang a bell and ordered tea and the Inverally deed box which an elderly clerk brought in and placed somewhat reverendly on the desk. She gazed at the green tin chest with Inverally Estate inscribed in large back letters on the side. Without looking at her he launched into speech.

'I had hoped to postpone what I am about to tell you, Mrs Myers, until a reasonable time had elapsed after Mr Myers' sad demise but now you are here, I really cannot, dare not, wait any longer.' He launched into a long explanation of the financial state of affairs which she only half understood. 'In a nutshell, Mrs Myers, the incomings from the tenants and other assets is less than the outgoings and has been for some time.'

'I thought the sale of Fisherton had helped.'

'For a short while, certainly, but without the income from the cottages that was never going to be a permanent solution.'

'So what are you suggesting, Mr Macmurtrie?' she asked.

'Unless a new source of income is found, there is only one solution. The estate will have to be sold. Every month the debt is mounting, alas. We can still sell off several properties, but without the income they generate, how will you live?'

She was appalled 'No!' she said shaking her head. 'Surely this can't be so.' She felt as if she were tied to a stake in the Firth with the tide coming in.

'What about the boy's father? Can he not be approached for assistance?'

Yes, she thought. There was always James. Surely he would want to keep the estate intact for Andrew. But James had remarried and had three small children. and a wife to support. He already paid for Andrew's education, sent generous cheques to cover his expenses. She knew, because Hilary his sister had told her, that owing to her father's profligacy, James would have only a little more than his pension when he retired. Hilary herself had a wealthy husband who had bought an estate in Essex. Would he be willing to save Inverally for a nephew when he already had a family of his own to support? What a nightmare. She had known her financial situation was bad but not this bad.

Now was the time to tell him about the other business, but she could not do it. 'What am I to do?' she said wretchedly. ''What can I do? '

'The estate was mortgaged before your father died. A re-mortgage is always possible, but that could only ever be a short term measure. I believe the time has come to let Inverally go before it becomes so encumbered with debt that

291

you will have nothing left from the sale to live on. As you know your own fortune has all but gone.'

'How much do I have left?' she asked. Perhaps it would be enough to pay off Josiah Higgins' mysterious client.

'A few thousand pounds, just enough to support you if you were you to move to the Dower house.'

She stood up. Her legs felt weak and she had to hold on to the edge of the desk to keep her balance. 'I need time to think,' she said.

He came round to take her hand. 'Of course you do, Mrs Myers. But I beg you, don't take too long.'

'Perhaps no one will want to buy,' she said dolefully.

'You need not worry on that account,' he said intending to reassure her. 'I already have one interested party.'

'Who?' she asked sharply.

'Alas, I promised confidentiality. It was only an inquiry, after all.'

She held back her tears until she was outside. Partly to hide them, mostly because she was desperate, she slipped into the cathedral across the road, found a pew behind a pillar and sank to her knees. She had given her time, her energy, her whole life to safeguarding the estate but it had not been enough. What a failure she had been. Surely if she had been more understanding of Victor, kinder, she could have prevented him from getting himself into so much trouble. Surely if she had been a better steward and less stubborn in the teeth of her father and the factor's disapproval, the estate would not be bankrupt now. She had spent unwisely, married unwisely, lost Andrew's inheritance, and was now about to bring her family name into disrepute, perhaps criminal charges, for she had made up her mind. She had no intention ever of paying blackmail to a crook.

Point House

Cynthia had dressed with extra care. Her maid had spent at least an hour on her hair, which shone more golden than her wedding ring. Sir Hector Macdonald, Member of Parliament for Highlands East and his bosomy wife Enid were coming to dinner and she still enjoyed dressing up.

Before going downstairs she visited the day nursery. Adela at nine was having her supper of bread and milk with her nurse. Adela went to a private girls' school in Point because her father refused to be parted from her until she was older. Her name was down for Cheltenham Ladies College when she was thirteen years old. She was a pretty precocious child, adored by the whole household including her grandmother.

Lady Morton senior was already downstairs when Cynthia arrived just in time to greet their guests. Resplendent in purple, the dowager cast a critical eye over her visibly pregnant daughter-in-law before moving forward, all smiles, to welcome the visitors. She and Lady Enid were by way of friends. Cynthia smiled at the older woman carefully averting her eyes from the enormous, bejewelled, semi-naked bosom and went forward to shake her hand but Lady Morton had already taken her by the arm and drawn her aside. Cynthia did not need Sir Hector's appreciative bow to know she looked her best. Violet was a good colour for her and the family amethysts round her white neck were only a little less dazzling than her eyes.

Donald too was satisfied. His glance was almost approving as she set herself out to charm their honourable guest. Apart from her gleaming hair, she had little other opportunity to shine. Her mother-in-law who sat at the foot of the long French-polished dining table opposite her son with Sir Hector on her right and Lady Enid on her left, dominated the conversation. Cynthia sat quietly between her

293

husband and Sir Hector. Conversation flowed but only included her when she was deliberately addressed. She had learned long ago that her Inverness accent which she had tried hard but unsuccessfully to eradicate, irritated her mother-in-law beyond words so she tended only to speak when she was spoken to. When the topic of suffragettes was raised, Sir Hector turned to her. 'You are very quiet, Lady Cynthia. Won't you share your views with us?'

'Cynthia does not concern herself with politics,' Lady Morton answered for her, dismissively. 'What do you think, Lady Enid? Would you not agree with me that we women have more than enough to do in the house and in the home without intruding into male preserves?'

'Nevertheless I should be glad to hear Lady Cynthia's views - as one of the younger generation?' Sir Hector persisted.

Cynthia had strong views on the subject which she discussed endlessly with her mother while they drank tea and shared fashion books. She liked to call herself a suffragette which delighted Mr Gallie and shocked her mother. She would have enjoyed sharing her views this evening but the opportunity was lost. Her mother-in-law had ruthlessly changed the subject. She leaned towards Sir Hector and murmured confidentially, 'I hear that Inverally is in trouble.'

'In trouble?' said Sir Hector. 'In what way?'

'It's common knowledge,' said Lord Morton 'The estate is close to bankruptcy. Hardly surprising. Overstretched themselves financially over the years. Perfect fool, that chap Myers, God rest his soul. Bad business altogether.'

'It's Mrs Myers I blame,' said the dowager. 'She made all the decisions, or so I'm told. A lesson to all those would-be suffragettes.' She stared provocatively at her daughter-in-law. 'If a woman can't manage her own household, how can she be expected to run a country?'

'I do so agree with you,' said Lady Enid. 'What will happen to Inverally now?'

'They'll have to sell, or so I've been told,' Lord Morton said.

'Good opportunity for someone. Fine situation, splendid view, good shoot,' said Sir Hector. 'If we weren't so well settled, I wouldn't at all mind living there, eh Enid?'

'Exactly,' said Lord Morton. 'I'm half thinking of offering. How would you like that?' he asked his wife.

His mother answered, 'I think not, my dear. I'm too old to consider moving.'

'Of course, Mother. I would never think of asking you to move. This is your home. I was in fact asking my wife.' He looked at her briefly. 'She spends most of her time in Inverally as it is.' He laughed a little joylessly.

Cynthia was about to answer when Sir Hector spoke. 'How could the factor fellow allow Myers to get into this state? Wedderburn, isn't it?'

'He's long gone. A chap called Wilkie. D'you know him? Decent enough fellow,' Lord Morton replied.

They spoke further on the subject then turned to other topics. The evening dragged on interminably. At eleven, they left. When they had gone Lady Morton turned to her son. 'You're not thinking seriously of acquiring Inverally, are you?'

'I might be. If only to settle the boundaries. Their shoot would be an excellent extension to my own.'

'It might be worth while if this time you have a son,' she said casting a cold look at her daughter-in-law. Her pregnancy was much in evidence. She yawned. 'Ah well, time for bed, I think. What about you, my dear?'

'Presently. Good night, mother.' He kissed her cheek and walked her to the door.

When she had gone he turned to Cynthia. 'I have some work to do. I might be late. You should go to bed.'

'I thought I might go out for a turn in the garden. It's a beautiful night.' Anything to get out of the house and its stifling atmosphere.

'You are out of the house altogether too often. I fear you may endanger my son's life. You should be resting in your boudoir not gallivanting off to Inverally when you feel like it,' he said coldly.

'I may not have a son,' she retorted. The remark, which she had made before, infuriated him as she knew it would.

'Then what use are you to me? Why else do you think I married you if not for an heir.'

'I know very well why you married me, Donald,' she said sweetly lifting her head to look him in the eye. 'And now if you will excuse me, I intend to take a turn in the moonlight.'

As she passed him he reached out to sieze her arm. 'And I intend that you go to your room.'

She stared pointedly at his hand as it gripped the long arm of her kid glove. She wore long gloves in the evening to hide old bruises. When he removed his hand she brushed past him without another word. There was a time when she had feared her husband. Now she merely hated him.

Drawing her shawl around her shoulders, she strolled out in bright moonlight as far as the old summer house. It was a beautiful night. Not a breath of wind... He had told her he would be there.

The Hill

Although Macmurtrie had already wired the other trustees, next morning Meg sat down to write to James and to Hilary to tell them that the estate was nearly bankrupt and that without a substantial inflow of capital the debts would only accumulate. She said nothing about Victor's connection to the disaster. She had no words and no inclination to repeat what he had allegedly done. She could barely let herself think of it.

'*Mea culpa*,' she wrote. *'I fear I have not been a good stewardess of Andrew's inheritance and without financial assistance the estate will go under. I don't expect you to solve the situation but it is my duty to make you aware of it. It is, after all, Andrew's future that is at stake. The sale of Fisherton seemingly only postponed the inevitable. Macmurtrie wants to put Inverally on the market before the debts accumulate further. I find the whole situation deeply distressing and I am sorry beyond words that it has come to this…'*

She put down her pen suddenly overwhelmed by the sadness of it all. She loved, had always loved Inverally from the top of Ben Fhuar, over the moors, down the Hurler, through the woods, down the avenues, the braes, past the churches, the houses, the cottages to the harbour and the zulus in the sea. She had a sudden longing to smell the wild flowers, gaze up at the new greening of the Spanish chestnuts, listen to the river Ally with its trout pools and water-gates. Abandoning the letter, she called for the dogs, found their leads because there were young lambs on the Hurler, changed into her walking boots and, choosing a stick to slash at burgeoning thistles, set off to follow the Ally to its source high on the Ben, a favourite walk she had not taken for a while.

It was a sparkling mid-April day. She walked fast, breathing in the air which enlivened her whole being like champagne after the stuffy misery of the past week. Primroses bunched in clumps on the lush river banks, celandine and dandelions carpeted the turf, whins in full bloom smelled of honey, everywhere she looked was green and gold. When she lifted her eyes, the sea was that particular pale blue that promised permanence for a day at least. A clump of yellow iris had her searching in her memory for their Gaelic names. *Seorbrach* – that was primrose, *am bearnan-bride* – dandelion, but she could not remember the word for celandine or whin. She must remember to ask Mr Vass.

Thinking of Hugh Vass reminded her of Victor and the horror of what had happened. She sat down in the shelter of the ancient boulder, her chosen refuge since her childhood days, and gradually the dance and tinkle of the nearby Ally and the high sweet song of a skylark calmed and comforted her. It was all too much to comprehend, the beauty of this her present world, and the sadness of what had happened and what was yet to come.

She heard his footsteps whip the heather before she saw the stranger striding across the moor towards the boulder where she sheltered. So deep in thought was he that he did not notice her at all and would have passed her by had she not moved. He started at the sight of her.

'Miss Megaidh?' he exclaimed. 'I did not see you there.'

Though she had no idea who he was, she was not surprised that he knew her. She had long ago realised that the inhabitants of the Hall were objects of interest and curiosity to the village. Nor was she displeased. The grouse moors were free for all to roam except during the shooting season. She rose to her feet to greet him on equal terms.

'Good day, Mr? I'm sorry I don't seem to remember your name.'

'Why should you? Even my own mother did not know me.' In spite of the lines on his strong weathered face, the leanness of his body, there was something familiar about his appearance and the intentness of his eyes as he looked at her. 'I'm Don King,' he told her in an American accented voice that overlay a lilting local tone. A strange accent. 'I was coming to inquire about your nephew. I found him and my'- he paused for an instant ' - his young friend Daniel on the Hurler yesterday.'

'It was you!' she exclaimed. 'I am so grateful to you, Mr King. He forgot to ask your name. We had no idea who had come to the rescue.'

'My pleasure,' he said politely. As she listened, it dawned on her who he was.

'I know who you are,' she declared. 'You are the new owner of Fisherton. Am I right? I am so pleased to meet you.'

'Indeed,' he said bowing slightly.'The pleasure is mine, Miss Megaidh.'

His American drawl was distracting. The more she looked at him the more familiar he seemed, yet how and where could she have met him? She knew so few Americans.

'We are all so pleased with the improvements you have made in Fisherton. It was always my - and my late husband's - wish to have made them myself but unfortunately...' She tried to inject some enthusiasm into her words but the loss of Fisherton was still a wound.

'I heard of Mr Myers' death,' he said politely. 'Please accept my condolences.'

The longer she looked at him, the more familiar he became. 'Thank you, Mr King. Do you plan to stay here long?'

'That rather depends....' He looked over her shoulder down to where Inverally lay spread out below them.

299

'On what, Mr King?'

'Several things. My mother for one,' he said a little hesitantly.

As soon as he mentioned his mother she knew exactly who he must be. But how was that possible? Surely he had drowned with her brother and Aaron Gallie? So Marsali had been right all these years! She had never believed him drowned; Marsali Gansey who was married to Ezra Macreedie who was also known as King.

'Donnaidh?' she asked uncertainly. 'Are you Donnaidh Macreedie?'

'I am,' he said simply.

Speechless, she sat down again on the springy turf and this time he sat down beside her.

'Can you ever forgive me, do you think?'

She thought he meant for buying Fisherton. 'For what? You and Mr Morton have done nothing but good - '

'For Master Andrew,' he interrupted her. 'For surviving.'

She looked him straight into the eyes. She thought suddenly she could forgive this man anything.

'What happened?' she asked. Almost she did not want to know.

He was silent for a while. 'I survived,' was all he said.

'I'm glad, Donnaidh. I'm so pleased for you, and for your mother. She must be delighted. What will you do now? Will you go back to America or stay with us?'

'First I need to make amends,' he told her.

'I'm sure your mother has forgiven you.'

'My mother, perhaps in time.' He rose to his feet. 'Please give my best wishes to young Master Andrew. I'm pleased he's on the mend.'

'Come and see him for yourself,' she said also rising. She felt a warm affinity to this stranger whom she had known as a child. 'I remember you so well.' An image of the barefoot boy with the unruly tangled hair cowering out of Cuthbertson's sight at the bottom of the steps leading up to the Hall strode into her mind. 'It's so good to have you back, Donnaidh.'

'Does that mean you forgive me?' he asked earnestly.

She was puzzled. 'For surviving? I never blamed you, Donnaidh. No one did.'

He shook his head. 'Thank you for that, but you're wrong. One person did and always will.'

She knew he must be talking about himself for no-one in her family, or in the village to her knowledge, had ever thought to cast a stone at him or any of the lads.

He lifted his hand briefly to his brow partly in farewell, partly as a gesture of respect. 'Good day to you, Miss Megaidh. If there's anything I can do for you, please ask.'

He was already several yards away from her before she remembered Jenkins. If the Hall was really to be lost to her, homes would have to be found not only for Jenkins but for all the servants one way or another. She was about to call him back but changed her mind. There would be time enough for that. The thought of meeting him again was a pleasure in store. Instead she roused the dogs and strode upwards, her energy restored.

Fisherton

Evie sat at the door of the cottage with her neighbours mending nets. The boaties had gone out early with the tide and would not be in till the following evening but none of the women were anxious. The sea was like a pond and the sky cloudless. She had no fish to sell. The older bairns, including her Cathy and Seth, were at the school. The toddlers played among themselves in the street. Chat flowed easily between the women. Most days they grumbled about the rents, the price of meat, the stubbornness of their men folk, the waywardness of their older children, the poverty of the fishing season, the doings of 'the Darkie' as they called Aaron Morton, but not this morning. This morning was all about the return of Don King.

He had called in last night to greet his brother. He had a new motor as big as a boat, too big to drive down the narrow streets of Fisherton so he had left it at the foot of the Brae. Everybody had seen it there or outside Marsali's door in Kirkton. Bairns hovered over it, awe-struck in admiration.

On this fine morning everybody had something to say and most of the remarks were directed either obliquely or directly at Evie.

'So Donnaidh King's back then.'

'Aye wi' his pockets full of' siller.'

'What's he been up to all they years ? Nothing good, I'll be bound.'

'They King brothers know well how to look after theirsels.'

There were sly glances in her direction. She concentrated on her net but she felt her cheeks go hot.

'Where has he been all these years, that's what I'd like to ken?'

'America, I heard tell,' said Evie's neighbour, a buxom woman with quiet bairns. 'But Evie will ken.'

'Aye, Evie will ken. Go on then, tell us Evie? Whaur's he been hiding himself all these years?'

'And nivver a word tae his mam.'

'Mistress Gansey never believed him drowned,' said Anna Munro, who having once been Marsali's closest neighbour, knew more, or thought she did. 'She always kenned he were alive.'

'Why did he no' let on to her, then? Don't tell me they canna send letters frae America because I get one every month from our Davie in Canada.'

'And how did he come by all that siller, I'd like to know.'

There was a pause which Evie felt bound to fill.

'He worked for it,' she said loudly. 'In a cattle ranch.'

'A cattle ranch?' said her neighbour scornfully. 'Fisher folk in a cattle ranch? Can you see Old Geordie at the Mains in sea boots!'

They all laughed.

'Maybe he found a gold mine.'

'He'll not need to put up the rent then.'

'Aye he will. That's how they keep their siller.'

They were silent for a moment as each of them pondered the remarkable fact; Marsali Gansey King also called Macreedie's youngest bairn was now owner of their homes, the streets where they lived, the ground under their feet and a big motor forbye.

'Fine for you, Evie,' said one of the younger wives, 'good-brother to the boss. You'll never end up in the Poor House.'

As soon as the woman had spoken she clapped her hand to her mouth. She had forgotten that Evie's father, old idle Ephraim Cooper had died last year in the Poor House.

Anna broke the uneasy silence. 'Aye well, times are changing right enough. I mind that old prophecy my mam used to tell us when we were bairns. *'Thig an latha ...the day is coming when the bonny lands of Inverally will fall into the hands of the son of fisherman.*

'Right enough. It was the *Fiosaiche* who said it.'

'I mind more' said another. *'the day is coming when the big sheep will chase the people from Glen Mhor.'*

'Whoever said it surely had the second sight for here we are.'

303

'Aye' said Anna, *and the day is coming when water and fire will flow freely through the streets of Inverally.*

'Did he say that?' said Evie who had never heard it before

'He did, lass.' Some of the older women nodded

'There was more,' said Anna, trembling from the palsy and with the wonder of it all. 'Do you not recall? *The day is coming when the very hearthstones stones of Inverally will weep for the children who are no more.*'

There was silence among the women while they contemplated the mystery.

'The preacher told us that was a black lie invented by the de'il,' one of the older women protested.

'It was not a lie though, was it?' said Evie quietly.

Suddenly everyone was laughing and Evie with them. One of the toddlers had got himself ravelled up in a neighbour's net. Someone had remarked dryly. 'If that's the quality of the fish this season it's no wonder the prices are down.' It wasn't particularly funny but it made her forget the about strange prophecies, the cheerless cottage with the pots still unwashed in the stone sink, the new water closet that spewed out filthy waste because she had put down potato peelings and other bits of rubbish. Nobody had told her different and it still hadn't been fixed. Then there was Jonas, sourer than rhubarb, his tongue as dangerous as his fists. You'd think he would be pleased to see his long lost brother, but no, not Jonas. Nothing pleased Jonas.

Evie remembered the previous evening with astonishment. They had been sat at their meat, bairns on the floor, Jonas in his chair, herself at the big pot with the oatmeal and tatties flavoured with the remains of one of Jonas' hogs, when the rap had come to the door. Who would rap? No one in Fisherton rapped. They chapped and walked in.

At a look from Jonas she sped out of the room into the narrow lobby and tentatively opened the door a crack. There he stood a fine sturdy figure of a man, dressed smart, with a strong face, brown and lined, and a smile on his mouth. That mouth with the chiselled lips distinctively bowed under the faintly aquiline nose reminded her of someone.

'Evie, is it?' he asked in a pleasant twangy voice that sounded like the Darkie and he was smiling. He had strong white teeth that glinted in the gloom of the doorway. 'I'm Don, Jonas's brother.'

She stood back astonished. She knew about Donnaidh of course and how he had been drowned all those years back though the *mathair* thought she knew different. Marsali had often talked to her about Donnaidh, what he did as a bairn, what a clever lad he had been, how he could have ended up a school teacher or even a minister like Mr Vass. She never spoke of him when Jonas was there, though, and Evie had long ago learned not to mention his name in Jonas' presence. For some reason Jonas did not like his brother. 'An idle cocky shite,' he once said, 'The boatie that drowned him did us all a favour.'

But it was the boatie seemingly that saved him. So he said with a cup of tea in his hand seated in her chair opposite his brother who had not moved to welcome him, nor held out his hand in greeting. Seth and Cathy sat at his feet, mouths open, the sweeties that he had brought them forgotten in their hands. Only when she saw them together she realised that his nose was exactly like Jonas', like an eagle's beak.

'So you've had it good,' said Jonas grudgingly after he had told them about the ranch. 'What's kept you all these years? Women or whisky?'

'Jonas!' she protested with an eye on the listening bairns.

'No,' Donnaidh said to her, unperturbed . 'Jonas is in the right of it. I should have told my mother. Truth is I was ashamed.'

305

'Ashamed of all that siller? A likely tale.' Jonas said with scorn.

Don opened his mouth then closed it again.

'Why should you be ashamed?' she asked him. Jonas shot her an evil look.

'Ashamed of what?' he interrupted her crudely 'Did you drown your precious foster brothers then?'

'Jonas!' she declared again as Donnaidh rose to his feet.

'He's not denying it,' Jonas said triumphantly. 'That's it, isn't it? No wonder you stayed away. Why did you bother coming home? The sooner you go back to your fancy ranch the better. We all manage fine without you.'

'You're right and you're wrong, Jonas,' Donnaidh told him quietly as he stood up and moved towards the door but Evie could see that he was angry.

One of the bairns, Cathy the eldest, called out after him, 'Will we see you again, then?'

He turned and smiled at her 'I'm not going anywhere in a hurry, quine,' he told her

Evie had seen him to the door. 'Pay no heed to Jonas. I'm glad your're back,' she told him shyly.

That had been yesterday. Donnaidh back felt like a blanket around her shoulders. She hugged it close.

Chapter Eight

Summer 1912

The Hall

On May 3 Andrew went back to school for the summer term, his last at the preparatory school before starting at Wellington in late September. Meg took him to Inverness and after a hefty 'last' lunch at the Caledonian Hotel saw him on to the 2.15 train to Perth. He was going to India to spend the long summer holidays with his father in the care of a professional lady companion who supplemented her income by escorting children on the voyages to and from India.

The farewell was not painful or protracted because there were several boys returning to school on the platform and although all of them felt as miserable as sin none of them wanted to show it. The goodbyes on his behalf at least were loud and cheerful. On hers, less so. She was on her way to see Macmurtrie to tell him she had made up her mind.

During the past week a letter had come from his office accountants stating exactly the state of the Trust's affairs and they were not good, worse than she could have imagined and ever since the funeral she had been imagining the worst. If the Trust dissolved and sold up now, there would be enough left over from the sale to pay the servants a small pension, keep her in the Dower house and support the Bothy. Colonel Moncrieff and Lady Harriet Barraclough had both wired to insist that the decision must be hers, but that reluctantly they could see no alternative. Of her own fortune there was less than £3000 pounds in Railway Stock left.

When she had come to a decision, she knew that she had to keep Andrew informed. The estate, after all, was his, she only a caretaker. It had been easier than she had believed possible. They had had dinner together in the dining room the previous evening, his favourite food, roast chicken and chocolate shape, and afterwards he had stayed up long enough to play three games of *Halma* and one very long *Beggar my Neighbour*.

'Will you miss coming here in the summer holidays?' she asked him as she paid out three cards to his King. He was going to India to be with his father.

'Sort of,' he had said non-committally, gathering them into his hand.

'Only sort of'? Truthfully?' He led two cards and then an ace.

'Father's going to teach me to shoot,' he replied as she paid out three cards followed by a knave.

'I thought Finlay had shown you how to shoot.' She paid him with a queen.

'Not grouse, Aunt,' he had said scornfully, dealing out the required two cards. 'Anyone can shoot birds. I mean shoot properly. Army shooting. I want to join the army as soon as I'm old enough.'

'What about the estate? You know your grandfather left it to you in his will. It will be your responsibility when you're twenty-one.' She had stopped playing.

He sighed and said nothing.

'Andrew?'

'Can't you just keep it? I want to be a Gunner like my father and my grandfather. It's your turn to play.'

'Suppose,' she said carefully, her cards held tight in her hand, 'I couldn't keep it either. Suppose it had to be sold? Would you mind dreadfully?'

'No', he said, 'but you would.' He was no fool, she realised. 'I'd be sad of course, but mainly for you - it's your turn to play, Aunt.'

The game which he eventually won continued for another ten minutes in silence. The grandfather clock struck and wheezed nine. 'Time for bed, I think,' she told him. 'A long day tomorrow.'

He rose, kissed her dutifully on the cheek, walked to the door then came back. 'I really don't mind, you know.'

It was then that she realised that he minded a great deal. To tell him she was sorry seemed inadequate, so all she said was, 'Good night.'

She stood waving to him on the Inverness platform until the train was out of sight then looked at the watch. She had three visits to make, the first to Macmurtrie. She took one of the motor cabs in Station Square.

'I think you are making the right decision, Mrs Myers,' he told her sounding so patronising that she felt angry.

'I presumed,' she said shortly, 'that it was the only decision possible under the circumstances.'

'It is, it is,' he reassured her, aware of her anger. He began to expound on the procedure but she cut him short.

'The twentieth of July,' she told him. 'I don't want it advertised until then.'

That would give her twelve weeks to inform and settle the servants, clear the attics and box her possessions. He prattled on but she was no longer listening.

'I need some money,' she told him, interrupting his instructions.

'Of course, of course. How much do you require?'

If he was surprised at the amount he did not show it. 'Give me a few moments.'

The bank notes stowed in her purse, she decided to walk across the Ness Bridge to the High Street. There she found the shipping offices and booked a passage to India on the SS APHRODITE, the same ship on which Andrew was travelling due to leave Liverpool on the twenty-first of July. It had been her brother-in-law's idea for her to visit. His wife Clarissa had written warmly to welcome her now that she had no ties: in other words 'find me a husband', Meg thought on a spurt of humour. After initially discarding the idea of India, she had slowly come round to thinking that she might quite like to get away for a while. Now she could not wait.

Her third visit was to the Police Station.

Inverness

Inspector Golland did not often have the 'quality' come to him in his office. When the desk sergeant showed her in, he rose to his feet, took out his handkerchief, fresh that morning thus fortunately clean and dusted the chair he brought forward somewhat deferentially for her to sit on.

Sergeant Grigor had forewarned him. 'There's a lady at the desk, one of the toffs, with a story you need to hear, sir.'

'Show her in then, Sergeant.'

She was not what he had expected. The word 'lady' conjured up the front rows of the Kirk, large broad-bosomed women married to councillors and other high-heid-yins, in furs, wide-brimmed feathered hats, rustling in silks and satins. Mrs Myers was small, presumably in mourning for she was dressed in a dark grey tweed coat and skirt, a simple untrimmed black felt hat, a black leather handbag and black hand-knitted gloves. She had a watch pinned to her lapel and a white silk blouse with a narrow black tie. She was not beautiful but she was not plain either. Inspector Golland, who always noticed everything, was particularly struck by her vulnerable mouth and pretty smile. He glanced down at the note his Sergeant had given him. Mrs Margaret Murray Myers of Inverally Hall: widow; d.o.b. 14.03.1877 which would make her thirty-five years old. Worn well. Figure of a girl. Not an ounce of surplus flesh on her. Inspector Golland noticed flesh perhaps because he had rather more than he liked. 'Awfie fat,' his mother called him; 'well-built,' his wife, who was no sylph herself, consoled. He leaned forwards clasping his massive hands together on his desk. 'How can I help you, Mrs Myers?'

'I'm being blackmailed,' she told him concisely.

It was a nasty story indeed. He listened carefully then asked her to repeat herself while he took copious notes.

'This Josiah Higgins. Have you parted with any money yet?'

'No,' she said. 'He called at the Hall last week. I was out but he left a verbal message with one of my servants.' Mima had repeated it verbatim. 'My good wishes to Mrs Myers. I will call back.'

'So let me see if I've got this straight. Your husband, Mr Victor Myers, an invalid recently deceased, has been paying this businessman Higgins large sums of money on a regular basis for some ten years. Higgins maintains that the late Mr Myers was responsible for the death of a certain Mr Anton d'Olio. How and when was that, Mrs Myers?'

'I don't exactly know, but that awful man told me that the death was listed as an unsolved crime in the police files. I presume you will know when it happened.'

'Uh huh,' the Inspector said evenly. 'And the money was to pay Higgins to hold his tongue?'

'He said that the money was to support the dead man's family, now that he was no longer able to earn a living.'

'And your husband believed him?'

She nodded. 'My husband was a ...' she hesitated. 'Believe it or not, Inspector, my husband was a kind man,' she said firmly. 'He would feel obliged.'

'But not obliged enough to come to the police?'

311

'He was probably thinking of what the scandal would do to the rest of us - me,' she said quietly and added even more quietly, 'he probably felt guilty.'

Scared more likely, the Inspector thought. What sort of a fool was this Victor Myers? But he kept his thinking to himself.

'You mentioned his servant, a Mr Jenkins. We would like to question him in due course. Meanwhile you can safely leave the matter in our hands, Mrs Myers. You did right to come to us in the first place. A pity Mr Myers did not do the same.'

'Yes,' she said quietly. 'My life would be very different now if he had.'

He saw her to the door. 'I or my sergeant will want to speak to you again, no doubt. We'll be in touch.'

When she had gone he summoned his sergeant. 'I want you in my office, Willie, right away and bring that file with all the unsolved crimes from 1900 to 1905. Oh and a cup of tea too. We've work to do.'

The Hall

Jenkins was sitting at the kitchen table with a cup of strong tea at his elbow watching Mrs Munro roll out a slab of pastry. Over the years Ina had risen from kitchen maid to cook but she was not married. 'Never had the time,' she explained in such a way as to plant in her listener's ear the belief that she had had many offers when indeed she had had none. She had grown into a bit of a tartar. No one below stairs, except for Jenkins, would dare call her Ina to her face.

Madam had just been down to tell them the Hall would be up for sale in the summer, that to find a buyer might take some considerable time, that she could not guarantee them work after July 20, that she and Master Andrew were going to India for the summer holidays, that she had not finalised her own future plans but that they, the servants, would not be left destitute.

'I'm more sorry than I can say,' she told them briskly, 'I had hoped that the Hall would be my home and yours for the foreseeable future, but that is not to happen. For those of you who are no longer able to work, the estate will continue to support you to the best of our ability. I wish I could be in a position to give you a more definite plan. This has been your home just as it's been mine and the thought of leaving it ...' She could not finish for the threat of tears that choked her throat.

The news was greeted by the small group of indoor staff in silence. Eventually Mima spoke for them all. Her voice was larded with reproach. 'It's a sad day indeed, Madam. I'm just thankful the Colonel did not live to see it. Broken his heart, it would have.'

'Will I get a pension then?' said Florrie, the fourteen-year kitchen maid from Fisherton, a remote cousin of Ina. She had meant it as a whisper to Mrs Munro but everyone heard.

'You, a pension!' said Mima, outraged. 'You've fifty years work ahead of you, girl.'

'I'll try to find you a new job, Florrie,' Madam told her kindly. 'I can't guarantee you work for me, but I can give you a good reference. I'll do my best for all of you, I promise you that.'

After she had finished speaking she had told Jenkins to see her upstairs. 'Immediately, if you please,' she had added firmly when he showed to inclination to move.

'That's you told,' said Mima tartly.

He shot her a look. He had never taken to the women folk below stairs, or above, come to think of it. Deliberately, slowly, he finished his cup of tea before climbing the stone steps, through the green baize door, along the dark passage to tap on the small sitting room door before entering.

'Sit down, won't you, Jenkins?' She seldom called him Jimmy like Mr Victor and young Andrew. Wouldn't dare, he thought as he took the chair she had indicated.

'I have been wondering, Jimmy - '

Oh ho. So I'm Jimmy now, he thought. She'll want something.

'Have you made any plans for the future?' she continued. When he didn't immediately answer (of course he had plans for the future which he was not prepared to share with anyone), she added, 'I don't know how I would have managed without you, Jimmy, first the colonel and then Mr Victor. Had things been different there would have been no thought of you ever leaving the Hall. This has been your home almost as long as it's been mine. I'm not sure what my own plans are. I might well stay on in India, for a while at least. I was wondering therefore if you would like me to find accommodation for you somewhere in the village? At the estate's expense of course.'

'Fisherton?' he asked, attempting to keep his voice even. I'll wager she'd have dumped me in Fisherton.

'That might be difficult but I can certainly ask Mr Morton.'

'Don't bother yourself on my account, Mrs Myers. I already have h'accommodation... in h'Inverness.' A two-roomed tenement flat nowhere near Inverness, but that she did not need to know. He could hear the crow of triumph in his tone.

'That is good news,' she told him. He sounded surprised. Did she really believe him incapable of sorting out his own future? Where the money had come from she didn't need to know.

'Do you plan to leave soon?' she asked.

314

'h'I'll stay till h'Im ready,' he said cryptically. 'h'I'll sort Mr Victor's things.' He had already sorted most of them into his own personal belongings.

'Thank you, Jimmy.' Huh, he thought. You wouldn't be thanking me if you knew what I know. You'd have the polis on to me.

The interview was over, or so he thought. They both rose to their feet. Thus, her next remark mirroring his own thoughts, came as a shock. 'One more thing, Jimmy. I'm afraid you'll be having a visit from the Inverness police within the next day or two.'

'And w'at would that be h'about, Ma'am?' he asked evenly. If he was surprised he did not show it. The good days were about to begin just a bit sooner than he had planned. He had a place of his own and what with his savings, his army pension and a few bob from the boss he'd be all right. As for the police they could ask what they liked. He didn't have to answer them.

Kirkton

Hugh Vass heard the horse in the small carriage-drive snort outside the schoolhouse   The whole class heard it. Seth Macreedie who sat nearest the window stood up and peered out. 'It's the lady from the big hoose.'

'Thank you, Seth' Hugh said mildly. 'Read on, please.'

Miss Megaidh at eleven in the morning? She did not usually call so early knowing his school hours. It would be Helen she was wanting on Bothy business, no doubt. He had intended to visit her later in the afternoon. He had heard rumours, or rather Helen had been told by someone, that the estate was definitely to be sold. Surely she would have told him if things had got so bad; perhaps that was why she had called.

315

Abruptly he told the class to continue reading in silence. 'Mr Gordon will keep the door and his ears open,' he warned them sternly. 'I want the chapter finished by the time I return.'

They were both standing in the parlour by the unlit fire, the two women he loved, when he joined them. They both turned their heads to look at him.

'Mrs Myers has sad news, for us, Hugh,' Helen said rising to go over to him. She took his arm a little possessively. 'She is leaving us to go to India.'

Hugh was shocked. Never in his life had he thought that the woman he had known and loved from her girlhood would ever leave her home. Yet the indications were all there. The estate had been limping along for some time now. Ever since she had got rid of Wylie, the factor, the hedges were uncut, the fences broken, bills unpaid or so he had heard. As for the house, he had noticed damp patches on the drawing room ceiling, scribbles of mould in the downstairs cloakroom, that sweet smell that he recognised as dry rot in the hall. Why had she let it get so bad? Where had all the money gone?

'I leave with Andrew at the end of the summer term. The ship sails on the 21st of July - the day after the Hall goes officially on the market.'

India, he thought aghast, did she have to go so far? Why did she have to leave Inverally? 'Is there nothing that can be done? Stay with us here,' he added impulsively.

Helen pressed his arm. 'Yes indeed,' she echoed kindly. 'Stay with us for as long as you like. Andrew too. We are very quiet without Hamish and we would love to have you.'

She smiled a little as she shook her head but her eyes were bright with tears. 'Such kindness!' she told them, but her mind was made up. 'I came to tell you both personally and also to speak to Mrs Vass about the Bothy.' They sat down together on the sofa and were soon deep in serious conversation.

Hugh was no longer listening. He looked at the two women he loved, from one to the other, and then the thought came to him, suppose it was Helen who had come to tell him she was leaving and not Megaidh. It was then that he knew where his heart lay. How strange, he thought. The reality of Megaidh leaving was sad but the idea of Helen leaving would have been a tragedy.

'Will you excuse me, ladies?' he interrupted. 'I have a class to manage.'

Meg stood up apologetically. 'I'm so sorry. It was a bad time to come. I'm afraid I can think of no one but myself these days. You must both come to dinner before I go.'

'Arrange it with my wife,' he said taking her hand. 'You know how much we will miss you.'

'And I you,' she said. 'Both of you.'

He knew then as she held his hand that just as his love for her had subtly changed into affection, (perhaps that was all it ever was) so hers for him had been nothing more than a youthful crush. He would miss her, of course he would, but his heart was not broken. He bent to kiss her cheek because he knew it was safe to do so, safe and right. Helen took her in her arms. Above her head, they caught and held each other's eyes.

The Road to Point

It had been Fanny's idea that Jared should take his brother to the Station saloon. Fanny liked Donnaidh, that was obvious. He could not help thinking that this was because he was wealthy, a success and generous. He had brought her chocolates and crystalised fruit in a gaudy package and she had been delighted. Would she have bothered to invite him to tea if he had come back a penniless vagabond? At the same time he was aware that he was not being fair to his wife. Rather he was projecting his own perceptions upon her. Fanny did not care about these niceties. She had married him, had she not, against her father's wishes? But he Jared, cared. He was Fisherton born and bred. So was his mother, so were Jonas and Effie. Where they lived made no difference to who they were. They carried Fisherton on their shoulders like a shawl. They only had to open their mouths for the world to recognise their origins. His cultivated accent might fool strangers but never himself. He preferred the company of big folk. Suddenly Cynthia stormed into his mind. She was seldom far away. Yes, he aspired high. He deliberately pushed the thought of Cynthia out of his mind if only for the space of an hour or two.

He did not know what he really thought about Donnaidh's return. He knew he should be pleased and of course he was pleased but at the same time he remembered his father's bitterness and his mother's grief when he had vanished; how hard she tried to convince anyone who would listen that he was still alive. Surely it would have been easy enough for Don to have let them all know he was safe.

He tried to say something of the kind to his brother as they walked the street towards the hotel.

Don was silent for a while. 'Can you not understand? I was ashamed,' he said at last.

'Ashamed?' Jared declared in astonishment, stopping and turning to face his brother. 'You survived. That surely was a matter for pride.'

'I am still ashamed.'

What else has he done, Jared wondered uneasily. He was an odd fellow this brother of his, playing the big man when it suited him, the quiet incomer at times. Without thinking, they passed the hotel entrance and carried on striding along the road to Point.

'What really happened, Don?'

'What is there left to say?' Donnaidh replied evenly. 'I told you of my passage in the galley. I told you how I was employed by Mr Gemmell on his ranch, how he took me into his home, how we were suited, how he left me his fortune.'

'Why this shame, then? I don't understand.'

Don turned on his brother. 'Must I spell it out to you? I let those two lads drown. Had it not been for me they would both be here now.'

Jared was astonished by his vehemence. How could his brother take the blame for what surely had been an accident of wind and waves.

'No one blamed you.'

'You all did. From the laird to Gallie at the timber yard right down to that hovel in Fisherton I once called home. You all blamed me. And you were right to do so. I was the only one who wanted to try out the boatie that night. Aaron and Andrew came because I wanted them to come. I let them drown as surely as if I had pushed them under the waves with my two hands.'

Had they blamed him? Not to Jared's knowledge. But what if he had returned alone? What then?

Without thought, the brothers stopped beside a stile. Jared sat on the step while Donnaidh leaned against one of the fence posts. A glimmer of understanding dawned on Jared, something of Don's pain and guilt and he was astonished that this seemingly arrogant brother of his who had been so obviously his mother's pet could have such feelings. Jared had never liked him more.

'What was this Mr Gemmell like, then?' he asked curiously.

Donnaidh was quiet for a moment as he thought. 'An old man with a temper on him like the squawl that drowned my brothers.'

'They were not your brothers,' Jared said a little resentfully. I was your brother, and Jonas; we were your brothers, he added in his head.

'My foster brothers then,' said Donnaidh.

'And this Mr Gemmell became your foster father. Is that it? You chose to stay with him and forget your true family. What did he promise you? A gold mine?'

Donnaidh's mouth twisted in a joyless smile. 'You're right about the gold mine. Mr Gemmell did not make his money out of ranching. He struck it rich a good while before I knew him.'

'And he left it all to you?' Jared was less resentful than impressed. 'Why?'

'He owed me...' he began reluctantly.

When Donnaidh hesitated. Jared knew there was more to his brother's past than he was telling. 'He owed you? Why? What did you do for him?' he asked curiously.

'I told you he had a temper on him that would burn a forest. He killed a man. I took the blame. The reason I stayed away so long was not entirely my fault. I spent the last ten years in Wyoming state penitentiary.'

Jared's mouth opened. 'For nothing?' he exclaimed. 'You spent ten years in jail for nothing? I can't believe it! Does my mother know?'

Donnaidh nodded. 'I told her myself.'

It was Jared's turn to be silent as he tried to digest the facts of his brother's life. 'So this Mr Gemmell paid you to go to jail for him?'

'Not exactly. He was an old man who had been good to me. His wife was sick and they had no family and few friends. I was as hot-headed as he was in those days. I was in a fight with another lad who was beating the daylights out of me. He had a knife. Mr Gemmell shot him dead on my behalf. Yes, I took the rap. He would have died in jail within the month. He died anyhow a few years later and left me every dollar in his will.' He paused then added, 'I came home as soon as I was released.'

'How does Aaron Morton come into all this?'

'We shared a cell for some five years. You get to know a man pretty well if you share a cell. He told me how his great grandmother had been slave to Lord Morton's ancestor, a much-loved slave by his account. He was curious to see his ancestral home so I employed him as my agent. The rest you know.'

But you don't know everything, Jared thought; there's things I'm not willing to share even with you, my fine brother.

'Why did you buy Fisherton?' he asked aloud.

'Because I could,' Donnaidh replied enigmatically. It was no answer really.

'And will you buy the Hall too? And the whole estate of Inverally?'

'Why do you ask?'

'Because it's up for sale as from the 20th of July. Effie and Sam and the house servants were all told yesterday morning.'

'Why?'.

'They're bankrupt,' Jared said. He could hear the ugly note of triumph in his voice. 'Owing money everywhere, the Emporium included. The estate is going to rack and ruin.'

'So I've seen. Why though? I thought there was plenty of money there.'

'There was,' said Jared. 'There was…' Jared hesitated. Would he tell him what he knew? If Donnaidh could admit to a ten year jail sentence for murder, then he could surely share his own secret which had, since the news of the sale of the estate, had become a burden to him. 'I reckon it was Mr Myers' blame.'

The words poured out of him like water. How once a month the package – a bottle he could tell – was delivered to the hotel from an apothecary in Inverness to be handed over personally and privately to Mr Myers by himself. 'I knew what it was of course. Nothing wrong in it; but Mr Jenkins said that Mrs Myers would not approve.'

'What was it?' Donnaidh asked. 'Alcohol?'

'Alcohol and opium. Mostly opium. Stronger than laudanum. Mr Myers was a sick man.'

Donnaidh shrugged. 'A little opium could not have bankrupted the estate, surely.'

'That was not the only package,' Jared lowered his voice. 'There were two in all. The opium and another envelope, one fat, one thin. The fat one was to be delivered personally and privately by me to the Hotel desk in exchange for the bottle. The thin one which contained a five pound note was a payment to me for my trouble…and to hold my tongue. The fat one contained a lot of money, every month or so for years. Years, Don! So you see? It's no wonder the estate is bankrupt.'

Donnaidh was silent. 'I thought the estate was held in trust for the young lad, Andrew. Where did the money come from?'

Jared shrugged. 'How would I know? I was just the go-between. Some said it was her money that kept the wages paid.'

'What sort of a man was Miss Megaidh's husband?' Donnaidh asked curiously.

'Victor, they called him. Nice enough I suppose. Simple though. Had a bad stutter on him too, poor fellow. We got on fine. Used to have a game of backgammon with him when I took up the package. Got a glass of brandy off him, too. He liked his brandy. Some said he was a pansy. I wouldn't know. I liked him well enough.'

'Poor Miss Megaidh – to lose her husband and the estate,' said Donnaidh.

'Aye, well,' said Jared. 'They were not that close, or so Fanny tells me. Little wonder if it was her money he took, so it's said, though how would I know? Anyways the police are on to it now. I've told them all I know.'

There he said it, the little secret that he had kept from Fanny and had not intended to share with his brother.

'The police?'

'Aye. An Inspector from Inverness. Seemingly he knows about the money. I told him about the arrangement and the stuff that Mr Myers needed for his health. I was just doing the poor wee mannie a favour... For God's sake don't tell Fanny.'

Automatically they stood up and began to retrace their steps back to the hotel. Jared still had one question burning a hole in his brain. 'Now you've got Fisherton, do you think you'll make an offer for the estate?'

It was a question too far. Don said nothing. It was as if he hadn't heard. Jared did not like to ask it again.

At the hotel Donnaidh was mobbed. All of Kirkton, it seemed, knew the story of his disappearance and return. Jared was pleased enough to show him off.

But a few hours later alone with Fanny in their big bed he was not so sanguine. 'I'll not have Don up at the Hall playing his lordship over me,' he told her bitterly but she was already asleep.

The Stables

At the kitchen table, Effie had a chance to study her brother. He looked older than his thirty-three years, weather-scarred, too thin, fined down to flesh and bone without a spare inch of fat on him. There were white flecks in his dark hair, lines around his eyes and his nose had been broken. What had he really been up to in those twenty long years, she wondered as she watched her son, Daniel, listening open-mouthed to his uncle's story about a rattlesnake. Sam was no better. Wee Donnaidh had become for them the hero straight out of the colourful penny bookies about pirates and explorers and cowboys that Danny devoured when he had the chance.

She caught her brother's eye over the head of her youngest. 'Will ye take more meat?' she interrupted.

'Mam!' protested Danny.

Don laughed as he held out his plate. 'There's plenty time for stories, Danny lad, but your Mam's good meat will not stay hot forever.'

'Plenty of time?" Don, man, does that mean you plan to stay in Inverally?' Sam asked.

'Long enough for a few more wee stories,' his brother-in-law replied enigmatically

That was not good enough for Effie. When Danny had come back bruised and shaken from the mishap on the Hurlers full of tales about the stranger and when that stranger turned out to be her long lost brother she had been dreaming foolish dreams. Marsali had told her not to go counting her chickens, that Donnaidh surely had other interests in America but Effie could not help herself. Her dreams grew bigger by the day. Eli, fifteen past, was apprenticed unwillingly to a builder from Point, Ruth nearly seventeen was homesick and unhappy in service in Inverness and Danny was only interested in those new fangled motorcars that were already beginning to appear in the High Street.

Donnaidh could maybe help them all, set Sam up in a new business now that the estate was about to be sold, take Danny over to America and get him into the motor industry and - why not? She had whispered her hopes privately to Sam who had flattened them in a sentence. 'Why would he do that? Likely he has a wife and five bairns waiting for him across the water.' She had not thought of that. There was an easy way to find out. Given the opportunity she would ask him.

'I'm away to the stables,' Sam said when they had eaten their fill. He pushed back his chair. 'The old mare is off her oats. I'd value your opinion, Don.'

'I'll come too,' said Danny eagerly unwilling to let his hero out of sight. 'can I get into your motor?'

'*De tha thu deanamb?* Not so fast, boyo,' said Effie sternly. 'You've school work to do. Away through to the room.' The room was the Sunday parlour kept strictly for visitors like Miss Megaidh, Sunday afternoons and homework. 'And you, Donnaidh, stay a wee while. I'm needing to speak to you.'

'Now you're for it,' Sam joked. 'Come by the stables when she releases you.'

Don did not laugh. Sam wondered for the moment what he had said to offend his brother-in-law. 'See you later,' he said as he left the kitchen to put on his boots.

When they were alone Effie plunged straight in. A great man he might be, but he was also her wee brother and she was not going to hold back now she finally had the opportunity to question him. 'What are your plans, Donnaidh?'

'What have you heard?' he countered.

A little spurt of anger puffed blew up in her head. She confronted him hands on her hips. 'It's been fine to see you again, Don, I'll not deny that, but you can't turn our lives upside down and then disappear again. My mother needs to know - we all need to know - what are your plans? There's a rumour going the rounds that you're wanting to buy the estate. Is that true? Some are saying you've a wife and five bairns in yon America and your're planning to set them up in the Hall.'

He stood up and moving towards her, put his hands on her shoulders. 'Effie, Effie, I'm not going to abandon any of you, at least not for a while. The fact is I don't yet know what I'm going to do, but this much I can tell you. I don't have a wife and I don't have any bairns anywhere. I don't even have a sweetheart, more's the pity.'

'Why not?' she retorted. 'You're thirty-three years old. What stopped you?'

'Not much opportunity where I've been for the past ten years,' he said shortly returning to his chair. 'Sit down, Effie, till I tell you the rest. I'd rather you kept it to yourself, but I can't force you.... I've been in jail for the past ten years.'

She opened her mouth but no words would come. She listened in appalled silence as he told the whole of his story. When he had finished she went over to him and bent down and, uncharacteristically, kissed his cheek. 'You're safe now,' she told him. 'Home and safe.'

Meanwhile her mind was racing. Her little brother was free in every sense of the word. He would look after them all when the estate was sold and she would look after him. 'I was thinking,' she said, beginning to clear the table. 'maybe you could set up a wee business down in Milton, a family business. Motors maybe? Sam would help you. Horses can't be so different from motors, can they? Danny is daft on motors.'

Maybe she had said too much. She didn't want to appear greedy, out for what she could get but with the estate going and Sam out of a job, life would be tough.

He stood up and moved to the door. 'Don't worry, Effy. You'll know my plans when I do. I'd better go and see that mare.'

'One more thing before you go,' she called out.

He paused.

'Is it true you might buy the estate?'

The door closed quietly in the face of her unanswered question.

The Hall

Meg had worked it out. She had also written down a list. Seventy days to clear the house of not only her own things but also a life-time of family possessions; she knew she would have to be ruthless. The two lads who looked after the garden could burn the old papers. Good clothing could go to the Bothy. Helen Vass would see to that. The furniture could remain at least until the Hall was sold. This, she realised, might take many months. When the time came, Macmutrie would organise an auction to clear the house. Hopefully she would be out of it all, the sadness of parting from her home and its possessions dimmed by the distance of several thousand miles. What she would do after India she had considered not at all, shied away from the very thought of it. Macmutrie advised that the Dower house in Kirkton should be kept for her use, but she had always disliked the place with its dark poky rooms and big heavy furniture.

She decided to start in Victor's suite. She had intended to get Jenkins on to that. but Jimmy had gone. Shortly after their conversation he had packed up, presented himself to her and told her he was ready to leave. 'I told you,' he said evasively, winking and waving his hands about as if to explain. 'I have a property… in Inverness.'

'Won't you be a bit lonely?' she asked. 'Have you friends in Inverness?'

'My first posting was h'Inverness before h'I worked for the Colonel. A mate h'arranged it,' he said somewhat cryptically. She didn't know that he had any 'mates'. It occurred to her how little she knew about the wizzened little monkey of a man who had given his life in service to her family. 'Can't see no point in 'anging on 'ere,' he told her when she protested that he would be missed. 'h'I've got a bit put by and the rainy day 'as come.'

'Indeed it has,' she told him sadly. 'You've been a wonderful help to my family, Jimmy, but I think you know that. If you leave your address, Mr Macmurtrie will be in touch with you about your pension. Do you want Sam to take you to the station when you leave?'

'The station wagon's coming at twelve sharp.'

'Oh!' she said surprised. 'As soon as that? Please do take what you want from Mr Victor's things and let me know when you're going.'

The staff all gathered when the wagon drew up. She could not help noting how many bags and boxes he had, but supposed that they were the accumulation of some thirty years of service to her family. She shook his hand, gave him an envelope containing twenty-five pounds and wished him well as did the small clutch of servants on the gravel outside the Hall. A twinge of sadness and regret touched her heart as she watched the driver assist his ageing spidery body up into the seat beside himself. Poor little Jimmy. She wished she could have liked him more.

'I hope he'll be all right,' she said to Mima as they climbed the stone steps back into the Hall.

'You need na worry your heid about that one,' said Mima scornfully.' He kens fine how to take care of himself.'

'I hope so,' she answered with a sigh.

'Did he tell you he had the polis at him on Monday?'

She turned round quickly. 'The police? Why? What did they want with him? Did he say?''

Mima shrugged. 'It's no' likely he'd tell me.' She sniffed. Meg knew there had been little love lost between the two of them. 'I thought he would hae mentioned it to you.' When she said nothing, Mima added nastily, 'maybe that's why he's hot-footed it off today.'

Though she said nothing, she could not help but wonder. Leave it to the police, she told herself. Whatever Jenkins had or had not done, she would not be prosecuting the old man. It occurred to her that she had forgotten to get his address.

After he had gone she discovered that he already cleared the drawers and cupboards of his master's things. His watches, cufflinks, tiepins, collar studs and better clothing had all gone. Only Victor's shabby old dressing-gown remained hanging in the wardrobe that had been stripped bare of suits and jackets. At the sight of that worn, frogged garment her eyes brimmed with tears. The loneliness of Victor's life filled her heart with sadness; the loneliness of her own. She could have been kinder to him but she had never loved him enough; never loved him at all. For that reason she felt guilty. For that reason, she had allowed him to squander her inheritance without question. She could not blame him for making a life for himself, disaster though it had proved to be, for he had had none with her. Had she been less critical, less impatient, more loving, he would not have had to find his entertainment elsewhere. So she thought.

All that was left to show for his life were some books and papers, darned underwear and old shoes polished to mirrors, Jimmy's handiwork; she had never doubted this, that he had been good at his job. Most of the books had belonged to her father, for Victor had not been a reader, finding letters as difficult to decipher as words to speak. His papers consisted mainly of old letters stuffed into a couple of cardboard boxes at the foot of the empty wardrobe. That night she forced herself to go through them. They included a bundle of love letters dating from when he was still a very young man living in the deanery from someone called Hilary. She glanced at one of them. Short, written in careful capitals as for a child or someone who could not read well, she knew these were not for her eyes. Poor Victor, she thought, but only for a moment. He no longer seemed so 'poor' in her eyes, for judging by these letters, some twenty of them, he had loved and he had been loved and she was glad of it. No wonder he had never wanted to come to her bed. Whoever this Hilary was, she had clearly adored him. A girl, she decided firmly. The alternative which touched the edges of her mind was unthinkable... One by one and with some sadness she had burned them in the empty summer grate.

Though she had scrutinized the rest of the papers carefully, there had been nothing from anyone by the name of Anton. No evidence to prove that he existed. She had no doubt that Jenkins had known more than he had ever told her. She hoped he had at least told the police.

Today was Thursday. She had not yet heard back from Inspector Golland which surprised her a little. He had assured her he would be in touch. She wondered continually if she had done the right thing in contacting him. One decision she had already reached. She would pay that odious Mr Higgins not one penny, whatever it cost the family reputation.

Starting in the attics with a scarf tied round her head to keep the dust out of her hair and with Jenny Paterson to help her, she began the mighty task of clearance. She had known Jenny from her infancy in the Lodge, through her childhood and employment at the Hall first as scullery maid and now housemaid. Jenny was engaged to be married to one of the garden lads so the contents of the attic were arranged into three piles; Bothy, bonfire and Jenny's bottom drawer.

'Keep what you like,' Meg had told her to her delight for to Jenny the attics were Aladdin's cave.

'What about this, Ma'am?' Jenny had found the leather case containing the family christening robe. She took it out of its layers of tissue paper, held it up and shook out its lace and silken folds. She had been about to tell Jenny to keep it and then remembered it was rightly Andrew's inheritance. A new pile of things to keep for Andrew was started.

It must have been close to teatime when Mima trudged up the three flights of stairs to the attic floor. 'There's someone to see you,' she said a little truculently. 'I told him you were busy but he wanted you asked.'

Inspector Golland, she thought. 'I'll come.'

As she went downstairs she took off the scarf knotted round her head to keep out the dust and shook out her hair. But it was not the Inspector standing in the hall, broad brimmed hat in hand, it was Mr King, or rather Donnaidh Macreedie as she had once known him. As she paused on the top stair, she could see him below her gazing intently at one of the hunting prints on the wall which had belonged to her father and she was suddenly overwhelmed by a strong sense of familiarity. It was as if she had known this man all her life, knew the way his mind worked, the way his body moved, the way his heart beat. It was an extraordinary sensation, the like of which she had never experienced. Of course she had known him as a twelve year-old boy, briefly, not intimately, but now it was as if he had never been away.

'Donnaidh,' she said with pleasure, informally, unthinkingly, forgetting altogether that he was now virtually a stranger.

'Miss Megaidh.' He took her outstretched hand to shake it. She held on a little longer than necessary. She found it hard to let him go. The touch of his skin was not only familiar, it was like an extension of herself.

She stepped back. 'How nice of you to call,' she said forcing formality into her tone. 'Is your mother quite well?' she asked, not knowing what to say because there was so much she would rather say, such as how good it was to see him .. How wonderful that he had come back….how fine he looked.

'My mother is very well. She sends you her kind regards. How is Master Andrew's ankle? He took a nasty tumble.'

'Still limping a bit, he writes, but not badly enough to keep away from the class room. Has Danny fully recovered?'

'Fighting fit, thank you.'

The formalities over Meg found herself asking him to stay for tea. Mima who was still hovering disapprovingly in the background said nothing when told to bring tea for two into the drawing room.

'Isn't it strange that our nephews should be such good friends – like you and my brother?'

'Not so strange perhaps when you remember what they shared.' He was not so indelicate as to spell it out.

'Foster brothers,' she said. Then she found herself voicing the unanswered question. 'Why did Andrew drown, Donnaidh? He could swim like a fish.'

He moved to the window and looked out over the lawns that were sprinkled with daisies. 'Because he could swim,' he answered. 'Andrew and Aaron both started to swim for the shore. I was left clinging to the wreckage because I could not swim. My father would not let me learn. He believed that it was better for a fisherman to drown quickly. Swimming only prolonged the agony of drowning. I survived because I could not swim.'

'Thank you,' she said quietly. She could see that it distressed him to remember and his distress moved her. She had long ago got over her brother's death but she realised then that Donnaidh had not. She touched his arm. 'It's over, Donnaidh. You need to forgive yourself.'

He swung round to face her. She could see green flecks in his dark blue eyes, a scar that followed a line in his taut cheek. She wanted to trace it with her finger and found her hand moving of its own accord to touch his face. 'How did you get that scar?'

He lifted his own hand to bring hers down from his face but did not immediately let it go. 'That was the cut that landed me in prison.'

'In prison?' she repeated unbelievingly.

Briefly he told her of the fight that caused his employer to shoot his fellow ranch hand dead; how he had taken responsibility for the crime and had been in jail for ten years. 'You had to know,' he told her. 'Bearing in mind why it took so long to come back, why I'm right here now. You need to know the truth.'

'Tell me.' It was as if her hand itself had been imprisoned. It felt warm and comfortable, wedded for life to his warm strong fingers.

'I came to ask you if you would object if I were to put in an offer for the Hall.'

She was astonished. Pulling her hand away, she replied instinctively, 'But why? Is Fisherton not enough for you? First my brother and now his inheritance! How can you ask it of me? My father must be turning in his grave.'

His face hardened and his back stiffened. 'I need to make myself clear, Mrs Myers. The reason why I bought Fisherton was not to take your family's inheritance but to improve the life of its inhabitants, my own people. The reason I want the estate is because you don't.'

But I do, she screamed at him in her heart. This is my beloved home. Do you think I want to lose it? The reality of what was happening appalled her. 'I'm sorry,' she said aloud, forcing herself to sound calm. 'Its hard to think of parting from my home'

'Especially to a son of Fisherton with a brother at sea, a brother in trade and a sister married to your groom. A jailbird. I understand,' he said evenly but she could hear the bitterness in his tone.

Was that how she felt? Perhaps a little. Although she had not given the future owner of Inverally much thought, she assumed that he would be a gentleman. Aloud she said quietly, 'I'm sorry you should think that.' She could not lie.

'You would prefer Lord Morton,' he said evenly. 'I understand.'

'Lord Morton?' She was horrified. 'He intends to offer? How do you know?'

'Have you forgotten? Aaron Morton is my agent in Fisherton.'

At that moment Mima came in with the tea things. She set the silver tray down on an occasional table with as much clatter as she could get away with. Her disapproval was evident from the set of her mouth to the tips of her fingers. On any other occasion Meg would have laughed, but not now. This, she thought with shame, is how she must appear to Donnaidh.

They waited in silence until Mima had finished and left the room, not exactly banging the door but shutting it a little too firmly.

Donnaidh was the first to speak. 'I guess she don't like me,' he said. His mouth closed firmly, but his eyes seemed to dance.

'Not much,' she said and suddenly they were both laughing.' Now that the tea is here, we had better have it.'

She took her seat at the occasional table and lifted the teapot. 'Milk and sugar?'

'Both, if you please.'

After a moment he sat down. She handed him the cup and saucer. Then both spoke at the same time. 'I do beg you pardon, Donnaidh, if I seemed - ' while he said, 'What has happened to the estate, Miss Megaidh? How has it come to this?'

Afterwards she wondered at herself for being so frank, but the words were out before she could stop them, nor indeed did she ever regret them. 'I think my husband was being blackmailed.'

He listened carefully as she told him all she knew. 'There was a man in Inverness called Anton who seemingly became my husband's friend. His family blame Victor for his death. He has been supporting them ever since. Otherwise they threatened to go to the police. Every month Victor seemingly was forced to pay out more than we could afford.'

'I know something of this.' He told her of Jared's part in the affair, the monthly delivery of laudunum from the apothecary in Inverness. 'I swear Jared knew nothing about blackmail.'

'Poor Victor,' she said. 'How can I blame him? He was a sick man. If the laudanum gave him relief I am glad of it and I'm grateful to Jared for making it possible. As for this Anton, I find it hard to believe that Victor could have been responsible for the death of anyone. It's all in the hands of the police now. No doubt it will all come out in the open and the whole of Ross will revel in the downfall of the Myers family. That is reason alone for selling up. Thankfully Andrew will be in India with his father and thus escape the scandal, and I with him.'

Up to that moment she had been glad of India, but now as she looked at his concerned expression, felt such comfort in his presence, she was not so sure.

They talked a little further before he stood up to go. She walked with him to the door and down the stone steps reluctant to see him leave. At the foot of the steps he took her hand to say goodbye. 'I'll not be putting in an offer,' he told her and she was aghast.

'Oh but I wish you would!' she cried spontaneously. 'I wish you would. Please reconsider.'

He lifted her hand to his mouth and to her surprise kissed it, but he said nothing.

'Goodbye Donnaidh,' were her formal words. Don't leave me, she cried in her heart. As she watched him drive away in his motor she knew for certain that which she had half recognised in her heart the moment they had met on the hill. She wanted him, needed him in her life. How ridiculous that was. Could this be love, she wondered with a sense of incredulity. Could she be in love? She knew now that she had never before been remotely in love. Her feelings for Mr Vass in comparison had been no more than admiration. How ridiculous! Now indeed her parents must be turning in their grave. The laird's daughter and a son of Fisherton! Impossible. Not to be contemplated. Besides, he was still young, he was strong and he was rich. Why would he ever look at her, a plain, thirty-five year old, penniless widow. Put him out of your head, she told herself as she watched him drive away. Putting him out of her heart was, however, another matter.

Milton

Marsali took her visitor into the parlour. She knew that Miss Megaidh had come to say goodbye and she was heartsick at

336

the thought, heartsick that the Myers' were being forced out of home and heritage by her family. So it seemed to her. That Donnaidh would do such a thing saddened her to the quick of her being.

Rumour was rife in Milton. Some said that Mr Myers had been mixed up in an unspeakable scandal, that Donnaidh was somehow bullying Miss Megaidh and forcing her to leave her home for India. In Fisherton, the rumours were equally hateful. Anna, her old friend and neighbou,r had told her that Donnaidh had come back to fulfil the old prophecy that the bonny lands of Inverally would one day be inherited by a son of Fisherton and did Marsali not remember how the prediction ended. '*Woe to that man for his house will surely perish*'

'A lot of nonsense is in it,' she told Anna with more conviction than she felt. 'Who pays heed these days to what an old seer once imagined he saw?'

'His other sayings have come true. '*The big sheep will chase the people from Glen Mhor. The lands of Culloden will be stained with the best blood of the Highlands.* Why should this one fail?' she retorted. 'Your Donnaidh is above himself.'

She had such mixed feelings. Partly she was proud of her son for all he had achieved, partly ashamed for aspiring so high. What must Miss Megaidh think?

'You'll take a refreshment, Miss Megaidh?' If she accepts, Marsali thought, she will have forgiven me and mine. If she refuses, how am I to bear it?

'Thank you, Marsali,' Miss Megaidh seated herself in one of the four big cushioned chairs that Donnaidh had bought for her in Inverness and Marsali, light-footed with relief, brought through a tray with two small glasses of elderflower wine which Missus Fanny had made herself. Missus Fanny was an unending source of admiration to Marsali.

They talked for a moment of Missus Fanny's energy and skills. 'You are indeed blessed in your family,' Miss Megaidh told her and the conversation came round inevitably to Donnaidh.

'*De chanas mi*? What can I say, Miss Megaidh. My heart is heavy that it has come to this.'

Miss Megaidh leaned forward in her chair and reached for Marsali's hands and held them reassuringly. 'But not mine, Marsali. I am sorry that I have to leave, but I am glad that Donnaidh is thinking of taking the Hall. Truly I am.'

Marsali looked at her closely and saw that she was telling the truth. Would she tell her of the prediction that was all over Fisherton? Evie had mentioned it again only yesterday. But it was all havers, was it not? Who believed in such nonsense these days? Certainly not an educated lady like Miss Megaidh.

'*Moran taing*. I thank you for that,' she said but now she could not hold back her anxieties. 'What does my Donnaidh know of managing a great place like the Hall? How will he do it?'

'He will do it well, Marsali,' she reassured her. 'Look how Fisherton flourishes.'

'That is Aaron Morton's doing,' she said quickly.

'And Aaron works for Donnaidh. I'm sure he will help him manage the rest of the estate. Your Donnaidh was running a great ranch in Canada was he not? Inverally is small in comparison.'

Marsali shook her head. 'I don't know what your dear mother, the *Aingeal*, would be thinking.'

'Who knows? But I believe my brother would have been pleased.'

'He would be the only one, then.' She knew that for a fact.

Miss Megaidh sipped the wine. 'This is delicious,' she said. 'Fanny has surpassed herself.'

They talked for a while of other matters, her grand-weans, the arthritis in her back, the future of the Bothy now in Mrs Vass's care, but always the subject came back to Donnaidh. It was still a wonder to her that he was here under her roof, at her table, sometimes under her feet as he had once been as a laddie. She spoke a lot about Donnaidh, perhaps too much but Miss Megaidh seemed happy to listen. Eventually she rose to her feet.

'I'm really here to say goodbye, Marsali. I leave for India on the twentieth.'

'Why?' Her throat tightened with tears. She could not say all the things that were in her heart but Miss Megaidh understood. She put her arms round her and held her close.

'Oh Marsali, when I'm here with you, I don't really know why,' she said. 'It seemed the right thing to do for Master Andrew. After all it was I who lost him his inheritance.'

'But you'll be back?'

'I don't know,' she said as the tears spilled over and fell down her own cheeks.

The Hall

Inspector Golland had taken the station cab up the Brae to the Hall. His case was almost complete. Only an arrest remained. In order to make an arrest he had with him the local police constable, who was aghast at what lay ahead. Constable Rossie was a big man, good at intimidating the local youths, fierce with poachers, but ill-at-ease when it came to dealing with the gentry.

The inspector directed the cabbie up to where the drive split into two lanes, the one, rhododendron-lined, ended in the sweep of gravel in front of the imposing flight of stone steps that led to the front door of the Hall, the other, weedy and overhung with sycamores and beeches, led to the servants' entrance at the back of the house. He chose the back entrance. Last time he had called, he had had words that broached on the insulting with the servant who had opened the front door.

'Mister Jenkins, if you please,' he told the young lassie who opened the back door She took one look at them and fled. After a while the older woman who had been so rude to him last time appeared. 'Well?' she said crossly.

'We're here to speak to James Jenkins. Please inform him of the fact.'

'Then you've had a wasted journey,' she told him smugly. 'Mister Jenkins is not here.'

'Perhaps you could inform us of his whereabouts?' The constable asked somewhat pedantically.

'No,' she said triumphantly, 'I cannot. He left the Hall the day after you spoke to him last. Took all his stuff too. He'll not be back.'

The inspector was not surprised. This, if nothing else, confirmed his suspicions.

'The lady of the house, if you please,' he told her briskly stepping firmly over the threshold . The local constable hung back. He knew Mima of old.

'She's busy.' Mima glared at them.

Constable Rossie turned to withdraw but the inspector held his ground. 'She'll not be too busy to see us,' he declared and reluctantly Mima stepped back.

'I'll have to see. Yous wait there, ' she commanded.

Five minutes later she reappeared cross and breathless. You've to go up.' She turned and they followed her up the flight of stone steps through a heavy curtained door and down a dark passage lined with paintings and into the hall. Once again he noticed the state of the place, peeling paint from the wainscot, the occasional patch of mould and the faint sweetish smell of decay.

'Madam will be down in a wee while,' she told them. 'I've to ask. Do yous want tea?'

Inspector Golland would have loved a cup of tea. The afternoon was warm and the train had been hot, but Constable Rossie refused. 'We're on duty,' he told her virtuously. She left them, and, choosing the least delicate of the beaded and cushioned chairs they sat down to wait.

What a wee thing she was, Inspector Golland thought as seconds later Meg appeared. The two men got to their feet. 'I apologise for keeping you waiting, gentlemen. Has Mima offered you some tea or would you rather something stronger?'

When he reluctantly refused, she begged them to be seated. 'I'm so glad to see you, Inspector. Did you find out anything about the person called Anton?'

It had all been remarkably easy. 'Indeed. Did your husband ever mention visiting the Bonnie Prince Club in Inverness?'

She shook her head. He was not surprised. The Bonnie Prince Club met regularly in a room above the tavern of the same name in a vennel off the High Street. Its members were mostly young gentlemen like Mr Myers who met to smoke and play backgammon and other games of chance. He had kept an eye on it over the years and and knew that from time to time large sums of money exchanged hands, though he had never caught anyone in the act of gambling. Let the young gentlemen enjoy themselves, was the Chief Constable's advice, so long as they behaved themselves..

'A Mr Anton d'Olio, a Spanish gentleman, was certainly a member of the Club some years ago,' he continued.

'Victor knew him?' she asked anxiously. 'What happened to him?'

Seemingly he had been a music teacher to several of the wealthier young ladies of Inverness. The inspector had interviewed one of his pupils, a pretty young wife now married to a prominent banker. She had told him that Mr Anton had been a popular choice of tutor for it was generally known that he was not interested in susceptible young ladies.

'Nothing happened to him, madam. He returned to Spain some eight years ago. I have already had confirmation from the Spanish police that he is very much alive and teaching music in Madrid.'

'Thank God,' she breathed out her relief. 'So Victor never harmed him. Who was blackmailing him, then? Who provided the laudanum?'

That too had been remarkably easy. There were several apothecaries in Inverness, one of whom readily admitted to making up prescriptions of opium for his customers. Yes indeed he had prepared a monthly order for a Mr Higgins, opium and alcohol, a particularly potent form of medication. His lad had delivered it regularly to a Mr Josiah Higgins - he had proof of that - who paid for it without fail about once a month. He had thought nothing of it. Opium was a strong drug, not to be taken lightly, but a blessed relief to certain sufferers. 'Mr Myers was a sufferer, was he not?'

'Indeed he was,' she agreed. 'I did not realise that opium was so expensive.'

'No indeed. I have already spoken to Mr Jared Macreedie who acted as courier for Mr Higgins. He informed me that once a month he received from Mr Jenkins two envelopes each containing money one of which held a small remuneration for his trouble, the other, addressed to a Mr Higgins, he was instructed to leave at the Royal Station Hotel. Macreedie never met this Mr Higgins. According to the receptionist at the hotel, the packages were deposited and recovered by an intermediary, usually a young lad, and not always the same one. This was not at all an unusual transaction. Packages were often left at the hotel desk for uplifting. The receptionist had presumed Josiah Higgins was the apothecary and the courier his lad.'

'And this man Higgins was my visitor, who called himself a man of business! Surely he can't have been a proper lawyer? Have you found him, Inspector?' She was twisting her hands together in anxiety.

Again it had not been hard. The inspector had his own 'friend' (an old potman) who kept an eye on the young members of the Bonnie Prince. According to this friend - spy might be nearer the mark - Joe Higgins had been employed by the tavern as wine waiter to the club members until the previous week.

'A wine waiter?' she exclaimed. 'He was the blackmailer?'

'Indeed, it seems that way,' he told her.

'Have you spoken to him?'

Now to tell her the worst. Joe Higgins had left in a hurry at a day's notice the previous week. He had been seen boarding a train to Glasgow with an old man who fitted the description of James Jenkins.

'My informer told me that Higgins had once boasted to him that he had an old relative who was sitting on a fortune which would all come to him in the not too distant future.'

'So that's who he reminded me of!' she declared. Jenkins had had a habit of illustrating his conversation not only with his winking eye but also with his hands. Now that she thought about it she realised that Higgins used the same gestures. 'I never knew that Jenkins had any relatives.'

'I have every confidence that the Glasgow force will find them,' he reassured her; but he was not at all certain. Finding two men who would not want to be found in the maelstrom of Glasgow would not be easy.

She looked down at her clasped hands. 'I don't want Jenkins prosecuted, ' she said quietly. 'He looked after my father and my husband.'

'I understand,' he told her, but he didn't. Not really. If he had been in her shoes, blackmailed for years by a deceiving servant, he would have wanted justice. Fortunately it was not her decision. 'The matter, however, is no longer in your hands, Mrs Myers. The law will take its course.'

She saw them to the front door, thanked them both and shook their hands.

'What a nice lady!' Constable Rossie remarked twice on their way back to the station.

The Estate Office

The deed was done. Papers signed; money orders arranged. From July 20 – Tuesday of the following week in fact, Inverally would be his, Hall, estate, fifteen properties including the Mains farm, half a mountain. His actual ownership had been fixed for the end of September after the roup sale of furniture and other appurtinances held on the premises had been completed. The auctioneer and his crew were due to enter the the Hall on the day after Miss Megaidh had left for India. Macmurtrie would continue to represent her interests in the sale of her possessions as he had done for the sale of the estate. Don had paid a little over the asking price - he knew that - but it suited him to do so. Aaron would have been mortified had his relative, Lord Morton, had a chance to bid. Where was Aaron? They had arranged to meet at two o clock.

Don had driven up to the office in his motor. He now owned a stable of ageing animals and a groom to take of them. He was not sure he needed any horses now that he had the motor, but there was Sam to consider. Young Danny could think of nothing but motors. He enjoyed the company of his young nephew.

Before he had time to glance at the game books and registers, the files of title deeds, accounts and letters, Aaron arrived on horseback.

'You got it?' he asked as he entered the office.

Don nodded. The two men shook hands. 'I'm pleased for you, man.' Aaron clapped him on the shoulders. 'Don King, laird of Inverally. You got what you wanted.'

'Almost,' he said. He felt strangely flat.

'Whadya mean 'almost'? You've got it all, man. From Fisherton upwards.'

'I could never have done it without your help,' he told him. It was true. Aaron gave him the confidence that only a comrade can provide

'And I would no doubt be back inside that penitentiary without yours.'

'So you're not thinking of going back home, Aaron? I thought maybe...'

'No way, man. I'm here to stay.'

'Thank God for that. We'll do this together. Get this place back to the way I remember it.' He was relieved. Aaron had always said he would go back to Wyoming when he, Don, was free to take over.

'Wait up,' Aaron said taking a step back and holding up a hand. 'You don't need me now, Don. You can manage the estate one-handed. I was only ever temporary, while you got yourself sorted. Besides, I got myself another job.'

Don was disappointed. He had been counting on Aaron's partnership and support for he knew that most of Inverally would turn their backs on him once it was generally known he had acquired the estate. Effie had already asked him if he knew what he was letting himself in for. With Aaron at his side he could have ridden out the disapproval which began with his own brothers. 'What job?' he asked roughly.

345

'At the timber yard. Mr Gallie has asked me to take over as manager. He wants to step back a bit from the business. He's gotten too old, or so he says.'

'I'll offer you twice what he's offering,' Don declared but Aaron shook his head.

'It's nothing to do with the money, man,' he said shifting his eyes sideways.

'Not money, then what?' Don asked, but he reckoned he knew. Aaron liked the ladies.

'Who is she?' he demanded to know. He had seen a lot of Aaron since his return but he had never seen him with a woman, or heard him speak of one. Surely he would have mentioned her. 'Does my mother know?'

'Know what?' he said evasively. 'Don't worry, Don. I'll stay with you till you're settled. Mr Gallie has given me six months to finish up in Fisherton. When do you officially take over the estate?'

The subject was changed to Fisherton and outstanding estate business. Eventually Aaron took his leave. Don watched him go. He was no happier than he had been when Aaron arrived. That talk of women had unsettled him further. He now acknowledged to himself why he felt so restless, out of sorts, dissatisfied. He was deceiving himself if he insisted he did not know. Inverally might now be his but it was incomplete and he knew why. He had known deep inside him since that day on the hill. Perhaps it was not too late. Not with what he had to offer.

He jammed his hat on his head. Don's hat had become his symbol. He was seldom to be seen without it on his head or in his hand. Wide-brimmed and battered, he loved his rancher's hat for it was all he had with him of Mr Gemmell's personal possessions. He wore it in memory of the man who had become his benefactor. He made up his mind and cranked up his motor.

'She's not in,' said Mima sharply when she answered the door. He knew that she too was deeply disapproving of his visits and that rightly his place was at the back door.

'When do you expect her back?' he asked bravely. Mima was terrifying in her dislike of him.

'How would I ken?' she remarked rudely, managing to imply she would never tell him even if she knew, as she shut the door in his face.

He would wait. Leaving his motor on the drive he decided to find her if she was to be found. One of the gardening lads, digging out a clogged ditch, told him she was in the walled garden and there she was, stooped over a clump of fading flowers whose name he never knew, with a pair of secateurs cutting off the dead stems.

She looked up and they looked at each other for a long moment. She was wearing a battered man's panama sun-hat and a bibbed apron over her white silk blouse and black skirt. She looked familiar, not unlike other working women, and yet entirely unlike them. He thought her beautiful in her uniqueness and at the same time in her familiarity.

'Miss Megaidh.' he began as he removed his hat.

'Donnaidh?' she shaded her eyes. 'How nice to see you. Is there anything I can do for you?'

He said the first thing that came into his head. 'Those prints in the Hall, the ones that the colonel liked. I would like to purchase them for the office.'

'Of course,' she told him. 'Please take them as a gift. I really am grateful to you, Donnaidh. It is good that the estate has gone to someone I know, a family I have always respected.'

'Even if we're from Fisherton?' he said dryly. He could not help himself.

She was silent for a moment as her eyes turned downwards. I've offended her, he thought, annoyed by his own stupidity.

Then she looked up. 'No, Donnaidh, you're wrong. Marsali has always been as dear to me as she was to my mother. You were my brother's hero. I didn't want to sell the estate but I can think of no one I'd rather have living here. Someone from Inverally born and bred.'

He took a step closer and again spoke straight from his heart. 'Don't go to India, Miss Megaidh. Stay. The Hall needs so much done to it. Help me get it right.'

Again she was quiet but it seemed to him that his offer had pleased her. After a moment, however, she shook her head. 'That is kind, Donnaidh. But I have to go. You know I do. I would only be a hindrance to you and your plans. Besides I don't think I could bear …'

She could not finish her sentence, so he did it for her. 'I understand. You could not bear to see your brother's killer, a jailbird, a fisher lad, sit in your father's chair.' He knew he sounded bitter but again he could not help himself.

'No, Donnaidh.' She took off her gardening gloves and reached out to touch his hand. 'Not that. I'm just finding it a bit hard to leave my home.'

He took her hand and entwined her fingers with his. 'Miss Megaidh…' he began, but now he could not say the words aloud he was shouting in his heart. This is your home. I love you. Stay with me, and then the unthinkable, marry me.

Instead he said, 'That other business with the police, did you get it sorted?'

She unwound her fingers He fancied she could feel his reluctance to let her go. . She told him about the fraud. 'Victor was being blackmailed by two rogues all these years. I feel so sad for him.'

He felt hot with anger. 'You are too forgiving. Your husband was surely much to blame.'

'No, Donnaidh, I am to blame. I only married him to keep the Hall.' She laughed a little, both of them aware of the irony of the situation. 'Come up to the house,' she said, changing the subject. 'I'd like to give you those prints.'

He protested that they should perhaps be valued but she spoke through him. 'A gift to your office. Anything else you might want, please let Macmurtrie know.'

Outside the garden he offered her his arm to walk up to the house. She took it without hesitation. In silence they walked slowly up weedy paths, over shaggy lawns. Inside his head he was shouting 'I love you,' but he could not say the words aloud. He was too afraid of her rejection. Of course she would reject him.

Indoors he unhooked the prints and she wrapped them in brown paper. 'Give my respects to Master Andrew,' he said when he had stowed them in the motor. 'He'll always be welcome here,' and so will you, he added silently.

'Good bye, Donnaidh,' she told him in a small unfamiliar voice but he was not yet prepared to let her go.

'When do you plan to come back?' he asked.

' I don't know.'

A thought struck him. 'But you are coming back.' It was not a question. It sounded a little like an order. She did not answer. Then, because he could not help himself, he took her hand and kissed it. She had tears in her eyes so he leaned over and kissed her cheek.

Invernally Station

The day had come. Her trunk had gone ahead the previous week. Her suitcases were packed. She had walked the policies, said goodbye to the indoor servants the previous day and had intended to climb up to the moor to say a final farewell to the village, but found that a step too painful. Her last act was to visit all the rooms, make sure they were secure and that all was made ready for the auctioneers and the roup to be held in a few weeks time after which Don would take full possession. Then Sam drove her in the trap to the station.

To her joyful surprise they were all there, or so it seemed, the whole of Inverally. The station platform was crowded. At first she thought they must all be waiting for the train but no, they were there to say goodbye and to wish her well. A group of wives from Fisherton, several carrying heavy creels for a boat had come in early that morning. There were Fanny and Jared with their children, Marsali with Evie and hers. There were the Reverend Solomon Carruthers and his sisters, the Vasses and what seemed like the whole of his school although it was holiday time. They had made little flags out of different coloured paper and waved them vigorously as she arrived. There were women she knew from the Bothy, families from the church, estate workers, gillies, gardeners who had finally been paid with small bonuses that had come out of her own dwindling fortune. There was Aaron Morton and the Gallies, no Lord or Lady Morton, however. Mrs Gallie had managed to whisper to her that Cynthia was due shortly to be confined. All of them wanted to pay their respects, show affection and gratitude, shake her hand and wish her well. Some brought small gifts of posies and sweeties, even buttered scones; many shed tears.

The train puffed away quietly on the platform. A porter took her luggage and stowed it in a first class compartment, courtesy of the station-master who escorted her through the crowd. Nor was she allowed to pay for a ticket. Hugh Vass stood on a carriage step and said a few words of prayer and good wishes. She hardly heard them for her eyes were busy scouring the crowd. He was not there. She would gladly have exchanged them all for a glimpse of him. Don't be ridiculous, she told herself. Be grateful. She was grateful. Helen kissed her. Hugh handed her into the train. She stood at the open window and in a voice thickened with emotion thanked everyone and wished them all well. Someone raised three cheers and the station-master waved his flag.

She stood at the window until the gathering was well out of sight then she walked down the corridor to her compartment. She had half hoped that he might be there, but of course he was not. Why should he be? She sat there alone and read the cards, smelled the posies and opened the little parcels. The Vasses had given her a small silver St Christopher medallion which she slipped around her neck. Her overweening feeling was not regret for the loss of the estate, not for the parting from old friends, but that Donnaidh had not bothered to come to say goodbye.

She had an hour to pass before her connection south. Macmurtrie met her in Inverness and took her into the Royal Hotel for tea. They had last minute business to discuss, a couple more papers to sign. He brought her up to date with Inspector Golland's inquiries. Nothing of Jenkins and Higgins had so far been seen or heard of in Glasgow. He would continue to look after her affairs at least until she was settled. He would be attending the roup himself and pay any over-looked debts. What capital remained from the sale of the estate and the contents of the Hall would of course be Andrew's in due course, though a portion of the interest, according to the Trust, would accrue to her during her life time. She thanked him and he promised to keep her regularly informed of all matters pertaining to the estate.

She caught the train south which would take her overnight to London where she had arranged to meet Andrew (who was to be escorted from Wellington) at four o'clock the

351

following day in the foyer of Green's Hotel. The next morning early they would travel together to the dock at Southampton.

To her complete and giddy surprise, Andrew was not alone. There he was, looking taller, chattering and laughing with someone whose back was turned and whose body was half-hidden by the high-backed chair. She waved and Andrew saw her and rose to greet her. His companion also rose and turned and she saw, not really too surprised, that it was Donnaidh. Officially he was in London on business. She wanted to believe he had really come to say goodbye.

They dined together that night. Andrew was full of tales of school life and Donnaidh entertained them both with stories of the ranch. It was a happy evening. Andrew was brimful of excitement at the prospect of the voyage, of seeing elephants and of being with his father again.

At nine o clock she had had enough. She had not slept much the previous night and she was emotionally drained. Andrew too had quietened. She got to her feet. 'Bedtime I think. We have an early start.' Andrew did not argue. After bidding them both goodnight, he kissed her cheek and left them alone. She too was about to say goodnight when Don offered her a *doch an doris* to which she repied *Gle mhath*

'You see? I have not forgotten my Gaelic,' he told her.

'Nor have I,' she replied and they both laughed. That strong sense of familiarity that she always felt in his presence overwhelmed her. Though she did not want a drink, she was unable to refuse him.

He ordered himself a whisky and for her a glass of hot water with lemon, her usual bedtime refreshment. She knew it was important to keep hold of some semblance of reality. She almost believed that he intended to make a declaration.

He did not. They talked of trivial matters. His hotel on the far side of the city, the business and bustle of London, the state of the railway. Nothing more. He did not ask her to cancel her trip to India. He did not ask if he could write to her. He did not touch her until at the foot of the staircase to her room on the first floor, he took her hand and kissed it. His feelings for her were palpable or so she believed, as, she was sure were hers for him, but he said nothing other than to wish her a good night, farewell and a pleasant voyage.

He was not there in the morning either at the hotel or at the station. She was vastly disappointed and so was Andrew. 'Mr King is nice, isn't he, Aunt?' he said once they were on their way. 'I wish he was still here.'

So do I, she said to herself. Her heart was full of regret. I could have spoken, she thought. Why did I not say something? It was too late now. She made a huge effort to cast him out of her thoughts but she was only partially successful.

The following five hours were busy, fraught and full of anxiety but eventually they stood on deck watching visitors crowd down the gangway to line up on the dock to wave goodbye.

'There's Mr King!' Andrew exclaimed as the ropes were cast off and the engine thrumming.

'Where?'

'Look. Over there at the back in front of that great shed.'

She saw him and he was waving with both hands as if to call her attention. She waved and waved until the great liner gently slipped out of the harbour.

India

Three months later three important letters from home arrived by the same boat.

Meanwhile she was getting used to the eternal sunshine, the smiling dark faces of Clarissa's servants, the early rides before the sun grew too hot, the tea parties, the dinner parties, the endless stream of callers, the interminable gossip, the exotic flowers, the terrifying insects, the smell of India - dust and drains and patchouli.

James was a charming host, what she saw of him, for he was often away on manoeuvres. He looked capable and distinguished in uniform and Clarissa was the right wife for him, accommodating and beautiful, dark where Isabella had been golden but equally handsome. Their children, two little girls both under five, spent much of their time with their Indian ayah. Andrew had by now returned to Wellington escorted by a family on furlough to England.

She and James spoke at length about the estate and its loss. He was kind and understanding which made her feel abject with guilt. She explained that she had put aside everything of family importance and value for Andrew when he came of age. 'Everything is stored in the Dower house which will be his in due course,' she assured him.

'Don't worry about Andrew,' he told her. 'I am eternally grateful for your care of him, but he's my responsibility now. What will you do?'

She shook her head. At that moment she had no idea.

'Well, well, there's no hurry, Meg,' he assured her kindly. 'There will always be a home for you here.'

She thanked him but they both knew that this was not the answer.

She was included in every outing, invited to every ball, expected to attend every function. It was immediately clear to her that Clarissa believed she was here for one reason; to find a husband. That both amused her and annoyed her.

To this end Clarissa gave her endless advice. 'Don't become involved with anyone below the rank of major. They can't afford to marry. Stick to the army, Civil Service if you must, but avoid trade.' She would look at Meg, her pretty dark head cocked critically and advise, 'A widower might be your best prospect. Major Thomas has recently lost his wife - she dined at the Club one night and was dead the next morning - that can happen, alas, in India - you met him last night at the mess gala. What did you think of him?'

She couldn't untangle him from the scrum of other eligible officers so all she replied was, 'he seemed nice.' Clarissa looked at her and raised her eyebrows. Poor Clarissa, Meg thought, she was trying so hard.

One day in late October James' batman brought over a sheaf of letters from the latest boat. Three of them were for her. One was from Helen Vass, one from Macmutrie with the results of the roup no doubt and the third, an official envelope marked Inverness Police. That one she opened first. It was a typed letter from Inspector Golland dated September 19 1911.

I have information on your late husband's servant, James Jenkins, which I think you will find of interest. He could not be traced in Glasgow. There was no evidence of his arrival there nor of his presence. However a colleague in the Metropolitan Force, Scotland Yard, contacted us to inform us that a body had been lifted the previous week from the Thames. The post mortem *described him as an elderly male, severely arthritic, who carried no papers or other means of identification. The coroner's report stated that the deceased had suffered three blows to the back of his head which had killed him, and his body deposited in the river where he had been, the doctor believed, not longer than forty-eight hours. He was, however, wearing a tweed jacket with the name of an Inverness tailor stitched to the lining bearing the name, MacDowell & Sons, Church Street, Inverness. The said garment was sent to us, and, on questioning Mr MacDowell Jr., it was established that the jacket had been part of an outfit bespoke for a Mr Victor Myers, Inverally Hall. As Constable Rossie was acquainted with Mr Jenkins, he travelled south and identified the body as that of your late husband's servant.*

It is thought that Mr Jenkins had been robbed and murdered by a person or persons unknown who had removed all means of identification except for that one vital piece of evidence. There has as yet been so sign of Josiah Higgins. I will let you know if there are any further developments...'

Poor Jmmy, she thought. He was a rogue, of course, but had she not always known that? Her father had also been aware of it, but he had known how to deal with him, liked him in spite of his roguery, perhaps even because of it. Jenkins would not have dared to steal from her father. Victor had liked him too, but, because Victor was who he was, Jenkins had manipulated him as he pleased. She believed herself to be at fault. Knowing him for a rogue, she had kept him on to look after Victor because it suited her to do so. She knew she should be angry, outraged by his behaviour as were James and Clarissa, but rather she blamed herself for allowing him to get away with what amounted to serious theft and blackmail.

The second letter dated several days after Inspector Golland's brief missive was from Macmurtrie. It shocked her profoundly, so much so that Clarissa immediately sent one of the servants to fetch Colonel Mackenzie from his office.

'Dear Mrs Myers,

I would ask you to prepare yourself. I have some very bad news, which indeed you may already have heard. I felt, however, it was my duty to let you know immediately. Two nights ago, 1 October, after the last remaining item of furnishing, (the damask curtains from the large drawing room) had been taken down and removed by the purchaser, the Hall was finally empty of all contents and persons. Sometime during the night, the Hall caught fire. Unfortunately it was not detected until early yesterday morning when Sam Stuart in attendance at the stables was aware of the smell of smoke. He discovered the fire and immediately alerted the police and the local fire station. (As you know this is run by volunteers and operates from a shed by the station in Inverally.) The motor engine came as soon as possible from Point and engines from Inverness were also summoned. Local inhabitants too did their best to quench the flames by running a chain of buckets from the Ally. Everything possible was done to save the Hall, but unfortunately the fire, fanned by a high wind, had taken such a firm hold that the estate office, stables and many fine trees were also destroyed.

You will be thankful to hear that Sam Stuart was able to save the horses now safely installed at the Station stables and the strong south wind kept the flames away from the village. I am extremely sorry to say that the Hall has gone but no person was hurt, which is a matter for thanksgiving. Mr King had not yet taken up residency. How the fire started is a matter of speculation. Arson cannot be ruled out, I fear. The matter is in the hands of the police.

On a more practical note, I am thankful to say that the property belongs legally to Mr King and though, naturally, I am sorry for his loss, I cannot but be grateful that the estate is no longer our responsibility.

To end with some happier news; the roup went satisfactorily. A great crowd attended and everything sold with the exception of some fire irons and a butter churn. You will receive a detailed statement in due course…'

Numb with horror, she handed the letter to Clarissa. All Meg could think of was Donnaidh. Aloud she said to Clarissa, 'I should go home.'

Clarissa did not argue with her. Instead she put her arms round her and held her. 'Dear Meg, I am so very sorry. How dreadful! I know how much the Hall meant to you. Thank God you were not there – and Andrew is safe. What can have happened?'

Meg tore open Helen's letter dated the October 4.

My dear Meg,

Macmurtrie assured me yesterday when I came across him in the village that he had written to you so you will already know about the Hall. It is too dreadful Your beautiful home destroyed overnight. I visited the site myself this morning and all that remains are a few blackened walls, the hot ash still smouldering. Indeed a pall of smoke continues to hang over the whole village reminding everyone of what has happened. The offices and the stables are gone, also that beautiful copper beech hedge that your father planted is completely destroyed. Thank God - and Hugh joins me in this - you and Andrew were not there at the time, nor indeed any of the servants. For the first time since you left Inverally, the Hall was empty of people and for that reason alone we must thank God. The estate cottages are untouched for the wind was from the south and near gale force.

Sam and Effie Stuart and their children have been stalwart as indeed you would expect. None of the horses or indeed any other animal was harmed. Tell Andrew when you write to him at Wellington that young Danny was there with his father pumping the stable hose while his father attended to the horses. Hugh and most of the townsfolk helped in whatever way they could but it was a losing battle by the time they got there The fire had taken hold before anyone

358

noticed. I am told Mr King and Aaron Morton were in the thick of it, directing the affair until the engines arrived. Poor Mr King. My heart goes out to him for that and other reasons.

I have debated with Hugh as to whether to repeat to you the ugly rumours that are flying around like midges on a summer night and he thinks it best that you should know. They are saying in the town that the fire was started deliberately. Mr King seemingly is not liked. He is thought to be above himself, that his fortune was somehow gained unlawfully, that he has escaped from an American jail, and more which I will not repeat for it concerns your late brother. Hugh has done his best to refute this unpleasant gossip for we both of us like and respect Mr King, what little we know of him, just as we like and respect the Macreedie family.

The gossip seems to have its origin in Fisherton, for two fisherwives I spoke with at the Bothy earlier this afternoon both quoted to me some old prediction made by one of those Highland seers of yore. You may already know it. The gist of it seems to be that Inverally would one day be owned by the son of a fisherman and that doom and disaster would come to the town when that happened. Mr King is, as you know, a son of Fisherton. It seems strange to me that in this day and age there are folk who still believe in these things. On the other hand we cannot deny that there are 'more things in heaven and earth' etcetera – I forget the precise quotation. It is perhaps a good thing that Mr King has decided to leave us and return to America where he owns a ranch in Wyoming, I believe. Aaron Morton is to take over the estate at least for the time being.

The Bothy is still well attended. Your old friends continue to inquire of you. We have your pretty postcard from

Gibraltar pinned to the wall for all to read. We look forward to hearing further news from you.

Before I close, I have another small item of news. Lady Morton has been confined. She has given birth to a son which must please even the old dowager! She - Lady Cynthia that is - with her baby have gone to stay with her mother and step-father at Timber House to recuperate. None of us has yet seen mother or baby, not even Hugh who called on them there last week. The child is very frail I am told.

Will you return home soon? You know you are very welcome to stay here with us until the Dower house is put in order.

Yours affectionately, Helen Vass

PS *Le durachdan, do deagh charaid, Hugh Vass*

She pushed the letter over to Clarissa. At the same time, James arrived and at Clarissa's request quickly read Macmurtrie's note.

'My God, how appalling!' he exclaimed and Clarissa agreed with tears in her eyes..

Meg was too upset for tears. Poor Donnadh, oh poor Donnaigh, she said over and over to herself 'I must go home immediately,' she said aloud. 'Can you please arrange it for me, James?'

'I can of course,' he told her, 'but why, Meg? What can you do? Think about it first. You are in shock and I don't wonder. It is a shocking business. But what can you do?'

'I have thought about it. I am thinking about it. Don't you see? I'm the one to blame. I have to go back.'

'Not true, Meg,' said Clarissa taking her hand. 'How can you be to blame?'

It was all so simple. How could they not see it? She had married Victor just to keep it all, had she not? She had left him to the devices of a crook, had she not? She had spent unwisely and had wasted her inheritance. Worse still she had allowed it all to happen. She had fallen in love with Donnaidh. There, she had admitted it. She had fallen in love with Donnaidh. Too late.

Aloud she said 'I wanted it all too much.'

'Of course you did,' said Clarissa.kindly. 'It was your home. You've done nothing wrong, Meg. Has she, James?'

He agreed with his wife. 'Your father once told me the estate was a millstone round his neck. You've done your best, Meg. You have to let it go. It's this fellow King's responsibility now.'

'There's nothing you can do, my dear,' Clarissa said firmly. She picked up the letters and handed them to her. 'Put these away for the time being. You can reply tomorrow or when you've had time to calm down.' She paused for a second. 'By the way Major Thomas is dining with us tonight. You like him, don't you?'

Meg almost smiled. Clarissa never gave up. But it was true. She did quite like Major Thomas much as she had quite liked Victor all those years ago. She would not make that mistake again.

Chapter Nine

1913

Milton

He should never have come back. He had seen the fire as the ultimate humiliation, a message which spelt out clearly to him, *you are not wanted here. Take your money. Go back to your ranch. Get out.* What had he been thinking of? During those long hours in jail he had planned to return not exactly in glory but certainly in triumph, make peace with his family, make amends to the Gallie and Myers families for what had happened on the night of the drowning and something else which he had not cared to define.

It had not worked out like that. His mother certainly had been glad to see him but what of his siblings? Jared and Effy and Jonas? They had not wanted him to acquire the estate. Jared who had climbed the social ladder on the back of his wife, did not want his younger brother lording it over him in the Hall. Effie and Sam had been pleasant enough until he had told them his plans for the estate. Then she had shaken her head and resurrected that old prophecy that no one seemingly had forgotten. *Tha an latha*....The day is coming....as indeed it had. Jonas had not wanted him as his landlord in Fisherton, had been hostile from the start, so hostile that it made him wonder about the fire. Inverally to a man was convinced it had been arson. Don knew of no one with such a troubled soul as Jonas. Those were the words his mother had used regarding his older brother. 'A troubled soul.' His own opinion of Jonas was far less sympathetic. He supposed his nephews and nieces had been glad enough to welcome him, but only because he had come bearing gifts.

362

'Why did you come back at all?' Jonas had thrown the words at him one day after the fire. 'We were doing fine without you and your grand airs. Was it just to spite your own folk?'

He had shouted something back, he couldn't remember the exact words but then he had sworn at his brother. 'Damnation, Jonas, I can do what I like with my own.' Something of the sort, but it had set him thinking, doubting his own motives.

It had been Aaron's connection to Lord Morton that had started the dream. As he had listened, flat on his back in the cell they had shared, to Aaron's tale of his great grandmother's ill-treatment, he remembered his own childhood. He had loved his foster brothers more dearly than his own siblings and he had never thought of them as in any way different or superior. They were just *caraidhan* – mates. Lying on his bunk, with Aaron's bitter tale in his head, he realised that of course they had been different. Maybe Aaron Gallie had not been a better scholar, but he had a bigger house, a richer father, better prospects. As for Andy, he was a gentle soul like his mother, the *Aingeal,* as they called her, whom his own mother had worshipped, but he was also richer, better born, one of the nobs in fact. They were no more 'brothers' than Aaron Morton and his lordship. He had been no more welcome at Mr Gallie's dinner table than he had been at Colonel Myers' front door or even his kitchen. That was how it had been and he had taken it for granted, skulking on the gravel at the Hall, lurking outside the back door of Timber House. In retrospect during the long hours in jail, he had found the memory irksome. The more he thought about it, the more irritated he had become. In those days he had been at the bottom of the social heap; now that he had inherited a fortune he could go back to Inverally more than equal to his foster brothers, superior even. The idea invigorated him, got him through the remaining years of that dreadful decade.

Meanwhile Aaron Morton had been released. He had dreamed of confronting his relative, Lord Morton. Don had encouraged him, given him his passage money and a bit more besides.

When Aaron told him that Fisherton was for sale and that the estate was in trouble financially, he became alive. For his mother's sake he would turn those misterable dank hovels into little palaces. He knew now that was not the sole reason. It was for his own sake, just as later he had bought the Hall, not just to make amends to Miss Meg for letting her brother drown, though there was that reason too. No. He would climb those stone steps leather-shod, take his ease in that great drawing room and welcome whom he chose to his dinner table.

But there were complications. He had not reckoned on his feelings for Miss Megaidh. Why her? he nagged at himself. Of all the eligible women in Inverally he had chosen her. She was not beautiful, older than he was, one of the nobs. No doubt she still saw him as a dirty, bare-footed cocky little fisher lad. What a fool he had been. After ten years of enforced abstinence he was so ready to fall in love, so much in need of a woman, a wife, but why her? Although their encounters had been pleasant, more than pleasant, he believed she must despise him for taking her home and thereby destroying it. She had run away to India to escape from what he had done, had she not? Humiliated and depressed, he too had run away, back to Wyoming.

He had only returned because Aaron had insisted. The six months he had promised to work for him were up. Don had a decision to make; either to find another factor or sell up and return to Wyoming for good.

He had told no one he was back. Turning up at Marsali's house on a wet January afternoon when the wind was from the east he found her not alone. Jonas' two bairns, Cathy and Seth, at ten and eleven years old, were doing school work at the kitchen table They glanced up briefly, mumbled answers to his questions and turned back to their books. No welcome there, he thought grimly. His three months on the ranch had, seemingly, not changed a thing.

Marsali had aged during the time he had been gone, but at least her welcome was warm. 'I knew you'd be back,' she cried triumphantly. 'Did I not say he'd be back?' she said turning to the children. 'Come away into the parlour and tell me everything. We'll leave the bairns to their school work.'

She brought him tea and scones and he told her about the cattle, the manager he had installed at the ranch who was as fat as a barrel but could outride any of his hands. When there was no more to tell, she asked him what he intended to do about the burned Hall. He had been dreading the question because he had not yet decided.

He was about to tell her of his indecision, when Cathy opened the door, her eyes lowered shyly. 'Come away in, *mo gradh*.' Her grandmother reached out for the little girl who hung back by the door. 'Is that you finished your school work, then?'

Cathy nodded, still not looking at either of them in the eye.

'Are ye not pleased to see your Uncle Donnaidh all the way back from America? Come over and give him a hug, then.'

The little girl, who was as dark haired and blue eyed as he was, suddenly began to cry. Fat tears rolled down her cheeks as she stood there by the door not moving.

'Tch tch. What is it lass? Come and tell your Nan. It cannot be that bad.'

'I'm sorry,' she said between sobs. 'I'm real sorry.'

'Sorry to see your uncle?' Marsali said disbelievingly. 'Is that what you're telling me?'

She shook her head and then lifted her tear-stained face to look him in the eye. 'I'm sorry,' was all she could say.

Marsali rose to comfort her but Donnaidh reached her first. 'Let me,' he told his mother. She nodded. 'I'll see to Seth,' she told him and left the room.

For an instant he had wondered what she had to be sorry about but reckoned he knew. 'You can tell me, Cathy. I won't be angry. Is this about your da?' he asked gently.

She looked up at him in genuine surprise. 'Pa?'

'Did he set fire to the Hall, Cathy? I need to know.'

The tears started again. 'No,' she burst out. 'It was us. Me and Seth. I'm sorry, Uncle Don. We didn't mean it. I promise you, it was an accident.'

At that moment Marsali came back this time with her hand on Seth's shoulder. 'Seth has something to tell you, Donnaidh.'

He looked at the two children, Seth pale with terror, Cathy red with tears, and he listened. Seemingly they had been curious about the Hall. Just as he, Don, had once been curious as a child. Now that it was empty they had decided secretly that they'd go and take a look. 'We just wanted to see inside,' Cathy pleaded, but it had been dark, so they had taken a stump of candle and a box of matches and gone up there after school. They had wandered through the empty rooms spilling hot grease on the stairs and then they had planted the guttering candle in the drawing room and somehow it had got knocked over and a pile of old newspaper lying about had caught fire. They had tried to put it out but it kept starting up elsewhere. In the end they had had to get out in a hurry.

When they had got back, Evie had gone to bed but Jonas was there, sitting by the embers of the kitchen stove. 'Where have you two been? Will you look at the time?' he had demanded. 'You stink of smoke, the pair of you.'

So they had told him. He had beaten them both and sent them to bed.

'We're sorry,' said Seth. 'We tried to put it out but it got too big so quickly.'

'We were scared,' said Cathy.

Don was speechless for a moment. Glancing at Marsali over Cathy's head, he asked 'What did your father do then?'

'I dunno. I suppose he got the fire engine,' Seth mumbled wretchedly while Cathy wailed anew.

But Sam had got the fire engine. Marsali said nothing. She could not look him in the eye.

'Will you tell?' Cathy asked them anxiously.

Masali had closed her eyes. Don could feel her misery. Perhaps she too had thought it was Jonas. Would it have made any difference if he had alerted the village? Probably not. The fire had taken hold by then. He looked at the children, their stricken faces and felt nothing but pity.

At that moment Evie came in. She had closed her fish stall and had come to take the children home. Her face lit up when she saw Donnaidh. He thought: she knows nothing of this. The children were still looking at him. 'It'll be our secret,' he told them for their mother's sake.

'Secrets?' asked Evie smiling. 'What secrets?'

'The contents of my baggage,' he said putting his finger to his nose.

Aaron came in after they left, clutching their gifts, an American Indian doll for Cathy, a fancy tomahawk for Seth and pretty silver brooches for Evie and his mother.

Marsali cooked them dinner and after a while she went to bed. Don and Aaron stayed talking long into the night about what had been done, (surprisingly more than Don had

367

expected) and what needed to be done, (a great deal). The blackened ruins of the Hall were as yet untouched.

'You need to come to a decision, Don,' he said. 'I've done my best with the grounds and the tenants' repairs but the Hall is like a festering wound. If you don't want to rebuild, I reckon you should sell up. Inverally needs the estate to be running properly. After the fishing and the timberyard it's a primary source of local employment. You're doing it no favours right now.'

' I realise that,' he said. 'I know you've got a good job waiting for you at Gallie's, but it's not too late to change your mind – '

'My plans have changed,' Aaron interrupted abruptly. 'I'm going back to the States.'

That surprised him. 'Why? I thought you were settled here.'

'I guess I was, but things change,' he said vaguely rising and going over to a brand new cabinet which Marsali had lately acquired mainly to hide the whisky Aaron occasionally enjoyed on an evening. He poured two generous measures into glasses and handed one to Don.

'What things?' Don asked.

'If I tell you, then it goes no further. Nobody knows outside her family.'

'Ah,' Don grinned, 'I understand. These 'things' you talk of concern your lady friend.'

'It's not a joke, Don,' he replied without a trace of a smile. 'I got a lady into trouble, massive trouble. The States is the only option, I reckon.'

'You've got to get out of town quick, is that it?' Don was still smiling.

'I guess so. Both of us. Soonest. Now you're back I can go ahead and book passages.'

'That quickly! When's the baby due?'

'The baby's born,' he said and now there was no hiding his pride. 'Joshua Aaron Morton's very much alive.'

'Morton?' Don asked. 'You married the lady, then?'

'She's married right enough,' he said, 'but not to me.'

The story was not long in the telling. He had met Cynthia Morton often enough when he was working at Gallie's. She had not been happy in her marriage. Aaron had not disguised the fact that he delighted in cuckolding Lord Morton, avenging his great grandother's rape - as he saw it. However, what had started off as a mild seduction had turned into love.

'No wonder at that,' Aaron continued.. 'She is the most beautiful creature in the whole of creation.'

That was why he had accepted another job with Mr Gallie rather than stay with Don, so that he could see her more often. They had both tried to put a stop to their feelings, Cynthia especially. She had her reputation and her position in society to lose. She already had a daughter but Lord Morton naturally wanted a son. He was said to have been delighted to hear that another child was expected.

'The baby was born. There was no doubting that he was mine.' He laughed a little grimly. 'The only darkie in town.'

Lord Morton had flung her out. No one was allowed to know why. She was returned to her mother but no one was invited to see her or the baby. Lord Morton now doubted the parentage of his daughter, Adela. She has been taken from her boarding school and returned directly to her mother at Timber House.

'I'm gonna take them all to the States to start over. Lord Morton is divorcing her and as soon as she's free we'll be hitched.'

'Are you happy to do this, Aaron?' Don asked. seriously He already knew something of Lady Morton's reputation. Jared had more than hinted at a flirtation. Don needed to know that his friend had not been conned into a false relationship.

'Happy?' said Aaron raising his glass to his lips and swallowing the dregs. 'Man, I'm over the moon - literally over the moon. A son, a daughter and a wife! What more does a man need?'

'A job?' said Don. 'High Cloud ranch could always do with another hand, if you want it, man.'

'I was hoping you'd say that.'

'Have you told my mother your news?'

'She knows.'

'I thought you said it was a secret.'

'Sure.' He laughed,' but you know how it is with a secret in Inverally. That's the thing everyone knows.'

They talked for a while about his plans then Aaron said as they rose to go to bed, 'So you'll stay and sort out the estate yourself? Mistress Macreedie will need you now.'

He could not answer because he did not know. They told each other good night. He stayed up for another hour, the whisky bottle at his elbow.

The Hall

It was coincidence, perhaps meaningful, that they had both returned to Inverally on the same day, though they did not know it at the time. Meg had caught the early train from Inverness off the night train from London. Don had caught a later one in the afternoon. He had been noticed but it would take a day or two for word to get around that he was back. She too had been noticed and the word spread like thistledown in a wind. The Reverend Hugh Vass had met her at the station and taken her and her luggage to the school house where Helen was waiting with a late breakfast prepared.

Hugh went off to his classroom. When Helen, after listening to her tales of beautiful warm India, asked her why had decided to come back, she had told her more perhaps than originally she had intended. Major Thomas, poor man, had asked her to marry him. 'He was - is - a nice man and desperately lonely.'

'Were you not tempted a little to accept?' Helen asked. 'From the purely practical point of view it would have solved so many of your problems.'

'Yes,' she said frankly, 'if I had stayed in Lahore any longer I might well have given him the answer he wanted, but then I remembered I had married Victor to solve my problems. Besides,' she added. 'I was homesick.' That was certainly true; homesick and heartsick, but the ruined Hall could wait a little longer. She wanted to see it, yet dreaded the sight. 'Tell me all the news.'

There was much to tell. 'We have two new helpers at the Bothy. Mrs Carruthers junior is proving to be a great support. She's quiet and kind and our visitors are growing to love her. Our other new helper is a somewhat opinionated unmarried lady who is housekeeper to her brother lately come to Kirkton....' And so the stories continued including the gossip surrounding Lady Morton. 'No one has been allowed to see the child. I find that very odd.'

'Not even the minister?'

Helen shook her head. 'Did I write to you about Sam Stuart? Mr King has apparently set him up with a garage in Milton. Our first in Inverally. He runs a motor cab service too which I'm told is doing well.'

'That will please young Danny.' She paused. 'What of the Hall?' she asked a little abruptly cutting through Helen's speculations about the new garage. It seemed to her that Helen was deliberately avoiding the subject.

'Ah, the Hall.' Helen sighed. 'I was coming to that. The truth is, Meg, nothing has happened to the Hall. The grounds are in better shape, thanks to Aaron Morton. The bills have all been paid, but the Hall itself is sorely missed. We have come to realise that along with the fishing and the timberyard, the estate was one of the main employers in the village. I hear it all the time in the Bothy. Young people can no longer find work locally. I dislike having to tell you this, because I know how much you care for the community, but I have to be honest. There is a lot of poverty about because of the loss of a major employer. Mr King is still away with no word of his return. Rumour has it that he is going to sell the estate. Hugh and I both think that would be best for the village.

My poor home, she thought with a stab of anguish. 'I should go there,' she said aloud, half rising.

'If you wait until this evening, Hugh and I will come with you,' said Helen kindly. 'You should not go up there by yourself.'

Meg thanked her but knew this was something she must do by herself so she changed the subject. 'It's so good of you and Hugh to have me to stay, Helen, but I can't impose on you forever. Would you visit the Dower house with me?'

'You intend to make that your home, then?'

I don't know, she thought, I have no plans. They arranged to go the following morning.

That afternoon while Helen was at the Bothy, she could wait no longer. After leaving a message for her, Meg slipped out of the front door of the school house and made her own way up the Brae to the south avenue by foot.. The countryside was dead, trees skeletal against a quiet grey sky, but wait, there were one or two golden buds on the dark green whin, the beech tree trunks were as grey as the hide of an Indian elephant but there in the dead grass below were the green ruffs of early aconites, and was that not a snowdrop almost in flower? Her heart lifted a little. The fences were mended, new posts everywhere, but the avenue, she noticed, was already sprouting sturdy dandelions and the gate needed a coat of paint.

The nearer she drew to her first sight of the Hall, the more anxious she became. It was worse, far worse, than she had imagined in her darkest moments. Parts of the walls remained like the blackened teeth of some mythical monster. A barbed wire fence had been erected round them and a warning notice attached which read *Danger*. Weeds were already thrusting through the fallen stones. She stood for a long time watching, remembering, conscious of the faint stink of ash, unaware that she was weeping.

After a while she turned away and without making a conscious decision found herself following the path that led through blackened stumps of trees up out on to the moor. There were long streaks of snow high on the Ben above her and the clumps of heather and dead bracken spattered cold drops of moisture on her boots. Climbing higher, she turned to look back and down on Inverally. The water in the firth gleamed like a looking glass in the fading light. There were no boats in the harbour apart from a couple of near wrecks that had been stuck there for as long as she could remember. A pall of peat reek hung over Fisherton with no one about. One motor crawled between the stationery carts on the High Street, another was parked outside the Emporium whose gaudy sign was almost legible even from this height. There below her were the quiet streets of Kirkton with its churches and its schools. Released from their classes the children ambled home. She could not see them but she could hear them shouting and laughing, a tone higher than the scratchy saws of the timbermill. At the station a whistle blew, two dogs barked at each other. All was as it should be, she

373

supposed, on a late January Wednesday afternoon. Then her eyes settled on the black devastation that had once been her home.

A wind had risen and the light was beginning to fade. She knew she should go, that Helen would be worried, but still she sat. It was almost as if she had known he was coming, though that was impossible. Yet there he was, stick in hand, familiar hat on his bowed head, striding down the hill by the Ally, not yards from where she sat in her favourite spot sheltered from the north by her old familiar boulder. He did not see her for he had eyes only for the heather at his feet. She stood up. 'Donnaidh?' she called not believing it could be him. He was in America, was he not? 'Donnaidh!' This time she shouted and he heard her. He stopped and turned towards her.

'I did not realise you were home!' they both exclaimed on the same breath. It was only afterwards that the significance of the word 'home' occurred to her.

They laughed. She was drenched in that glowing feeling of familiarity that she now recognised for what it was. In spite of her regrets at the loss of her home, her sense of helplessness, she was suddenly clad in joy.

Did he seem pleased to see her? He certainly was in no hurry to move on. They inquired conventionally of each other's journey, health, well being. Then she said because she could not stop herself, 'What happened, Donnaidh? Did you ever find out how the fire started?'

He ignored her question. His brow furrowed, then he said, 'The truth is I should never have come home in the first place. I see that now.'

'What nonsense is this?' she said, but gently, and sat down again for her limbs had grown weak. 'Tell me,' she insisted softly.

After a moment, he sat down beside her. Then he said, 'We had a teacher at Vass's school, Miss Rosie, who taught us a song. The words went something like this: '*The rich man at his castle, the poor man at his gate, God ordered their estate.* Do you know it at all?'

'*All things bright and beautiful,*' she said. 'We sometimes sang it in church. Why do you ask?'

But she knew the answer. She also knew that Mr Vass hated that hymn. 'God had nothing to do with it,' he would insist. Thus it was seldom sung at St Moluag's.

'I broke the rules,' he said. '*The poor man at the gate*, that was me. I thought I could become *the rich man in the castle.* It's time I realised I was wrong.'

'Bad rules are meant to be broken,' she said. 'Your mother is glad you broke them. Your family must be glad... I'm glad.'

How truly glad I am, she thought with a rush of warmth.

He looked at her then. 'Are you, Miss Megaidh?' he asked. 'How can you be? I took your home and I destroyed it.'

'No,' she shook her head. 'Not you. I managed to do that all by myself. Let me tell you how.'

So she told him the whole story of how she had mismanaged the estate, by overspending, neglecting her husband, allowing her fortune to be blackmailed away by a servant and a crook.

'Jenkins is dead,' she said. 'That too could be put at my door. I knew he was untrustworthy but it suited me to trust him with my husband.'

'Surely Mr Myers was at fault - '

She would not let him finish the sentence. 'No, Donnaidh. Victor was a child when I married him and a child when he died. He was lost in the adult world.'

'It was not Mr Myers who set fire to your home, was it? It was not your rascal of a servant who destroyed it. Two

375

children playing silly beggars managed to do that all by themselves. Two children from my family, Miss Megaidh.'

'I'm sure it was an accident,' she said calmly as she listened to the sorry tale. It was a relief to know the truth. She had wondered if it might perhaps have been Mima in a fit of pique or someone from the Bothy. 'It was not your fault, Donnaidh.'

'Oh indeed it was. I grew up on that prophecy. Do you know it? *The day is coming when the bonny lands of Inverally will fall into the hands of the son of a fisheman.'*

'I have heard of it'

'Aye, but have you heard it all? *Woe to that man for his house will surely perish.* I have come to believe I was that man. I should have known what would happen. I defied tradition. I rejected the wisdom of centuries and you have had to bear the consequences.'

She was so close to him that she could once again see the livid scar across his cheek, every line on his face. 'Mr Vass once told me that prophecies if they are known before hand can become self-fulfiling. He would also say that those lines from that pretty hymn are blasphemous. The important thing is what happens now.'

'I came home to sell the estate. My life is at High Cloud in Wyoming.'

'But why?'she protested.

'Because I broke the rules. Because I'm not wanted in Inverally. Because I should never have presumed in the first place.' His breath was on her face

She could not not help herself; she kissed him. In an instant his arms were round her shoulders and his mouth open on hers.

After a long moment he was the first to break away. Before he could apologise she was hushing him. 'I love you,' she said.

He broke from her suddenly and held her at arm's distance. 'Me?' he asked roughly, 'or Inverally?'

She saw immediately what he must think. She had married Victor to inherit the estate; had she not as good as told him so? Maybe he spoke the truth. She was stricken.

'You of course,' she protested.

'Then come to America with me as my wife,' he said roughly.

Was he testing her? Let him. She did not have to think twice. 'Yes,' she said, 'of course I will.'

Afterwards

1920

Meg looked down at the place where she and Don had sat together all those years ago, remembering. She often walked here usually with the dogs or the children. Today, January 25, on the anniversary of that special meeting, she was on her own. She sat under the boulder and looked down on Inverally. In spite of the war years and all that had happened, nothing much seemed changed. There was Fisherton, its little cottages gable end to the sea looking much as they had always looked from the outside, yet deeply different within. Every house had lost at least one family member to the war, either father, husband, brother or son. There were fewer boats, yet more fisherwives on the street trying to make a living. Life was no easier than it had ever been, for some a great deal harder. How well she understood their grief, for she too had suffered loss.

Jonas Macreedie was a skipper now, a bitter man in spite of his brother Don's generosity, and no wonder. His son Seth had joined the navy and had been killed at Jutland, barely eighteen years old His poor wife Evie had died of a broken heart, so it was said. In fact she had fallen and broken her hip and died of blood poisoning. But Cathy was doing well. She had gone to a secretarial college (Don had seen to that too. He had a close reltionship with his niece) and now she had a good job in the office at Gallie's timbermill, except that it no longer belonged to Mr Gallie. He too had died suddenly of an apoplectic fit and the mill sold to strangers. Mrs Gallie had joined her daughter who had - to the delighted scandal of Inverally - gone off to America with Aaron Morton. They were married, or so she had heard, and there was another baby in the cradle. Now that Lord Morton's mother had gone, he had become reconciled to his daughter. He had told Meg himself at the last meeting of the County Council of which he was chair and she the first woman councillor, that he had high hopes of Adela's imminent return. As someone remarked somewhat unnecessarily, he was in need of an unpaid housekeeper. There was still no love lost between the Mortons and the Myers, except there were no Myers left. She had taken Don's name, not Macreedie but King, which Don had used now for many years. Mrs Don King

When Aaron left, Marsali had moved into the flat above the Emporium with Jared and Fanny. Don had wanted her with them at the Dower house so the brothers had agreed to share her, three months at a time but that had never happened. She had caught 'flu' at the close of the war like many others in Inverally and had died suddenly just when she had seemed to be getting better. Meg missed Marsali for she had been almost the last link with her family, the last person to have known her mother.

The Reverend Hugh and Mrs Vass had left the parish, gone to Inverness where Hugh was now a canon of the cathedral. He had decided to leave the schoolhouse after the war for his son Hamish had been killed on the Somme. There were too many reminders of him in Inverally. Meg saw him and Helen from time to time but not often enough. Her own fault, she knew that, for her life had become impossibly full.

The Bothy had gone. Physically destroyed in a storm that had blown hen-coops out into the firth and thrown fully grown trees on to their backs. It was not that the need had gone. In some ways the need was greater than ever. So many families without sons or fathers, so many broken men traumatised by war, so many girls in trouble. Fanny now headed the Ladies' Charitable Fund which helped in the worst cases, but several women on that committee, including the Misses Carruthers, had declined to give support where it was most needed to what they termed as the 'undeserving' poor. In other words, they turned away unmarried mothers, alcoholics and the workshy. Meg had fallen out with that particular organisation. How she hated that word 'deserving'. In her opinion either no one was 'deserving' or everyone was.

Milton looked just a little shabby as if it could do with a new coat of paint. There were a lot more motorcars in the High Street, a van or two but she could clearly see the old coal cart, the patient horse with his nose in his feedbag.

Fanny and Jared were grandparents twice over Connie had married a Cornishman recuperating from war wounds at Point House which had been commissioned during the war as a convalescent home. The term 'had to get married' applied to Connie, but she and Caradoc seemed happy. Though still disabled, he had taken over the ordering at the Emporium thus freeing Fanny from one of her many responsibilities. Kenny had survived the war and was training to become a teacher in Glasgow. Jared, impossibly pompous these days, (she smiled at the thought) served as a town councillor.

She could just see the sole petrol pump at Sam's garage. Stuart and Son Ltd was now a thriving local business. Sam had enlisted in the Royal Engineers and there learned the rudiments of car maintenance. Danny too had been lucky though he did not think it at the time An appendectomy had set back his enlistment by six months by which time the war was over. He had trained in Inverness as a mechanic and was now back working in his father's garage. Thanks to Don, the family lived in a new built stone bouse next to their business. They were thinking of employing a couple of apprentices. Effie was still the same warm kindly woman she had always been and grown remarkably stout.

Kirkton, too, looked much the same. Now that Dr Anderson had retired and moved to Edinburgh, there were two new unmarried doctors living in the late Miss Agnes Gallie's house, cousins called Watson, war veterans. Doctor Paul held his surgery in Point and Doctor Sandy in Inverally, not young either of them, both ardent fishermen, which was why they had come north. As Dr Sandy told her, the Ally had beckoned. The new priest at St Moluag's was still in lodgings. Hugh's assistant teacher had been appointed headmaster at the school and now lived in the schoolhouse. The congregation was in the process of finding a suitable new rectory.

Meg's eyes shifted. It was still strange to her, that great, green, open space that had once supported the Hall. Nothing now was left of the building or the walled garden and most of the woodland had been blown down in the same gale that had destroyed the Bothy. It was as if it had never been. Sometimes admittedly she still felt sad about it. Then she remembered. It had been her idea.

Of course they did not go to Wyoming. At least they did, but only for three month's honeymoon and she had loved it. Don never had any real intention of settling in High Cloud. He employed Aaron and Cynthia to run the ranch where her love of horses had blossomed. He had planned to rebuild the Hall. Those plans! She could laugh now but it had been a dream they had shared for months before the war; two turrets, castellated walls, a medieval castle with modern conveniences. They had even spoken to the architect of the day and he had shared their enthusiasm. So the site had been cleared, the shoot re-established, the gardens redug, and then had come the war. Masons, builders, stalkers, gardeners all had been called up. Don himself had enlisted. Plans were put on hold. To her utter amazement she had become pregnant.

The twins were born in the Dower house in January 1915, miracle babies that neither of them had expected. They had lived and thrived and grown into sturdy toddlers by the time their father had seen them for the first time. Grizel and Andrew - yes, another Andrew in spite of the fact that her brother and nephew had both died so untimely, Andy, as a young lieutenant, in that last Christmas of war.

With the twins to care for and Don to worry about, the war years crawled to a close and the new house all but forgotten. Her eyes lingered on the site, a lush green field, the ground slightly elevated on the place where the Hall had stood. However it was not the site that engaged her crritrical attention, but what was on the site; cattle, long- haired, shaggy, with wide horns and gentle faces.

'Mamma! mamma!' She heard them before she saw them, her five year-old twins, Grizel, dark haired and blue-eyed, the image of her father, Andrew, red-haired and green-eyed, like Marsali, she thought. The dogs barked excitedly. She rose and held out her arms to her bairns.

'There you are,' said Don. His hair had gone prematuarely grey but otherwise he was unchanged, still bronze-complectioned, upright and, in her opinion, entirely beautiful. 'So this is where you got to.'

She looked up at him over her children's heads. 'They look good from here,' she said her eyes shifting from his to the cattle below.

'We moved them into the Hall field this morning.'

The cattle ranch had been her idea. She had asked him once when he had come home, restless and unsettled, after the war what he liked most in the world, for at that time she hardly knew the man she had been married to for six years.

'Cattle,' he had told her instantly 'the smell of them, the feel of them, the nature of them, their stubbornness and their fads. I know about cattle for Mr Gemmell taught me. We shared that love… You will laugh at me now but cattle are in my blood.'

'I'm not laughing, Don. I'm thinking perhaps we should go back to High Cloud,' she had said.

He had nodded slowly. 'Perhaps,' he had replied but without much enthusiasm, and they had turned off the lamp, and gone up to bed but she had not slept. At two in the morning she had woken him.

'We don't have to move back to Wyoming. We can bring High Cloud to Inverally.'

He knew exactly what she meant. They were silent for a few moments as the idea took hold of both of them. Then he said, 'I remember my father telling me I would never make a fisherman. My mother would have made me a teacher but truthfully I was always a crofter at heart.'

A crofter he had become, or so he told everyone. High Cloud Farm, as it became known, was a bit bigger than a croft and still growing for it now incorporated the Mains. The tenant farmer having retired, Don and Meg moved out of the Dower and into the farm house. Don was now the second biggest employer in the area. Men who had once been gardeners and stalkers were now cattlemen; women worked with the poultry or in the spanking new dairy.

'I knew you'd be here,' he said easing himself down beside her under the boulder while the children jumped over tussocks of heather on this deceptively calm January afternoon.

'No you didn't,' she said affectionately.

'Did you think I'd forgotten?' he asked her.

'Probably,' she told him

They both laughed. Then he said seriously, 'I've forgotten nothing, Mrs King. Nothing.'

She had a sudden image of the bare-foot boy skulking by the stone pillars at the foot of the Hall steps as he waited for her brother. I loved him then, she thought.

She took his hand. 'Nor have I,' she told him.

As for the predictions, they are still repeated at the hearths and in the taverns of Inverally. There was even a book written about the mysterious (some say mythical) *Fiosaiche*. Don King was indeed the son of a fisherman and certainly his days were stained with the blood of the Great War. Most often quoted since the Hall had been turned into a farm goes thus: *I see into the far future when the ancient inhabitants of Glen Mhor shall return and take possession of the lands of their ancestors.* The cattle were back were they not?

The latest to tease the folk of Inverally goes thus: T*he day is coming when water and fire will flow together through the streets of Inverally.*

The water was there already in the pipes. Recently there had been talk of subscribing to gas lighting in Kirkton. That was the fire, was it not?

Coincidence? Self fulfilment? Lies? Maybe, but as Inverally folk say to each other a little smugly, 'It makes you think.'